ASK NOT HOW

Ask Not How

Book Two of
'The Corncrakes of Skye'

LUCY MONTGOMERY

ECOLE ALOUETTE

For Hugo, Owen, Camilla and Clementine

ACKNOWLEDGEMENTS

This book would not have been possible without the wisdom, encouragement, advice and knowledge of the following people:

My editor *Sarah Illingworth* whose eye for detail, organisational skills and patience have kept me going. *Shelagh Parlane,* the legendary RSPB Corncrake project officer, for her enthusiastic dedication to the survival of corncrakes on Skye. *Sarah Alyson Smart* for artistically bringing Kilbackie to life on a map. Our small *Free Church of Scotland* congregation for their faith and friendship. My husband, *Robert's* unswerving support, tolerance and belief in Kilbackie. Without his encouragement, I would never have finished the script.

PROLOGUE

The explosive start to Book One **'Ask Not Why'** may seem unacceptably harsh to modern readers but the incident was in keeping with the Reformed Christian teaching of the era. Rev Tommy Nicolson's reaction to his daughters' dancing, giggling and new hair styles was both religious and personal. As the autocratic head of the family, he insisted on total obedience. Any sign of disobedience threatened his authority and had to be dealt with swiftly. Despite his overbearing intolerance, he was genuinely concerned for the souls of his wife and children. The ease in which they had embraced frivolity, pleasure and vanity was living proof they were back-sliding from the True faith. Punishment was his way of protecting his family from the World, the Flesh and the Devil. Eternal damnation was a very real and terrifying prospect.

My great-grandparents were members of the Plymouth Brethren. They possessed immense faith and a phenomenal self-discipline. Isolated from the outside world, they focussed their lives on 'saving souls'. Over a period of fifty years, my great-grandfather criss-crossed India as an indefatigable open-air preacher and tract distributor. He put up with discomfort, illness and pain and like Mairi in 'Ask Not How', his son, my grandfather, suffered humiliation, separation, hardship and material deprivation at the hands of his devout father. The First World War came at just the right time. It provided him with the perfect excuse to escape the suffocating confines of religious fundamentalism. As soon as he was old enough to leave school, he travelled to France and joined the Friends' Ambulance Unit (Section Sanitaire Anglaise 13) as a conscientious objector.

Mairi was brought up in a strict religious world of service, humility, modesty and self-denial. '**Ask Not How**' describes her difficult journey coming to terms with her complex past. As she pieces together her story, she faces goodness and evil, self-doubt and confidence, love and rejection. Through the whole painful experience, she realises just how much her husband, Johnny, loves and supports her.

I hope you will learn to admire Mairi's courage as she tackles her new life on Kilbackie. She isn't without fault. At times she is irritating and irrational but she refuses to play the blame game. To her credit she perseveres and becomes a finer more confident person as a result.

PREFACE

Ask Not How is the second book in the trilogy *The Corncrakes of Skye*.

Why 'Corncrakes'?

Our family farms a remote corner of Scotland where for centuries, Corncrakes were part of the crofting way of life, repeating their rasping call throughout the long summer days and short summer nights. Since 1945, their numbers have plummeted, in fact the elusive birds are now so rare in the British Isles, they have been placed on the endangered red list. We are working hard to care for the wildflower meadows that provide the perfect habitat for this elusive, secretive bird. Our meadows are grazed by a herd of Lowline Angus cattle whose small size and light weight are ideally suited to our ground conditions. Corncrakes (Crex Crex) have a distinctive, irritating, repetitive call, similar to the sound of a credit card running across a comb.

They over-winter in Africa and return to the West Coast of Scotland every May where they breed and rear their young. To protect the ground-nesting birds that breed on the farm, we cut our only crop of silage after 1st September. By this time the fledglings should have flown their nests and the wildflowers have gone to seed.

Ask Not How has taken far longer to write than I intended. For three years, the characters remained undeveloped - the story sat in a folder on my computer. It was so frustrating! Here was a book waiting to be written and I was the only one who could bring it to life but my mind was blank. In the end, I accepted that **Ask Not Why** was going to be my only novel and my vision for a trilogy would never be realised. It was sad but there it was! Move on and get over it!

Then one day I met a friend for coffee in my local community café and everything changed. After the usual chat about nothing in particular, she asked when the second book was out as she wanted to read it. Reluctantly I had to admit there never would be a second book.

Unfazed and persistent, she urged me to put the book to one side and start writing something quite different. Her words were timely and apt. After a few chapters of a thriller set on Skye, my thoughts kept turning to Mairi, wondering how she was coping with her new life on Kilbackie. It discovered I cared for her and wanted her to succeed. With fresh eyes, I started writing and never looked back.

Writing for me has always been a winter occupation when the days draw in and darkness descends over a wet and windy land. Few visitors venture north during the inhospitable stormy weather that blows in from the Atlantic and sweeps across the Outer and Inner Hebrides. The tourists are put off by the heavy rain, poor light and short days.

As winter turns to summer, the swallows and visitors flock back to Skye. The island is energised and bustling, friends and family call in to stay, meadows fill with wildflowers, the grass grows and the corncrakes return.

During these long days of almost permanent daylight, my time is spent ironing, making beds, serving coffee and cake, talking about conservation and conducting farm walks. Kilbackie never leaves me but it has to take a back seat until once again, summer turns to autumn, the visitors tail off, the clocks go back, the cattle eat silage, the world turns dark and the fires roar.

I hope you enjoy *Ask Not How* and feel, for a short time, part of the rich, dramatic, remote and mysterious world of Kilbackie.

FAMILY TREE

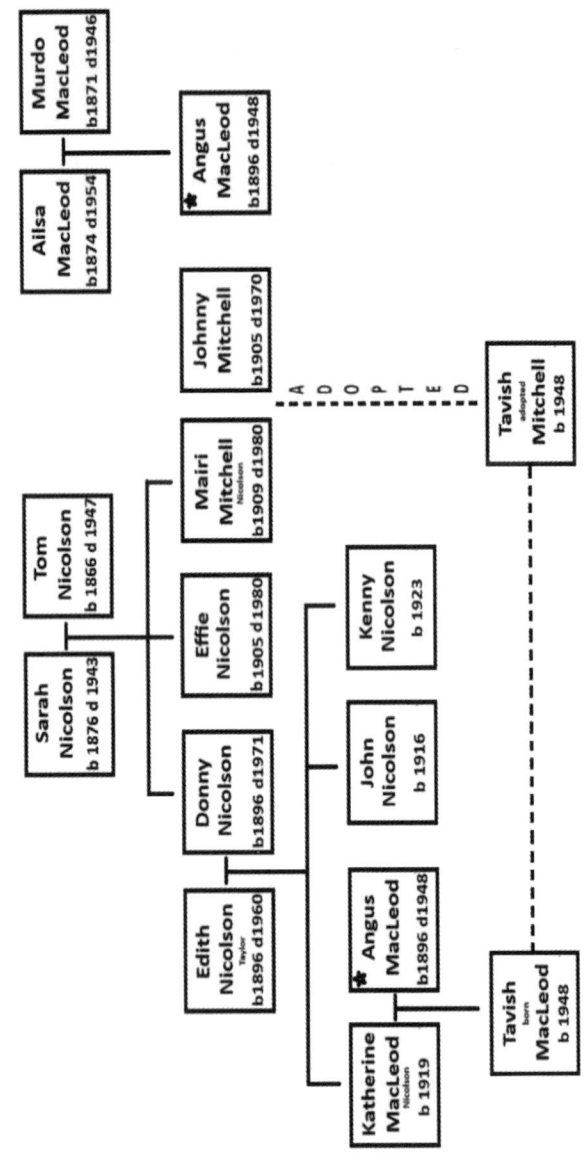

CHARACTERS FROM BOOK 1 'ASK NOT WHY'

Colonel Sir Hugh Hollister: The owner of the Shottenden Estate in Yorkshire.

He joined 4th Battalion Queen's Highlanders in 1915 and became Donny Nicolson and Angus MacLeod's Commanding Officer.

Unmarried and wealthy, he took a keen interest in Angus MacLeod's education and future prospects, treating him like a brother.

At the end of his life, Sir Hugh bequeathed Shottenden House to the National Trust and bought, with private funds, the Kilbackie Estate on the Isle of Skye for Angus and his wife, Katherine née Nicolson. Proceeds from the sale of the land were divided between the Kilbackie Trust and the Applecross Trust. The former to maintain Kilbackie, the latter to support Katherine, Alexander and Tavish.

Shottenden Estate: The historic Georgian home of Sir Hugh Hollister.

The estate was managed by Angus MacLeod until his untimely death on the Kilbackie causeway in 1948. Shottenden House was bequeathed to the National Trust in 1953 and the land sold to create the Kilbackie and Applecross Trusts.

Kilbackie Estate: The former home of the Urquhart family.

It was sold after the death of Major Urquhart in 1947 and bought by Sir Hugh Hollister who planned to give the Estate to Angus MacLeod. Sir Hugh intended to live in a renovated redundant outbuilding and leave the running of the farm to Angus.

Angus MacLeod: Born on the Kilbackie Estate, Angus was the only son of crofters, Murdo and Ailsa MacLeod. He joined 4th Battalion Queen's Highlanders with his friend Donny Nicolson in 1914 and became Sir Hugh Hollister's batman. Instead of returning to Skye after the war, he accepted an invitation to visit the Shottenden Estate, eventually becoming its farm manager.

At the age of fifty, Angus married Katherine Nicolson the only daughter of his friend Donny. They had one son, Tavish, born December 1948.

Angus died on the causeway leading to Kilbackie House in 1948 aged fifty-two.

Donny Nicolson: Born on the Kilbackie Estate, Donny was the only son of Rev Tommy Nicolson, the fiery minister of Kilbackie and the brother of Mairi Mitchell and Effie Nicolson.

In 1914, he joined 4th Battalion Queen's Highlanders with his friend Angus MacLeod and was badly injured and lost a leg at the Battle of Festubert. He was eventually invalided back to Kilbackie where he and his wife Edith took up crofting. Eventually he decided to train for the Ministry and succeed his father.

He married Edith in 1917 and had three children – John, Katherine and Kenny.

Katherine MacLeod (née Nicolson): Born on the Kilbackie Estate, Katherine was the only daughter of Rev Donny and Edith Nicolson. She trained as a nurse before leaving Skye to marry her father's oldest friend, Angus MacLeod. She had one son, Tavish, born December 1948, a few months after her husband's death on the Kilbackie causeway. Without Angus by her side, she had a breakdown and was encouraged to give up her son, Tavish for adoption. The pain of separation led her to withdraw from the world and entered Malvingborough Abbey where she dedicated her life to the care of traumatised soldiers.

Tavish was officially adopted by Katherine's aunt Mairi Mitchell (née Nicolson) and her husband Johnny.

Mairi Mitchell (née Nicolson): Born on the Kilbackie Estate, Mairi was the youngest daughter of Rev Tommy Nicolson. She was also the sister of Rev Donny Nicolson and Effie Nicolson. After Angus MacLeod's funeral, she left Kilbackie to join Katherine at Shottenden where she became Sir Hugh Hollister's mother's lady's maid. It was there she met her husband, Johnny Mitchell.

Angus' untimely death and Katherine's retreat from the world left Tavish without parents. With Katherine's consent, Mairi and Johnny adopted the young boy and moved to the Kilbackie Estate which Sir Hugh had initially bought for Angus and Katherine.

Johnny Mitchell: Born at Matchings, a tenanted farm on the Shottenden Estate. His parents lost the tenancy through no fault of their own and moved to a cottage on the estate where Johnny became the dairy manager. It was there he met and married Mairi Nicolson.

He and Mairi adopted Tavish, the son of Katherine and Angus MacLeod both of whom originated from Kilbackie.

CHAPTER 1

As the black Ford Anglia crawled over the track towards the low stone bridge marking the beginning of the Kilbackie Estate, Mairi grew quiet. There was no turning back. She had crossed the Rubicon into a land she must now call home.

"You all right?" Johnny asked, hardly able to hide the excitement that shone through his tired eyes.

A brief glance at his wife told him she didn't share his mood.

Kilbackie

She repeated the word to herself as memories of a troubled past wove fear through her fragile mind.

Rain continued to pour out of a leaden sky. It bounced off the bonnet, surged down narrow gullies cut deep into the hillside and gurgled its way along the open ditches.

"I've never seen rain like it," Johnny commented as they motored past a few white cottages.

Mairi smiled and squeezed his arm affectionately.

"It doesn't usually rain this hard! Just most of the time."

They reached the causeway linking the mainland to their island home just as dusk was closing in. Ankle deep, the inky waters of the rising tide were already swirling over the track.

"This is madness!" he said, hesitating before driving his wife and child into the sea. "Are you sure it's safe to cross?"

"It'll be fine. Head out between the boulders that mark the edge of the road but you'll need to get a move on. The incoming tides rise dangerously fast."

Johnny took a deep breath, slipped the car into first gear and cautiously entered the water.

"Keep going, Johnny! Don't stop!"

Water was everywhere - beneath, around and above them. The family seemed to be disappearing into a murky grave.

Mairi peered tenderly over her shoulder to catch a glimpse of her son lying peacefully on the back seat, wrapped in blankets and pillows. Every now and then his eyes twitched and his forehead creased as if he were dreaming.

Much to Johnny's relief, the car eventually emerged onto dry land.

"Not long now," he said, remembering the precise directions he had written down before leaving. "The house should be at the end of this track."

The car continued to carry the family through the incessant rain, eventually coming to a halt in front of a tall building half obscured by the low cloud swirling around its massive stones.

Kilbackie House

Its imposing structure stood above a stony beach, an eerie presence in a desolate spot.

"It's huge!" Mairi gasped.

Johnny switched off the engine hoping for a moment's peace after the long journey north but the force of the howling gale shook the vehicle so violently, he wondered how he was expected to provide for his family in such a wild unforgiving place.

"Come on," he said, plucking up the courage to move. "Let's see what we've taken on."

Mairi put on a brave face for the sake of her husband but deep down she, too, wondered how she was going to cope with the move back to Skye.

"You go and open up while I stay here with Tavish just in case he wakes up. It wouldn't be fair to leave him alone in this gale. He'd be terrified."

Johnny summoned the courage to leave the safety of the car. He dashed across the driveway, skipping over puddles until finally he reached the foreboding front door.

It was locked.

'Just my luck!' he thought, unsure what to do next. Donny, his brother-in-law had promised to open up the house before their arrival and leave the key on the kitchen table, together with a few provisions to tide them over. Either he had forgotten or they had misread his letter. He looked back at Mairi sitting in the steamed-up car minding their sleeping son who was the main reason for their move to Scotland.

"It's locked!" he shouted but his words were drowned out by the relentless wind that pounded the beach and drove the rain. It was no use. He would have to run back to the car and ask Mairi if she knew where her brother might leave the key.

"I've no idea! Are you sure it's locked?" she said. "He promised he'd open up and leave the key on the kitchen table."

They looked back at the house where the torrential rain tumbled through the broken guttering onto the doorstep.

"I'll have another look. That old stone pot beside the drainpipe looks a possibility."

He ran back to the house and lifted the pot.

"Found it!" he cried in triumph.

It took a while for his freezing hands to turn the lock but when he finally entered the house and discovered the light switch, he found himself in a vast panelled entrance hall decorated with stag heads and heraldry. Rising from the hall to a balustraded first floor landing was a stately staircase.

"Oh, my goodness!" he whispered, gazing up at the magnificent chandelier. "What have we taken on?"

He returned to the car to share his first impressions with Mairi while Tavish lay half-awake on the back seat, hypnotised by the rain that continued to cascade down the windows. He had never seen rain like it.

"Are you awake?"

The young boy nodded.

"It's time we made a move."

Reluctantly Tavish stretched his arm towards Johnny who wrapped his muscular fingers firmly round the tiny wrist and gently pulled his son clear of the luggage.

"Ready?"

Tavish nodded.

Mairi didn't answer. The size of the building left her speechless - the house quite literally took her breath away. Although she had been brought up on the Kilbackie Estate, she had never been allowed to visit the big house, the family home of the Urquharts, a reclusive couple whose only son, Douglas, had been killed in the Great War.

Mairi's father, the Free Church Minister at the time, tried to convince the grieving couple that Douglas' death was part of God's great plan but the Major and his wife refused to believe that a loving God could be so cruel. The more the Minister tried to bring them round to his way of thinking, the more they resisted until eventually they stopped attending church altogether. As a child, Mairi was constantly reminded that the Urquharts were wicked and Kilbackie House was off limits, a place inhabited by the 'unsaved'.

The house had been built in a prominent position above the beach, a testament to the absolute power of the Urquharts over the lives of those living on the Estate. The Crofting Act of 1886 weakened autocratic rule by giving the crofters security of tenure and rights over their land.

Better roads and cheaper cars drew remote communities closer to the cities where accessible legal systems and lawyers held the lairds to account. The Highlands gradually opened up to tourism and landlords could no longer banish a family from their croft on a whim.

Johnny slipped his arm through Mairi's and felt the warmth of her body through his wet coat. It felt surprisingly reassuring and intimate. To his delight, she nudged closer to him.

"I hope Donny's remembered we were arriving this evening," she sighed wearily. "It would be just our luck if he's forgotten his promise."

"You run on ahead," Johnny said, "Tavish and I will follow."

When they finally found the kitchen, it was bare - no food, no fuel, no fire, no welcoming note.

"Maybe he got the day wrong or was delayed by a parishioner," Johnny suggested, rubbing his hands to get the circulation going. "Let's give him the benefit of the doubt."

Mairi conceded gracelessly.

The kitchen was dominated by a monster range with cast iron doors, ovens and hot plates. When alight, it was the beating heart of the room but without the fire, the freezing kitchen was lifeless. Johnny arched his back and moved his neck to relax the tension after the long drive. He lowered Tavish into an old armchair and wrapped him loosely in a blanket. "Stay there while I unpack the car."

"There's nothing here," Mairi said, busying herself to look for fuel and matches. She opened the scullery door which was a mistake. A vicious draught hurtled across the kitchen, whipping their legs and dropping the temperature by several degrees.

"This isn't the welcome I'd expected!" she sighed, looking at Tavish who was staring into space. "Let's have something to eat before we decide what to do next."

She took a willow-patterned plate down off the dresser and unpacked the few things she had brought to eat. "I'm afraid supper won't be warm!"

By the time Johnny had taken the luggage upstairs, Mairi had hastily prepared a simple supper which they ate in silence, too numb to talk, too cold to move. Occasionally Johnny glanced in her direction but she remained focussed on Tavish who yawned for the third time.

"Come on, young lad!" she said at last. "It's time you were tucked up in bed."

Upstairs, the ill-lit bedroom was sparsely furnished with two iron beds and a wardrobe. A pair of faded curtains thinly veiled the rotten windows.

"Don't bother getting undressed. The bed is bound to be damp. Slip under the blankets and try to get warm. I'll sort out dry bedding and hot water bottles tomorrow."

She kissed her son's forehead and returned to the kitchen, leaving the bedroom door slightly ajar.

"I'm so disappointed in Donny!" she cried, berating her brother. "All he had to do was unlock the front door, leave a few things for us to eat and light the range. Was that too much to ask?"

The cold seeped through her body like a virus attacking her morale. She became too weak to fight. Everything about Kilbackie House reeked of decay. It was a joyless arrival.

"There's no point unpacking now," she said. "I'm done for! Let's call it a day."

They climbed the stairs and entered the spartanly-furnished master bedroom, too tired to undress. Johnny fell into an exhausted sleep within minutes of his head hitting the pillow but Mairi lay awake wondering if their move to Scotland had been foolish.

CHAPTER 2

Outside, huge waves pounded the beach below the bedroom window.

From memory, Mairi knew that storms on Skye could last for days. She was prepared for the worst but by daylight, the wind had died down and the rain ceased. An orange glow of the rising dawn formed a halo over the distant hills. She slipped out of bed and wrapped her winter coat tightly across her chest.

It was six o'clock.

"Anything the matter?" Johnny murmured deep within the bedclothes.

"Shhh! Go back to sleep. Everything's fine. I've been awake for ages so I thought I'd get up and look for some wood to burn."

"Don't get cold," came the groggy reply.

Downstairs Mairi stood in front of the unlit range watching her breath form clouds in the chilly air. The room was filled with an unpleasant acrid smell of mould. All she wanted was a large cup of tea to make her feel warm and welcome.

After a futile search for fuel, she began to lose heart, wishing she had never agreed to travel north to support Johnny's farming dream.

"Feeling overwhelmed?" a voice asked from the doorway. Johnny walked over to where his wife stood shivering in the middle of the room and gently enfolded her in his arms. She nodded. He planted a tender kiss on top of her head. "We'll make it work – after all, Rome wasn't built in a day."

Mairi straightened her back and took a deep breath.

"Where shall we begin?"

"How about I look for some logs or coal while you go and check on Tavish. I don't want him to wake up wondering where he is."

Johnny stepped out of the back door straight onto a pile of rotten leaves. Decay was everywhere. Neglected outbuildings stood forlorn as raindrops trickled down their thick rough slates onto saturated ground. It was a desolate scene. He walked over to a dilapidated byre where rising damp had turned the whitewashed walls green. Most of the roofing sheets had blown away, exposing the rotting rafters.

There was no sign of any logs. While Mairi was dealing with Tavish, Johnny walked up the hill behind the house to get a better view of the land he had come so far to farm. Stretching down to the sea was a strange wasteland of stunted trees bent double by the prevailing wind, their gnarled branches covered with pale green lichen. Clumps of rush choked the boggy ground, tussocky grass stagnated in the fields where once potatoes and oats had grown in abundance.

The farm was in a terrible state.

Johnny's thoughts were interrupted by the sound of dogs barking on the wet causeway.

"Someone's coming!" he shouted back at Mairi who had already heard the excited yapping.

"It's Effie!" she cried, waving her hands in the air.

A sturdy woman in her late forties, with grey curly hair, a weather-beaten face and a smile that lit the creases across her broad attractive face, walked up to the house, followed by three energetic border collies. It was difficult to tell who was more excited, Effie or her dogs.

"You've come!" Mairi said, showing her delight. "I can't believe it! You've actually come."

Effie placed her backpack on the ground and gave her sister a generous unconditional hug.

"It's good to see you back," she exclaimed, catching sight of Tavish who remained half-hidden behind his mother's skirt.

"Who's this wee chap?" she asked, pointing him out.

"It's Tavish," Mairi explained in Gaelic. "Tavish, come and meet your Aunt Effie."

The small boy stepped shyly forward and rather formally held out a hand to greet his aunt. He said nothing.

"Does he have the Gaelic?" Effie whispered.

"Of course he does! He's fluent but he's only used to speaking to me."

She crouched down and drew her son close.

"Say 'hello'."

"Hello," he replied with little enthusiasm.

Effie lifted the little boy up and wrapped her arms tightly round his slight frame, embracing him warmly. He felt the coarseness of her salty hair against his soft skin and smelt the dog hairs on her woollen cardigan.

"Come and meet the dogs," she said, lowering him gently to the ground. He held her hand, terrified the dogs would jump up.

Effie let out a long low whistle. Immediately, the three panting collies dropped to the ground, waiting for the next command.

"You can stroke them if you want. They won't mind."

The small child tentatively ran his fingers through the animals' glossy coats and patted their heads as Effie introduced them.

"The one with a black eye is Nell and next to her is Peg," she said proudly. "And that one over there with the white tipped ears is my champion, Bess.

"There now! That wasn't so bad, was it? You've just made three new friends and I can tell from their faces that they are pleased to meet you."

The boy beamed with delight and stuck close to his aunt as Johnny carried her backpack into the house.

"I hope I've brought enough," she said. "I had a feeling Donny might leave you in the lurch. You know what he's like. Promises the earth and delivers nothing."

"Do you know if there's any coal or wood here?" Johnny asked. "I've looked everywhere but can't find any. The kitchen's freezing."

"I think there's a stack of wood in one of the sheds. Hang on a minute and I'll show you."

The thought of heat and a meal lifted Mairi's spirit.

CHAPTER 3

The rambling old house was stuck in a time warp.

Whilst Johnny took Tavish outside to explore the farm, Mairi and Effie spent the morning discovering rooms that hadn't been touched since the Great War. The house was a warren of corridors leading to bedrooms, attics, sculleries and formal reception rooms. Evidence of mice was everywhere. Their black droppings lay scattered over the floor boards and beds.

"This place must cost a fortune to run," Effie said, as they entered yet another room. "You never did explain how you came to live here."

The comments were well meant but left Mairi feeling defensive.

"I don't like talking about it," she replied shyly. "Johnny and I were asked by the Kilbackie Trust if we would like to farm the estate on Tavish's behalf until he reaches twenty-five. We've been given a twenty-year tenancy."

"I'm not sure what that means but you certainly seem to have landed on your feet."

"I'm not sure I would call it 'landing on our feet,'" Mairi confessed, showing a few misgivings. "I find Kilbackie House strangely unsettling. I can't put my finger on it, but there's something not quite right about the place. It's as if the ghosts of the past are still living here, dragging me down."

Effie listened attentively. "I don't know anything about ghosts, Mairi, but I don't find Kilbackie House unsettling. Old-fashioned maybe, but definitely not unsettling."

Mairi frowned. Despite Effie's positive first impressions, she remained apprehensive.

Kilbackie House 1914

At the outbreak of the Great War, Major Urquhart had made enquiries about buying a large quantity of explosives from Vabost Quarry. His aim was to blow up the Kilbackie causeway and break the island's tidal link to the mainland to prevent his only child Douglas from joining up. Douglas Urquhart was a painfully shy young man of eighteen who had lived an isolated life under the watchful eye of his neurotic parents who were convinced he would come to harm without their protection. From sunrise to sunset, they kept a careful eye on him, watched his every move and never let him out of their sight.

The Major's eccentric plan would probably have succeeded, had the Defence of the Realm Act not been passed on 8th August 1914, giving the government wide-ranging powers to restrict the possession of explosives near railways, docks and harbours. The quarry foreman, Mr Mackenzie, a fastidious Free Presbyterian, dutifully read the Act and informed the authorities of the Major's unusual request. The Major was summoned before a military panel and asked to explain his improbable need for such a large amount of high explosives.

He was immediately put on the spot because he had no intention of telling the panel the real reason for his request. Standing to attention before the three-man committee, the Highland officer delivered a spluttering, preposterous speech about his fear of a German invasion and the need to build a defensive wall around his property. He had assumed that status, rank and authority would win the argument.

His application was turned down with immediate effect.

Under normal circumstances, Douglas would have remained quietly at home but in August 1914, his father agreed to let a 4th Cameron Highlanders' recruiting officer visit Kilbackie, a decision he would regret for the rest of his life. Across the Highlands and Islands, tales of heroism, adventure and chivalry helped create a frenzy of patriotic zeal. Major Urquhart, in his role as laird, was keen to show off the fit, resourceful sons of his tenants. There was no doubt in his mind that the youths of Kilbackie were capable of teaching the arrogant strutting Prussians a lesson or two about resilience. He relished the thought of his young men giving the Kaiser a 'bloody nose'.

Resplendent in Urquhart ancient tartan, tweed and plaid, the Major stood to attention next to the recruiting officer in the steadings' courtyard and proudly watched a line of young crofters enter through the large stone archway. The highly polished silver top of his sgian-dubh glinted in the sun and the effervescent song of a blackbird sang from the fruit trees in the well-tended walled garden.

The recruiting officer looked out across the sparkling Minch and for a brief moment felt overcome by the intensity of the colours and the breath-taking beauty of the Highlands in August. The men were keen to get back to work. They impatiently shuffled their feet, waiting for the young officer to speak, but he took his time, and gazed deep into the eyes of each face staring back at him.

When eventually he opened his mouth, he delivered a passionate, masterful speech in elegant Gaelic, urging those standing in the courtyard to join up, defend freedom and return as heroes.

His words fell on open ears.

Unbeknownst to the Major, Douglas had taken advantage of an unguarded moment and slipped behind the stone arch of the courtyard's bell tower from where he listened spellbound to the rallying cry of the recruiting officer. He decided, there and then, to defy his parents, travel to France and fight for his country.

The scene that followed his announcement was heart-wrenching. His mother let out a long, terrified cry which filled the room with such despair that her husband was unable to offer any words of comfort. Slowly, like a mortally wounded animal, she sank to her knees sobbing. Before Douglas could stretch out his hand to support her, she collapsed on the floor. No amount of protest, pleading or tears would make Douglas change his mind. His father desperately thought of ways to stop his son joining the army. In the end, he devised the plan to blow up the causeway to prevent Douglas from leaving Kilbackie.

A few weeks later, Douglas and a dozen young men from the Kilbackie Estate caught the train from the Kyle of Lochalsh to Inverness where they were billeted, kitted out and assessed ahead of training in Bedford. Sixty-seven troop trains packed with 17,000 recruits of the Territorial Force arrived in Bedford for three months of military discipline, drill practice and lessons on fighting with a rifle and bayonet. After twelve weeks of good food and vigorous exercise, Douglas put on weight and built up his muscle strength. He was fitter than he had ever been and felt optimistic about the future. From time to time, he came across Donny Nicolson and Angus MacLeod from Kilbackie but he didn't seek their friendship, preferring to spend his free time reading and writing home. In February 1915, the 4th Battalion Queen's Own Cameron Highlanders left Bedford for France, landing in Le Havre. Three months later on 18th May 1915, Douglas Urquhart was killed at the Battle of Festubert, aged nineteen.

Every night until her death, his grieving mother would read aloud the condolence letter written by Douglas' Commanding Officer, Col. Sir Hugh Hollister, in which he assured her that her son had suffered no pain and had died a hero.

'Douglas,' he wrote, 'was dependable and unceasingly cheerful, lifting morale with kindness, humour and song. He showed selfless leadership and bravery in the heat of battle and his loss has affected everyone. The world has lost a fine Christian soldier who served his country faithfully in the trenches and always put the needs of others before his own. May such a good and faithful servant find everlasting peace in the loving arms of his Saviour.'

'*A fine Christian soldier!*' the Major repeated in disgust. "Bah! Douglas was still a child when he died. He knew nothing about the wickedness of men or the cruelty of war."

The Major didn't recognise his son in the condolence letter and doubted whether the Colonel knew who he was. Reading between the lines, he concluded that the Colonel was an honourable man who tried his best to lessen the pain of loss by writing what he thought the parents would want to hear.

Although the Major took no comfort from the Colonel's letter, his wife certainly did. She thanked God that her only child hadn't suffered and that his fellow soldiers thought highly of him. She read and re-read the words 'good' and 'faithful' and cherished the fact that he had died a Christian.

The Urquharts never recovered from the shock of losing Douglas. They spent the next thirty years shut away from the world that had so cruelly stolen their future hopes and dreams. The causeway was their only protection from the horrors of the outside world. If anyone was seen wandering up the stony path at low tide, the Major would race upstairs, fling open a window brandishing a shotgun and shout expletives at the poor unsuspecting visitor. Most turned round and fled but the few who ignored the crazed man's warnings soon turned back when he fired into the air.

CHAPTER 4

Mairi moved through the main reception rooms, aware of a sadness lingering beneath the dust sheets.

Johnny sensed her change of mood. She looked grave, almost fearful.

"Come on, Tavish," he said, urging his son to get ready. "It's time you and I went out to inspect the farm again. You'll need to put on your coat and boots."

He squeezed Mairi's hand and kissed her cheek.

"With us out of the way, you can have a few hours to yourself!"

She managed a weak smile but didn't squeeze his hand back.

Tavish's excited chatter faded to a whisper as he skipped towards the front door where the outdoor clothing was kept. He held up a small pair of black wellington boots and asked his father to help him put them on.

"Not now," came the reply. "If you want to be a big boy and help me on the farm, you'll have to learn to dress yourself."

The child sat on the muddy floor, trying to work out his left from his right, desperate to show his father that he was big enough to help him.

Eventually he got dressed and followed his father outside, closing the heavy front door behind him. By this time, Mairi stood alone in the cosy kitchen, overwhelmed with a sadness she didn't understand. Although the range was lit, its glowing embers produced little comfort.

She had a choice. Either to slump into the large armchair and forget whatever it was she wanted to forget or to take charge of the morning and do something productive. She chose the latter.

Collecting some polish, a mop, a bucket of water and a dustpan and brush, she entered the drawing room where white calico dust-sheets hung grotesquely over the furniture like ghosts from a former age.

Two bottle-green Chesterfields stood on an Urquhart tartan carpet opposite a huge fireplace. There was a generous-sized bookcase flanked by two half-moon tables on the far wall. A rosewood card table fitted neatly between two long sash windows, each draped in rich red velvet curtains and swept back with tasselled cords. Above the card table hung a painting by Sidney Percy, depicting a romantic view of the Scottish Highlands, complete with mountain, loch, cattle and brooding sky.

On the wall hung two portraits of the Major and Mrs Urquhart but there was no painting of Douglas. Perhaps he had died too young or his distraught parents had removed his picture to relieve their pain.

The only evidence of his existence was a photo of him in uniform, taken a few months before his death. Mairi ran her fingers over the silver frame. She stroked the glass behind which stared a sensitive, thoughtful young man of slender build with bright eyes that smiled through a solemn gaze. She gave the frame a quick dusting and placed it back on the bookcase next to a small Venetian vase.

Mairi knotted a scarf over her head to protect her hair from the dust that would soon leap around the room. She picked up the small stiff brush in her right hand, dropped to her knees and started to brush every square inch of the tightly woven carpet, heaving and pushing the two sofas, chairs and tables so she could brush away the dirt underneath. It was slow, tiring work but hugely satisfying. When the last dustpan had been emptied into the bucket, she straightened her aching back to inspect her work. The difference was enormous. Years of grime had been removed to reveal the carpet's original deep rich colours.

Very carefully, so as not to disturb the thick dust that had settled on the sheets, she folded the corners into the centre and gathered the edges together to create a parcel. Most of the dust remained trapped in the folds, but enough escaped to form clouds of fine particles that danced in the diagonal shafts of sunlight beaming through the tall sash windows.

The Urquharts' fine collection of art and furniture was slowly being unveiled. The room's décor might have been the height of fashion in 1915 but compared with Shottenden's pastel elegance, Kilbackie appeared old-fashioned and distinctly Victorian.

Mairi flung open the windows to fill the room with the fragrance of spring. A gentle salt breeze blew over the furniture, breathing new life into a room that had suffocated through neglect.

To complete the transformation, she wiped the skirting boards and ledges with a damp cloth, cleaned the windows and removed the dead bluebottles. The dank air gradually turned sweet as the wax and soap lifted decades of grime.

It was half past eleven.

Mairi rubbed her chafed hands. They hurt. The dust had dried the skin and cracked the soft lines that ran across her palms, making them bleed. It was time to stop.

Down the long corridor linking the entrance hall to the drawing room she heard voices.

Johnny and Tavish were back.

She picked up the cleaning things, took off her head scarf and headed to the kitchen where they were waiting for her, their cheeks glowing from the bracing sea air.

Johnny's latest inspection of the farm confirmed his worst fears. The once fertile grasslands were choked with rush and bracken and an eerie silence hung over the fields where expectant ewes and new born lambs should have been grazing. The outbuildings were empty, all the machinery appeared to have been sold and the drystone walls needed repairing. They were no longer stock proof.

Without financial support, Johnny couldn't see a future for them on Skye but now wasn't the time to discuss his findings with Mairi. The move north had been just as much his choice as hers, so it was up to him to make a go of what they had.

"Are you all right?" he asked, noticing her red face. "You look a bit flushed."

"I'm fine - just a bit hot having given the drawing room a thorough spring clean." She tried to sound positive but Johnny sensed something was on her mind.

"And?..." he asked.

"and nothing."

"Come on, Mairi. I know you well enough to know something's not right!"

She gave a long, drawn-out sigh, holding back the tears. "I've spent all morning trying to bring the drawing room back to life but it still looks dreary. I hate this house and its decor. Everything is so depressingly old-fashioned. It's as if the Urquharts are still living here, pouring their grief into every nook and cranny."

She tugged at his sleeve. "Come and see for yourself."

She led him down the ill-lit corridor to the drawing room.

"Well! Be honest! What do you think?"

He stood in the doorway and breathed in the sweet smell of beeswax, noticing the swept carpet, polished surfaces and washed paintwork. "What a difference!" he said, putting an arm round her shoulder. "You've done a magnificent job. Everything is so much cleaner."

He agreed that the room was old-fashioned and lacked elegance, but tried to cheer her up by saying things could be changed in time. The main thing was that she had made a start.

His words of encouragement were lost on Mairi. As far as she was concerned, Kilbackie would never be elegant.

"What am I going to do?" she sighed. "Moving back to Kilbackie was my dream but I don't think I'll ever be happy here. It's all so gloomy."

She was interrupted by the sound of a car crunching over the stony track. The Rev Donny Nicolson had come to call on his sister.

"That's all I need," she shuddered. "Tell him to go away. I'm not at home."

"I can't do that; it would be rude. In any case, I've never met Donny."

"You haven't missed much!" she said returning to the kitchen.

Johnny waited at the front door to greet the brother-in-law he had never met. He was curious to know why Mairi became so angry and nervous whenever his name was mentioned. She never had a good word to say about her brother.

Johnny imagined a charismatic, domineering character but the man who stepped out of the car was surprisingly frail. He had a slight stoop and walked with a pronounced limp.

"Is she in?" he barked without introducing himself.

"Good morning," Johnny said graciously, holding out a hand to welcome his brother-in-law. "You must be Donny. We haven't been introduced before but I'm Johnny Mitchell, Mairi's husband. It's good to meet you at last."

Donny had no time for niceties.

"Where is she?" he shouted, refusing to shake Johnny's hand.

"If you would like to follow me, I'll take you to her," Johnny said tactfully, leading the way but Donny pushed past his host, calling for his sister in Gaelic, his booming voice filling the vast echoing entrance hall. Mairi cowered further into the corner of the kitchen, fearing the voice that bore an uncanny resemblance to her father's. A frisson of dread crawled over her as she waited for the man behind the voice to appear. Whatever she was expecting after an absence of six years, it wasn't the gaunt figure glowering at her through the doorway. Her proud opinionated brother had lost much of his charm yet the sight of him standing in her kitchen still unnerved her. Before he had time to open his mouth, she launched in, accusing him of disowning his daughter Katherine and refusing to accept Angus as his son-in-law.

Donny blanched.

"Don't ever mention Katherine's or Angus' names again. As far as I'm concerned, they are both dead."

"But Donny," Mairi replied indignantly. "Katherine isn't dead. She might have withdrawn into an Abbey but she's very much alive."

Donny put his hand up to stop her.

"My daughter is dead to me. End of story. And as for Angus, we might have been friends before and during the Great War but when he chose to leave Kilbackie and live in England, we lost touch."

"You might have lost touch with him," Mairi said, "but

he never abandoned you. Every time he returned home to visit his parents, he made an effort to see you. You were his dearest friend, his companion-in-arms. He tried to help you but you never gave him a chance."

Donny looked at his sister, clearly annoyed that the conversation was taking place.

"That man was an opportunist who enjoyed humiliating me!" he retorted, his voice revealing uncharacteristic emotions. "He refused to support my church, rejected my God, stole my only daughter and now you expect me to forgive him?"

"Angus never wanted to hurt you," Mairi said. "He wanted to show you a wider world outside the church and Kilbackie but you refused to engage with him. Your problem, Donny, is that you bully anyone who questions your authority. Although you will never admit it, your decision to go into the church was power-driven, just as it was with our father. Once in power, you used your biblical knowledge of hell and judgement to silence all opposition and belittle alternative points of view. You are no better than the worst Highland lairds who used their power to exploit their tenants."

Donny turned puce.

"Jezebel!" he retorted.

Mairi clenched her rough cracked hands to steady her nerves.

"Enough!" she replied bitterly, attempting to end the hurtful exchange of words that were getting them nowhere. "We cannot change the past but small acts of kindness like unlocking the front door ahead of our arrival, lighting the stove and placing a loaf of bread on the table would have made all the difference."

"If you thought for one moment that I was going to warm the hearth of a sinner then you were mistaken," he replied tersely.

Mairi covered her ears with her hands, blinking back the tears of anger that blurred her vision. Had she been stronger, she would have ordered her brother out of the house but his vicious attack had taken her completely by surprise. In her haste to leave the room, she failed to notice a small face hidden behind the door leading to the hall.

Donny stared into a pair of large terrified eyes. Eyes he had seen before, familiar eyes that belonged to a past he preferred to forget. He took a step nearer the boy who stared back at him with a look that bore deep into his consciousness. Donny enjoyed watching the child shrink back into the corner of the room like an animal caught in a trap. For a brief moment, he managed to smile at the child cowering in terror.

"Come over here!" he said as gently as he knew how. "I won't bite."

Tavish looked unconvinced. He remained alert, watchful, on his guard.

"Do you know who I am?" Donny asked.

He shook his head, his wide-open blue eyes staring through Donny.

"I'm your Uncle Donny," he continued in Gaelic, trying to sound pleased with the familial connection. "And I'm a Minister of God. Have you heard of me?"

Again, Tavish shook his head.

"Well, now you know I'm your uncle perhaps we could get to know each other," he said, hesitating just long enough for the boy to relax before adding, "Perhaps you could tell me who your real mother is, not my sister Mairi, but the other one."

Tavish looked confused, not knowing how to reply. He had vague memories of a lady called Katherine whom he used to call 'Mummy' but she had disappeared and been replaced by Mairi who hugged him, read him stories and kissed him goodnight. It was her scent that lay on his pillow as he fell asleep, her arms that surrounded him with love when he hurt himself, her cooking that filled his tummy when he was hungry.

He looked up at his uncle.

"Mairi."

Donny let out a long sigh and shook his head, making it perfectly clear that Tavish had given the wrong answer.

"Oh dear! dear! dear! You've just told a little lie and do you know what happens to boys who tell lies?"

Tavish shook his head in terror.

"Their tongues are cut out and they are thrown into a pit of burning coals."

The Minister spoke slowly, emphasising each word for maximum effect, a trick he had learned early in his career. Being a spokesman for God was the best job in the world, it gave him the authority to encourage his parishioners or scare them witless. Tavish fell into the second camp.

He slumped to the floor, lowering his blue eyes to avoid the menacing gaze of his accuser.

Donny was just getting into his stride when the sudden imposing presence of Johnny appeared in the doorway and interrupted his flow.

"Where is he?" Johnny cried. "Where's Tavish?"

From behind the door came a low whimpering sound.

"Daddy!" he whispered with relief. "You've come! You've come at last."

"Of course I've come. You're safe now!" his father said, gathering the boy into his arms and stroking his thick black hair. "It's all right, your uncle is leaving and I promise he'll never come back.

"You bullying bastard!" Johnny hissed, exaggerating the six-inch difference in their heights. "Get out! If you're not on the causeway by the time I count to ten, you'll have to wait here until the tide turns which may be another six hours. I can't guarantee your safety for that length of time. Do I make myself clear?"

The white-haired visitor nodded and dragging his artificial leg, hurried out of the room towards the parked car.

CHAPTER 5

Donny's disastrous visit to Kilbackie had a profound effect on Mairi. She became restless, flitting from task to task, obsessively cleaning.

"Come and sit down!" Johnny pleaded, encouraging his wife to stop cleaning the spotless kitchen.

"I can't!" she sighed, leaning heavily on her broom. "There's so much work to do. If I sit down, I'm afraid I'll never get up."

"Please, Mairi! For my sake. Sundays are meant to be days of rest but apart from cooking this delicious breakfast, you haven't stopped sweeping. If you carry on like this, you'll probably get one of your migraines so why not put the broom down and spend a few moments with me and Tavish?"

"I'd love to stop and put my feet up but I want everything clean and tidy before church at 11.00 am."

Johnny put his fork down.

"What do you mean *before church*?" he cried, thumping his fist slightly harder than he intended. "You can't be serious after the way your brother treated Tavish. There's no way we are attending one of his services."

"But I want to go," Mairi said firmly, unwilling to change her mind. "And I want my family there with me."

"I'll do anything for you, Mairi," Johnny pleaded, tipping a spoonful of sugar into his tea. "Anything except attend your brother's church. The man's a charlatan, a disgrace! He should be dropped on a remote island and left to rot."

Johnny should have stopped there, having made his point but he was rattled.

"Look at this place!" he taunted, sweeping his arm round the room in an exaggerated manner. "It's a bloody nightmare."

He paused to see if Mairi was paying attention but she had turned her face away from him the moment he started swearing.

"Let's face it, Kilbackie isn't exactly the dream we were hoping for. Our move north is turning into a disaster. God, what a mess!"

It was the first time Mairi had heard her husband blaspheme and the effect was shattering. She knew the score. It had been drummed into her since childhood; 'blasphemers went to hell'. The thought of Johnny suffering an eternal torment terrified her. Flashes of light darted in front of her eyes. She felt sick and the throbbing in her head grew worse. She tried to ease the pain by rubbing her temple with the palm of her hand but it didn't work. *'This is punishment,'* she thought, leaning on the broom handle to steady herself. *'Punishment for marrying a non-believer.'*

She started sweeping again, hoping the migraine would eventually go away but the throbbing increased to such a level she felt the room sway and her legs buckle.

Tavish peered over the table to see what was going on.

"What's happening to Mummy?" he asked with concern.

"She's shaking."

"There's nothing to worry about," Johnny said, calmly. "Mummy's not feeling very well, that's all. Finish your breakfast and wipe your mouth with a damp cloth. You've got ketchup all over your chin."

The boy ate his last piece of toast while Johnny crouched down to comfort his wife.

"Get me a bowl, quick! I'm going to be sick!"

She vomited into the mixing bowl then slumped to the floor, one arm draped over her head to try and stop the throbbing.

Closing her eyes to concentrate on her headache, she felt the warm strength of Johnny's hand wrap round hers.

"What brought this on? Donny's visit?"

Mairi gave the faintest of nods.

"I need you with me when I go to church."

"Of course, I'll be there for you but you are asking a lot of me." he said, stroking her hair. "I promise everything will work out. Neither of us understood what we were taking on when we moved. It's bound to take time to adjust and settle in."

Quietly and unnoticed, Tavish slipped down from his chair, determined to do something useful to help his mother. It upset him seeing her lying on the floor looking so pale. He fetched a glass of water. "Drink this, Mummy," he said in Gaelic, dipping his small fingers into the water and letting the cool droplets seep through her dry lips. The tenderness of the small child revived Mairi. She attempted to lift her head and smiled weakly.

"Thank you, darling! That was just what I needed."

Johnny remained at his wife's side, determined to support her as best he could. He enjoyed watching the close bond between mother and son. Two humans bound together by a common language as old as the tide that lapped the island's rocky shore.

Tavish's touching act of kindness strengthened Mairi's resolve to get up. She heaved herself into a sitting position, refusing Johnny's offer of help but the pain swirling around her head made her giddy. She held out her hand and whispered, "I'd really like you to come to church with me, Johnny. I know it's a big ask but I want us to be part of the community."

Johnny had no choice but to agree to his wife's demands. An hour's service was a small price to pay to make her happy.

He offered to clear away the breakfast things and do the washing up whilst she went upstairs to rest.

"I'll come up later to see if you are feeling any better."

Much to his relief, Mairi reappeared a while later looking pale but determined.

"Are you sure you are feeling well enough to go to church?" he asked.

"It doesn't matter how I feel, Johnny. Church attendance is part of island life. We go to church for God in the same way we plant potatoes for food, cut peat for warmth and shear sheep for wool. Our lives revolve around faith and work, it's what makes our community thrive.

"As I've mentioned before, those you meet at church

are honest and trustworthy, qualities you may one day come to rely on. Of course I'm up to going. Church will be good for us all."

"I'll be the judge of that!" Johnny replied, unconvinced any good could come from a service led by Donny.

Mairi gave her husband a look that showed her decision was final.

"All right, you win! I'll join you this once but that doesn't mean I've forgiven your brother."

They got in the car and drove in silence across the causeway. High above the brooding Minch, slender white gannets circled the grey waters hunting for fish. Mairi pointed them out to Tavish, hoping they would cheer him up.

"There!" she said suddenly, pointing to a bird torpedoing headfirst into the murky water. "Did you see that?" Tavish shook his head. He was in no mood for birdwatching. "Try to follow one and see what it does," Mairi persisted, watching his reaction in the car mirror. He stared out of the window and for a brief moment, smiled.

On the gentle slopes above the church, newborn lambs with trembling tails nestled close to their mothers, waiting for the mist to clear. Clumps of golden daffodils shone through the gloom. Rows of newly-planted potatoes waited expectantly for the first warm rays of sunshine to draw their sprouts through the soil. Mairi marvelled at the timeless rhythm of crofting life, its familiar patterns weaving a thread through the spring landscape.

It only took fifteen minutes to reach the plain white

church in which she and her family had worshipped for generations.

Mairi held Tavish's hand and together they walked cautiously towards the Minister who was standing in the entrance welcoming his flock. The green eyes that had once glinted with mischief had lost their sparkle and the thick flaxen hair that had attracted so many women when he was young, had turned snow white.

"You've come, then!" he grunted, showing no pleasure at seeing his sister again. Mairi looked at her brother and felt nothing but pity mixed with loathing.

"Yes, Donny, I've come," she said, placing a protective arm around her son who was hiding in the folds of her coat. "You've already met my husband, Johnny, and our son, Tavish, so introductions aren't necessary."

The remark was met with a chilly silence.

Standing to her full height, Mairi adjusted her hat, brushed down her skirt and entered a plain room full of tight-lipped men in dark suits and solemn women wearing mid-length skirts and hats. It was just as she had described it to Johnny; a proud place devoid of music and beauty but fiercely independent, focussed solely on the reformed teachings of the Protestant Church.

Johnny had never seen anything like it. Austere and cold, the people sat ramrod-straight in their pews, their eyes facing forward in a frightening display of self-discipline. They seemed bewitched, under a spell. No-one spoke. Not a muscle moved. Any temptation to glance round was resisted. From the porch at the back of the church, the Minister and elders could be heard praying in hushed voices. It was impossible to make sense of the words but there was no mistaking the loud, confident 'Amen' at the end. The small entourage led the Minister slowly and purposefully down the aisle to the stairs leading up to the pulpit from where Donny wiped the sweat off his brow with a large white handkerchief. He placed a large well-thumbed leather-bound bible firmly on the small lectern in front of him and gazed theatrically down at his people.

Johnny watched in amazement as his weak, bullying brother-in-law transformed into a man of conviction and stature, holding everyone in the palm of his hand. He spoke with an authority that made Johnny unexpectedly sit up and listen.

This was Johnny's first introduction to the Free Church of Scotland which had started in 1843 when a hundred and twenty-one ministers and seventy-three elders left the Church of Scotland on a point of principle concerning patronage. The Scottish Church had always claimed the right to exercise independent spiritual jurisdiction over its own affairs without royal or parliamentary interference and yet under the system of patronage, landowners were able to nominate and present ministers to their congregations without any consultation.

Although Johnny had been brought up in the Protestant Faith and considered himself vaguely Christian, he had no idea that some Christians actually read the Bible every day and believed it to be the inspired, inerrant and infallible word of God. Justification, salvation and sanctification were foreign words to him. His fragile faith celebrated poetry, art, architecture and music, concepts far removed from the teachings of original sin and predestination. It never occurred to him that he was too sinful to be accepted by God and that his salvation depended on God's grace.

Johnny had never read the Bible. His sparse knowledge came from a few Old Testament stories learned at school and the great Christian festivals of Christmas and Easter. He had been brought up on a farm on the outskirts of Kirkdale, a small village nestling in the lee of the Yorkshire Moors. From his parents' kitchen window, he could see the fine mediaeval Parish Church of St Swithin, half-hidden in the yew trees that grew among the gravestones. The tranquillity of this timeless English setting was only disturbed by the cawing rooks roosting high in the stone buttresses and on Sunday mornings by the peel of bells ringing from the ancient tower. Agnostic by nature but Christian by birth, he maintained a deep respect for the King James' Bible and the Anglican liturgy.

As a teenager, he liked nothing better than to sit at the kitchen table after milking and watch his parents and neighbours walk in their finery to the Great West Door. On still days, he could hear the reedy chords of an organ playing old familiar hymns, the words of which he knew by heart.

He had lived in the shadows of mainstream faith but made an effort to keep Sundays special by spending time with his parents, walking in the rolling countryside or reading poetry. All this changed when he married Mairi for whom faith was an anchor and church a rock. As a dutiful husband, when they lived in Shottenden, he attended Matins every Sunday. Whilst she knelt humbly in prayer, he sat admiring the massive oak beams that formed the mediaeval roof of the parish church.

That was yesterday's world. Today their future lay in the Highlands, the land of Knox and Calvin, where churches were stripped of all papal signs - crucifixes, candles, stained glass. In Mairi's church, the congregation sat for psalm singing and stood for extempore prayer. There was no liturgy, no organ, no music, no hymns.

Johnny felt a surge of anger as the minister announced the first psalm.

'*Bloody hypocrite!*' he thought uncharitably, remembering the way Donny had bullied his way into the house and terrified Tavish.

'*The man's a fraud, a coward who uses a dog collar to spread fear among the faithful.*'

His far from holy thoughts were interrupted by the precentor singing the first line of the psalm. Before long the room was filled with the haunting sounds of unaccompanied singing as bleak as the treeless landscape that rolled across the heather.

This was a truly strange land.

After the psalm, Donny read from Paul's Letter to Galatians.

Mairi gripped the edge of her pew until her knuckles turned white. She watched her brother stab the air with his index finger as he spat out each sin on the list of immoral works of the flesh. There was no doubt he had chosen the passage with her in mind but instead of his usual brand of explosive oratory, he appeared hesitant and weary, even dull. Something wasn't right.

He lowered his eyes to gauge his sister's reaction but she held his stare, forcing him to look briefly away. She was not going to be cowed by her brother. If he had hoped to embarrass her in front of the congregation, he had failed.

Johnny had switched off before the minister started his rant on sin. He took his wife's hand and tenderly wound his fingers round her wedding ring, distracting her from the intensity of Donny's accusing gaze. She closed her ears to her brother's words and watched the billowing dark clouds amass beside the church.

Johnny wasn't the only one struggling to cope with the long service. Tavish was bored. He started to swing his feet higher and higher until one particularly high kick caught the edge of the book shelf, sending a clattering sound through the church. Mairi placed her hand on Tavish's knee and brought her finger to her lips to remind him that church was a place of worship, not play. The boy thrust his chin onto his chest and folded his arms in a huff, letting out a short indignant snort that made her smile.

If her brother was looking for a sign from God, he received it towards the end of his sermon, when a fierce storm broke over the church, unleashing a torrent of water that cascaded down the hillside like an unstoppable tsunami. The flash flood that followed was deep enough to prevent those walking home from leaving the church.

"Did you bring the car?" Effie whispered.

Mairi nodded.

"Could you give Ailsa a lift back home?"

CHAPTER 6

The folds in Ailsa's Sunday coat hung loosely round her tiny frame. In her younger days it had been the most fashionable item in her spartan wardrobe. It had fitted her like a glove, not that she was ever aware how stylish she looked. True modesty made her oblivious to her shapely figure and good looks but those around her were drawn by her graceful beauty. Now, fifty years later, osteoporosis had diminished her stature and weakened her bones but her piercing blue eyes remained as lovely as ever.

Johnny parked the car outside No. 4 Garros, a thatched black house perched on a rocky hillside, surrounded by stone walls that glistened in the relentless rain. The single-storey dwelling had been Ailsa's home all her married life. It stood as a monument to an era when houses were built by hand using local stone.

She stepped cautiously out of the car, taking hold of Johnny's arm for support as strong gusts of wind hounded the hillside around her croft. The small group battled against the weather with their heads bowed until they reached the low door which opened into a cosy room warmed by the dying embers of a peat fire.

Mairi had known Ailsa's house for as long as she could remember. It had always been a welcoming place, a place of sanctuary in times of trouble. She watched Johnny follow the diminutive woman to her favourite chair by the fire where she settled comfortably among the deep cushions, pausing to catch her breath.

"You're back!" she said, over and over again, caressing Mairi's cheeks with her deformed arthritic fingers. "You're back!"

Mairi stoked the fire with a poker and added a fresh peat brick to increase the warmth. Before long the room was filled with a sweet earthy smell.

"Can I help in any way?" Johnny asked, feeling at a loose end. The last thing he wanted after the long, tedious service was to spend time with an old lady. If he'd had his way, they would have driven straight home but Mairi's frosty look gave him no option but to drive Ailsa to No. 4.

"I'm fine," she said, lacing her fingers with Mairi's in a gesture of solidarity. "If you want to make yourself useful, perhaps you could check the range has enough fuel and fill the kettle. I'm sure we could all do with a cup of tea."

The two ladies sat in silence, unsure where to start.

It was Ailsa who finally broke the ice. "Did Sir Hugh tell you anything about his plans for the Estate?"

Mairi shook her head. "Johnny and I leapt at the opportunity of moving up here without fully understanding what was required of us. To be honest, it has all come as rather a shock. Have you ever been into the house? It's enormous!"

Ailsa gave an enigmatic smile.

"Sir Hugh wrote to me about Kilbackie. Would you like to know what he said?"

"Of course I would!" Mairi replied.

"You'll have to let go of my hand for a moment whilst I get the letter," Ailsa continued. "I keep it in my bible."

She opened her bible and pulled out a well-worn letter.

Mairi began to read. The first part was personal to Ailsa but Sir Hugh went on to describe how thrilled he was of being in a position to buy Kilbackie.

'Buying the Kilbackie Estate was an inspired, impulsive decision, one I will never regret. It has given Angus and Katherine the opportunity to return to Skye and start their own business, breathing life into a neglected farm and house. I'm sure they will achieve their goals and make a success of the challenge. While Angus and Katherine do all the work, I have every intention of spending the rest of my days in blissful peace, reading, birdwatching and hopefully offering advice when needed. I can't think of a finer man than Angus to run the estate and I have you to thank, Mrs MacLeod.'

"Every word Sir Hugh wrote is true," Ailsa said, grasping Mairi's arm. "Angus was the perfect son - kind, patient and hardworking. He certainly didn't deserve to die the way he did. Everyone tells me it was an accident. That he fell and hit his head on the causeway but I don't believe it. I believe he was murdered and I know who killed him."

"You don't know what you are saying!" Mairi replied in total shock. "What do you mean he was murdered?"

"I can't tell you on the Sabbath," she replied. "Perhaps another day."

Mairi felt the colour drain from her face. She didn't believe it! No-one could have deliberately murdered Angus. It was impossible!

"Did you know Sir Hugh came to see me on the day of the funeral?" Ailsa continued, trying to control her tears. "He only stayed a few minutes but during that short time, he gave me a photo. Look, it's over there on the dresser. Be a dear and fetch it for me."

Mairi released Ailsa's hand and walked across the room to the silver photo frame standing in front of the hanging cups on the dresser. Staring at her through the glass was a lanky, good-looking lad with tousled hair and rolled-up sleeves. He was leaning against a farm gate, surrounded by Aberdeen Angus cows. Mairi had forgotten how impish his smile had been and felt a surge of pride that the son of a Kilbackie crofter had risen to become the well-respected manager of a huge English estate.

"It's my most treasured possession," Ailsa sighed, wiping the protective glass with her sleeve. Mairi looked over towards Johnny and Tavish who were waiting for the water to boil. She had enough time to ask the one question that was rankling her.

"Ailsa!" she said, feeling her throat go dry. "Have you heard from Katherine recently?" The mention of Katherine's name made Ailsa start. She shifted uncomfortably in her chair, her face visibly drawn, as if the journey back in time troubled her. Mairi watched her friend's eyes focus on the photo of Angus then begin to close. She gently shook Ailsa's arm and repeated the question, choosing her words with care.

This time, Ailsa stirred and opened her sunken eyes, blinking regularly to keep herself awake. She fumbled

for Angus' photo and clasped it to her before telling
Mairi everything she wanted to know. Katherine had
only written once since entering the Abbey. In the letter
she had explained her reasons for retiring from the
world and had assured Ailsa that Tavish would be well
loved by Mairi and Johnny. Knowing she was unfit to
care for him, Katherine fully supported their decision
to adopt her son.

Mairi let out a loud sigh of relief which Johnny took
as the sign they were ready for tea. He brought the tray
over to the fire and poured out four cups, one for each
adult and one for Tavish, who had decided to be grown
up and try some tea.

Ailsa made an effort to stay awake but she wasn't used
to company and it didn't take long for her eyes to grow
heavy and her head slump onto her scrawny chest.

"Best leave her be," Mairi said, clearing away the tea
things whilst Johnny paced restlessly up and down the
room, checking the time. He had had enough of old
ladies, church and Gaelic. If they left now, they could be
back home before the high tide blocked the causeway.
He urged Mairi and Tavish to get a move on but Mairi
showed no sign of wanting to leave.

"I think we've tired her out, poor thing," she said,
settling back in her chair by the fire. "Let's wait a bit
longer to see if she wakes up."

Johnny was in no mood to wait. In the end it was the
tired voice of a six-year-old that decided things. "I'm
hungry and want to go home!" he whined. Mairi looked

at her watch. It was nearly two o'clock and the boy hadn't eaten since breakfast.

"My goodness! I had no idea it was so late," she exclaimed. "You must be famished! Johnny, take Tavish to the car and I'll join you in a minute." But Tavish refused to go. He wanted to stay with Mairi and the tiny old lady who sat by the open fire with her eyes shut.

His mother gave her a gentle nudge.

"Ailsa, are you awake? I'm afraid we have to leave. The tide's coming in and we need to get home."

At first Ailsa seemed unresponsive but gradually she perked up and stared lovingly at Tavish, her wrinkled face breaking into a radiant smile. She recognised the raven black hair, freckles and piercing blue eyes that stared shyly back at her; it was a face she knew well, a face that brought back a thousand memories and ten thousand tears.

"Angus? Is it really you?"

Mairi put her arm round Tavish to assure him everything was all right but he was curious to know why the old lady was calling him Angus.

"Who's Angus?" he asked, shifting awkwardly from one leg to the other, his hands in his pockets.

"Never you mind," Mairi said rather shortly. "Ailsa is getting you confused with someone else."

She gently explained to Ailsa that the child standing beside her wasn't Angus but her son, Tavish.

"Your son. I'm sorry," Ailsa apologised. "For a moment I thought Angus had come back but it must have been a dream."

"We must go!" Mairi repeated, "but we'll be back soon."

"Does Tavish still have the small brass and enamel clock I gave him?" Ailsa asked.

Mairi nodded.

"Keep it safe," she pleaded. "I gave it to Katherine the day we buried Angus. It belonged to my mother. The ticking movement is meant to represent the beating heart of a loved-one."

CHAPTER 7

Early the next morning the telephone rang.

Johnny picked up the receiver.

"Rosvaig 914"

The man at the other end introduced himself as Mr Fergus Buchanan, a Trustee of the Kilbackie Estate.

"My apologies for phoning out of the blue but I've only just learned that you and Mrs Mitchell have arrived.

"It would be lovely to meet you both. As it happens, I will be in the area tomorrow. Would it be convenient to visit you at about midday or is that too short notice? I expect you are feeling daunted by the challenge you face but hopefully I can answer some questions and explain the role of the Trust."

Johnny was encouraged by Mr Buchanan's amiable, easy manner.

"Tomorrow at midday would be fine," Johnny agreed, keen to learn as much as he could about the Estate.

"Twelve noon tomorrow - perfect!"

The phone went dead before Johnny had a chance to ask whether he wanted to stay for lunch.

"Who was that?" Mairi shouted from the kitchen.

"Someone called Mr Buchanan. He didn't say much other than he's a Trustee and wants to call in tomorrow."

"Did he mention a time?"

"Yes, about midday," Johnny said.

At last, he was going to have someone to talk to. Someone to share his concerns about the farm's viability and find out what was expected of him, now he had arrived on Skye.

He rummaged through a box of papers and brought out a detailed map of the Estate which he rolled out on the kitchen table and weighted down.

"Tavish?" he asked. "Could I borrow your crayons? I've got some colouring to do. If you are very careful, you can help me."

The boy nodded cheerfully and ran over to the cupboard where he kept his precious things. Tucked among his books, games and puzzles was a wooden pencil-case with a sliding top. He handed it to Johnny.

"The sharpener and rubber are inside," he added helpfully.

Father and son sat side by side colouring in the map of the Estate; fertile land red, hill ground green and crofts blue.

"It's good to see you back in gear," Mairi said, wrapping her arms around Johnny's neck and giving the top of his head an affectionate kiss.

"Did Mr Buchanan mention lunch?"

"No," Johnny replied. "And before you get annoyed, I forgot to ask but I assume he'll eat with us."

Kilbackie Estate 1939
★★★

In 1939, the Ministry of Agriculture and Fisheries had set

up a plan to increase food production throughout the UK. Letters were sent to farmers instructing them to plough up ten per cent of their grassland and plant wheat, barley, oats and potatoes ready for the 1940 harvest.

Major Urquhart had no time for grey-suited bureaucrats. He burnt the letter thinking that would be the last he'd hear about it, but in 1942, an inspector from the Agricultural Executive Committee paid an unexpected call. Armed with a clipboard, he spent the entire day asking questions about the land, its crops and yields. Throughout the interrogation, the grey man never smiled.

By the end of the visit, the inspector appeared satisfied with the Major's answers. He thanked him for his time, remarked on the beauty of Kilbackie and said the Department would post its decision in due course. Sure enough, a fortnight later, a rather curt letter arrived in the post, informing the Major that the farm had failed its inspection and would be requisitioned by the War Office with immediate effect.

The Major was furious.

Waving the incriminating piece of paper in his hand, he shouted, "Damn those Whitehall buffoons! Damn the whole interfering lot of them! How dare they tell me what I can or can't do with my own land! My family's been farming this Estate since before the Jacobite Rebellion. Has Whitehall nothing better to do than poke its nose where it's not wanted?"

In a fit of autocratic rage, he tore up the letter and

ceremoniously threw the pieces into the waste paper basket.

Fortunately for the Major, the letter was never followed up. Kilbackie was considered too sparsely populated and remote to grow surplus food.

With so many young men fighting in France, the responsibility of food production on Skye fell on the shoulders of the women and elderly men. Undaunted by the challenge, they diligently worked the fields, cultivated crops, tended to their livestock, harvested peat, salted fish and milked cows to ensure there was enough to eat.

After the war, Major Urquhart finally gave up farming but decided, for nostalgic reasons, to keep a small fold of Highland cattle. Although he knew little about stock keeping, cattle were part of the Highland way of life and he liked seeing them grazing the fields.

The Major's decision to keep cattle would not have been possible without Iain MacKinnon agreeing to stay on. The 72-year-old stockman had been looking forward to spending more time in his vegetable garden but when the Major asked him to carry on working, he dutifully consented. Fifty-five years of service and bouts of arthritis had taken their toll on his body. By the end of each day, his swollen joints were so painful, he was forced to retire to bed, often too tired to eat.

The bitter winter months brought nothing but misery. Biting winds whipped the snow into sculpted drifts. The day-time temperatures dropped below freezing. Soft boggy ground turned as hard as iron. Yet every morning

Iain dutifully braved the cold to feed his cattle. It was back-breaking work for an elderly man.

And still the snow fell.

One morning, he woke up delirious, his flesh felt on fire. Distorted images of wild animals with paper teeth and glass fur appeared across his bedroom, their outlines contorting to the rhythm of his throbbing head. He tossed to and fro, too feverish to eat, too frail to get up.

He couldn't move.

Less than five hundred yards from his wretched dwelling sat the self-pitying laird wrapped in a blanket beside a hot range, oblivious to the tragedy unfolding on his doorstep. The Major, who hadn't worked since 1915, never gave a moment's thought to his stockman whose increasing ill-health went unnoticed.

It was only by chance that Ronnie the postman called in on Iain on his way to Kilbackie House. Usually, if the tide were high or the weather wild, he would leave Major Urquhart's post in a special box at the end of the causeway, but on this occasion, he decided to deliver the official-looking letters in person, even if it meant pushing his bike through the snow. Overnight, the stockman's humble black house had eerily disappeared under graceful curves and sweeping arcs of fine powdery snow. The unusual stillness bore the hallmarks of death.

"Dear God! What's happened?" Ronnie exclaimed. "Something's not right."

Using his bare hands, he frantically clawed at the huge snowdrift blocking Iain's door. Ronnie had never seen snow like it. He tried to imagine Iain's panic being trapped inside his home, unable to feed his beloved cattle. The silence around the cottage bore no signs of life. Ronnie prepared for the worst. He lifted the frozen latch and squeezed his way into the sparsely-furnished dwelling.

"Anyone at home?"

No answer.

"Is everything all right, Iain? Can I get you anything?"

Still no answer.

The muffled sound of the wind was all that could be heard inside the stockman's freezing home.

Ronnie instinctively knew what to expect as he walked into the adjoining bedroom. Stretched out on the bed under a threadbare blanket lay the emaciated corpse of Iain MacKinnon, his sunken cheeks and hollow eyes testifying to an unspeakably lonely death. Ronnie had seen dead men before but none as pathetic as Iain. His immediate reaction was to rush out of the room, open the door and vomit green bile onto the snow.

The thought of a gentle old man being left to die in such appalling conditions filled him with rage. He cried aloud, laying the blame squarely at the feet of Major Urquart who, for over thirty years, had hidden behind the stout walls of his fortress, unable to empathize. Such self-indulgence! He wasn't the only father to lose a son in the Great War. Old Duncan Grant, for example, had lost three sons fighting at Festubert where Douglas Urquhart had lost his life. Unlike the Major, Duncan had to continue working to provide for his wife and remaining son. Ronnie never understood how someone as privileged as the Major could become so heartlessly dysfunctional.

Once Ronnie had recovered from the shock of seeing Iain's lifeless body, he returned to the bedroom determined to show the old man the respect he lacked during his final days. With great tenderness, he swept the few strands of hair away from his sunken eyes before closing them.

"Rest in peace, Iain," he whispered, tucking the old man into his bed. He knew it was a pointless act of kindness but Ronnie hoped the loving gesture would remind Iain, wherever he was, that someone had cared for him at the end of his life.

Ronnie bowed his head and recited the 23rd Psalm before covering his face.

An overwhelming sense of injustice seized him as he pushed his bike up the frozen path towards Kilbackie House. It was time the Major understood that he had failed in his moral duty of care towards those working for him.

Ronnie usually left the post in an outside box but today he wanted to hand over the letters in person. He knocked on the front door, feeling tense, on his guard, ready for a fight but the pale man who greeted him was not the powerful man he remembered. Far from it. Major Urquhart appeared frail with bloodless lips, watery blue eyes and swollen, reddened hands. A large drip hung precariously to the end of his red veiny nose. He was wrapped from head to toe in a large woollen blanket.

On his head he wore what can only be described as a knitted tea cosy!

It was a forlorn sight.

"You needn't have gone to so much trouble," he said with genuine gratitude, "but I'm glad you did. I get so few visitors these days. Come inside and get warm."

The Major shuffled across the lofty hall in a pair of oversized slippers. The air was so cold it hurt to breathe. Once inside the warm kitchen, he bustled about trying to make space for his unexpected guest. The room was chaotic. Piles of magazines and papers littered the table, dirty plates, cups and saucepans were piled high on the draining board. Overhead, damp clothes dangled from a Shiela Maid and in a dark corner of the musty room there was a large stack of logs - enough to keep the range alight for several days. The Major cleared the table and drew a chair in front of the range that exhaled wisps of smoke from its ill-fitting doors.

Ronnie thought of Iain's pitiful, freezing death.

"Give me your coat," the Major said. "I'll hang it over the back of the chair and with any luck it'll be dry by the time you leave. While you wait, you may as well take off your socks and warm your feet. The last thing you need is a bout of chilblains - horrid beastly things!"

He rummaged in a large oak chest and pulled out two Black Watch tartan blankets.

"You might be wondering why an Urquhart tolerates Black Watch tartan in his house especially when his clan sided with the Jacobites at Culloden. I won't bore you with history other than to say that my wife was a Grant and these blankets belonged to her!"

Ronnie had no idea what the Grants had to do with blankets nor was he interested on which side the Urquharts fought at Culloden. As far as he cared, they could or should have been killed, taken prisoner, executed or transported to the Americas. He didn't care! His mind was focussed on Iain MacKinnon, whose emaciated body was still lying under a single frayed blanket in a freezing black house. Culloden, Jacobites, Grants and the Black Watch were never going to bring him back. Instead of worrying about clan history, the Major should have offered the Black Watch blankets to Iain.

The Major handed Ronnie the larger of the two blankets. "This one is made of good quality wool" he said. "Wrap it round your shoulders to get warm."

The second blanket was thinner. It was riddled with moth holes and had definitely seen better days but wrapped round Ronnie's feet it protected his toes from the freezing flagstones.

"Can I get you something hot to drink?"

Ronnie declined. The sight of the Major's voluminous, stained underwear hanging overhead made him queasy. He had no intention of staying any longer than necessary.

Ronnie sat down by the fire wondering how best to break the news of Iain's death. In the end it was the Major who broached the subject, asking if he had dropped in to see Iain on his way. Ronnie told him the grizzly details of the poor man's wretched end.

On hearing about Iain's demise, the laird sank his head into the folds of the blanket wrapped around his shoulders and wept.

"Oh, God! What have I done? Poor kind Iain! What have I done?"

It was difficult to tell if the Major's tears were genuine or just an act but Ronnie gave him the benefit of the doubt and looked kindly on the selfish entitled old relic sitting opposite him. He had nothing to say to the Major whose watery eyes were fixed on the cold stone floor beneath his feet.

"Iain dead!" he muttered over and over again. "I can't believe it."

The Major lost interest in Ronnie's presence. All he could think about was the great hole Iain's death would leave in his life. The two of them had grown up together. Without this irreplaceable, unique man who had served the Urquhart family for over fifty years, the cattle would have to be sold.

In the end there was nothing left for Ronnie to do, or say. He put on his clothes and slipped out into the snow, leaving the Major to reflect upon a wasted life filled with regrets.

The following day, a few neighbours from the mainland walked across the causeway to check on Ronnie's starving cattle. They were in a bad way but there was enough hay stored in the barn to keep them fed until spring. The fold made a dramatic recovery and grew stronger with every lengthening day. During a burst of spring growth in early

May when dull winter tones exploded into colour, the Major took his last breath and was buried alongside his wife on the hill overlooking the Outer Isles.

The cattle were sold in the market at Portree and the Estate was finally put up for sale.

CHAPTER 8

Mairi leant out of an upstairs window where musty blankets hung over the sill to air. The westerly winds had finally abated, making way for a gentle southerly.

Nature was straining at the leash, creaking in the rising temperatures. Great black-backed gulls, the kings of the Atlantic waterfront, hopped noisily over the stones on the rocky shore scavenging for food. The air was filled with optimistic energy. It was electrifying.

She rushed from room to room pushing hard to open windows that hadn't been touched for years. Faded curtains fluttered in the breeze that swept through unused corridors, scattering piles of dead flies and woodlice.

When all the upstairs windows were open, she returned to the kitchen while Johnny and Tavish stood by the front door waiting for their guest to arrive.

"He's coming! I can see his car," Tavish squealed with excitement. The eagerly awaited car crawled cautiously over the rough track, swerving from side to side to avoid the many potholes. Eventually, it came to a halt opposite the house and a tall upright man in his mid-fifties stepped confidently onto the stony drive.

He wore a beautifully fitted tweed suit and highly polished brogues that shrieked of quality, their muted colours blending effortlessly into the surrounding hills.

Tavish gave a sudden gasp and nudged his father.

"What's happened to his face, Daddy? It's all wrong!" he whispered.

Johnny squeezed his son's hand as if to say, 'Shhh! We'll talk about it later, not now.'

Mr Buchanan's badly burned face was covered in tight scarring that had transformed the skin into a mask. Johnny knew of several pilots who had suffered facial burns in the last war, mostly due to ruptured fuel tanks. He suspected that Mr Buchanan's reconstructed face was the work of Sir Archibald McIndoe, the plastic surgeon who had pioneered new techniques for treating burns to the face and hands. Sir Archibald recognised the importance of social interaction to draw the scarred pilots back into normal life. Fortunately for Johnny, Mr Buchanan wasn't the least bit fazed by his looks. He immediately introduced himself with humour and charm. After cordial handshakes and a lengthy pause to admire the view, Johnny led his guest into the hall. Mairi, who was rolling pastry to cover an enamel dish packed with tender venison, bacon and onion, caught snippets of their conversation.

"Welcome ... yes, we are fortunate ... I've worked with cattle all my life ... never been to Scotland before ... it's all new ... not possible without Mairi ... she's a rock ... wonderful place to bring up a child."

She felt herself blush with pride.

"Lunch will be ready in about an hour," she announced as the two men walked towards the drawing room.

Mr Buchanan's affable nature immediately put Johnny at ease. Despite his facial deformities, he was reassuringly positive with a natural authority that inspired confidence. Johnny fell under his spell.

They entered the bright, clean drawing room where warm rays of sunshine streamed onto the richly coloured carpet.

Johnny had never formally entertained anyone in the drawing room before. He badly wanted to make a good impression but was terrified of appearing ignorant or worse still stupid. He sat awkwardly on the sofa, aware that his posture was all wrong. It was far too rigid. He could feel his muscles tighten, his neck stiffen. Opposite him sat Mr Buchanan - relaxed, impeccably mannered and at ease. A man of the world who was used to gracious living.

"No wonder the privileged few still hold all the power," Johnny thought. *"They are so bloody charming and articulate."*

Mairi poked her head round the door to see if they would like something to drink.

"Come in, Mrs Mitchell!" the Trustee said, introducing himself properly, making her feel instantly at home in her own drawing room. "What a lovely thought! A cup of coffee for me, please. Milk, no sugar. And you Johnny, what would you like?"

"The same," came the rather terse reply.

"Splendid! Two coffees please, Mrs Mitchell."

Mairi closed the door and returned to the kitchen, delighted the Trustee had acknowledged her as the mistress of the house. As lunchtime approached, she reminded Tavish not to stare at their guest.

"I won't stare," he promised, his mind fixed on the Spitfire he was building out of Meccano. To give the plane extra firepower, he attached axle rods to the wings to imitate machine gun barrels and fixed a rubber band to the propeller within the fuselage so it would spin.

"I like Mr Buchanan, he's nice," he added, swooping the plane round the room making the 'tac' 'tac' 'tac' sounds of a machine gun.

"Stop that racket and tell your father lunch is ready," Mairi said, adding the finishing touches to the meal. Tavish reluctantly put down the plane and walked to the huge drawing room door. It was closed. He gave a hesitant knock.

No answer.

He knocked again, only this time louder.

"Come in!" came his father's familiar voice.

Inside the enormous room, the atmosphere was relaxed. His father and Mr Buchanan were chatting amicably surrounded by piles of paper.

"Mummy says that lunch is ready."

"My goodness!" Mr Buchanan said looking at his watch. "Is it one o'clock already? Your father and I have been so engrossed, we've completely lost track of time." He stood up, put the empty coffee cups and plates on the tray and followed Tavish back to the kitchen.

"Thank you for the mouth-watering shortbread," he said with total sincerity, placing the tray on the draining board. "It was just how I like it. Pale and buttery!"

Mairi welcomed the compliment but Johnny found Mr Buchanan's courtesy irritating. How could a man with such a sharp financial brain become an expert on shortbread all of a sudden? It didn't make sense. While he pondered the dichotomy, Mr Buchanan caught sight of the model Spitfire lying on the table.

"Is that yours?" he exclaimed, looking at Tavish. "I like the way you have added a wind-up propeller. Can I try it?" He picked up the plane, wound the elastic band as tight as he dared, then released it. The propeller whirred into action.

"Have you ever flown a Spitfire?" Tavish asked, hoping to meet a real fighter pilot but Mr Buchanan shook his head. "I'd loved to have been a pilot but I was too old to fight in the last war."

"So, what happened to your face?" Tavish asked in the matter-of-fact way children adopt when they are curious and want answers.

There was a stunned silence, a look of horror on Johnny and Mairi's faces but Mr Buchanan seemed undaunted.

"That's a fair question," he said, "I look different to most people, don't I?"

Tavish nodded enthusiastically.

"It all happened a long time ago when I was a soldier in what we now call the Great War. I was crossing 'No Man's Land'. Do you know what 'No Man's Land' means?

Tavish shook his head.

Mr Buchanan placed the salt cellar and pepper pot opposite each other on the table.

"Imagine the salt is our army and the pepper is the enemy. The space in between is called 'No Man's Land' because it doesn't belong to anyone. It is usually flat and very dangerous. My friend and I were running across this wide-open space when an enemy shell landed a few yards from us.

"A shell in this context means an explosive, an enormous bullet fired from a canon, not the ones you find on the beach.

"Anyway, back to the story. There was nowhere to hide when the shell whistled towards us. It landed and exploded close to where we were running, shattering my jaw and burning the skin off my face."

"Did it hurt?" Tavish asked matter-of-factly.

"Not at first because I was unconscious but when I woke up it really hurt. I was in hospital for two years."

"Wow!" Tavish exclaimed. "That's a long time!"

"That's enough, Tavish!" Mairi exclaimed, worried his persistent questioning would upset Mr Buchanan but her fears were unfounded. He was happy to talk about his wartime experience and used simple words to explain what happened without sounding patronising.

"Did the injury make you sad?" Tavish continued, despite his mother's objections.

"At first, I *was* sad but then one day a nurse told me a little story that changed my life and made me realise that I still had a lot to give."

"Tell me the story," Tavish pleaded. "Pleeeease! I love stories."

Mr Buchanan looked at Mairi for permission to recount his story, mouthing it wouldn't take long.

"Once upon a time there was an old lady who had two large water pots that hung on the ends of a long pole. One was perfect, the other was cracked.

"Every morning, she carried the pole and pots across her neck to the stream that flowed at the bottom of her village. Here she filled the pots with water. By the time she reached home, one of the pots, the cracked one, was only half full.

"For two years the lady filled her pots with water from the stream. For two years she returned home to find one of the pots only half full. The perfect pot boasted it was always full. The cracked pot apologised for being half empty.

After two years of failure, the cracked pot spoke to the woman.

'I am useless at holding water. The crack in my side makes me imperfect. Half the water spills onto the ground and is wasted by the time you reach home. Why don't you replace me with a perfect pot?'

The old woman smiled.

'Have you never noticed that there are flowers on your side of the path, but not on the perfect pot's side? I have always known you weren't perfect, so I planted flower seeds on your side of the path and every day when we walk back, you water them. Without you being just the way you are, there wouldn't be any beautiful flowers.'

Tavish listened spell-bound and when Mr Buchanan had finished, he remarked, "That's a really good story. Now I understand why it doesn't matter what you look like."

"Exactly!" Mr Buchanan smiled. "So, you see, Tavish, after the nurse told me that story, I stopped feeling sorry for myself."

Tavish spent a few moments reflecting on what Mr Buchanan had said, then asked if he could sit next to him.

Mairi's potato pastry venison pie was a triumph.

"My goodness, this is good!" Mr Buchanan said, savouring every mouthful of the succulent pie. "What a treat after so many years of rationing. Thank you, Mrs Mitchell!"

"You're a lucky man, Johnny!" he added.

Mairi glowed with pride.

The conversation around the kitchen table focussed entirely on the farm, with Mr Buchanan taking the dominant role. Mairi remained in awe of his perfect manners. Johnny sat mesmerised by his intellectual grasp of the facts. Tavish liked his stories.

"And you, Mrs. Mitchell?" He asked, dabbing the corners of his mouth with the napkin. "Do you have any plans for Kilbackie?"

The unexpected question took Mairi by surprise. She didn't know how to reply as no-one had ever asked for her opinion before. "I haven't really thought about it," she replied meekly. "All I want to do is look after the house and bring up Tavish." She left out the fact that her dreary cold home made her so depressed, she had even considered leaving Skye to return south, where the climate was gentler. How could she admit to the visitor that Kilbackie House's haunting history was weighing her down?

"Put it this way," he said optimistically, aware she was struggling. "Sir Hugh was passionate about saving this ancient, damp old pile but he was a realist. He knew it wouldn't be easy. To be perfectly frank, he believed you had the linguistic and cultural skills necessary to drag Kilbackie House into the twentieth century. He had faith in you, Mrs Mitchell and he was an excellent judge of character."

Mairi hung on Mr Buchanan's every word. His eloquence worked like a charm, convincing her that she was capable of reviving Kilbackie House.

"Sir Hugh was a romantic but not a hopeless one," Mr Buchanan continued. "Beneath his easy-going charm there was a steely determination to modernise Kilbackie and make it a home to be proud of. If you are happy to play your part in his vision, I'll get a surveyor to come over next week and inspect the roof, guttering, flashing and windows. Johnny told me about the damp. I'm so sorry."

He paused to take a sip of water.

"And while we're on the subject of the house, perhaps you could make a list of labour-saving devices that would make your life easier."

He flipped over a page in his note book.

"I've jotted down a few things - vacuum cleaner, twin tub, fridge, cooker and iron but I'm sure you will think of others.

"Sir Hugh was keen to install a hot water system to feed the new bathroom adjoining your bedroom. The present bathroom will be modernised for Tavish."

Mairi looked incredulous. Hot water, new roof, twin tub, fridge, bathroom all courtesy of the Trust? It was incredible.

"Lastly," Mr Buchanan said, "and I really mean lastly. Sir Hugh's life was based on the twin virtues of humility and forgiveness. It was his dearest wish that these virtues would continue to be valued at Kilbackie."

Mairi thought back over her past. It seemed very unlikely she could ever fulfil this wish.

"Are you all right, Mrs Mitchell? You've gone very pale all of a sudden!"

"I'm fine," she assured him. "It's been rather a long morning with lots to take in."

"I quite understand. Give yourself a breather and if Johnny can spare you for a few minutes, I'd like to show you a room that is very dear to my heart."

"Don't mind me," Johnny replied. "I've got enough paperwork to last me weeks!"

Mr Buchanan led Mairi down the corridor to the locked room.

"I've been looking everywhere for the key," she said. "It's the one room I haven't been able to open up and air."

"This should do it," he said producing a key from his trouser pocket.

CHAPTER 9

Mairi walked into a pitch-black room.

"Wait while I open up the shutters. It shouldn't take long."

One by one the wooden shutters folded back, flooding the room in a golden light. The sun's rays beamed into a magnificent library - a replica of the jewel in Shottenden's crown. Compared to the mournful Edwardian drawing room, the library was a masterpiece of elegant beauty crafted by men whose creative skills had produced oak bookcases, pilasters and mouldings. No expense had been spared. Rows of red, blue and green leather-bound books blended with the rich colours of a woven carpet that spread across the floor like a warm exotic tide. Sir Hugh's leather-topped reading desk stood in the centre of the room just as it had at Shottenden. Carved into the limestone fireplace were the intertwining initials A and K.

'Angus and Katherine,' Mairi thought. *'All this was for them, not for me and Johnny. Kilbackie was to be their home, their future with Tavish, not ours. We're only here because Angus died and Katherine withdrew into an abbey.'*

She thought of Mr Buchanan's words and the trust he was putting in her and Johnny. Despite her desire to please, she questioned whether she was truly the most suitable person for the task.

Sir Hugh had gone to extraordinary lengths to recreate Shottenden's exquisite library in Kilbackie House. It was the one room he chose to preserve after he had bequeathed his family home to the National Trust. He must have planned the whole transfer with extreme care. It was an eccentric, crazy idea but behind the madness, lay a noble dream that Mairi wanted to honour.

In pride of place on the wall opposite the north facing window hung a majestic full-length portrait of Sir Hugh, swathed in MacKenzie tartan. Arrogant and proud, he stood against a rugged Highland moor with his beloved Jack Russell, Tats, lying at his feet.

It was a remarkable portrait but then Sir Hugh had been a remarkable man.

Mr Buchanan remained by the reading desk to allow Mairi more time to take in the full impact of the room but her eyes never left the painting of Sir Hugh, whose extraordinary presence was changing her life.

Mr Buchanan went over to a bookcase and pulled out an illustrated volume of Highland Wildflowers. He opened it at Tufted Vetch, a purple flower described as a legume, a member of the pea and clover family, with spikes of bluish-violet flowers.

"The books in this library cover a wide range of subjects," he explained, "but the largest section is dedicated to natural history. There are many beautiful wildflower illustrations like this watercolour."

He turned a page to show Mairi a picture of red clover.

"Stop me if I'm telling you things you already know. I

tend to get carried away when talking about grassland and soil. It is such a fascinating subject.

"Very few people give much thought to soil other than it's dirty. We take it for granted and yet without healthy soil, life as we know it would cease to exist.

"Unfortunately, the soil on Kilbackie is low in nitrogen, an essential mineral for plant growth. Legumes, like this red clover and tufted vetch play a vital role enriching the soil by drawing nitrogen from the air and storing it in special root nodules. These nitrogen-fixing plants add important nutrients to the soil.

"Sir Hugh was a man ahead of his time, a great admirer of the Russian, Vasily Dokuchaev, who is often called 'the Father of Soil.' This book will help you identify the huge range of wild flowers found on the farm."

Mairi traced her finger over the intricate details of the red clover, noticing for the first time, its tiny tubular-shaped flowers. It never occurred to her that such an insignificant weed could enrich the soil with nitrogen, attract pollinators and play a crucial role in supporting biodiversity.

"I don't know what to say," she replied honestly. "This is all completely new to me."

"You don't have to say anything. There are plenty of books here to teach you about flowers, soil and the natural environment. There are also books on history, philosophy, religion and a small selection of novels. The world is now your oyster."

He closed the book and returned it to the bookshelf under the watchful eye of Sir Hugh.

"Take it!" he said, placing a chunky key in the palm of her hand. "It's yours. I already have a copy."

On the whole, Mr Buchanan's visit had a positive effect on Johnny and Mairi. They were relieved to learn that the Trust had sufficient funds to modernise the house and support the Estate.

"What did you make of Mr Buchanan?" Johnny asked as the Trustee's car crawled over the causeway.

"I liked him," she answered truthfully. "But he wasn't at all how I imagined he would be. He was much nicer."

She wanted to add that he was the first person who believed she had a brain but thought better of it.

"You spent a long time with him after lunch. What were you up to?"

"We weren't up to anything," she replied indignantly. "He wanted to show me the locked room. You know, the one that had no key. You'll never guess what's inside. It's amazing! If you have a spare minute, I'd love to show you."

Johnny had no wish to visit the locked room but he followed her all the same.

"Just a peep, then I promise I'll leave you in peace."

She turned the key, longing to see Johnny's face when he laid eyes on the beautiful library.

"Is that it?" he exclaimed, unimpressed by the vast collection of leather-bound books.

"All that money wasted on books when it could have been spent on the farm! It's not right!"

"That's a matter of opinion!" Mairi said, unaware of her husband's deep fear of reading. "Without learning, there wouldn't be progress. This library holds enough knowledge to change the way we farm! Look, I'll show you."

She pulled out the copy of Highland Wildflowers and opened it at the page describing tufted vetch. Much to her surprise she enjoyed talking about the importance of nitrogen and the effect legumes had on the soil.

Her words fell on deaf ears.

Johnny was in no mood to take lessons from his wife especially when the information came from books. He had disliked books ever since he was forced to read aloud at school, a humiliation he never forgot. Instead of staying in lines, the words seemed to jump around the page, rearranging themselves in ways that made no sense.

"Did you read about nitrogen in a book or did Mr Buchanan teach you?" he asked, unsure if he liked the idea of his wife using the library to educate herself. With so much knowledge at her fingertips, she could easily become an expert on soil nutrition and plant growth and put him to shame. He would have to keep up with her by asking Mr Buchanan lots of questions. The library was the one room in the house he was determined to avoid.

"Mr Buchanan told me about the benefits of clover and vetch on the land and showed me where I could learn more if I was interested."

"I suppose you will soon be running the farm!" her husband said facetiously.

The unnecessary comment hurt. Mairi couldn't understand why he was undermining her enthusiasm. She was only trying to help! Despite the temptation to hit back, she held her tongue for the sake of harmony, comforted in the knowledge that Sir Hugh had faith in her.

"I think you'd better go!" she said, placing the book back on the shelf. "Let's talk when you're in a better mood."

"What's got into you?" Johnny retorted. "I've never seen you like this before."

He closed the door, leaving Mairi shaking with rage.

CHAPTER 10

The next morning was wet.

Johnny woke early having spent a fitful night tossing and turning in bed. He and Mairi hadn't exchanged a word since the incident in the library. Looking back, he wondered if he had been too harsh. Perhaps he should apologise but that would mean admitting he was wrong, something he didn't want to do. Hopefully her mood would improve with the day.

He slipped downstairs into the kitchen where droplets of condensation ran down the window panes onto the sills.

Damp was everywhere. He wanted to squeeze the house dry, wring the water out of stonework, start afresh. No words in the English language could accurately describe the wetness of Skye.

He put a match to the dry sticks and moss in the range and stepped back to watch them burst into flames. The kitchen would soon warm up. He settled down to decipher the scribbled notes he had taken during his time with Mr Buchanan. Some of the words were illegible but slowly he managed to read back what he had written. The farming potential was enormous, the possibilities endless. In return for financial support, the Trustees had asked Johnny to produce a set of monthly accounts, something he would enjoy preparing. Whereas he found reading difficult, he had no problem with maths. Percentages, ratios and arithmetic came easily to him. Although the Trust respected his skills and credentials, it reserved the right to question any decision that could be detrimental to the farm's future.

Ambition drove Johnny forward. He was determined to make the farm profitable, fit for the twentieth century, a beacon of modernity. Alone in the peace of the emerging day, he started work on his grand plan, putting into words his frenzied thinking, creating columns of costs and forecasts.

By the time Mairi came down, his notebook was filling up with figures and field plans. The more his pencil moved up and down the page, the more excluded Mairi felt.

The joy she experienced learning about clover and tufted vetch slowly evaporated into the misty morn. Johnny had no interest in soil. He was preoccupied with numbers and accounting. Profit was all that mattered.

When Tavish eventually emerged for breakfast, it was clear from the start that he had got out of bed the wrong side. The child who had reassured his mother he would never be unkind had been replaced by a sulky individual for whom nothing was right.

"Mummeeee!" he whined sleepily. "I want a drink."

"What do you say?" Mairi replied, praying there wouldn't be a scene.

"I want a drink!"

"Not until you say *'please'*."

Tavish banged his cup on the table.

"I want a drink!"

"Not until you say *'please'*," Mairi insisted.

Tavish continued banging his cup on the table.

"Stop that awful noise!" Johnny cried, looking up from his paperwork. "I can't think clearly with all that banging!"

He turned to Mairi. "Can't you do something to stop him?"

She looked at Johnny, then at her disgruntled son who was in no mood to see reason. She doubted there was anything she could do to placate him.

"If you don't do as your mother asks," Johnny threatened, "you'll go straight back to bed! Do I make myself clear?"

The threat had no effect on Tavish - if anything, it made things worse. Mairi tried everything to lighten his mood but he still refused to say *'please'*. Eventually his fractious whining turned into screams.

"I want Daddy to play with me!" he shrieked, flinging himself onto the floor. "And I want a drink," he added, drumming his feet on the cold flagstones.

"Stop it!" Johnny cried. "I can't concentrate with you screaming like that! What's got into you?"

He picked Tavish up by the scruff of the neck and shook him, not violently but enough to make the child realise his behaviour was unacceptable.

"Go to your room!"

But Tavish had no intention of doing as he was told. He was ready for a fight.

"No!" he retorted, turning a deep crimson. "Not until you start playing with me again. You never play with me. All you do is work, work, work! It's not fair."

Johnny had had enough of the screams and sobs. He pushed his angry son aside, scooped up his papers and stormed out of the room, saying he was off to the office. Mairi let out a long sigh of relief once Johnny had left. With him out of the way, she could relax. No more obsessive accounting.

She rolled up her sleeves ready to start the daily chores but first she needed to focus on Tavish who was sitting hunched at the kitchen table, spinning a knife to see which way it would point. He had become sullenly quiet since the confrontation with his father.

She started sweeping the kitchen while Tavish continued to spin the knife, wondering why grown-ups spent most of their time arguing or working.

His thoughts were broken by a knock at the front door.

"Hang on a minute. I'm coming!" Mairi shouted, slapping her hand down on the knife to stop it spinning. Tavish glowered at her.

Standing in the doorway was a girl no older than sixteen, someone Mairi would have recognized anywhere. She was a carbon copy of her mother, Margaret MacPhee, (or MacLean as she now was). Margaret, although five years younger than Mairi, had been her best friend at school. Their friendship had ended when Mairi's father, Revd. Tommy Nicolson, publicly denounced the entire MacPhee family for their intentional and consistent absence from church. Such was his loathing for the MacPhee clan that he had banned his daughter from ever seeing Margaret again.

"Rhona! What are you doing here!? Is everything all right?"

The girl nodded and smiled. Oh! that smile. It brought back memories of Margaret's auburn-haired brother, David, whom she first saw when she was thirteen. He wore a pair of baggy trousers held up with string and was helping the crofters roll up the fleeces as they were shorn off the sheep. Most of the community from the very old to the very young were out on the hill that day, enjoying one of the highlights of the crofting year. Everywhere she looked, men were marking, penning, shearing or releasing sheep. For a girl brought up in the protected confines of the Manse, the sight of hard physical labour both appalled and thrilled her.

"Come and say '*hi*' to my brother," Margaret had said, dragging her towards a cacophony of baaing sheep and clipping shears. Mairi held back. Even though there were plenty of familiar faces from church, she still felt uneasy.

"Let's go home," she pleaded. "Please, Margaret. My father will be furious if he finds out I've been playing with you."

"Don't be silly! Your father can't stop us seeing people at shearing time!"

Mairi wasn't convinced. She felt on edge, afraid of what her father would say and even more afraid of what he would do if he discovered she'd spoken to Margaret and her brother. In the end she needn't have worried. David had no wish to chat to his little sister or her friend but Margaret had other ideas.

"What's got into you?" she mocked. "Trying to look older than you are now you've learned to smoke? You'll need more hair on your chin before you can call yourself a man."

David sauntered over to the two girls, drew in a lungful of smoke and exhaled in his sister's face.

Mairi looked on in utter amazement.

Margaret was furious.

"Come on, Mairi. It's no use trying to talk to him. He thinks he's too grown up for us. Let's go."

The two girls picked up their shoes and ran across the moor, laughing at the tickling heather under their feet.

"Ahem!" the visitor coughed, bringing Mairi back to the present with a jolt. The composure of the girl standing in the doorway was extraordinary. It unnerved Mairi. She stuttered to say something appropriate but, in the end, it was Rhona who spoke. "I've come to help you in the house, Mrs Mitchell."

Mairi was speechless. Her cheeks flushed at the sight of David's niece standing in the doorway of her huge house. "But I'm not looking for any help," she replied.

The girl handed over an envelope addressed to Mrs. Johnny Mitchell, Kilbackie House. It was from Mr Buchanan, informing her that the Trust had employed Rhona to work in the house for seven hours a day, Mondays to Fridays and, if required to baby sit for Tavish. She was to have an hour off for lunch and be allowed to stay overnight if the tide or a storm prevented her from returning home during daylight hours.

This was the first Mairi knew of such an arrangement.

"You'd better come in," she said, beckoning the young girl into the entrance hall. Rhona stood staring up at the ceiling, wondering what lay in store for her.

CHAPTER 11

"You're joking!"

"I'm not. I'm perfectly serious. The Trust has employed Rhona to help me in the house and look after Tavish."

"What will you do with all the spare time if Rhona does all the work?" her sister asked scornfully. "Surely you've lived long enough in a Manse to know that the Devil makes work for idle hands."

Mairi was slightly taken aback by Effie's barbed comment, but she had a point. What was she meant to do with so much time on her hands? Way back, Kilbackie House would have employed an army of servants to do the work but times had changed since the Great War. The entire house was run by her and Rhona. Two women were expected to wash and iron the sheets for eight bedrooms, prepare and cook daily meals, clean and polish three grand reception rooms and sweep the corridors, sculleries, hall and front porch. The days of Kilbackie's famed dances and house parties were over. What heady occasions they must have been! A whirlwind of fashionable ladies enjoying the delights of Highland hospitality. The dining room table would have been adorned with crystal glass, candles, flowers and sparkling cutlery, endless courses of seasonally cooked food, chopped, gutted, peeled, hulled, skinned, plucked and cored in the steamy hot kitchen. Servants would have bustled up and down the corridors, fuelling fires, serving, clearing up. It was hard, exhausting work and at the end of a long day, they would have retired to bed in the cheerless freezing attic rooms where the sun never shone and rotten window frames let in the cold.

Mairi shuddered at the thought of entertaining. The only people she knew well enough to ask over for supper were the crofting folk who attended her father's church, most of whom would feel awkward in such a formal setting. Dinner parties were set-pieces, run according to an etiquette she neither knew nor understood. Creative recipes, wine lists, flower arrangements and dress codes were beyond her understanding. She couldn't turn to Johnny for help because he would only scoff at the idea and probably refuse to make an appearance. Mairi tried to imagine ten crofters, dressed in their Sunday-best, trying to make polite conversation surrounded by silver and porcelain. The whole idea was ludicrous - a grotesque display of wealth and privilege.

She would have to justify Rhona's presence in the house another way.

"As from tomorrow," she announced the next morning, "we're going to eat breakfast and lunch in the dining room, using the formal dinner service. Rhona will lay the table and clear up after each meal, leaving us more time to talk to each other."

Johnny looked up from his farming journal, horrified at the thought of having to make conversation at breakfast.

"You can leave me out of this mad idea," he complained. "I have no wish to play the part of a laird, whatever that means. Give me a warm kitchen, muddy boots, old clothes and a smelly dog any day. What am I expected to do in this new world of yours? Shampoo the dog and change into a tweed suit?!"

"Don't be silly," Mairi replied with remarkable patience. "Everything will be just the same. All I'm asking is that you change out of your muddy clothes to protect the dining room chairs, wash your hands and leave Jess in the kitchen. Is that too much to ask?"

Johnny wasn't sure. He loved the shabby kitchen with its worn flagstones and scrubbed table. It was the beating heart of the house where he could relax with Jess. A place where no-one cared if his work clothes were dirty or his elbows were on the table. Now Mairi was asking him to become someone he wasn't. As a Yorkshireman, he had no time for dainty manners. Small talk was out of the question.

The next day, Mairi made a special effort with her appearance. She chose a white blouse, a tweed skirt and a powder blue cardigan that matched her eyes. A dab of lipstick brought colour to her lips. She looked in the mirror and was pleasantly surprised at the younger, more confident face staring back. Tavish immediately noticed the change.

"You look really nice today, Mummy. Is there anything I can do to help?"

He suddenly sounded grown up, as if he were making a special effort to earn his place at the formal table where delicate porcelain shone on the highly polished mahogany.

Such compliments were rare for Mairi who considered herself unremarkable.

"Let's go downstairs and see if everything's ready."

The dining room table was already set by the time Johnny had completed his early morning chores. Rhona was well underway cooking breakfast, her flushed cheeks radiating heat as she sang 'Dheanainn Sùgradh', the well-known waulking song sung by women in the Western Isles as they rhythmically pummelled and transformed newly-woven cloth into the famous tweeds known throughout the world.

Tavish tugged at her blouse and asked if he could help.

"Thank you," she said with genuine warmth. "Could you carry the porridge through to the dining room and put it on the sideboard? I've almost finished. I've just got the last two slices of bread to fry."

Tavish took the creamy mixture to the sideboard and waited for breakfast to begin.

He was hungry!

At the far end of the corridor, he could hear his parents arguing over something he didn't understand. Mairi and Johnny weren't exactly shouting but their disagreement was loud enough to be heard beyond the sitting room walls. They seemed to be bickering more recently; mostly about unimportant things like the arrival of Rhona, the expensive library, the size of the house but sometimes things got out of hand and words were said that were later regretted. Tavish closed his ears to the pointless squabble and retreated to the safe place he had created deep within his inner being. It was his special place. A place where he could be left in peace.

'*They can argue as much as they want,*' he thought, '*but I wish they'd hurry up. I'm famished.*'

He took a mouthful of porridge straight from the ladle and felt the warm oaty mixture trickle into his empty stomach just as a red-faced Mairi walked in, followed by Johnny who looked as if he'd rather be anywhere other than the formal dining room.

"I see you've already started," she frowned. "You should have waited."

Tavish didn't bother replying.

"Take this to Daddy," she said, handing him a bowl. "And Tavish," she warned, "don't eat out of the saucepan again!"

Johnny settled down at the table with his elbows conspicuously splayed out to annoy his wife. Although his hands were clean and he'd taken off his boots, he hadn't bothered to change out of his filthy trousers. This small act of rebellion was his way of telling Mairi that the 'eating-in-the-dining room' experiment was an embarrassment. He looked up at the row of Urquharts gazing down at him, wondering how their ancestral home had ended up in the hands of an Englishman with no Highland roots or Gaelic.

Johnny longed to return to the anonymous comfort of the cluttered kitchen with its lit range and uneven floor but while his wife was on a mission to upgrade the family's social status, he had to contend with sitting at a table designed for fourteen. It was so ludicrous he wanted to laugh but Mairi would never see the funny side of the pantomime performance. She was deadly serious. In all the time he had known her, she had never laughed or joked. He doubted she would understand a joke if he told her one. He studied the intensity of her face and saw an enigmatic beauty shining through the fragile mask. Perhaps he had judged her too harshly, after all, it had taken immense courage to organise such a formal breakfast and in a strange way, she had succeeded with extraordinary poise.

Like a chameleon, she managed to blend into her surroundings, eating dainty portions with an elegance he had never seen before.

Rhona stood hesitantly in the doorway.

"I'm sorry to interrupt, Madam, but shall I bring in the cooked food?"

Johnny writhed with embarrassment at the word 'Madam' but Mairi took it in her stride, checking to see everyone had finished before giving a nod of approval. When breakfast was over, she dabbed the corners of her mouth with the napkin and stood up as if to say 'we're done'.

"Is it all right if I use the car this afternoon? Effie wants to talk and I thought I could stock up with some food on my way home."

Johnny had planned to spend the whole day on the farm so had no need of the car.

"What do you want to do while Mummy is with Aunt Effie?" he asked his son.

"Stay with you," came the instant reply.

"Rhona will help look after him if you're busy but I know, for choice he'd prefer to be with you." Mairi said. "He won't be any trouble. While I'm out, I thought I'd visit the school. It's time he made friends with children his own age and learned how to read and write. I'll see if he can start next week."

"Come on, young man," Johnny said, ruffling the boy's unruly hair. "Let's go and find Willie."

Mairi gave a look of total surprise at the mention of Willie.

"I'm sorry," Johnny apologised. "With all that's been going on recently, I totally forgot to tell you that the Trust has asked Willie Morrison to help me on the farm. He won't be full-time as he has his own croft to run but he'll be a useful extra pair of hands when needed. I've already discovered he's a man of many talents. What that man doesn't know about cattle isn't worth knowing!"

The Morrisons and Nicolsons had known each other for generations. Willie had been at school with Mairi although they hardly knew each other. She had been studious by nature, spending most of her free time reading, whilst Willie had found reading and writing difficult. His school attendance had been patchy and his grasp of English poor, yet despite his academic struggles he had excelled in husbandry, possessing a unique bond with animals. He was a man at peace with himself. A deeply Christian man who was content speaking Gaelic and working the family croft.

A shy man of few words, he was hardworking and as honest as the day was long. It would have been difficult to find a kinder, more conscientious man to teach Johnny how to farm the land. The Trust had chosen well.

"Willie's a natural with animals," she said generously, aware that the breakfast hadn't gone as well as planned. "His natural language is Gaelic so he'll be the perfect person to help you understand the community. Did he mention the boat?"

Johnny nodded, trying to stop Tavish tugging at his jumper.

"All right. I'm coming!" he said, holding the little boy's hand. "Be patient!"

He looked at Mairi. "Have fun with Effie!" he said, then whistled for Jess and headed out of the dining room with Tavish in tow.

"You and I are going to check the cattle and fencing with Willie while Mummy visits your new school. Deal?"

"Deal!" echoed a small voice.

Mairi was pleased the way the morning had turned out despite Johnny's lukewarm reaction to the new breakfast arrangements. At least he had joined her, albeit reluctantly, and had shown a hint of admiration for the way she had behaved and dressed.

Crossing the causeway in bright sunshine, her senses were alive and responsive. Nature was finally emerging from the long Hebridean winter.

She drove over the moor and parked near her sister's croft where hens energetically pecked the ground beneath jagged strands of a rusty barbed wire fence. The last pregnant ewes staggered among grassy tufts, weighed down by their unborn lambs. A cat lay curled on the doorstep, sheltering from the wind that blew through the laundry pegged on the washing line. It was a timeless sight. One that reminded Mairi of the comforting way of life she remembered so well.

She turned the handle of the door and walked in without knocking.

"You've come, then!" Effie said with unexpected surprise. "I didn't think you would."

"Thanks a lot!" Mairi said with a degree of exasperation. "I thought you wanted us to talk but I'll go if you don't want me here."

"Don't be silly! Of course, I want you here! Come on in. Do you want a coffee?"

Mairi nodded as she made her way into the familiar front room where a thick layer of dog hair covered the orange swirls on the brown carpet. It smelt strongly of dog and fox but Effie had grown accustomed to the pungent smells. She loved her isolated croft on the barren hillside, far removed from the idle gossip that spread across the lower slopes of the township. She had inherited it from her maternal grandfather, Alasdair MacSwan, who, as far as she knew, had been the third generation to live there. The only records of the family's existence were found carved on various headstones in the remote cemetery set high on a hill overlooking Kilbackie Island.

One Sunday morning in 1578, a group of men from Clan MacDonald of South Uist rowed across the Minch and landed on the shores of Kilbackie while the inhabitants were in church. Under a covering of fog, they blocked the heavy wooden door and set light to the thatched roof, killing all but one of the worshippers. Ever since that dreadful Sunday, the church has lain in ruins - a testament to the brutality of clan warfare and the total disregard of the sanctity of life.

The original house owned by Effie's grandfather, had been a windowless, thatched black house heated by a peat fire that burned day and night in the centre of the main room. Its smoke filtered through the thatched roof, leaving a layer of sticky tar. Every year the thatch was stripped off the rafters and carted off to the raised potato beds to enrich the soil.

For centuries, crofting remained unchanged but the carnage of the First World War ended a traditional way of life. Hundreds of fresh volunteers from Skye, Lochaber and Wester Ross joined 4th Battalion Queen's Own Cameron Highlanders and saw action at Neuve Chapelle, Aubers and Festubert. In the fields and trenches of Northern France, miles from home, they were gassed, shot or blown up. Those who returned home determined to build a better future were thwarted by the twin evils of unemployment and poverty. Many chose to cut their losses and emigrate to distant lands where the future looked bright and the sun shone. The Highland exodus left crofts struggling to cope with the demands of subsistence living. Roofs were left to rot. Houses became uninhabitable.

Some were officially declared unfit for human dwelling. Effie and Mairi's grandparents had been forced to leave their decaying home but they were fortunate enough to receive a government grant to help build a new house next to the old one. Over time, the black house collapsed and its stones were used to build a fank.

Effie's front room hadn't changed - the dog hair, well-worn sofa, fire and display cabinet were just as Mairi remembered them.

'It's as if I've never been away,' she thought, pleased that Effie had finally got rid of the faded curtains that used to hang in her front room.

Half a dozen brightly coloured cushions added warmth to the well-worn sofa where, after an exhausting day out on the hills, Effie would curl up with her dogs and relax.

Mairi looked round the familiar room and noticed for the first time, a small photo perched on the mantelpiece. She had never seen it before. It showed a much younger Effie gazing adoringly at David on a picnic rug somewhere on the hill above the church. The tip of the bell tower could just be seen in the corner of the photo. A single moment caught on camera by an unknown photographer. The sight of David sent goose bumps crawling across Mairi's skin. However much she had tried to draw a line under her past, he haunted her waking hours, denying her closure and peace.

Mairi could hear Effie's footsteps walk the short distance between the kitchen and the front room. She hastily returned to the sofa and re-arranged her skirt over her knees, keeping her back straight.

"Do you want any help?" she called but her words were drowned out by the arrival of three boisterous border collies who took it in turns to sniff her ankles, rub their wet noses against her dark woollen skirt and jump on the sofa.

"Shoo!" she hissed. "Get down!" But the dogs ignored her command. They nuzzled up to her cardigan, leaving a trail of mucus across her sleeves. She tried pushing them away but they wouldn't leave.

Effie poked her head round the door. "I've forgotten the biscuits. Won't be a mo. If the dogs annoy you, feel free to push them off. They tend to get over-excited when I have visitors but with any luck, they'll soon settle down."

Mairi tried to ignore the dogs but it was impossible. They worked as a pack, taking turns to poke, paw and nudge her. No sooner had she pushed one off than another jumped up to take its place. By the time Effie returned with a tray, Mairi had given up trying to control the dogs and was sitting anxiously on the edge of the sofa surrounded by three very alert collies.

"Peg! Nell! Bess! Down girls!" Effie commanded, placing the tray of hot drinks and biscuits on a low coffee table.

It only took two words from their mistress for the dogs to spring off the cushions and re-assemble themselves at her feet. Effie sat down next to her sister, deciding now was the perfect time to bring up the subject that had troubled her ever since Mairi's return.

"How well did you know David?" she asked.

The abrupt question touched a raw nerve with Mairi who helped herself to a biscuit to steady her nerves.

"What a strange question after all these years!" she replied. "The last time I saw David was in 1933, just before he was lost at sea. Why bring up his name after all this time?"

Effie put her hand down to stroke Peg's silky coat. She was in no hurry to talk but the silence carried a pain she didn't want to bear any more.

"I'm not sure, really," she said reluctantly. "No particular reason other than I've been doing a lot of thinking since you've come back."

She walked over to the mantelpiece and picked up the photo. "I came across this the other day and have been racking my brain trying to think who took it. It wasn't you, was it?"

Mairi stared at the now familiar photo.

"I doubt it," she said in a soft voice. "You and David never invited me on any of your picnics. It must have been taken by Margaret. She was much more part of your life than I ever was. Don't tell me I've come all this way because you want to know who took a photo of you and David over twenty years ago!?"

Effie mused on her words, lost in memories. She seemed perplexed.

"I'm sure it was you!" she replied. "You were always hanging around me and David, trying to catch his attention and act older than you were."

"I never hung around you!" Mairi said, indignantly. "David was your fiancé. Yes, I found him good-looking and fun to be with but no, I never followed you around."

"Perhaps we see the past differently," came her sister's weary reply.

"What's got into you, Effie?" Mairi pleaded. "Why all the gloom about things that happened such a long time ago? Let it be. It's past history."

"I wish I could but something's always niggled me. You remember the St Andrew's Night dance at the Rosvaig Hotel when I was ill in bed? What exactly happened between you and David after the dance? Call it feminine intuition or something else, I don't mind, but I know something happened that night."

"Not that again!" Mairi exclaimed. "When will you get it into your head that nothing happened! Absolutely nothing! We've been over this time and time again and no matter what I say, you are determined to cause mischief by making a mountain out of a molehill!"

"All right! Fair enough, I half believe you but why don't you satisfy my curiosity and tell me once more exactly what happened."

Mairi began to wish she had never paid her sister a visit. Their so-called relaxed conversations always revolved around David and the St Andrew's Night Dance. Mairi wanted to move on but Effie would have none of it. She was like a dog with a bone and never gave up.

"You, David and Margaret," Mairi said, "secretly bought tickets for the St Andrew's Night Dance at the Rosvaig Hotel, knowing our father would have gone mad if he heard you were planning to dance with David, especially as he was a MacPhee. You were in bed, feeling unwell so rather than waste the ticket, you persuaded me to take your place even though I hated dances and was terrified our father would find out."

"David and Margaret were lucky. Their family broke away from our church, leaving them free of all the Presbyterian guilt that kept me in a permanent state of fear. Relaxed and in a party mood, they chatted and danced with friends, leaving me nervously hidden in the shadows wishing I'd never agreed to go. When it was time to leave, Margaret announced she was going to stay the night with her friend, Seonaid, rather than join David and me on the long walk home. She had drunk too much, felt sick and needed to lie down. Fortunately for her, Seonaid only lived five minutes from the hotel, so it was pointless trying to make her change her mind. She left the dance and David and I started the long trek home over the moor.

It was a freezing night with a huge moon that kept disappearing behind the clouds, plunging the moor into darkness. David saw me safely home just before it started to snow. End of story!"

The canine smell in the room and the sight of mucus smeared across her sleeve made Mairi queasy. She had outstayed her welcome and longed to leave the acrid whiff of damp dog.

Effie's eyes never left her sister.

"I don't believe you," she replied.

CHAPTER 12

Kilbackie School was a single-storey building built on a wind-swept hill where Highland cattle grazed the spring grass and nesting grouse and curlew fluttered their wings over large swathes of heather. Mairi hadn't been on this moor for over six years and had forgotten how much the sparsely populated landscape, with its dramatic rock formations, had shaped her earliest memories.

She remembered standing in the playground on the first day of school. A painfully shy five-year-old in awe of the vastness of the view that stretched across the bay to the steep rugged cliffs at Rosvaig Point. Her teacher, Miss McKenzie, had been extraordinarily kind and patient. She encouraged her young protégée to take a pride in her work, focus on accuracy and read as much as possible. There had been something dependable about this impressive middle-aged lady who had dedicated her life to the school. Throughout the year, no matter what the weather, she would turn up for work in her signature blue and grey Harris tweed suit, stout polished shoes and thick stockings.

Mairi had been brought up speaking Gaelic so her arrival in an English-speaking school had been utterly bewildering. Miss McKenzie was sensitive to the needs of the new intake and allowed a few older children to act as translators for the first week only. After that, the five-year-olds had to rely on their scant knowledge of English to get through each day. It didn't take long to learn the new language and by the end of her first term, Mairi was confident speaking and reading books in English. Her reading skills were exceptional. Within weeks she was devouring books aimed at much older children. Among her favourites were 'Five Children and It', 'The Secret Garden' and 'The Railway Children'. She read them over and over again, never tiring of the familiar stories which she knew by heart. Books were her passion. She spent most of her free time reading on the carpet beside the large oak cupboard that housed the school library. During the long dark winter months, the pungent heat of burning peat from the school fire radiated across the classroom, drying the neat row of wet shoes and boots laid out on the hearth.

Mairi's voracious appetite for learning never waned. By the time she left school she was remarkably well-read. Had her parents been more ambitious for their youngest child, they might have encouraged her to apply for a place at college or even university but, instead, they insisted she stayed at home to look after their daily needs, teach in the Sunday School and carry out parish visiting with a meekness of spirit and a quiet sense of duty. The stifling confines of the Manse sapped her creativity and stunted her dreams. Months turned to years and nothing happened to relieve the boredom of her exemplary life.

And now here she was, Mairi Mitchell, waiting in the car to enrol her son at the same school.

Despite the sunshine and clear skies, a strong wind blew across the moor between the crofting communities of Lussa and Rogart. It buffeted the car, shaking it from side to side but Mairi seemed unusually preoccupied. She sat in the driver's seat, summoning the courage to leave the safety of her private space and enter the wide world. She pushed hard at the door but it remained firmly shut. She tried again. The force of the wind was pressing hard against the side of the car, trapping her inside. After several failed attempts, she managed to lever herself onto the passenger seat and open the door on the lee side.

"Good afternoon, Mairi," Mrs Campbell said warmly, delighted to be welcoming a former pupil back to the school. "Please, take a seat."

Instead of acknowledging the generous welcome with a few kind words, Mairi chose to distance herself from the informal greeting.

"It's Mrs Mitchell," she said coolly. "I'd prefer to be called Mrs Mitchell at school if you don't mind."

"As you wish, Mrs Mitchell," Mrs Campbell said, surprised by the unexpected stiffness of the meeting. "My apologies!" She glanced at her notebook. "Have you come to enrol your son, Tavish?"

'Your son ...'

It took Mairi a minute to let the words sink in. Tavish was her son, emotionally and more importantly, officially. The adoption papers had been signed by all the necessary authorities and Katherine had given up all legal rights over her son. No one could remove the small boy from

Mairi. He was safely hers, yet instead of feeling ecstatic, she felt inexplicably sad.

"It's good to know that Kilbackie House is being lived in once more," Mrs Campbell said, trying to sound positive. "It's been a long time since a young family lived there. You are just what it needs. A Gaelic-speaking local family who will breathe new life into the place."

"Thank you!" Mairi replied softly, feeling uncomfortable talking about a house that made her feel so inadequate.

"How old is Tavish?" the Head Teacher asked, aware the meeting wasn't going as well as she had hoped.

"Six," Mairi replied. "Seven in December."

"Six," Mrs Campbell repeated, writing down his name, address and age on a piece of paper. "So, he was born in 1948."

"That's right," Mairi replied, "15th December 1948."

"Thank you," Mrs Campbell said, looking up from her desk, keen to end the awkward meeting. "I think that's all I need for now. I'll be in touch in a couple of days but I can't see why Tavish shouldn't start next week."

The two ladies shook hands and Mairi left the room just as parents were arriving to collect their children. The stares and nudges started before she had time to leave the front door.

'Psst! Look who's coming out of the school! The minister's sister.'

'I hear she's back with a husband and a six-year-old son. Not bad for a spinster who left the island with nothing, seven years ago.'

'I wonder how she managed to bag Kilbackie House. Probably robbed a bank!'

The unkind comments continued to cause ripples of laughter.

"You're back then, Mairi Nicolson," Janet Cameron sniggered. "I hear you've got a wee bairn."

Mairi didn't reply. Holding her head up high, she walked through the crowd, closely followed by Margaret, whose youngest child was still at the school.

"Don't let them get to you, Mairi," she whispered. "They're all mouth, especially Janet Cameron. She's the worst. I don't know how her husband puts up with her but she must be doing something right. She's expecting their fifth child in a couple of months. Her daughter, Annie will be in Tavish's class but you needn't worry, she's a bonnie wee lass.

"If you show a flicker of fear, Janet will twist the knife. Best ignore her. After all, it's you who's living in the big house, not her."

"Thanks, Margaret, but I'm fine, really I am."

Their conversation was interrupted by the arrival of a tall lanky boy of about nine who sprinted across the playground towards his mother. Margaret threw her arms round his skinny frame and hugged him tightly.

"How was your day?" she asked, beaming with pride.

"Good!" Allan replied with impish confidence. It was obvious from his easy manner that Allan was a popular, outgoing pupil.

"Come and meet Mrs Mitchell, the lady I was telling you

about. You probably don't remember her. You were only a baby when she left Skye but she's the one who lives in Kilbackie House where Rhona works. Her son Tavish is starting school next week so perhaps you could keep an eye on him, at least until he has settled in."

Allan wasn't in the least bit interested in Tavish. He wanted to leave.

By the time Mairi reached home, Johnny and Tavish were back in the kitchen, their faces flushed with exercise and sunlight. They had obviously spent an enjoyable afternoon together, unlike Mairi whose visit to Effie and the school had been strained.

"How did you get on?" Johnny enquired. Without waiting to hear Mairi's reply, he added, "We've had a great time, haven't we, son?"

The word 'son' struck Mairi as faintly odd although there was no reason why he shouldn't refer to Tavish as his son, after all, he was officially theirs.

"Excuse me, Madam," Rhona said, gently tapping on the door. "A letter arrived for you in today's post. I put it on the hall table. I hope that was all right."

"Thank you, Rhona, I must have missed it. The hall table is perfect. Are you off now?"

"In about half an hour, Madam, once I've finished cleaning the silver."

"Letters on the hall table, cleaning the silver!" Johnny mimicked, when Rhona had left the room. "Whatever next, Madam?"

"Stop mocking everything I'm trying to achieve, Johnny! Rhona's a diligent worker and whether you like it or not, cleaning silver happens to be one of her jobs. As for calling me Madam, it just happened. I never requested nor expected it."

"I've got nothing against Rhona. She's a lovely girl," Johnny retorted, rubbing his chin to distract himself from what he really wanted to say. "But ever since we arrived, you've been acting like a haughty duchess, putting on airs and graces, telling me and Tavish what to wear and how to behave. We've had enough, haven't we, son?!"

He glanced down at the boy, hoping for a nod or wink of support but Tavish's thoughts were far away. He hadn't heard a word.

"Don't you dare bring our son into this!" Mairi said defiantly, her cheeks flushed with rage. "Any disagreement between us, stays with us. Is that clear? It has nothing to do with Tavish!"

Johnny's criticism lit a touch paper that set off an explosion of suppressed emotions.

Despite her objections, he had a point.

It was absurd for two adults and a child to eat breakfast on a table designed for fourteen but Mairi had no intention of ending the new arrangement. She had invested too much time and energy into bringing the formal dining room back to life. Progress had been slow but with Rhona's youthful help, the musty old Edwardian rooms were being dragged into the modern era.

Johnny gathered his papers and marched indignantly out of the room leaving an air of despondency in his wake. Mairi wandered over to the hall table where Rhona had placed the envelope addressed to Mrs Johnny Mitchell, Kilbackie House. She slipped it into her pocket and disappeared to the library, the one room in the house where she felt at peace.

The letter was from Daisy.

"Last week", she wrote, *"the National Trust invited me back to Shottenden to see the changes they had made to the house. I went out of curiosity but left wishing I had never gone. On the plus side, the house was well-cared for and clean but the Trust had ripped its heart out, leaving a sanitised void where once there had been energy.*

Imagine! The kitchen had been turned into a museum to educate the paying public on how meals were prepared in 'the old days!' Gladys' highly polished copper pans hung unused on large meat hooks in order of size. Her rolling pins, pastry cutters and jelly moulds were neatly labelled and displayed on the kitchen table beside a plastic loaf and a fake pie. I'm sure, like me, you would have hated it!

"The sterile room lacked the daily drama that took place among the hot ovens and steaming saucepans. No more Gladys singing hymns and shouting at poor little Amy Pritchard. Instead of the mouthwatering smells of freshly baked bread, cakes, pies and sizzling roasts, the soulless room smelled of pot pouri, a mixture of herbs, spices, seeds and cones displayed in wooden bowls. It was so depressing I wished I could have turned back the clock and returned to the good old days!

"That world has gone and we are the poorer for it.

"Do you remember how Sir Hugh's study always smelt of wood smoke, wet dog and cigars? Well, it doesn't any more. It's been so thoroughly cleaned; it smells of nothing. Perhaps the saddest change of all was Lady Hollister's bedroom which looked like an upmarket brothel! Two of her silk night dresses had been laid across her bed in a rather seductive way. Her fabulous evening dresses were vulgarly displayed on hangers around the large open wardrobe. Not surprising, they attracted comments from gawping visitors.

"Not a day goes by when I don't think of Sir Hugh and Angus and wonder what Katherine is up to now, tucked away in her remote abbey. I haven't heard a word from her since she retreated from the world but I suppose that was all part of her plan. Total seclusion and no communication.

"How are you doing on Skye? I often think of you all and wish you lived nearer. It would be lovely to catch up and see Tavish again. Perhaps one day we will come and visit, although Bill rarely goes out these days. William and Dorothy are both well and live nearby which is a bonus.

Did I tell you they are expecting a baby? My first grandchild. Imagine, me a grandmother! I'm not old enough.

I miss the old days and wish you were here!

With much love to you, Johnny and Tavish,

Daisy"

CHAPTER 13

"Who was the letter from?" Johnny mumbled, with his mouth full.

He wasn't particularly interested in his question but the letter was the first they had received since moving to Kilbackie and he was intrigued to know who it was from. Mairi was still smarting at Johnny's refusal to eat lunch as well as breakfast in the dining room although deep down she accepted the kitchen was cosier. He had agreed to go along with the formal breakfast in order to keep the peace but he put his foot down when she suggested extending the experiment to include lunch.

"One meal is enough," he exclaimed. "Two is out of the question!"

He had no intention of giving up the one room in the house where he could sit in his socks and enjoy a cheese and pickle sandwich.

"Daisy," Mairi eventually said, annoyed at the way Johnny continued to speak with his mouth full.

"What do you mean, Daisy?"

"I mean the letter was from Daisy."

"Oh! What did she want?"

Mairi wished Johnny wouldn't speak with his mouth full. She tried to ignore the habit but when food stuck to his upper lip, she couldn't stay quiet.

"What are you staring at?" he asked with a hint of annoyance. "Can't a man eat a sandwich in peace?"

Mairi raised an eyebrow and tapped the side of her mouth. The use of sign language seemed particularly prissy but he had no energy for a fight. Obediently he licked the top of his lip and removed the errant piece of butter.

"Satisfied?" he said.

Mairi knew it was futile discussing table manners with Johnny especially when he believed relaxation was the most important part of home life. As far as he was concerned, manners were a middle-class obsession and he'd have none of it. He was proud of his Yorkshire roots with little time for niceties.

Mairi, on the other hand, regarded manners as a universal language of order and courtesy. Without manners the world would become ruder and more selfish.

Johnny took a large slurp of tea and rubbed his mouth with his sleeve to get rid of any surplus food.

"Did Daisy have anything to say?"

"Not much, other than there have been lots of changes at Shottenden."

"Ahh! I bet the place is dead without Sir Hugh," he replied. "Talking of Shottenden, I forgot to tell you. Fergus Buchanan rang yesterday. He may call round sometime tomorrow morning but said nothing about lunch. As far as I could tell, he was staying at Rosvaig Castle tonight ahead of an early meeting tomorrow.

"I still can't make that man out," he said, rising from the table and whistling for Jess who was fast asleep in front of the range. "He's easy to talk to but comes over as a bit of a 'know-all'. I can't put my finger on it but there's something odd about him. He's very polite but his politeness borders on the creepy."

Rhona and Tavish came in from the farmyard in high spirits, ready for lunch.

"Could you look after Tavish for a couple of hours tomorrow morning?" Mairi asked.

"Of course!" came the enthusiastic reply. "I'll take him down to the beach. He enjoys collecting coloured shells and pebbles."

"That would be wonderful!" Mairi said. "I'm sure he'd love to spend a morning on the beach with you but don't stay too long. I've got a few things to do and might call on Ailsa while I'm out and about. I should be back about 11.30 a.m. Are you sure you'll be all right with him on your own?"

"We'll be fine, won't we, Tavish?" she said ruffling the boy's hair. He looked up and smiled.

The two of them got on extremely well, sharing an enthusiasm for games, nature and exploration. Under her tutelage, Tavish had learned to play Snap, Snakes and Ladders and Ludo. He had also begun to read a few simple sentences, do some sums and, best of all, explore the farm. Nature walks with Rhona were both educational and fun. It didn't take him long to learn the names of wildflowers and birds.

The next morning Mairi left the house confident that her son was in capable hands. Her trip didn't take as long as expected so rather than hurry home, she decided to park the car below Gillen Moor, a wild windswept area high above the crofting township of Stradal. It was a place full of memories she wished to forget yet some inner demon told her it would be the perfect spot to stretch her legs. She should have known better. Matted heather and clumps of bog myrtle hindered her climb but eventually she came to an ancient sheep path that wound its way through the bracken until it reached an abandoned shieling. Long ago, women and children would spend their summers in such places, milking cows and making dairy products to send down to the menfolk working on the crofts. The building was structurally sound although its original thatch roof had been replaced by corrugated sheeting that had gradually turned red.

Mairi lifted the rusty latch and crept gingerly into the dimly lit room. Its only source of light came from a single window built into the stone wall. It took a while for her eyes to adjust to the dark but gradually she made out a couple of broken chairs and a rickety table covered in bird droppings. Maidenhair spleenwort grew in the damp crevices of the old stone walls, their bright green leaves splayed out like octopus' tentacles. The charred remains of a peat fire lay cold in the grate. It was a forlorn sight. One of decay and neglect. The interior reminded her of the last time she had visited the shieling on St Andrew's Day 1932.

Memories she had tried to forget came flooding back. Memories of David.

Always David.

Through the tiny window she saw a flock of golden plovers tumble like autumn leaves against a menacing sky. She closed her eyes and saw a young woman dressed in a cotton dress and knitted woollen cardigan, staggering towards the shelter, her hands blue with cold and her feet numb with pain. The strong arms that held her in a protective embrace, provided her first experience of intimacy. The softness of touch, the taste of lips, the smell of sweat thrilled her. What started as two cold human beings seeking warmth on a winter's night turned into an all-absorbing journey of discovery. They experienced the thrill of love-making and slept till dawn wrapped tightly in each other's arms.

Her memories were interrupted by the sudden sound of curlews crying over the moor.

No more memories. They were too painful.

It was time to go.

She drove through a rising tide and arrived home just before 11.30 a.m. The return journey had been a challenge. High tides, gales and general wear and tear was taking its toll on the causeway. It was gradually breaking up. Losing the road would be unimaginable. It was the farm's lifeline. She wasn't sure whether to mention the problem to Mr Buchanan but he was no fool. He must have been aware of the fragile state of the structure every time his car struggled to make the crossing.

She slowed to a halt in front of the house and was pleased to see that Mr Buchanan hadn't left. His car was still there. Unlike Johnny, she enjoyed his company.

His old-fashioned manners were a welcome contrast to Johnny's bluffness. As she mulled over the differences between the two men, she caught sight of Rhona standing ashen-faced by the front door.

There was no sign of Tavish.

"Oh God!" Mairi screamed, leaping out of the car. "Where's Tavish?"

"He's inside. Come quick!" Rhona wailed, running back to the kitchen where the young boy was sitting on a chair, a towel pressed tightly against his knee. There was blood everywhere.

"What happened?" Mairi cried, turning on the poor girl, accusing her of neglect without allowing her time to explain. Rhona broke down in tears. Between the sobs, she explained that Tavish had been scrambling on the rocks when he slipped and cut his knee.

"He wasn't very high," she assured the distraught mother, "and I was holding his hand when he fell. It all happened so quickly. One moment he was laughing, the next he was lying on the ground with a gash in his knee. It must have caught something sharp when he slipped."

Rhona was beside herself with remorse.

"I took off my shirt and tied the sleeve tightly round the wound to stop it bleeding. Then I carried him back to the house. He was so brave."

"He wasn't brave," Mairi hissed unkindly. "He was in shock! How could you have let a small child climb onto the rocks when you were meant to be on a nature walk looking for different coloured pebbles. This is serious,

Rhona. You've let me down. I've a good mind to end your employment right now."

"Please don't sack me," Rhona sobbed, rubbing her runny nose across her sleeve. "I'm so sorry, Mrs Mitchell. I promise nothing like this will happen again."

"Nothing like this will ever happen again because there won't be another time. Now hurry up and find Mr Mitchell," Mairi shouted, embracing her son more roughly than she intended but the sight of him in pain sent her into a frenzied panic.

"What are you waiting for, Rhona? Go!"

The scared girl raced out of the kitchen leaving Mairi alone with her injured son, who remained strangely mute. His legs shook uncontrollably - his teeth chattered. His vacant eyes stared far ahead, lost in a haze of pain. She eased the bloodied towel away from his clenched fists to examine the wound. The jagged cut was deep enough to expose the bone underneath. She let out a muffled cry of horror.

"Oh God!" she cried, grabbing a fresh towel from the cupboard in the dresser. "Stay brave, Tavish. Daddy will soon be here. He'll know what to do."

The traumatised child said nothing.

"Are you cold?" Mairi whispered, feeling the need to say something. Her heart rate rocketed as a surge of adrenaline fired her into a state of hyperactivity.

Tavish nodded sleepily.

"Blankets! We need blankets," she exclaimed rushing over to the large wooden chest where generations of rugs and blankets were stored to keep them dry. Rummaging through the chest, she threw out anything that looked thread-bare or moth-eaten.

"I know there are some good quality rugs somewhere," she muttered, conscious that the chest needed a good sort out. "Ah! Here they are!"

At the bottom of the pile were three neatly folded thick woollen rugs.

"Just what I'm looking for," she said, taking them over to Tavish and cocooning his slender shoulders in Black Watch tartan.

She hoped the extra warmth would cure his clammy skin but there was nothing she could do to break his unnatural stare.

"Daddy will be here soon. He'll know what to do," she said, wiping wisps of damp hair away from the boy's eyes.

At last, the sound of clattering footsteps could be heard in the hall. Johnny appeared panting hard and looking flustered, followed closely by Mr Buchanan who looked calm, athletic and totally focussed.

"Thank God you've arrived," she said on the verge of tears. "There's so much blood and his knee's in a terrible state. I didn't know what to do for the best. I've tried to keep him warm but he keeps shaking."

Mr Buchanan untied the bandage and examined the knee, re-assuring Tavish that everything was going to be all right. The tone of his voice was measured, possessing the quiet authority of someone used to dealing with crises.

"The cut will need stitching," he explained, turning

to Johnny and Mairi. "We could leave things as they are and hope for the best but open wounds are particularly vulnerable to infection and complications. High tide makes it unlikely that a doctor will be able to cross the causeway so you have two choices - to wait until the tide recedes or close the cut here and now."

Johnny was hesitant to give the go-ahead but Mairi replied for them both. "Do whatever you feel is necessary, Mr Buchanan. We trust you."

Mr Buchanan showed no sign of panic. Choosing his words with care, he explained everything he planned to do to make Tavish better. Mairi hung on his every word, convinced he knew what he was doing.

The gentleness of his concern had a calming influence on the unfolding drama and pacified Mairi who felt surprisingly moved when he raised his head and enveloped her fear with a look of unexpected tenderness. For a brief moment she saw a different face through the scars. A face at peace, having conquered pain.

"I will need clean strips of sheeting, a saucepan of boiling water, a pair of tweezers, a needle, some strong thread and some antiseptic," he said firmly.

Mairi set about collecting the necessary items whilst Rhona stood unnoticed in the corner. When everything was ready, Mr Buchanan knelt down beside Tavish and carefully explained the procedure, sparing the child no detail and warning him that the stitches would hurt. He then asked if he had understood what was going to happen to him. Tavish gave a subdued nod.

Mr Buchanan placed the tweezers and needle in the pan of boiling water and washed his hands thoroughly with soap before drying them and rinsing them with whisky. He soaked the cotton strips in TCP and swabbed the wound thoroughly, picking out the dirt with the sterilised tweezers. He started threading the eye of the needle with the delicate precision of an embroiderer. Mairi noticed with interest his long artistic fingers. They were the fingers of a pianist or a poet so unlike Johnny's muscular ones. Years of working with livestock and hard manual labour had hardened the skin, making them tough and strong. Tavish looked terrified as the needle slowly approached the gash in his knee. He pleaded with Mr Buchanan not to hurt him.

"I need you to hold his arms tight," Mr Buchanan whispered to Mairi. "I can't close the wound if he keeps trying to grab the needle."

Turning to Johnny, he pointed at the boy's legs.

"Keep them still for me."

Johnny clamped his large rough hands around the unnaturally white shaking legs and closed his eyes.

Mairi whispered loving words of encouragement to calm her son but to no avail. His whimpering turned to screams of terror as the needle perforated his delicate skin. Mairi turned her head away from her son's suffering as he fought to free himself from her grip.

"Let me go!" he pleaded. "You're hurting me, Mummy. Let me go!"

Despite the protests and tears, Mr Buchanan successfully

completed the first suture. Tavish struggled, fought and writhed to avoid further pain but as long as Johnny and Mairi held him down, Mr Buchanan was free to carry out his work. He effortlessly re-threaded the needle and kept a steady hand whilst completing the second suture. This time Tavish didn't scream, in fact the stitch was made so quickly he didn't have time to react.

When all the sutures had been knotted and disinfected, Mr Buchanan turned to Rhona who had remained hidden, too afraid to show her face.

"It's all right now, Rhona," he said, beckoning her to join them. "You can come and have a look if you want. Tavish's knee is all stitched up."

The girl stood in a state of shock, tears streaming down her cheeks, mumbling the words, "I'm sorry! I'm so sorry!"

"It wasn't all your fault," Mr Buchanan said, trying to reassure her. "Accidents happen but thankfully Tavish hasn't come to any real harm. Come and have a look. His knee will soon be as good as new."

Mairi couldn't let his words go unchallenged.

"It's not all right," she said louder than she meant. "Tavish could have been killed out there on the rocks. It was Rhona's job to care for him and keep him safe."

"Woah!" Mr Buchanan replied softly. "Don't be too hard on her, Mairi. Yes, she let him scramble on the rocks but then all Kilbackie children scramble on the rocks. And for a very good reason. It's fun and exhilarating! Children love testing their agility and balance. I'm sure Tavish was having the time of his life before he slipped. We'll never know why it happened but I'm sure he and Rhona have learned a lesson they'll never forget."

Mairi wasn't convinced.

"He's only six. Rhona should have been more careful and put her foot down when he insisted on climbing. Her judgement was wrong. She was irresponsible and I think it would be best for all concerned if she ceased working here."

Mr Buchanan looked surprised.

"You don't mean that!" he said, showing a rare flash of anger through the tightness of his scarred face.

"I do, and I won't be changing my mind."

Mr Buchanan beckoned to Rhona. "It's time you were back home with your family but I'm afraid you will have to wait until the tide turns. Is there anything you can get on with while you wait?"

Rhona nodded her face still blotchy from crying. With quiet efficiency, she boiled some water and poured it into a galvanised bucket with a cap full of bleach. After sweeping the kitchen floor, she washed it thoroughly until every stone slab sparkled and smelt like a hospital. Finally, she wiped down the table and chairs with disinfectant. Nothing was left to chance. By the time she finished, the room was glistening clean.

'Mairi has no idea how hard Rhona works,' Mr Buchanan thought as he led the unhappy girl to his car. 'She will rue the day she let her go.'

"Well!" Johnny exclaimed, once Mr Buchanan and

Rhona had left. "Are you sure you've done the right thing, dismissing Rhona? You were very certain of your views without even listening to her side of the story. Personally, I think she showed great maturity and presence of mind when dealing with Tavish after the accident. She applied a tourniquet, carried him home, waited for you to arrive, then ran to find me. I agree she was with Tavish when he fell, but as she said, she was still holding his hand. It was an accident.

"You focussed on Rhona's one mistake whilst ignoring Mr Buchanan who was utterly brilliant. Without his quick thinking and practical help, the wound could easily have become infected and who knows what would have happened then? I'm totally speechless and can't work out what came over you, Mairi!"

Mairi stood stock still, bearing her humiliation in silence. She knew she had behaved badly but had no idea why. Leaving a subdued Tavish in the care of his father, she crept out of the kitchen and made her way down to the beach, needing air and space to think.

CHAPTER 14

"I had no option," Mairi explained a few days later. "Rhona couldn't be trusted. She had to go."

Johnny wanted to reason with his wife but the more he defended Rhona, the more she dug her heels in.

"What about her work ethic, cheerful disposition and friendship with Tavish?" he asked. "Don't they count for anything?"

Mairi shook her head. As far as she was concerned, Rhona was irresponsible and a malign influence on Tavish. They were better off without her.

"She's sixteen," he argued. "When I mentioned the accident to Willie, he said all the children brought up on Kilbackie scrambled over the rocks at some time or other. It was a favourite pastime."

"You told Willie about the accident!" Mairi cried. "How could you? Nothing remains secret around here. Now everyone will know I can't be trusted to look after my son. I'll be a laughing stock."

"Mairi, for goodness' sake, calm down! Willie was very sympathetic and as far as I know he isn't a gossip. He said that any babysitter worth her salt would have done what Rhona did; it was just unfortunate Tavish got hurt."

"It wasn't unfortunate!" Mairi cried, raising her voice. "How many times do I have to remind you that Rhona was irresponsible and, by the way, we're talking about our son, not just any child. You saw the mess his knee was in after the fall. It was awful!"

If Mairi had been less self-obsessed, she would have noticed the black circles round Tavish's eyes and the tears that too often welled up. The six-year-old was full of nerves ahead of his first day at school. He sought assurance, a hand to hold, a hug, anything to take away the tightening knot in his stomach but his mother was too preoccupied to notice. He stared in bewilderment at his warring parents, wishing he had never come to Skye.

He excused himself from the table and limped over to the range where he sat on the floor and placed his arms lovingly round Jess who nuzzled his neck and licked him with unconditional love.

Since Rhona's departure, Jess had become his only friend.

A few days after the accident, Mairi had nagged Johnny to take Tavish to the doctor to get his knee checked before starting school. Twice a day, she had diligently cleaned the stitches with disinfectant and was fairly sure there was no sign of infection but she wanted to be sure. The doctor was sympathetic. He gently examined the knee and prodded the skin around the stitches to see if it hurt. Tavish showed no emotion. When asked how the accident had happened, Johnny explained that he had been scrambling over the rocks and fell.

"You're not the first child I've seen with a rock wound," he smiled, ruffling Tavish's hair the way grown-ups do. "And I doubt very much you'll be the last. I don't think there's a child on Kilbackie who hasn't come to grief at some time or other climbing over rocks.

"It must have really hurt," he added, the deep lines across his brow creasing with concern. "Your cut was very deep so whoever stitched it up did a really good job. With any luck you'll only be left with a faint scar. A permanent reminder of your bravery!"

Johnny wished Mairi had been with them to hear what the doctor had said.

The good news did nothing to alleviate Tavish's fear of starting school with a bandaged knee. The other children were bound to notice and ask questions. If his mother had been less preoccupied with her problems, she could have advised him. He became withdrawn, convinced his parents would be happier without him. Isolated and alone, he tried to remember his life before Kilbackie but the memories were a blur - soft green grass, daisy chains, flowers especially roses, walks, sunshine and story books. And then there was Katherine, whose smile had made him feel safe.

"It's time we were off," Mairi shouted from upstairs. "Make sure you've brushed your teeth and washed behind your ears!"

There was a throaty gurgling sound of water running down the bathroom pipes followed by a sharp clunk as the cold tap was turned off. The cacophony of plumbing fixtures and fittings reverberated around the house. It was a strange phenomenon but each basin created its own idiosyncratic sound.

"Will you come with me to see my teacher?" Tavish asked nervously as the car bumped over the uneven track.

"Of course I will," Mairi promised, but as they cleared the brow of the hill, she saw Margaret and Rhona deep in conversation with a tight-knit circle of friends and relatives. The thought they were all discussing Rhona's dismissal was too awful. Her courage failed her and in a moment of panic she brought the car to a halt a little way from the school.

"This is where you have to get out, I'm afraid," she said firmly. "There's no room to park by the school so I'll have to park here. Now off you go and have a wonderful day and I'll pick you up just after three."

"Aren't you coming with me?" Tavish asked. "Please, Mummy! Please come with me. I don't know what to do."

"Of course you do! Look! Over there," she said, pointing to a small crowd. "Can you see Margaret and Rhona? They'll be really pleased to see you."

Tavish raised his head to get a better view and saw Rhona glance briefly in his direction. She didn't look particularly pleased to see him.

"I don't want to go!" he cried, clutching his bag. "Please don't make me go without you."

"Don't be silly, Tavish. All you have to do is walk over to Rhona and Mrs Campbell will take you into the school. There's nothing more to it."

Tavish remained unconvinced.

"But Rhona isn't my friend anymore and Mrs Campbell doesn't know who I am. She may leave me behind."

"Of course she won't. She's expecting you."

Mairi leant across the passenger seat and opened the door to let the nervous boy out.

"Off you go, you're a big boy now."

He limped timidly along the grassy verge, keeping his eyes firmly fixed on Rhona, who, when she saw him, rushed forward and swept him lovingly in her arms.

"Where's your mother?" she cried, feeling the child's thin arms tighten their grip round her neck. He nodded in the direction of the half-hidden car where Mairi sat watching the demonstrative signs of affection with a twinge of jealousy.

Rhona's mother Margaret had been her best friend at school. They had been inseparable, always giggling. Oh, the giggling! The two of them would double up laughing, tears streaming down their cheeks, their tummies aching with joyous pain. Together they felt alive and happy, released from the complications of family life. Then, out of the blue, Mairi's father forbade them from seeing each other. No explanation was given, just the threat of punishment if he saw them together or heard Margaret's name mentioned. It was quite clear from the look on his face that the Rev Tommy Nicolson meant what he said.

Mairi obeyed his order but turned in on herself.

It was only much later that she discovered the real cause of the rift between her father and the MacPhee family. Old Granny MacPhee had been confined to bed with bronchitis, an ailment she had suffered from all her life. The deep chesty coughing fits were more tiring than dangerous. Wrapped warmly in a woollen shawl and propped up against a pile of soft pillows, she spent her days looking out of the window, observing the clouds and listening to the birds. The first snowdrops and aconites were already braving the winter weather, adding colour to the short dreich days. Instead of improving with the lengthening daylight, Granny MacPhee remained bedbound unable to shift her cough. She felt awful.

It was at this time that the minister, hearing she was unwell, decided to pay an unannounced visit.

He dragged a chair next to the old lady's bed and held her bony hands in his.

"How are you feeling?" he asked, giving her hand a gentle squeeze.

Mrs MacPhee broke into a long throaty coughing fit that dislodged a lungful of phlegm.

The minister hastily reclaimed his outstretched hand in disgust and edged away from the intimate proximity to the bedside.

There was an awkward moment of silence before he meekly bowed his head and proceeded to deliver a masterful prayer, weaving together the subjects close to his heart – repentance, commitment, salvation and hell. It was not a prayer for the fainthearted.

He opened his eyes with a curious, malevolent smile; the kind a cat might give before pouncing on an unsuspecting mouse.

Despite his doom-laden prayer, the minister's bedside manner was caring, his approach to illness sympathetic.

Granny MacPhee began to relax.

Until the recent chest infection, she had regularly attended church. Her simple faith had sustained her and kept her grounded during a long and difficult life. She had no fear of death, in fact the idea of dying and going to Heaven appealed to her. There were times when she would willingly have crossed over to the other side just to experience a healthy body and peace of mind. Despite her loyalty to the church, she refused to attend the weekly prayer meeting, saying it was nothing more than an audience drawn together to witness the minister's gift of oratory. Her decision to stay away from these meetings infuriated the Rev Nicolson who took advantage of the pulpit to announce that anyone failing to attend his prayer meetings was not of the true faith.

"Will you or any of your family be attending the next meeting?" he asked provocatively.

Granny MacPhee shook her head.

"No," she replied, breathlessly. "None of us will be there."

"Think very carefully before refusing," the minister urged. "Only God knows the time or the day when you will face Judgement. Repent of your sins now or face eternity in Hell separated from those you love."

He wagged his finger, reminding her of the punishment that awaited her for not attending the prayer meetings.

"Let us pray for God's forgiveness," he continued bowing his head for the second time. But before he could utter another word, Granny MacPhee hauled herself into an upright sitting position and hissed, "Get out of my room!"

The minister looked aghast. No-one had ever dared interrupt his devotional prayers for the sick and dying before. He was lost for words, unsure how to regain the moral high ground. It was clear from her feisty outburst that Granny MacPhee had reached the end of her tether. She wanted sleep not more prayers.

"If you don't leave now, I'll call my son." She hissed.

"Anger won't protect you from the wrath of God," the minister continued, using his quiet reassuring voice. "It's no use calling your son. He can't save you. As I have told you many times before, the consequences of an unrepentant life are too awful to contemplate."

The minister continued bullying his sick parishioner until her screams reached her son who bounded upstairs to find out what was going on.

"Get him out of here!" the old lady cried. "Get him out of my bedroom!"

"I think you had better leave," her son said, leading the clergyman downstairs.

The minister's warning was aptly timed. That night Granny MacPhee died unexpectedly in her sleep. The lead-up to her demise was so distressing, her furious family stopped attending church altogether, blaming the minister for frightening their mother to death. The minister retaliated by breaking up the friendship between Mairi and Margaret.

As far as Rev Tommy Nicolson was concerned, the MacPhee family had chosen the broad road that led to destruction. He would do everything possible to stop his youngest daughter from being led away from the True Path. Her soul was too precious to lose.

On reflection Mairi wondered if her father had been right all along when he warned her that the MacPhees were not of the true faith and could never be trusted. If true; it could explain Tavish's injury on the rocks and the misery she experienced after the St Andrew's Night Dance.

By the time Johnny returned home for lunch, Mairi had finished her morning chores and was writing to Daisy.

"Did Tavish go off all right? Any tears?"

"Sshhh! I'm writing to Daisy," she replied, trying to think of words to entice her up to Skye - dramatic scenery, wild flowers, deer, otters, eagles, an historic house by the sea.

Now that Tavish was at school full time and Rhona no longer came to the house, Mairi's days were longer and lonelier. A visit from Daisy would do her good.

"Put your pen down and tell me about Tavish." Johnny said, looking quizzically at his wife. "I haven't got long and am longing to know how things went. Was he all right going in?"

Mairi didn't know how to reply. She wanted to tell Johnny that she'd been the perfect mother and given their son all the reassurance he needed to walk through the front door of his new school and face the unknown, but she couldn't lie.

"I messed up!" she said, not daring to look into her husband's eyes. "Margaret and Rhona were waiting at the gate and I couldn't face them. Not after the accident. I made Tavish go in on his own."

A large tear dropped onto Daisy's letter, smudging the ink.

"Bother!" she sighed. "I'll have to re-write the whole letter."

"Is that all you can think about, Daisy's bloody letter?" Johnny exclaimed in disgust. "What about our son? He didn't deserve to be abandoned this morning on his first day of school?"

Mairi froze.

"I didn't mean to swear but at times you are so thoughtless I find it hard to stay calm! You need to get a grip, Mairi. You've been so preoccupied recently you haven't even noticed that Tavish isn't eating. This morning was the third day this week he hasn't eaten any breakfast. Rhona would never have allowed him to go to school on an empty stomach."

His words hit home. They hurt.

"Leave me alone," Mairi cried. "I know I'm an awful mother and don't deserve Tavish. There are times I wish we'd never adopted him! He would have been better off staying with Katherine. Everyone loves Katherine."

Johnny had had enough of the self-pity. He grabbed a sandwich and left the house, leaving Mairi to re-write Daisy's letter.

By three o'clock, she had made up her mind to wait at the school gate to greet Tavish at the end of his first day. Nothing, not even the sneering looks of other mothers, would put her off. It was time to show the doubters that she, Mairi Mitchell, was mistress of Kilbackie House and proud of her position. She parked the car and walked towards Margaret and Rhona who were in deep conversation with Janet Cameron. There was a moment's hesitation as Mairi approached but they soon ignored her and hastily returned to the latest gossip concerning Kirsty MacLeod whose wild antics at a ceilidh had caused quite a stir.

"That girl will come to no good, if you know what I mean," Janet whispered with a knowing wink.

The focus on Kirsty MacLeod ended with the ringing of the school bell and squeals of joy from thirty-five excited children pouring out of the school building. Tavish ran straight up to Mairi and wrapped his arms round her waist, nuzzling into her coat.

"You've come!" he said, handing her a picture.

CHAPTER 15

"Mummy?" Tavish asked before getting down from the breakfast table. "Why do people keep asking me funny things?"

Mairi tried not to show her alarm. "What sort of things, darling?"

"Well, yesterday at play time, Ruairidh's mummy asked me who my mummy was and I didn't know what to say, so I told her that you were my mummy. Is that right?"

"Of course it is!" Mairi replied. "Some grown-ups ask very silly questions! Who else did they think your mummy was?"

The rhetorical question rekindled a fear that had never left her. It was irrational but she genuinely believed she wasn't good enough to be Tavish's mother. She did her best to love and care for him but her devotion to the little boy never seemed good enough.

"Who else has been asking questions?"

"Only Mrs. Cameron, Mrs MacPhee and Ruairidh's mummy," he replied nonchalantly.

"What about Aunt Effie?"

"No, not Aunt Effie! She's really nice. She never asks questions," he said, helping himself to a slice of toast. "When can I see her again?"

"Actually, darling, the tide will be too high for you to get home after school today so Aunt Effie said she'll meet you and take you back to her croft for the night. Is that all right?"

"Goody!" he beamed, his face lighting up with delight. "I like her house. It's snug and warm."

'That's because it's small and the fire quickly heats up the living room,' thought Mairi with a tinge of jealousy. A cosy house that didn't need much cleaning sounded appealing.

"Listen to this," Johnny said from the chair by the range, ending Mairi's conversation with Tavish. He shook the paper to keep it firm.

'Seventy-seven spectators have been killed at the Le Mans car race in France. A Mercedes travelling over 150mph, crashed into another car. It flew through the air, hit a bank and exploded, sending burning wreckage into the crowd.'

Tavish immediately switched his attention to Johnny.

"Is 150 mph very fast?" he asked out of curiosity.

"Yes! It's very, very fast!" Johnny replied.

"Faster than my Spitfire?"

"No, not as fast as that but imagine driving across the causeway ten times faster than usual."

Tavish racked his brains trying to think how fast that would be but such speed was beyond his understanding.

"Those poor people!" Johnny muttered. "One minute they were enjoying a day out, the next minute they were dead. It just shows, you never know what lies around the corner."

'You never know what lies around the corner'

The words struck a chord with Mairi. It was time to pay

Ailsa a visit after dropping Tavish off at school.

The old lady was sitting in her usual chair with a copy of the King James Bible balanced on her lap. Hearing Mairi enter the house, she lifted her head and stretched out an arm.

"Katherine, my darling, you've come!"

Mairi retreated into the shadows waiting to hear what Ailsa would say next.

"I *knew* you'd come," she said, resting her outstretched arm back on her knee.

"I've missed you so much. Where have you been?"

Unaware that Katherine wasn't in the room to reply, she continued her musings.

"You were such a bonnie wee thing, always smiling. I can still see you out on the hill with my Murdo, helping him during peat cutting. You were hardly big enough to lift the slabs off the ground, yet you never gave up trying. I always hoped Angus would find someone like you but I never imagined he would actually fall in love with you and want to marry you. It was the happiest day of my life when he told me you had accepted his proposal. I had gained the daughter I'd always wanted. When Tavish was born, I had everything I could ask for but joy is fickle and happiness is short-lived."

She paused to reflect on the past. All those memories. Memories that could never be changed.

Mairi hadn't the heart to interrupt.

"If it's no trouble, could you bring Tavish to see me before I die. I'd love to carry a picture of him on my final journey? He's the only link I have left to my darling Angus."

Mairi shrank further back into the dark recesses, unsettled by Ailsa's obvious love for Katherine. Did she know that Katherine had withdrawn from the world and given Tavish up for adoption?

She took a tentative step forward, treading on the ghosts of the past.

"It's not Katherine," she stammered, "it's me, Mairi. I hope I'm not disturbing you."

"Ah, Mairi, not at all. Come and sit down. I thought for a moment Katherine had come to say goodbye."

There was no sign of disappointment in her voice, far from it. She radiated a serenity that left Mairi transfixed. Time stood still as they sat together in the familiar half-light, drifting into a past inhabited by memories of lost loved ones. The two ladies lingered on the edge of existence, questioning what might have been.

"How's life at Taigh Mòr?" she asked, referring to the big house. "It can't be easy moving into the Urquhart's family home with all the responsibilities that go with privilege. You look worn out, poor thing. Are you sure everything is all right?"

Everything was quite clearly not all right. For the past few days, Mairi had woken up with puffy eyes and pasty skin; her face looked drawn, with a few extra lines etched across her brow. Staring in the mirror she was confronted by a frumpy, downcast woman, far from the gracious, elegant lady she had hoped to become. Beneath the worry lines lay the persistent dread of failure.

Over the past month, particularly since Tavish's accident, she had grown short-tempered and not very likeable. Too quick to criticise the smallest faults in others but never ready to admit to her own. Johnny deserved better.

"I'm fine!" she said not knowing what else to say.

"Really?" came the perceptive reply.

Mairi felt torn by her need to talk and her desire for privacy but she needn't have worried. Ailsa already knew what she was going to say, it was just a question of waiting until Mairi was ready.

"I'm not coping, Ailsa. My life's a mess! I want to leave Kilbackie but I can't go without Johnny who's determined to make a success of the farm and I can't leave without Tavish even though I sometimes think he would be better off without me. What should I do?"

She blinked away her tears and sniffed as she told Ailsa the reasons for her unhappiness. She left nothing out.

Ailsa listened sympathetically without saying a word. Her silence had a healing effect. It drew the pain out of Mairi like a poultice.

"You speak of past failings, judgment, Tavish's injury on the rocks, damaged friendships and a lack of trust," Ailsa finally said, choosing her words with care. "You're struggling to understand where God fits in to your life."

She paused to think carefully what to say next.

"You're making faith far more complicated than it need be, Mairi.

"Your brother stands and preaches from his pulpit every Sabbath but he isn't God, neither is he your judge.

Leave judgement to God's mercy and learn from his unconditional love. You have nothing to prove and nothing to lose."

Ailsa paused to let her head sink onto her chest. "Will you do something for me?" she said, letting out a long deep sigh. "On that dresser there's a large blue jug and inside is an envelope. Could you bring it to me?"

Mairi did as she was asked and waited. The old lady was in no hurry.

"I don't know if I'm doing the right thing," she said eventually. "God forgive me for breaking a confidence but I'm near the end of my life and don't want to take this secret with me to the grave. Keep the letter safe, Mairi. Open it once you are home. You'll know what to do once you've read it. It isn't long, more a short note. Leave me now. I've talked too much and I'm tired."

Her head drooped forward and she appeared to nod off to sleep.

Mairi stood up to leave and kissed the top of Ailsa's head.

"Thank you!" she whispered and left the room more at peace than she had been for a very long time.

The temperature had dropped a few degrees by the time she left Ailsa's croft. Over the Uists, menacing dark clouds threatened rain. Mairi started her journey home across the bay where the wind whipped the water into corrugated ripples.

There was something about the light and the movement of the water that reminded her of the last time she saw David over twenty years ago. They had been sitting in his car looking out across the exact same spot under the glare of a low winter sun; its blinding rays streamed through the windscreen. They had been arguing. Nothing terrible, just differing views about whether she should stay on Skye or leave. David tried to encourage her to move away but she had already made up her mind to stay where, she said, she would be happier. It was a lie and she knew it. Probably he knew it as well.

Once indoors, Mairi walked across the hall, turning the envelope over in her pocket, feeling its soft edges, wondering what was inside. For once she was glad Tavish was not around to disturb her. She put the kettle on and settled down to read the letter Ailsa had given her.

'1935

Dear Ailsa

Please excuse the letter but I need to tell someone about what really happened the day my boat was found abandoned in the loch. To put it bluntly, I faked my disappearance, hoping people would believe I was dead. My life had become too complicated and I couldn't cope. I have joined the Merchant Navy and am enjoying my new life sailing across the Atlantic. However, a day doesn't pass without me thinking of all the pain I have caused my family and friends. Especially Effie and Mairi. I never meant to hurt anyone.

I had a good reason for leaving although I can't tell you about it. Perhaps one day the truth will come out but not yet. Promise me you won't tell anyone that I am alive. I need closure.

Yours, David'

Mairi read the words over and over again before folding the paper in half and replacing it in its envelope. She didn't know what to feel. In many ways the short letter came as no surprise. She had always suspected that David was still alive but there were so many unanswered questions.

Where was he now? What happened to him during the war? Did he survive?

The next morning Mairi woke to the joyous sound of the dawn chorus rising above the silent rays of a new sun.

The effervescent burst of song lifted her spirits. For the first time she lay in bed unconcerned by the holes in the ceiling where chunks of plaster had fallen off the damp lath due to a leak somewhere in the attic. Johnny had spent a fruitless afternoon pulling up the floorboards but he never found the source of the leak. He tried, with little success, to reassure Mairi that the ceiling was safe. The next time Mr Buchanan paid them a visit, she would tell him about the damp ceiling. Until then, all she could do was pray it didn't fall down while they were asleep.

Eventually she eased herself out bed. The sun had slowly evaporated the low mist that hung over the grass like wisps of candy floss. Oyster catchers scurried along the water's edge displaying their bright red legs and beaks while out in the grassy meadows, a male corncrake repeatedly announced the beginning of a new day.

"You're looking brighter this morning," Johnny remarked as they sat having breakfast in the dining room. "Perhaps Tavish should stay away more often!"

Mairi returned a sheepish smile.

"What time are you picking him up?" he asked, carrying the dirty plates to the kitchen, a task he had taken on since Rhona left.

"Not 'til 3.00 p.m."

"Well, be careful what you say to Margaret because, according to Willie, she's still mad at you for sacking Rhona. Apparently, you are just like your father, whatever that means."

Mairi knew exactly what it meant. The bad feeling between the Nicolsons and the MacPhees had gone on long enough. It needed to be put right and the sooner the better.

"I'll try and have a quiet word with her at school although it won't be easy. She's always surrounded by a large group of family and friends. I swear that woman is related to every child in the school!"

The weather took a turn for the worse. Freezing rain slid off the roofs, down slimy walls onto the soggy ground. Mairi drove cautiously, barely able to see where she was going even with the windscreen wipers working at full speed. She parked opposite the school where the usual gathering of mothers huddled together, their heads bowed to keep the sleet off their faces. Mairi remained in the driver's seat unsure whether to move or wait. It wasn't going to be easy to catch Margaret on her own. She was deeply engrossed in conversation with one of her many cousins.

The children had been kept inside all day so by the time they were let out to play, they were like tightly sprung coils, desperate to be released. Despite the weather, they tore round the playground, skipping, kicking balls and jumping puddles. The youngest children, tired after a full day at school, were allowed to sit on a bench. Mairi searched for Tavish but couldn't find him.

She edged her way nearer Margaret.

"Have you seen Tavish?" she asked, trying to sound calm.

"Not this afternoon. I thought Effie was picking him up."

"No, that was yesterday. He should be here waiting for me. Are you sure you haven't seen him?"

"Quite sure!"

A terrifying thought suddenly occurred to Mairi. Tavish had been taken by the MacPhees as punishment for dismissing Rhona. It all made sense. Willie had warned Johnny that Margaret was furious and now Tavish was missing. It was all her fault. She looked again at the children caught up in a wild game of tag. He definitely wasn't there. The realisation that he may have been taken was too much to bear. She began to sway, holding onto Margaret to keep her steady,

"Are you all right?" Margaret gasped, pushing away a couple of gawping onlookers. "Give her some space."

A few minutes later Janet Cameron arrived, with a glass of water.

"Come on, Mairi," she said kindly. "Take a sip. It'll do you good."

Mairi drank the water, never taking her eyes off the playground where she hoped to spot Tavish but he was still nowhere to be seen.

"Thank you, Janet, I needed that!" she said with gratitude. "Have you seen Tavish?"

"No!" came the puzzled reply, "but I expect he's playing football with the older boys behind the school."

"Of course," Mairi groaned. "I'd forgotten the playground extended round the back of the buildings. I thought something had happened to him."

She made a huge effort to stand up, relying on Margaret for support.

Then she saw him! Kicking a ball at the far end of the playground behind the classroom. It was clear from the big grin on his face that he was thoroughly enjoying himself.

"Oh, Margaret!" she groaned. "I've been such a fool. I'm so sorry! I'll explain everything later but for now, will you stay with me until I feel better? I don't want Tavish to see me like this."

She held onto Margaret's arm her head bowed in shame. A heavy silence hung between them.

"I must say, for one so young, your boy has guts," Margaret said generously, trying to think of something positive to say. "He ran straight up to Jamie Finlayson, who must be at least ten and asked if he could join in his game of football. He's by far the youngest out there but the older boys clearly like him."

The clanging sound of the school bell rang across the playground ending free play. Mairi watched Tavish jostling in line to get nearer the older boys under the watchful eye of Mrs Campbell.

"Are you sure you're in a fit state to go home?" Margaret asked. "Why not come back with me for a cup of tea?"

The generous offer was tempting.

"Donald, Murdo, Flora, Lexy!" Mrs Campbell called out, dismissing the children in order of age. Mairi had barely a minute to reply before Tavish rushed over to her.

"I don't know," she hesitated. "I'm really sorry for the way I treated Rhona. I was too hasty and didn't handle things well but I still believe she should have taken more care of Tavish when he was climbing the rocks."

Margaret remained calm.

"So how about coming back with me to talk about it and hopefully we can start again?"

Margaret's generous olive branch should have put an end to the tension between them but Mairi wasn't prepared to forgive - not yet.

"Another time," she replied.

CHAPTER 16

After Tavish's accident Willie offered to teach Johnny to sail.

"I'm not sure!" he hesitated, showing little enthusiasm.

"But you must learn," Willie urged. "It would be irresponsible not to. It was pure luck that Mr Buchanan was here when Tavish cut his knee but boys are boys. They like testing their limits so it's likely there will be other times when a doctor is prevented from crossing the causeway because of the high tide."

Willie had a point. Without Mr Buchanan's calm leadership, Johnny wouldn't have known what to do.

"All right," he said, reluctantly. "I'm willing to learn, if you'll teach me."

Willie seemed pleased with the idea but Johnny remained unconvinced.

"You'll have your job cut out," he smiled anxiously. "I hate water."

The two men walked through the farm's grand stone archway, a monument to past wealth when labour was cheap.

The arch opened into a cobblestone courtyard surrounded on three sides by barns. Opposite the entrance was a flight of steps leading up to an abandoned walled garden, where in former times, half a dozen gardeners had tended the orchard and harvested the soft fruits. Now there was no-one left to prune the trees or gather in the produce. Despite the garden's dilapidated state, nature persisted in fighting back. A few forsaken apple trees still bore fruit among the nettles and raspberry plants growing wild in the rough areas of the garden.

The punishing wind and rain had taken their toll on the outbuildings and garden walls, wearing away the lime mortar that held the stones in place. The historic gardens and mill ponds were choked with wild fuchsia and water mint. The fine overshot watermill was missing its buckets and large sections of its circular cast iron wheel. It was a pitiful sight yet despite the damage, peaty water still poured down the chute over the remains of the wheel before disappearing down a culvert into the burn.

Willie lifted the latch of a barn and squeezed through the rotten half-hanging door, closely followed by Johnny.

Inside lay a 15ft clinker sailing boat surrounded by old tins of varnish, paint brushes and sheets of newspaper dated 26th April 1933. Johnny could just make out an article describing the expulsion of a group of Jewish students from their school in Germany.

"Whose is it?" he asked, looking at the boat.

"David MacPhee's," Willie replied, pensively. "How much do you know about him?"

"Almost nothing," Johnny replied, hoping to learn more.

"Well, you may as well hear it from me but don't tell Mairi I told you. She's very touchy about David. He was a good man, dependable, honest, hardworking. Good-looking too if you believe what people said but I wouldn't know. Anyway, he was engaged to your sister-in-law, Effie, but no date was ever fixed for the wedding. The lack of commitment was highly disapproved of by Effie's father, Rev Tommy Nicolson. Did you ever meet him?"

Johnny shook his head.

"He was something else! A copycat version of Donny or rather Donny is the image of his father, whichever way you look at it. Rev Tommy Nicolson was extremely strict, especially when it came to religion. He thought a wedding date should be set on the day of the engagement. But with David it never was!

"No amount of bullying would persuade him to name the day.

"He and Effie were engaged for three years when in April 1933, he disappeared and has never been seen since. We know he intended to go fishing because Iain MacLean spoke to him at the water's edge about nine o'clock just before he stepped into that boat," he said, pointing to the upturned dinghy.

"Iain even remembered wishing David luck which was a strange thing to say to someone who knew the currents, tides and rocks around Kilbackie better than anyone. He was a natural seaman, having fished the local waters since childhood and, unlike most fishermen, he was a strong swimmer. The morning of 20th April was clear and calm. Perfect conditions for a day's fishing out in the bay but something must have gone wrong because by nightfall he hadn't returned home and his friends and Effie started to worry. Around one o'clock the following afternoon,

Iain MacLean found David's empty boat floating on the other side of the islands. There was no sign of David. Even after an extensive search, his body was never found.

"The police were extremely helpful at the beginning, treating his disappearance as a missing person case but with limited manpower and a tight budget, they eventually lost interest. The trail grew cold. Mairi still believes David is alive and that he had his reasons for disappearing. Effie, on the other hand, believes he died at sea and will never be seen again.

"After he vanished, the Major allowed us to store the abandoned boat here where it has been ever since."

He ran his hand across the wood, reflecting on happier times.

"Let's get her back in the water!" he said with enthusiasm.

"What now!" Johnny exclaimed.

"Why not."

Johnny baulked at the idea. There was no certainty the dinghy was still seaworthy after twenty years lying in a barn. The thought of launching it into the unpredictable waters around Kilbackie, really scared him.

He desperately sought a plausible reason to decline the offer but the gleam in Willie's eye persuaded him that 'no' would never be accepted.

"Don't just stand there. Help me get the tarpaulin off." Willie said, grabbing the corners of the large canvas sheet covering the boat.

"Take hold of the other corners!" he commanded in his

soft Highland way. "And try not to spill any of the bird droppings. I'll scoop them up later for next year's potato crop. They make excellent fertilizer."

Once the tarpaulin was off, Johnny didn't have the heart to refuse Willie's offer.

"I'll help you get this thing launched," he said hesitantly, "but then I need to get back to work."

"Fair enough," Willie replied.

Johnny's fear of water had started when he was six.

He was playing happily in his parents' garden with his Jack Russell, Acorn, when the small dog caught the scent of a rabbit and disappeared into the wooded 'no-go' area beyond the privet hedge. Johnny knew the trees beyond the hedge were out of bounds but he wanted to make sure the rabbit was all right. A number of headless rabbits had been discovered on the lawn much to his mother's distress. In his haste to rescue the creature, Johnny disobeyed his parents' rule and ventured into the thick undergrowth near the towering beech trees. The excited dog ran across a nettle patch into an open expanse of green which he soon discovered was a pond covered in duckweed and water mint. Acorn managed to stop in time but Johnny ran straight into the pond and got the shock of his life. He couldn't swim. Matted clumps of water mint wrapped themselves around his dangling legs, preventing him from reaching the edge of the pond. He thrashed around in the water, desperately trying to keep afloat but after a while, he grew tired and sank deeper into the muddy sediment. Slowly the stagnant water rose above his chin, trickled into his mouth and crept up his nose whilst the world around him grew dim. Eventually he stopped struggling and slipped into a dreamy sleep. His last memory was the distant sound of a barking dog.

Johnny owed his life to Acorn whose intelligent loyalty had sensed his young master was in danger. The small dog raced back to the house where Johnny's parents were enjoying a few moments of rest away from the demands of daily milking. They were totally unaware of the drama unfolding in the woods. The little dog ran round in circles barking furiously to attract their attention. His agitated state and continuous yapping irritated Johnny's mother but caught the attention of Mr Mitchell, who realised that Johnny was missing. In a panic, he followed Acorn through the hedge, reaching the pond in time to haul his son's lifeless body clear of the duck weed and mint.

Johnny felt himself being stretched out on the grass, his face licked clean by a soothing tongue. A heavy fist thumped his chest until his small frame shook with involuntary spasms, replacing lungfuls of dirty pond water with fresh air.

His father's quick thinking saved Johnny's life but left him afraid of water.

He had refused to learn to swim.

Unlike Johnny, Willie had no fear of water. He had been born into a family of crofters and fishermen dependent on the sea for their food and income. As a child he accompanied his father and uncle on fishing trips around the peninsula. Kilbackie's turbulent waters and rocky shoreline were his playground, the salt winds that blew across the Minch toughened his character, climbing cliffs kept him agile and fearless. From an early age he lived close to nature, knowing the names of the plants that grew on the croft and the natural dyes they produced - red from the roots of Tormentil, yellow from Bog Myrtle, brown from Crottle, salmon pink from Ladies' Bedstraw. At low tide, during the short summer months, he would dry armfuls of deep red Dulse for his mother's cooking. His parents taught him how to milk cows, make butter, cut peat, plant potatoes, reap hay and feed cattle.

Johnny looked at the boat and immediately regretted his decision. Although he trusted the rugged crofter, the thought of sailing on the sea terrified him. He tried pulling himself together, putting on a brave face but it was no use. No amount of cajoling would make him step on board the dinghy.

He needed air!

A few steps short of the door, he felt a hand press down on his shoulder.

"Where are you off to?" Willie asked. "You can't leave yet. There's a trailer under that huge pile of fishing tackle and I need a hand shifting it. I can't do it on my own."

Willie had sensed Johnny's reluctance to go out in the boat. He knew something was wrong but couldn't put his finger on it. Johnny appeared tough and resilient, not someone who would scare easily. The demons haunting him in the barn had to be ones he had had for a long time.

Running away wasn't an option.

Johnny didn't want to abandon Willie. He had always prided himself on being the reliable type, the one who could be trusted to stand firm when others floundered. He had been chosen by Sir Hugh Hollister to modernise the dairy business and look for innovative ways to increase the value of Shottenden milk. Dragging an antiquated system into a post-war era demanded nerve and vision, both of which Johnny had in abundance. He had served Sir Hugh well and had been considered an asset to the business. Unfortunately, those days were over, never to return.

He took in a few deep breaths and felt his body relax. The hot clammy sweat that had previously paralysed him, finally cooled down.

"Come on!" he said, flexing his muscles. "Let's get this stuff shifted,"

Willie silently smiled.

Beneath the chaotic pile of buoys, floats, lobster pots, fishing tackle and nets, lay a rusty yellow trailer with flat threadbare tyres.

It was going nowhere.

"Let's see if we can move it," Willie said, clearing a path in front of the trailer. "When I say 'push', push as hard as you can."

The first attempt failed but after more heaving and pushing, it finally lurched forward and rolled easily across the floor of the barn.

"That was easier than expected," Willie said, arching his back. "Have you time to help me take her down to the sea?"

Johnny took a sharp intake of breath.

"Won't the flat tyres damage the wheel rims?"

"I think they'll be all right. After all, the combined weight of the boat and trailer isn't huge. I know it's not ideal but I'm willing to give it a go if you are."

It didn't take long for the trailer to be pulled across a field to the secluded stony beach half hidden at the bottom of the burn.

"I'll hold the painter whilst you clamber on board," Willie said, keeping the boat as close to the shore as possible. Once the flapping mainsail was in place, he pushed the boat further into the water and jumped in.

The dinghy cut through the water, propelled by the wind filling its taut sails. Johnny grasped the sides, too afraid to let go as the boat tilted and water sloshed against the hull. As the dinghy gained speed, the bow lifted, sending a fine sea spray across Johnny's face. He could taste the salt on his lips.

Instead of fear, he experienced an unexpected sense of euphoria.

Willie was in his element, responding to the wind and adjusting the sail to optimise speed and control.

"It's the best feeling in the world," he said, navigating the vessel deftly into Loch Rosvaig where a small row of whitewashed shops and houses lined the edge of the shore. "You see how easy it is to reach the shops by boat?"

Johnny could clearly see the white tower of the Church of Scotland, a prominent fixture on the horizon since 1832. In front of the church stood MacAllister's, the long-established agricultural merchant.

"Do you want anything while we're here?" Willie shouted, steering the boat into the wind to slow her down.

Johnny shook his head.

The short trip to Rosvaig had given him an indescribable sense of freedom. It was an experience he would never forget. Thanks to Willie's seamanship Johnny had been cured of a life-long fear of water. As the small dinghy sliced through the waves, he felt the tensions of the past few days ease.

Not long after the relaunch of David's boat, Willie asked Johnny if he would like to spend the morning exploring the coastline. The reply was instant and positive.

Ever since the short journey to Rosvaig by sea, he had wanted to return to the loch where seals basked on small rocks, sleek otters slithered through the water, plunging gannets sliced through the surface of the sea and moon jellyfish with pink rings floated in the shallows.

"I may be late home," Johnny said, raising his voice to be heard above 'Music while you work' the radio programme that lifted Mairi's spirits and kept her company as she carried out her daily chores.

"Willie's taking me out in the boat."

Mairi trusted Willie. He was cautious but she hated the thought of her husband learning to sail in David's boat. His presence was everywhere, his closeness unnerving.

'Where are you?' she sighed, looking out at the bay. If only Willie had left the boat in the old barn.

CHAPTER 17

As they hauled the dinghy ashore, Johnny pointed to the scratched-out name on the side of the boat.

Willie's demeanour grew serious. He paused before answering.

"You remember me telling you about David's disappearance? Well, there's more to the story. The MacPhee family was, as I said, honest and hardworking but, in the eyes of the Church, they were 'unsaved'."

"Why?" Johnny asked with surprise.

"Because they refused to go to church," Willie replied. "Rev Tommy Nicolson, Mairi's father, enjoyed causing mischief. He was ruthless and charismatic, adored by those who believed his message and loathed by those who questioned his teaching.

"The MacPhees were very much in the second camp. They refused to believe in a loving God that condemned people to everlasting torment and pain."

He paused to smile. "I can see from your face that you don't believe me but I know what I'm talking about because my mother was a MacPhee. My father paid a heavy price for marrying her.

"It was always assumed that David would marry Effie even though the union would have alienated her from her father. Maybe David hesitated to make a commitment because of the rumpus it would have caused. Whatever the reason, the perfect couple never formalised their love.

Then David disappeared. We spent weeks searching the coastline for his body but it was never found. As you can imagine, Effie was heartbroken but to her credit she never complained or showed her grief in public. She just got on with her life and made a success of it."

"What do you think happened?" Johnny asked, looking Willie straight in the eye.

"I honestly don't know. He was an excellent seaman so there was no way he would have fallen overboard on a flat sea. The only explanation that makes any sense is that he chose to disappear."

"But why?"

"Your guess is as good as mine. Whatever the reason, he must have been in a terrible state to leave Effie. He adored her. That's why I painted over the boat's name after he disappeared. She used to be called the *Effie Joan*."

Johnny took a while to digest the story and wondered how David's disappearance had affected Mairi. It was strange she had never mentioned him.

"Where does Mairi fit into the story?"

"She doesn't really. Obviously as Effie's younger sister she saw a lot of David but in March 1933, a month before David went missing, she left Skye for Inverness. I don't think the two events were connected but Effie has always maintained there was a link, although she has never given her reasons for thinking this way."

He sighed.

"It's probably best we never know what happened!"

"I think we should rename the boat out of respect for Effie," Johnny said, breaking the sombre mood of the

X

conversation. "She must hate seeing us out in the *Effie Joan* especially after everything she's been through."

"I wouldn't worry about Effie. I've already talked to her and she's quite happy seeing the boat back on the water but I agree we ought to change the name even if re-naming a boat brings bad luck.

"Any suggestions?"

"How about *Skye Belle*?"

Willie stroked his chin and repeated the name to himself, frowning.

"I'm not sure," he replied. "*Skye Belle* sounds like a music hall performer!"

"*Gannet Flight*?" Johnny suggested, keen to find a name that Willie would like.

"No! Definitely not *Gannet Flight*! 'Gannet' has a harsh ring to it. Although the birds are beautifully streamlined and built for speed, they plunge into the depths of the sea, making them a bad omen. Any others?"

Johnny racked his brain trying to think of a soft sounding name that would combine wildness, grace and speed. He sifted through a list of birds, girls' names and mythical creatures. All were possible yet none sounded right. After a few minutes, he lifted his head smiling broadly, as if to say '*You'll love this one*!'

"I've got it!" he said. "How about *Arctic Tern*?"

Willie looked doubtful at first, repeating the name several times.

'Arctic Tern'.

Eventually he nodded with approval. *Arctic Tern*, or

the Sea Swallow as it was sometimes called, had a good ring to it.

"Let me suggest the name to Effie and see what she thinks. If she agrees, I'll rename the boat."

The evening light was clear and bright when Johnny arrived home, still undecided whether to quiz Mairi about David's disappearance or leave it until he had given the subject more thought. He grabbed an unopened letter lying on the hall table and headed for the kitchen where he was met by a scene of utter misery. Mairi was sobbing at the kitchen table with Tavish sitting beside her, his arm around her shoulder for comfort.

"What's going on?" Johnny asked with a hint of alarm in his voice. "What's happened?"

"Something terrible!" came the muffled reply.

"What? Tell me!"

Johnny tried to think what could possibly have produced such distress. He feared the worst.

"It's Ailsa," Mairi whispered. "She's dead! Effie's only just told me. She died this morning in her sleep." Her words were lost in a maelstrom of grief.

"Oh, Johnny! I shall never forgive myself for not taking Tavish to see her. She knew she was dying. Her last wish was to see her grandson. How could I have been so heartless? I deprived a wonderful lady of her last wish and now it's too late."

She hung her head in shame.

Johnny knew there was no point saying anything. He had learned from experience that silence was the best way of dealing with Mairi's moods. He held his tongue, made two cups of tea and sat down beside his weeping wife, wondering if this was an occasion when he should break his silence and say something comforting. He could explain the workings of the internal combustion engine and the three-point hitch on a tractor but emotions left him tongue-tied.

"Will she forgive me?" she asked.

He couldn't answer truthfully because he had no idea what happened after death but the subject had always intrigued him.

'*Was death the end of everything, a brick wall or the beginning of a new world, an opening?*' As far as Ailsa was concerned, he had no doubts she had gone to a better place, somewhere good where her loving spirit would be re-united with her husband and son. He told Mairi his thoughts and assured her that Ailsa was now at peace.

"I do hope you're right," she replied. "If anyone deserves Heaven, it's Ailsa."

Johnny waited until Mairi had quietened down before mentioning the letter he had in his hand.

"Who's it from?"

"I don't know but the post mark is Richmond."

"You open it! I'm not in the mood!"

He slid his finger under the folded edge of the envelope and pulled out four thin sheets of blue writing paper. The handwriting was childish but neat.

"It's from Daisy."

Her letter was more of a confession than a conversation

between friends. She wrote with candour about her dreary life with Bill, their failing marriage and her urgent need to escape. Her tenor was depressing yet Mairi found it strangely comforting to know that she wasn't the only one struggling to cope with the difficulties of life. She couldn't care less if Bill reeked of tobacco and beer after work or preferred the smoked-filled bars of the local Working Men's Club to home but she felt a tinge of sympathy for Daisy when she learned he no longer ate the evening meals she had prepared.

'He's shutting me out of his life,' she wrote.

After months of loneliness, wasted food and tears, Daisy gave Bill an ultimatum. Either he sat down at the table and ate with her four evenings a week or she would start to build a new life for herself. It was up to him – his choice. Bill never gave a direct answer but the next day he came home late, saying he was too tired to eat the shepherd's pie she had kept warm for him.

"She's arriving this Saturday," Johnny said with surprise. "She could have given us a bit more notice."

'That's Daisy for you!' Mairi said. 'Self-centred and good fun. At least I've got three days to get everything ready.'

The news of Daisy's imminent arrival, ended her bout of self-pitying sadness. Slowly but surely, she roused herself to focus what little energy she had on preparing for her friend's visit.

"Come on, Tavish!" she said. "We have work to do."

Mairi racked her brain to think how she could make the bleak spare room more welcoming. Then she remembered the three colourful paintings that lay forgotten in the attic. All were dated 1912 and signed by D. A. MacKenzie. Vibrant, confident brush strokes criss-crossed the canvases creating vivid impressions of the local landscape. Mairi had no idea who D. A. MacKenzie was. The fact his paintings were stored in the attic meant he was likely to have been a local or a relative of the Urquharts. Although the art could best be described as modern and messy, there was something about its composition that appealed to her. Hidden in the chaotic patchwork of colour were gannets, oystercatchers, heather, cotton-grass, and foxgloves. The painter had created an optimistic, energetic representation of nature, in stark contrast to the sterile empty spare room with its heavy drab furniture.

She removed years of grime and cobwebs from the large wooden frames before carrying them down, with Tavish's help, to the room where Daisy was going to sleep. Propped against the wall, the pictures immediately added a vibrancy to the otherwise sombre room. Once the windows had been thoroughly cleaned, they set about enhancing the wood's natural shine by applying beeswax. Encouraged by the sweeter, fresher air, Mairi placed the pictures around the room ready for Johnny to hang them. Later on, she would place a vase of wildflowers beside Daisy's bed as a welcoming gesture.

Cleaning the spare room had a calming effect on Mairi. The physical work proved the perfect antidote to grief. The earlier shock of Ailsa's death gradually subsided, leaving her time to think clearly. It was comforting to know that Ailsa had no fear of dying. In fact, she was looking forward to her final journey and being reunited with her son, Angus, and husband, Murdo. If Mairi hadn't been so wrapped up in her own troubles, Ailsa's wish to spend time with her grandson would have been granted.

"I'll write to Katherine and tell her about Ailsa's death when I know the day and time of the funeral," she said.

"Do you think she will attend?" Johnny asked.

"I hope not!" came Mairi's surprising reply. "It's a long way to come and if I know my brother, he will use the occasion to remind everyone of the horrors of hell and the need to repent before death.

"You've never been to a Highland funeral, have you?" she continued.

Johnny shook his head.

"They are not for the faint-hearted! You probably think I'm being unfair but I'm not. They are cold, joyless occasions, devoid of love. The deceased are rarely mentioned and there are no comforting words for the bereaved."

Johnny looked aghast.

"Really?"

"Really," Mairi replied.

That evening she asked Johnny what she should do about the photo Sir Hugh had given Ailsa. The one of Angus as a young man.

"I want to do the right thing, especially after failing to carry out her final wish."

Johnny thought a while.

"You could place the photo in Ailsa's coffin so the two of them are never separated or send it to Katherine as a memento of her husband."

He paused before adding, "or you could keep it for Tavish so when he is older, he has a photo of his biological father."

There was no rancour in his voice, no sadness or resentment. Typical Johnny! He was thinking what would be best for his son.

Mairi threw her arms round his neck.

"I'll keep it safe for Tavish," she replied. "One day he will need to know the truth."

CHAPTER 18

On the day of Daisy's arrival, Skye shone beneath a cloudless blue sky. Johnny and Tavish drove to Kyleakin to meet their visitor off the ferry, leaving Mairi at home to add a few finishing touches.

As the turn-table ferry 'Lochalsh' cautiously approached the slipway, two crewmen jumped ashore to wrap the mooring line round a bollard. They worked fast, nimbly skipping over the lobster pots, chains and anchors that lay on the quay. When the ferry was still, they heaved and pushed the turn-table to face the slipway and lowered the ramp to allow vehicles to drive ashore. Johnny strained to see if he could spot a travel-weary foot passenger but the only solo woman who alighted off the ferry was a slim woman in a full-skirted floral dress, wearing a tailored coat and a neat hat perched on the side of her head.

It was Daisy.

During the brief crossing from the Kyle of Lochalsh to Kyleakin, her elegant poise had turned a few heads. For a woman in her forties, she possessed an enviable figure and radiated a natural beauty that left a lasting impression on those around her.

Johnny wasn't sure whether to be proud or embarrassed when she waved enthusiastically in his direction. He smiled back, not wishing to draw attention to himself.

She stepped ashore, aided by two willing volunteers who carried her luggage like porters at Victoria Station. Once on dry land she filled her lungs with sea air and remarked how good it was to be on Skye.

Johnny stepped forward to welcome her. The softness of her skin against his rough, calloused hand triggered an unexpected reaction. He had fallen under her spell, smitten by the allure of her clothing and perfume.

"And you, young man!" she said, sweeping Tavish up in her arms, "You must be Tavish. My, you've grown at least two inches since I last saw you!"

Tavish was acutely embarrassed by the stares he received from passengers and workers on the pier. He tried to wriggle free of Daisy's welcoming hug but her grasp was too tight. Eventually, she slackened her grip and lowered him gently to the ground leaving a lingering waft of *l'Air du Temps* clinging to his clothes.

"Welcome to Skye!" was all Johnny could think of saying.

"Thank you," came the quiet confident reply.

She nodded at the two young men who were still holding her luggage.

"You can put them down now," she smiled. "I can carry them from here. Thanks for all your help."

"Allow me," Johnny said, picking up the bags in spite of Daisy's protests. They walked to the car in silence with Tavish dragging behind, unsure what to make of their new visitor.

"What a place!" she exclaimed. "I imagined Skye would be beautiful but not as beautiful as this! Can we get going? I can't wait to see Kilbackie."

The car drove past a row of white cottages built beside a single track that led to the ruins of Castle Moil, the ancient seat of clan MacKinnon. From its vantage point on a modest mound overlooking Kyle Akin, the castle could keep an eye on every vessel navigating the narrow strait between Skye and the mainland. Sgùrr na Coinnich and its smaller neighbour, Beinn na Caillich were the highest peaks in the area, both dominating the rugged wilderness surrounding the castle.

In 1263, Haakon Haakonsson, King of Norway, moored his entire war fleet in Kyle Akin before the Battle of Largs which ended five hundred years of Norse invasions of Scotland.

According to legend, Castle Moil was built by 'Saucy Mary', a Norwegian Princess who married a MacKinnon chief. She accumulated great wealth by stretching a large chain across the Kyle and demanding tolls from every ship that passed through the strait. Norwegian ships were exempt. After her death, she was buried on Beinn na Caillich where the winds from her native Norway were said to blow across her grave.

Daisy's good humour and genuine interest in Johnny's vision for the farm helped pass the time. She listened attentively as he explained the importance of feeding hay to the cattle during the long winter months. Johnny found talking to Daisy easy. She was receptive and intelligent.

Her wide attractive hazel eyes sparkled with laughter as he rambled on about cows, grass and crops. During the moments of silence, she leant her head against the side of the car and gazed at the dramatic scenery unfolding around her.

Mairi was still wearing her apron when the ferry party stumbled through the front door, chatting like old friends. Compared to the slim, stylish lady talking amicably to her husband, Mairi felt positively frumpy. Her weighty tweed skirt and coarse Fair Isle jumper clung awkwardly to her ample frame. Neither garment flattered her and, to add insult to injury, her sensible lace-up shoes made her look like a dowdy great aunt. Daisy, on the other hand, was as fragrant and light as a summer's day. Her presence filled the entrance hall with lemon, jasmine and rose.

She was out of Mairi's league.

It was hard to believe that the refined creature standing in her hall was Daisy Smith, Lady Hollister's former maid. The tilt of her head when she laughed was the same, but her couture definitely wasn't.

Mairi thought back to the letter in which she described her failing marriage and unhappy home life. The thought of welcoming a depressed, down-at-heel friend had appealed to her. She imagined the two of them would find solace in each other's company, sharing common anxieties and fears for the future. Had she known about Daisy's transformation, she would have thought twice about letting her stay.

Johnny tried to break the ice by taking Daisy's suitcase upstairs.

"You must be exhausted," Mairi said, taking her coat. "Would you like a cup of tea now or later, once you've freshened up?"

Daisy said she would like to freshen up first but wouldn't be long. They walked up the main staircase to a wide corridor that ran the full length of the house. Leading off the corridor were five large formal bedrooms and two bathrooms.

"Your bathroom is down there, the third door on the left. I'm afraid the plumbing is rather primitive but there is usually enough hot water for a bath although the pressure varies. Come down when you're ready. There's tea and cake in the kitchen."

"Thank you, Mairi!" Daisy said with genuine gratitude. "And thank you for having me to stay. I'm afraid I've rather imposed myself on you but you'll never know how much this visit means to me."

She opened the lid of her suitcase to reveal a pile of clothes neatly folded in tissue paper.

"I know it's wrong to covet your neighbour's goods but you are so lucky living here on Skye."

The remark seemed genuine but words weren't enough to pacify Mairi.

Once downstairs, she confronted Johnny.

"You obviously enjoyed bringing Daisy home from the ferry!" she said sarcastically as he stood by the range waiting for the kettle to boil. "I saw the look on your face as you walked into the hall."

Johnny was in no mood for confrontation. "I don't know what you're talking about! Daisy's a nice woman who asked a few questions about the farm and yes, I was flattered she showed an interest in my work but that was all. As for the journey home, she spent most of the time looking out of the window."

He poured the boiling water into the teapot and left the kitchen just before Daisy popped her head round the door to see if she had found the right room. She looked relaxed, almost glowing, in a pair of navy slacks which accentuated her slim figure. Mairi caught another whiff of the French perfume and winced.

CHAPTER 19

Daisy had no difficulty adapting to Kilbackie's slow pace of life. She amused Mairi with tales of her failing marriage describing with wit and humour Bill's dislike of all things cultural, especially the architectural gems of North Yorkshire - The Shambles, York Minster and Castle Howard. The more Daisy took him out, the less interested he became until one day she'd had enough.

"You've absolutely no interest in history," she complained during a visit to Fountains Abbey. "All you do is sit in the car and eat. Why not stay at home next time? You'd be much happier."

During a regular check-up, the doctor warned Bill that he had become clinically obese and if he didn't do something about his weight, he could develop Type 2 diabetes or have a heart attack.

Daisy and Bill's marriage had started happily enough but arguments about finance, how to spend their free time, household duties and meals soon muddied the clear waters of married life. Rather than address these issues straight away, they let their differences fester, preferring to ignore the hairline cracks that were appearing on the surface. It wasn't long before their bearable relationship had turned into a dysfunctional torment. Both found it hard to communicate with words. The passion that had been the glue in their relationship became unstuck, leaving their marriage in tatters, dependent on drink and lust for its survival. As time went by, they found themselves trapped in a loveless co-existence.

Daisy refused to live with regrets. She was an optimist, with ambitions to improve her life but in 1945 her life changed forever. Allied troops launched a series of offensives that ended Japanese rule in Burma. Her only son William was finally liberated after three horrific years incarcerated in a prisoner of war camp. He never spoke of his ordeal but some inmates were more vocal, describing systematic torture, starvation and beatings. Thousands died of dysentery, beriberi and malaria but William miraculously survived.

When he eventually returned home, his once robust muscular body was reduced to skin and bone. He weighed no more than seven stone. His existence was nothing more than a living hell of nightmares and flashbacks.

Kind neighbours and friends remarked how lucky he was to make it home alive but they had no understanding of the daily struggles he faced living with pain while trying to adapt to civilian life. Their kind words were well-meant but short-lived. All too quickly William became yesterday's hero, a tragic victim of a war they all wanted to forget.

Daisy took matters in hand and devoted the next chapter of her life to restoring William to full health. She cocooned him in maternal love, praying he would gain weight. Day and night she sat by his bed, pouring teaspoons of nutritious soup through his parched lips. The road to recovery was slow, hampered by ugly red marks that developed on his lower back, elbows and hips. He often cried out in pain, tossing and turning to get comfortable. Daisy had never seen anything like them before.

On a chance meeting with the District Nurse, she described the broken patches of skin that were giving William so much trouble. The nurse nodded thoughtfully, showing great sympathy.

"Does he ever spend time out of bed, helping you in the house or going for short walks outside?" she asked.

"No!" Daisy replied rather tersely. "He returned home from the Far East, a walking skeleton. It was heart-breaking. You've no idea how awful it's been trying to get him to eat and build up his strength. He's far too weak to get out of bed."

The nurse looked sceptical. She had heard it all before - over-protective mothers relishing the close bond they had formed with their sick children. Over time, their offspring became addicted to being needed and were reluctant to let go, for fear of losing the close maternal ties.

"I'll call round and visit him," she said, taking out an appointment book. "How about Wednesday morning at 10.30 a.m.?"

"That sounds fine to me," Daisy replied, relieved that someone was taking her seriously.

Wednesday eventually arrived.

At precisely 10.30 a.m. Nurse Symonds knocked on the front door and was ushered in by Daisy. After a brief examination of William's damaged body, she gave a nod of satisfaction. Her diagnosis had been correct.

"Don't look so worried, William," she chirped. "You've got bedsores. Beastly painful things but very common on patients who spend a lot of time in bed and don't walk about. Do you know anything about them?"

William shook his head, unsure if he wanted to know about bedsores.

"They occur when pressure is placed on the bony parts of the body, preventing blood from delivering oxygen to the skin and tissue. They are curable but it takes time. Each sore needs to be washed daily."

She took several bottles and packages out of her bag, then turned her attention to Daisy.

"Have you got a small hand towel I could use? I'm afraid it will have to be boiled once I've finished with it."

She wet a wodge of cotton wool with a saline solution and gently washed the infected areas on his lower back, elbows and hips before dabbing them dry with the soft towel.

"All finished!" she smiled, encouraging William to take heart. "You should feel more comfortable now they are clean."

She handed Mairi the stainless-steel bowl containing the soiled cotton wool.

"Could you dispose of the contents for me and wash the bowl in soapy water? It's vital you prevent infection by washing your hands and keeping the sheets, towels and bandages spotlessly clean.

"Now if you'll excuse me, I need to wash my hands."

She walked across the landing to the bathroom, leaving Daisy alone with her son.

"How are you feeling?"

For the first time since arriving home, William replied with genuine warmth.

"Great!"

The nurse returned, smelling strongly of carbolic soap.

"Before I leave," she said, rummaging in her bag, "I have one more job to do."

She took out a pot of honey.

"I know this sounds strange, but a small amount of honey smeared on the infected areas will improve the healing process."

Daisy looked surprised.

"Honey!" she exclaimed. "Why honey?"

"It's one of nature's miracle cures. Very few people know that it draws bacteria out of wounds and seals them with a protective coating, keeping the skin moist. But a word of warning. The word 'miracle' does not mean 'instant'. You will need a lot of patience before the bedsores finally heal."

Nurse Symonds told William that he was spending too much time in bed with nothing to do.

"It's time you got up and exercised your limbs. Weeks of inactivity have reduced your muscle mass and the natural padding around your bones.

"No more pandering!" she added, patting the soft eiderdown. "You need to get up, walk as much as possible."

William scowled at the thought of leaving the comfortable laundered sheets that smelt of temperate winds and green grass. No well-meaning nurse would ever succeed in cajoling him out of bed when his body still bore the scars of cigarette burns and beatings.

He turned his sallow face towards the magnificent chestnut tree that took in pride of place in his parents' garden. As the days grew warmer, he watched its swollen buds burst into leaf and listened to the melodious song of a blackbird perched high in its canopy.

Every evening Daisy kept vigil beside her son's bed, catching sleep whenever she could. During the day, she opened the bedroom window and filled the room with the sweet smells of nature. Ounce by ounce William began to gain weight. His grey sunken cheeks fleshed out and turned pink. Physically he was on the mend but his mind was still troubled. Spring turned to summer - summer to autumn. Armistice, Christmas and the New Year passed with signs that William was healing under his mother's watchful eye.

On 3rd February 1947 the outside temperature plummeted and it started to snow. At first the flakes were large and soft but as the night drew on, the weather deteriorated and the flurry turned into a blinding blizzard.

Seven years of food and fuel rationing had taken their toll on a war-weary population struggling to make ends meet. The arctic wind that arrived in February showed no mercy as it swept across the land, paralysing daily life. Daisy had stopped working for Sir Hugh's mother as soon as it became clear that William needed a full-time nurse. The Great Freeze brought a weakened economy to its knees. Businesses and factories closed, men were laid off, transport and delivery systems ground to a halt, roads were blocked by abandoned vehicles but Bill was lucky. His factory managed to stay open by reducing employment to a three-day week. With Daisy no longer earning, their weekly income was pitiful, barely enough to feed a family of three. At the beginning of the cold snap, Daisy had the energy to drag a sheet of corrugated iron through the snow to the woods at the end of the village where she foraged for kindling and logs. The exhausting two-mile round trip provided enough wood to keep the kitchen stove burning for two days. With careful rationing, she could make a large stew or soup last three days by storing it in a freezing cupboard and reheating small amounts each day. Fresh bread, meat, eggs and milk were still rationed but the village stores stocked vegetables, oats, tea, powdered milk and eggs.

Huddled round the table in their tiny kitchen, Daisy served the lion's share of every meal to William, unaware that Bill needed energy to walk to the factory and put in a full day's work. Her obsession with William fractured the bond between father and son. Bill became an extra, an irrelevance in her fight for survival. Daisy never thought to thank him for persevering at work and bringing back a wage that kept them all alive. The mood in the house was grim, with all three struggling to cope in their different ways with poverty, hunger and cold.

Although William was healing physically, his mind remained a blank page, his beautiful eyes stared listlessly out of their dark sockets.

Bill watched his wife grow thinner and paler as the subzero temperatures entered a second week.

"You must eat more," he said, concerned by her weight loss and general state of apathy. "Perhaps you should take William next time you collect wood. It's too much for one person."

Daisy shook her head. "He's not strong enough yet and it's far too cold outside. I'm fine, Bill, honestly, I am!" she said defiantly.

"At least let me help you when I'm not working," Bill insisted but Daisy would have none of it. Collecting wood was her responsibility. It was her contribution to William's welfare.

The thrice weekly trips to the woods were taking longer, due to her swollen feet. She stoically trudged through the snow trying to ignore the pain in her fingers and toes. The snow clung to her shoes, stockings and skirt. Its freezing grip took her breath away. By the time she reached home she had nothing left to give.

Eventually she collapsed.

The doctor prescribed total rest and better nourishment which Daisy continued to ignore in favour of her son. Cold and hungry, she spent the day sitting in the kitchen with newspaper stuffed into her winter clothes to ward off the worst of the winter chill. When Katherine made an unannounced visit to check everything was all right, she was horrified to find an emaciated woman half-hidden under a pile of clothing and newspaper.

"It was unbelievable!" she related to Lady Hollister.

"Daisy looked so thin and tired. She's destitute, even with Bill working three days a week. Is there any way we could help her during this exceptionally cold snap?"

Lady Hollister thought for a while, then suggested they could put together a weekly supply of logs and food from the kitchen garden. It wouldn't be much - some potatoes, onions and cabbages but at least it would see Daisy's family through the worst of the winter. The rescue package could be revised once the snow had melted.

This act of kindness probably saved Daisy's life.

The harsh winter had brought her to her knees. In a rare moment of contrition, she admitted she could no longer cope on her own. Caring full-time for William had placed immense financial and emotional pressure on Bill. Every day he struggled to help his exhausted wife while privately grieving for his lost son. The small boy who used to giggle when he tried to hoot like an owl through cupped hands; the boy who snuggled up to him, spellbound by stories of pirates and explorers; the boy who pleaded with him to delay bedtime until he had seen the vast array of stars in an infinite sky. This was the adorable inquisitive child he had loved with all his heart but who had now withdrawn into a world Bill couldn't reach.

"I can't do this anymore," Daisy told Bill, her eyes filled with tears. "I thought I had enough love to make him better but I don't. Do you remember when he was little? He would run up to me whenever he fell over, pointing to the cut or graze on his knee, saying 'Mummy kiss it better!' Everything was so much simpler then but now

I seem to be making matters worse. It isn't fair on you or William."

Bill listened, relieved she was beginning to see the folly of trying to do everything on her own. They discussed Malvingborough Abbey, a residential home for war veterans whose minds had been damaged by cruelty and trauma. They put the idea to William, and much to their surprise, he agreed he needed help. A visit was arranged for the following week and William was accepted for a trial period of six months.

CHAPTER 20

Life without William was particularly hard for Daisy, who for the past eighteen months, had focussed solely on his survival. She had nursed his sores, fed him, washed him and held his thin bony hand twenty-four hours a day, seven days a week. Nurse Symonds consoled her by saying his road to recovery had been due to her perseverance. With William away from home, Daisy needed a reason to get up in the morning. The answer came in the form of an advertisement placed in the Post Office window: '*Assistant Wanted - Davidson's. Book-keeping skills an advantage - Phone 376 or write to Davidsons, 24 High Street, Craventhorpe'*.

Davidsons was the local haberdasher's owned by Mr Davidson, who had recently been widowed after forty years of marriage. The sudden death of his wife had deeply affected the mild, unassuming man and it didn't take long for his regular customers to notice subtle changes in the shop. The weekly display of accessories so creatively put together by Mrs. Davidson ceased to tempt. The empty space in its place, denied shoppers the thrill of seeing the latest fashions first hand. A few loyal customers continued visiting the shop but the gloom that descended over the poorly stocked shelves tested their patience until one by one they took their custom elsewhere.

Women with money to spend no longer visited Davidson's. One evening, whilst checking the monthly takings, Mr Davidson realised how serious things had become. Rather than keep the information to himself, he had the good sense to confide in his daughter, Shirley, who was horrified.

"For goodness' sake, Dad! You've got to do something or else you'll lose the shop," she said in exasperation.

"Why not put a notice in the Post Office window asking for a shop manager with book- keeping skills? We could write it together and if it would help, I'll take the advert to the post office this afternoon."

Reluctantly Mr Davidson listened to his daughter's advice. Once the wording had been agreed, the advertisement was placed in the window, although Mr Davidson couldn't see how a small card could improve his business' cash flow. By the end of the day, he had received three phone calls from women keen to work in his shop. By the end of the week, he had received eight letters.

"What did I tell you?" Shirley laughed when he told her about the responses. "I'm sure the ladies are genuine and not just after your body, Dad!"

Mr Davidson didn't find the flippant comment very funny. He took everything literally so the thought of being eyed by a woman when his beloved wife had only just been laid to rest, appalled him.

"Don't look so shocked," she said, trying not to laugh. "The war has changed everything. You'd be surprised how many women are trying to find work to make ends meet."

Her father forced a smile although he still had no idea why so many women would want to work in his shop.

"For money," his daughter replied. "No-one wants to remain drab now that rationing is over. The war deprived us of colour and fun. With extra money in our pockets, we have more choice, more variety. We want a brighter future and are prepared to work for it."

"I honestly didn't think anyone would contact me," he replied. "I'm amazed."

"Did you like the sound of anyone in particular?" Shirley asked, clacketing her knitting needles as she spoke. "It's amazing how much you can learn about someone over the phone or in a letter."

Her father thought a while, unsure whether to mention Daisy, the one who had stood head and shoulders above the rest. Her intelligent confidence had taken him by surprise. Compared to his quiet submissive wife, Daisy was sharp, with an unexpected reassuring manner. For the first time in his life, he realised just how insular he had become, shut away in his shop for hours and days on end, worrying about cash-flow, product quality and service. He had lost touch with the changing attitudes to wealth, work and equality. His dutiful wife had stood by his side without complaining. In all the years they had been together, he never heard her utter a cross word. Her temperament was calm and loyal, the perfect soulmate for an awkward workaholic.

"There was one who sounded more alert than the others," he said with surprising enthusiasm. "She definitely caught my attention. I don't know if she has the right skills but she came across well."

"You see!" Shirley exclaimed. "You're becoming aware of the type of person you want for the shop. It's a start."

The interviews took place the following week for all the candidates except Frau Huber, whose poor grasp of English and thick German accent was considered a disadvantage in a country still smarting from the war.

Daisy arrived punctually, wearing discreet makeup, a woollen belted jacket, a pleated skirt and a pert hat set neatly on the side of her head. She sat elegantly in front of Mr Davidson, answering his questions in an attractive fluent manner. When it came to the mental arithmetic test, she passed with flying colours, finding addition, subtraction, percentages and multiplication easy. The interview came to a promising close.

"Thank you, Mrs. Smith," he said, shaking her firmly by the hand. "I think that will be all for now. Do you have any further questions?"

He felt confident she would shake her head, satisfied that everything had been covered but to his astonishment, she looked him straight in the eye and said, "I'd love to work in your shop, Mr Davidson, and I think I could make a difference but I would need an extra eight pence an hour if I were offered the job."

Mr Davidson looked aghast at the suggestion he should pay an extra eight pence per hour. It was lot of money. Probably more than he could afford in the current climate but Daisy was adamant. She smiled graciously, completely wrong-footing him.

"But you haven't started yet!" he stuttered, still reeling from her brazenness.

"I know!" she replied. "You must think me very greedy but I know I'm worth the extra, especially if you want me to take control of the stock and keep the accounts. That's a lot of responsibility, more than a shop girl would be expected to do."

"I'll think about it," he added, stretching out an arm to open the door for her to leave.

Back inside everything seemed duller without Daisy. Mr Davidson looked round the gloomy shop that had once been his pride and joy and noticed for the first time the dirty floor, the dusty counter and the half-filled shelves. He was savvy enough to know that an under-stocked, dirty shop would never draw in the ladies whose daily presence had played such an important role in the business' success. He had taken for granted the colourful artistic displays of lace, ribbons, buttons, zips and cotton reels, cleverly put together by his modest wife who instinctively understood how to draw in the wealthy ladies with time to waste and money to spend. One look at the forlorn shop convinced him that he needed Daisy.

Under her management, Davidson's flourished. From the moment the doors opened at nine o'clock, the tills started ringing. Laughter returned to the shop, gossip was exchanged and Daisy's elaborate displays drew gasps of admiration. They were full of the latest accessories, all irresistibly tempting, all reasonably priced. Freed from the constraints of work, Mr Davidson took on a new lease of life. He started visiting the Social Club where, much to his daughter's amusement, he befriended a widow called Anthea Eastburn who was outgoing, sociable and fun. The last thing she wanted was to live in a tiny flat above a haberdasher's, so after a whirlwind courtship, the two got married and put the shop up for sale, ending Daisy's employment.

News that the Craventhorpe's long-established haberdasher's had finally closed its doors spread quickly and several affluent ladies, too lazy or proud to clean their own large houses, approached Daisy with offers of work. At first, she turned them down, hoping to find something more challenging but nothing turned up. She didn't have the luxury of choice. Memories of cold, hunger and destitution forced her to take the next job that came her way.

Providence was kind. She was approached by Mrs Lewis, the bank manager's wife, who was looking for a competent, cheerful person to run her busy household. The following Monday, Daisy started work at 12 Victoria Avenue, a large Edwardian Villa on the outskirts of the town. It was a job she loved and it paid well.

After six months, she was summoned into the drawing room.

"Sit down," Mrs Lewis said, gazing intently at Daisy who sat obediently with her shoulders forced back to accentuate her perfect deportment. "Would you like a cup of tea?"

Daisy was so surprised to be ushered into the drawing room, she temporarily lost her tongue and could only reply with a nod. She looked around the elegant sunlit room, taking in the soft furnishings, photos of smiling children in silver frames, the row of embossed invitations prominently displayed on the mantelpiece. The room exuded affluence, a far cry from the humble terraced cottage she shared with Bill. Things didn't feel right. Mrs Lewis kept a professional distance from her staff, not wishing to become involved in their lives and yet here she was, refined and fashionable, pouring tea into a delicate porcelain teacup for her 'daily'.

"Milk, sugar?" she enquired, spreading her full skirt over her knees.

"Just milk please," Daisy replied, having finally found her tongue. She took a freshly baked almond slice and placed it on a plate, unsure what to do or say next.

"Relax!" Mrs. Lewis said, trying to put Daisy at her ease. "You've done nothing wrong. On the contrary, you've done everything right and I don't know what I would do without you.

"The reason I've asked you for tea is to make a suggestion which you can reject if you want. Tell me to mind my own business but have you ever thought about learning shorthand and typing?" She reddened as she spoke, unsure if she was saying the right thing.

"I'm probably shooting myself in the foot," she continued, "but you are so competent. I'd hate to hold you back."

This was not the conversation Daisy was expecting. From time to time, she and Bill had discussed further education but Daisy had never pursued it because she liked working for the Lewises and had grown to rely on the generous pay and flexible working hours.

The seed planted by Mrs. Lewis started to grow.

A few days later she brought up the subject with Bill.

"I'd love to attend night school," she said. "But who will look after William when he's at home?"

Bill looked blank. He had no idea what she was talking about.

"Think about it, Bill!" she said. "Someone will need to stay with him on the evenings I'm out. He's not fit enough to be left on his own. At least that's what we've been told."

Her husband's face grew dark. His fists clenched.

"Well, you can count me out!" he said, resenting the fact he might have to give up some free time to look after his damaged son. The whole idea appalled him and he wasn't shy in expressing his views but Daisy held her ground. The more he shouted and swore, the more determined she was to study at night school.

"Well?" Mrs Lewis enquired the next time they met. "Have you made up your mind?"

Daisy nodded.

"I'd love to learn shorthand and typing but I haven't found anyone willing to care for my son who's had a few problems since returning from the Far East."

"Have you asked your husband? If he's anything like mine, he'll promise the earth and deliver nothing especially if his cooked supper, glass of claret, armchair and relaxation are compromised!"

Daisy stared in amazement. It was the first time she had heard a woman speak candidly about her marriage and admit to imperfections.

"They're all the same," Mrs Lewis continued with a sigh, noticing the look of surprise on Daisy's face. "Little autocrats enjoying their power. Look at us, Daisy! We've got brains that could make a difference to the world but you end up cleaning and I end up breeding. Where's the sense in that?"

Daisy smiled. "Is that really what you think?"

"It's not what I think, it's what I know and before you say anything, I'll help look after William if Bill ever lets you down. He can come over here and play with the children. They love meeting new people and an extra mouth to feed at supper time won't make any difference."

Her mood was feisty but there were dark patches round her fiery eyes.

"I don't know what to say," Daisy replied, genuinely moved by Mrs Lewis' generosity.

"Say you agree," came the hasty reply, "And before you start worrying about lessons, I've arranged for you to learn with a friend's mother who is a retired shorthand typist. She spends each day sitting at home, bored out of her mind. She'd love to teach you and doesn't want to be remunerated."

Mrs. Lewis' overwhelming kindness left Daisy tongue-tied.

"This is incredible," she said. "How can I ever thank you?"

"By agreeing to take up my offer," came the swift reply.

"Why are you helping me?" Daisy asked. "You hardly know me."

Mrs Lewis' shoulders drooped. Her eyes filled with tears.

"I'm pregnant!" she said flatly.

"But that's great news!" Daisy exclaimed enthusiastically. "You must be so excited."

Mrs Lewis shook her head.

"Why does everyone think I must be excited when I'm not! I don't want another child. Four is enough but Derek has always wanted a large family and is obviously thrilled with the news."

Daisy hesitated before getting up off the sofa. Kneeling silently in front of the crumpled woman, she took her hands in hers and allowed the warmth of her affection to flow through them.

"Do you want to talk?"

Mrs Lewis gave the slightest of nods but kept her head hung low.

"You see," she began. "I wasn't born into a professional family. I came from a small Nottinghamshire mining town where everything was grey - the clothes, the street, the sky, the houses. My parents were decent hard-working people who did their best to clothe and feed five children but life was hard. I don't mean we were starving or anything like that, but resources were scarce and there was very little money for treats.

"I, unlike all my sisters, argued and fought to be heard. I challenged established views, debated with my father and drove my mother to distraction.

"'She's the son we never had,'" my father used to say, exasperated by my fierce determination. I don't think he ever understood me but I believe he admired my pluck and came to accept I was an inquisitive oddity who liked reading, got top marks at school and always completed her homework on time.

"The breakthrough that changed my life came in the form of Miss Owens the young maths teacher who arrived at our school full of intellectual zeal. Single-handedly, she transformed our lessons by combining clarity of thought with infinite patience. What's more, she believed in me. She went that extra mile to get me into university and, much to everyone's surprise, I won a scholarship to Girton College, the first pupil in our school ever to go to Oxford or Cambridge. Quite an achievement for a small-town girl!

"I'll never forget my first day in that great city of learning, walking among its beautiful mellow buildings surrounded by exquisite flower gardens, meadows and lawns. I cried with joy for a week!

"For the next three years I debated, studied, read and researched for up to fifteen hours a day. Sleep was a waste of time, learning was everything. I left university starry-eyed with optimism, ambitious to make a difference in the field of science, medicine or industry. I wanted to repay society for the educational opportunity I had been given."

Mrs Lewis slowly lifted her head as memories of her time at university came flooding back.

"Would you like a drink? It's the least I can offer while you patiently listen to me talking about myself! I might even find some cake. Let's go through to the kitchen."

While the kettle boiled, she took a tin off the shelf and cut two slices of Victoria sponge.

"Milk? Sugar?"

"Just a dash of milk, please. No sugar."

The warmth of the drink and the sweetness of the cake calmed Mrs. Lewis into a more relaxed frame of mind.

"Am I boring you?" she asked, unused to an audience.

Daisy shook her head, savouring the deliciously light sponge and jam.

Mrs Lewis resumed her story.

"I moved to London hoping to find a job but it was much harder than I thought. Perhaps I was too naïve. Who knows? But the desire to be successful, away from my home town, drove me. Before long I found somewhere to live, if you can call a tiny unheated attic room, suitable accommodation. Rejection letters fell through the letter box at an alarming rate. One after another, all polite, full of apologies explaining that I was either too young, too inexperienced or had the wrong academic qualifications.

"Then, quite by chance, I came across an advertisement for a teaching job at a girls' day school, a short bus ride from my dismal digs. It was a decision that changed my life but not in the way I was expecting. The full-time position gave me financial security. I earned enough to move out of the dingy attic into a more comfortable lodging within easy reach of the school but teaching young children was a bit of an anti-climax after three exhilarating years in academia. My sweet-natured, polite pupils led charmed frivolous lives far removed from the harsh realities of the world around them. Theirs was the childhood I had dreamt of, yet close up, it appeared strangely hollow, over-protected.

"Job applications were consistently rejected. Little girls continued to be taught mathematics. Then one glorious day, the miracle I'd been praying for actually happened. I was offered an interview at the Building Research Establishment for a job looking into the behaviour of reinforced concrete flooring in new buildings. This was the work I was looking for. Serious research requiring a high level of mathematics that would make a difference to people's lives. I was ecstatic and felt confident my headmistress, Miss Watson, would be equally delighted with my good news and allow me time off to attend the interview. How wrong could I be? She stood by her desk and lectured me on the virtues of loyalty and commitment, accusing me of being a lightweight, lacking moral fibre, a modern woman who thought more about herself than others. Little wonder, with that attitude, my request was turned down.

"In many ways she had a point. I was employed by the school to do a job and couldn't expect another teacher to cover my lessons especially when I was thinking of leaving but even so, it wasn't easy turning down the interview.

"The blow must have been etched on my face because Peggy Mason, the English teacher, took pity on me and invited me to a concert in the Town Hall, hoping to ease my disappointment. It was there that I first met Derek, the one person who has never stopped being proud of me!"

Mrs Lewis sighed as she recounted her courtship and marriage to the man she described as her rock.

"Why are you telling me this?" Daisy asked uncomfortably, taking another sip of tea.

"I thought it was obvious! I want you to experience further education without having to worry about William."

"But why?" Daisy asked.

"I can't really explain," she replied, her eyes still swollen with tears. "Perhaps it's because I recognise in you a hunger to succeed. The same hunger I had before I had children. And this little one," she said, patting her stomach, "has finally put an end to my dreams of one day returning to work and making a difference. The razor-sharp mathematical mind that once showed so much potential has dissolved into a fuddled fog of baby talk, nappies, school runs and games of Snap.

"And that's where you come in!"

"Me?" Daisy exclaimed, still trying to understand why Mrs Lewis was speaking so freely to her.

"Yes! You!"

For the first time since opening up, Mrs Lewis seemed to regain control of her emotions.

"I want you to take my place and make a difference to this world."

Daisy looked aghast!

"What do you mean?" she asked, still unsure what was going on.

"You've got an opportunity to get some qualifications and move on with your life. Take it! I'm here to help you."

For two hours, every Tuesday and Thursday evening, Daisy sat at Mrs. Tasker's kitchen table with a well-thumbed copy of *Pitman's Shorthand Instructor* and a typewriter. Mrs. Tasker was a born teacher. She set the bar extremely high, demanding perfection in everything. *'Practice makes perfect'* was the motto she lived by and Daisy certainly practised hard, writing letters and taking dictation. She strove for perfection, always hungry to learn more.

Mrs Lewis remained true to her word. She allowed William to visit whenever Bill was too busy to keep him company, which was increasingly often. William had a rare knack for bedtime stories and was surprisingly patient when playing with the children. He was adored by them all. Even Freddy, the eldest boy, a spectacular cheat, learned to respect him. One look from William and he would blush with shame and mumble an apology.

As the weeks turned to months, Daisy became more proficient, more confident. Her skin glowed, her energy increased. She lost weight, became elegant and took a pride in her looks. It didn't take long for her diligence to be rewarded. Mr Warburton, the senior partner of the solicitors, Warburton, Clark and Paine, placed an advertisement in the local newspaper seeking a secretary to replace Miss Dickson who was retiring after thirty-five years' devoted service to the firm. Pernickety by nature and precise in manner, she had worked tirelessly to keep the busy office running smoothly. Eventually the day came when she was forced to retire. She had reached sixty and was crippled with arthritis in her hands.

Daisy's interview went well, considering her lack of experience. Her dress-sense and the way she composed herself had impressed Mr Warburton so much, he asked her back for a practical test which she sailed through, achieving top marks in all the disciplines.

After interviewing the other candidates there was only one clear winner.

Daisy

Around this time, she became an active member of the Women's Institute, kept herself socially and politically informed and started reading novels, which was where her fascination for the Highlands started. Quite by chance, she read Walter Scott's 'Waverley' the book that fired her imagination and unlocked passions that had laid dormant for years. She became obsessed with images of misty lochs, castles, hills and rugged coastlines. They overwhelmed her waking senses and haunted her dreams.

When Johnny and Mairi had given her an open invitation to visit Kilbackie, she knew she couldn't refuse.

Kilbackie 1955
★★★

Daisy settled effortlessly into her new surroundings, grasping every opportunity to wander round the farm and explore the island's coastline. The fickle weather never worried her. Invigorating walks made her flawless skin glow, accentuating her natural looks. From the brightness in her eyes, it was clear she was loving her stay at Kilbackie.

"Come out with me," she urged one glorious morning. "The fields are carpeted with wildflowers and you deserve a break. Put down your duster, hang up your pinny and join me outside. It's such a beautiful day and I'd love the company. We could even take a picnic down to the cove. How about it?"

Mairi declined even though she would have loved a break from her daily chores.

"Please, Mairi! It will do you the world of good," Daisy pleaded. "You can't spend all day shut away in this huge house. If you're not careful, you'll wake up and find your dream has turned into a nightmare."

Despite her pleas, Mairi chose not to exchange her dustpan and brush for a walk through the meadows. Daisy's prophetic words hit home later that afternoon when she returned from her daily walk with Johnny by her side. Mairi couldn't help notice how relaxed they looked in each other's company, laughing and talking with no sign of awkwardness, just as they had done the day Johnny picked her up from the ferry.

"Any chance of a cuppa before you pick up Tavish?" Johnny asked his wife. "I'm parched. What about you, Daisy? Would you like something to drink?"

"I'd love a cup of tea if there's one going!" she smiled, running her fingers through her thick wavy hair.

Her glowing cheeks and Johnny's furtive look made Mairi uneasy. Something was going on between the two of them, she knew it but now wasn't the time for a showdown. It would have to wait. Much to her surprise, the seeds of suspicion left her overwhelmed with a jealousy that took her by surprise.

That evening when Johnny came up to bed, Mairi turned her back on him.

"I'm off to Inverness for a couple of days and will be taking the car," she said coldly. "You'll have to do the school run and look after Tavish while I'm away but don't worry, I'm sure Daisy will help."

She wanted to add that Daisy would be far better company than she could ever be but refrained from sounding too bitter.

"What's brought this on?" Johnny asked, tracing his fingers lightly down her bare back, hoping to arouse her. It had been a long time since they had been truly intimate, losing themselves in a love that cleared the air and restored calm.

She flinched.

"Nothing!"

"Something must have upset you to make you want to

leave. Is it me? Have I done something wrong? Whatever it is, I'm sure we can sort it out."

"It's not you," she said. "It's me. You have no idea what's going on in my head!"

"So why don't you tell me? Talk to me, Mairi, please!" Johnny pleaded, aware of the increasing tension growing between them as she lay rigid beside him. "Is it Daisy?"

"Daisy? No, it has nothing to do with her although I'm sure she'll find plenty to do when I'm away. If she gets bored, she can always help you on the farm. The two of you are made for each other!"

"That's cheap and totally beneath you," Johnny said, picking up his pillow and throwing it down between them.

Mairi realised she might have gone too far but was in no mood to apologise.

"You won't starve," she said, trying to sound positive. "There's plenty of cold meat and vegetables in the larder and I've made an apple crumble, your favourite. If you get peckish there's a fruit cake in the tin. I promise I'll be back before you've had time to miss me."

Johnny was too tired for an emotional disagreement but he couldn't let the matter rest.

"Why? Just tell me why you have to go to Inverness."

"I can't," she replied. "But trust me, it's something I have to do. Please let me go, Johnny, and don't ask any more questions."

Outside the window, a full moon turned the night sky silver, its shimmering rays shone on a dog fox slinking silently through the dew, while up above, a barn owl glided noiselessly in search of mice. The mysterious night-time world seemed eerily bright. Inside, the mood was dark.

Mairi appeared to be in the grip of a lunar madness that was slowly destroying her sense of reason. Johnny wanted to explain that there was nothing going on between him and Daisy, nor would there ever be, but Mairi was in no mood to listen. A chilly loneliness descended over the marital bed. Johnny edged nearer his wife for warmth, tenderly enclosing her tense body in his arms and rubbing his cheek across her hair.

She lay unresponsive.

"There's nothing going on between me and Daisy," he repeated, trying to get her to face him. "It's all in your head. She is fun and enthusiastic but I'm not attracted to her - far from it. She's too self-centred and shallow for my taste. If you would only turn over and look me in the eye, you would see that I love you Mairi and you alone."

Mairi listened to Johnny's words and felt the heat of a tear trickle down her cheek. She longed to respond to his touch, to love him and be the person she'd always wanted to be, noble in character, hospitable, supportive and a role model for Tavish but the past few weeks had exposed her failings and robbed her of courage.

"I'm going away for a day or two," she announced to Tavish at breakfast the following morning. "Daddy will look after you, so you'll have nothing to worry about."

Tavish looked far from worried.

"Have fun!" was all he could say between mouthfuls of cereal. After a moment's reflection he added, "If you're going away, does that mean Daddy will be taking me to school?"

"Yes, darling!" Mairi replied, hurt by her son's apparent indifference.

"Goody!" he squealed, taking everyone by surprise. "That means you can come too, Daisy. I'll persuade Daddy to take the boat. It's such fun, you'll love it!"

CHAPTER 21

Rain water ran down the gutters just as it had in April 1933 when Mairi last walked along the wet pavements of Inverness. Like then, the towering granite buildings cast long shadows over the street. She sought solace in the warm glow of Maggie's Teashop on Queensgate just as she had done all those years ago. After ordering a cup of tea, she took a seat at the only free table next to the window. It didn't take long to realise why no-one had taken the table set for two. It was littered with half-eaten scones, undrunk cups of tea, dollops of jam and crumbs on the Formica top and dirty napkins. One bore the distinct impression of crimson lips. Mairi hoped the lady wearing red lipstick had enjoyed her tea, although it looked as if she had left in a hurry. Perhaps she had argued with her friend or he had finished with her. Whatever had happened, the cluttered table showed signs of an unhappy encounter.

The lipstick reminded her of Daisy.

Her thoughts were interrupted by the arrival of an efficient-looking waitress wearing a light blue belted dress and an apron trimmed with lace. In her hands she carried a tray and a damp cloth.

"Sorry about the dirty table," she apologised, stacking the crockery on the tray and wiping the table top clean.

"We're a bit short-staffed today and the couple sitting here had a blazing row and left in rather a hurry."

'Ah!' thought Mairi. '*The lady with the crimson lips had not enjoyed her tea at Maggie's.*'

She enquired about Maggie Gillies, the former proprietor.

"Do you know her?" the waitress asked, buffing the table with a soft cloth.

Mairi nodded.

"She was very kind to me once. It was a long time ago but I have never forgotten her."

"I can believe that," the girl replied, picking up the tray of crockery. "I'll just get rid of these dirties, then I'll be back to take your order."

She hurried through the tea room into the kitchen and returned with a notebook and pencil.

"Just a tea and some shortbread," Mairi said with a smile, watching the girl write it down. "You were telling me about Maggie."

"Ah yes! I was fortunate to work for her in her final year. She was a lovely lady. Totally fair, without a mean bone in her body."

"Is she still alive?" Mairi asked, keen to learn as much as she could about the woman who had saved her life.

"Good Lord, yes! Very much so. She occasionally drops in to see us but spends most of her time with her daughter who is unwell with something like... oh bother! I keep forgetting what she has. It begins with R. Something like rumour. Sorry! It's gone. Perhaps I'll remember it when I bring you your tea."

The girl remained calmly efficient, obviously trying to get on with her work without appearing rude.

"Tea and shortbread you said?"

Mairi smiled encouragingly. "Yes! Tea and shortbread."

The waitress left Mairi gazing at the nameless passers-by bustling along the wet pavements, their heads bowed, trying to avoid umbrella spokes and puddles. Everything looked so achingly drab.

The waitress returned with the order.

"I've remembered!" she said triumphantly. "Maggie's daughter suffers from Rheumatoid Arthritis which I think has something to do with swollen joints."

"When you next see Maggie, could you mention that Mairi Nicolson was asking after her. I think she will remember me but perhaps you could add that I have never forgotten her kindness."

The waitress promised she would pass on the message.

Twenty-two years had passed since she last saw David and yet here she was, back in Inverness dredging up the past, trying to find out what happened to him after he faked his death. Although she was glad, finally, to have discovered the truth about his disappearance, she found it hard to forgive him for the deception. A postcard or a brief note explaining that he was alive would have made all the difference.

Sitting in the warmth of Maggie's Tearoom, Mairi wondered why she had arranged a meeting with the matron at Saint Joseph's House. It was sheer madness digging up the past she had chosen to bury. Perhaps it had something to do with Daisy's arrival, her easy manner and the way she charmed Johnny and Tavish with her confident elegance. Mairi's lack of poise and humour made her appear dull in comparison. She urgently needed to get a grip on her life if she wanted to become a more likeable person.

She paid for her tea and stepped wearily into the half-light, trudging down Fraser Street to find her lodgings for the night. It hadn't stopped raining since she arrived in Inverness. The drains were barely big enough to take the volume of water pouring off the roofs and down the streets. The next morning, after very little sleep, she drove to Saint Joseph's House, an imposing pile built in the style of a large Edwardian manor but even the most creative architect couldn't disguise its institutional use. It was here that Mairi chose to delve into her painful past and face up to the truths she wished to bury. Was she making the right decision? Only time would tell. She parked the car outside the wrought iron gates marking the entrance to the children's home and walked down the long drive to give herself time to reflect on what she was going to say. The grounds were beautifully maintained with a profusion of flowering shrubs and bulbs set among immaculate lawns. The knot in her stomach grew tighter as her sturdy shoes crunched the loose gravel carrying her nearer the one place she never wanted to see again. She dragged her reluctant body up the steps to the oak front door. Despite the long journey and the expense of staying overnight, she prayed the door would remain closed.

'*I can't do this,*' she told herself, shaking uncontrollably. '*It's too painful. I need to go home.*'

She was on the point of leaving when the door opened, revealing a woman aged about sixty, dressed in comfortable, homely tweeds. The warmth of her smile persuaded Mairi to stay.

"Good morning!" she said, trying to appear confident. "I have a 10.30 appointment with Mrs Douglas."

"I'm Mrs. Douglas," the lady replied, putting Mairi instantly at her ease. "You must be Mrs Mitchell. Please, come in."

The matron led Mairi down a long corridor, past sturdy cast iron radiators set against bare cream walls. Her soft shoes moved silently over the hardwearing floor, whereas Mairi, in her best shoes, made a loud clackety sound as she followed Mrs Douglas through the soulless building that smelled of disinfectant, cabbage and urine. It was the same unhealthy smell that made her retch when she had cradled her newborn son for the very last time. The memory of leaving Alexander in a place that reeked of poor nourishment, poor sanitation and neglect had broken her heart.

Saint Joseph's House was where she had taken her son and put him up for adoption when he was barely two days old. She had buried her guilt for too long. It was time to face the truth and discover what had happened to him.

"You didn't say much in your phone call," Mrs Douglas said when they finally reached her spartan office. "But I have managed to find the file you were interested in. I'm afraid there isn't much in it."

She handed a manila folder over to Mairi who stared at its blue cover with a mixture of relief and fear. It was difficult to tell if the colour was significant to her case but written in neat handwriting on the cover page were the words *Baby N* and his date of birth. No mention of the child's name. She took a peep inside. A few sheets of ageing paper lay within the folded cardboard, the sum total of her shameful past.

Mrs Douglas stared at Mairi through a large pair of tortoiseshell spectacles, trying to gauge her reaction but Mairi's thoughts were well hidden.

"Before we look further into the case of Baby N, I wonder if you could answer a few questions. Just to verify that you really are the mother.

"Would you mind passing me the folder? I need to make notes," she said stretching out her hand. "You can have it back at the end of the interview although I'm afraid you won't be able to take it home with you.

Mairi meekly did as she was asked.

"When did you say you brought Baby N to us?"

Mairi hesitated before answering although she knew the date by heart.

"3rd August 1933."

"How old was the baby when you brought it to us?"

Mairi winced at the use of the word 'it' to describe the most beautiful boy in the world.

"Two days," she winced.

"Was Baby N male or female?"

The impersonal line of questioning made her hackles rise but matron had interviewed hundreds of distressed mothers in her time and wasn't in the least bit fazed.

"My baby was a beautiful, dearly loved, little boy."

"Just answer the question please, Mrs Mitchell. Was the baby male or female?"

"Male."

It soon became clear that Mrs Douglas was only interested in ticking the relevant boxes on her questionnaire. She wasn't an uncaring person but had learned to distance herself from the heart-breaking stories that filled the filing cabinets in her office.

In her younger days she had been driven by an idealistic resolve to make a difference. To care for abandoned children and give them the love and support they deserved but as the years rolled on, the presence of so much despair and poverty had taken its toll on her health. The orphanage continued to grow but society placed little value on its work and without sufficient funding, the small team of committed helpers struggled to give the children the attentive care they so badly needed.

Mrs Douglas bore the increased workload with admirable stoicism. Single-handedly she dealt with the home's clerical, administrative and financial affairs. To preserve her sanity, she focussed on the facts of each tragic case, distancing herself from the people involved.

"Did you leave anything of personal value when you brought your baby to us?"

Mairi tried to think back to what she had left with Alexander. Her mind went blank, her memory clouded by confusion and fear.

Then it came to her.

"A shawl"

Mrs Douglas didn't bat an eyelid.

"Can you describe the shawl?"

Like an open dam, the memories started pouring in.

"It was beige and blue, made of Harris tweed with tasselled edges. I swaddled him in the blanket to keep him safe, taking extra care to keep the woollen fringe away from his eyes and mouth. He was fast asleep the last time I was here."

"Please keep your replies short," Mrs Douglas said officiously. "Beige and blue tweed is all I needed to know."

Mairi wanted to scream, to make Mrs Douglas understand the importance of every small detail relating to Alexander. She wanted to tell the world that she had been a good mother and only handed her son over for adoption because she was desperate.

"You mentioned in your phone call that you wanted to know what happened to Baby N after you left him with us," Mrs Douglas said, peering over her glasses.

Mairi nodded, trying to keep calm. The whole process was taking too long.

Mrs Douglas referred once again to her folder.

"I'm not sure how to tell you this," she continued, her eyes glued to the open file. "But when you left Baby N with us, you signed a form surrendering all rights to the child."

Mairi looked puzzled.

"I don't know what you mean."

"It means that once Baby N was adopted, you could never find out what happened to him," Mrs Douglas explained. Mairi opened her mouth to say something but was interrupted. "You must forget about your son, Mrs Mitchell, even though you are his biological mother, you are not the woman bringing him up. I'm so sorry."

There was a long heavy pause.

The large iron radiator smothered the room with waves of uncontrollable heat. Mairi felt her neck prickle and itch. She wanted to run.

"Is there anything you can do to help me find him?"

"None," the matron replied emphatically. "However, looking at the paperwork, I see your son was born in 1933 which means he's legally old enough to find you if he wants to. Fingers crossed, eh?"

Mairi buried her head in her hands. The weight of two decades of sorrow bore down on her slumped shoulders. She half-lifted her head and pleaded with the emotionally detached matron.

"Please, Mrs Douglas. Help me! I need hope."

The despair on the mother's worn-out face touched Mrs Douglas deeply. She had dealt with countless desperate mothers over the years. Mothers who had lost everything, unable to care for their children, at their wits' end. She had seen it all. Babies born as a result of incest and domestic violence - abandoned, neglected, starved and beaten. None of them had asked to come into the world yet their continuing existence was an embarrassment to society, an irritant to moral sensitivities. They were to be kept in institutions out of sight, out of mind until respectable married couples could be found to adopt them and alleviate the shame.

Baby N was lucky. He had been adopted soon after birth and had been given a chance but those left behind, the unwanted ones, were less fortunate. They quickly became withdrawn and institutionalised, walking silently down long corridors for fear of being punished. Theirs was an artificial world of control, queues and whispers. With so many children in their care, the staff were quick to discipline the rebels and quash early signs of individualism. Saint Joseph's House wasn't a brutal place but in order to keep everyone safe, rules had to be obeyed and offenders punished. Mrs Douglas was known to be fair and compassionate. She rarely took sides, preferring to listen and advise but no matter how hard she and her staff tried, they were never able to give the orphans the love they craved.

Tired and battle-hardened after thirty-five years' service, Mrs Douglas was nearing the end of her time at Saint Joseph's. She was retiring in two weeks and keen to mark the occasion in a memorable way.

She looked up at Mairi and saw a mother crushed by guilt, desperate to find her child.

'*I'm going to throw away the rule book,*" she told herself. *and make a difference to this woman's life! For years, I've done everything the authorities have asked of me and never put a foot wrong. Now it's my turn to make the decisions.*'

An unexpected surge of excitement burst through her body, releasing the restraints that had controlled her every move for so long. For the first time, she saw the world in a different light. It shone!

"Would you like something to drink?" she asked, thumbing through the papers in Baby N's file.

Mairi nodded.

"Tea or Coffee?"

"Tea, please, milk, no sugar."

Mrs Douglas pressed the small circular brass bell on her desk and a young girl, no older than fifteen, made an appearance.

"Ah! Sandy," she said settling back into her chair. "Could you bring two teas. Both with milk and sugar."

Mairi looked bemused.

"The sugar will do you good. You look as if you could do with the extra energy."

Mrs Douglas paused to steady her nerves before deliberately breaking the rules that had guided her whole career.

"Did your son have a name?" she asked. "I can't keep calling him Baby N."

For a brief moment Mairi showed a flicker of hope

"I called him Alexander, after my grandfather," she whispered, her words barely audible.

Mrs Douglas pulled out a sheet of paper. "It says here that Alexander was born with Mongolism. Did you know this when you brought him to us?"

Mairi lifted her head accusingly but didn't reply

"Your son wasn't born normal," Mrs Douglas explained, unsure how much Mairi was taking in.

"You're wrong," came the terse reply. "When I left Alexander in your care, he was a perfect little boy with pink cheeks, dimples on the back of his hands, strong kicking legs and blue eyes. How dare you sit there and tell me after all these years that he wasn't normal!"

Mrs Douglas remained serenely unmoved. She was used to the reactions of worn-out mothers weighed down by guilt and despair. Her office was the final destination of a child who had suffered the slings and arrows of a cruel, unjust world.

Unsure how much Mairi was taking in, she went on to explain that Mongolism or Down's Syndrome, as it was sometimes called, was a congenital disorder caused by the presence of an extra chromosome. Its sufferers were prone to heart defects and often had problems with vision and hearing.

"I'm really sorry, Mrs Mitchell. I know this information must be painful to hear."

Mairi sat deflated, her dreams in tatters as she tried to process the unwelcome news of Alexander's condition.

Mrs Douglas courteously gave Mairi time to reflect.

Mongolism wasn't the best news for a mother to receive out of the blue but the matron, battle-scarred after years of delivering unpalatable truths, gave Mairi the time and space to assimilate her thoughts.

"On a brighter note," she added as an aside. "It says here that Alexander was adopted in November 1933 aged twelve weeks."

Mairi sat up straight. Here was the glimmer of hope she had been waiting for. Someone had chosen Alexander despite him being abnormal.

"Does his file say who adopted him?"

"It gives a name but I'm afraid that's classified information which I cannot legally divulge, even if I wanted to."

Mairi wanted to snatch the file out of Mrs Douglas' hand. How dare she sit there smugly talking about classified information and the law, when Alexander suffered from Mongolism and had been taken away by a complete stranger. She set herself a mission - to find out who had adopted Alexander and where he was living.

"Do you know where he was taken? Any clue would help. A county, town or village? Anything."

"I honestly don't know how I can help without compromising my authority," came the weak response. "I've given you more information than I should have done but my hands are tied."

"Then don't bother!" Mairi retorted. "Right now, you have the chance to make a difference. You can either help me find my son or hinder my search.

"Now, if you don't mind," she said, standing up from her chair. "I have a son to find."

She walked towards the door without looking back but was stopped from leaving by Mrs Douglas.

"I have two important questions for you, Mrs Mitchell. You may find the answers help you in the quest to find Alexander. They are both relevant to an address here in Inverness. First, what number follows fifteen? Second, on which Scottish island is the town Rothesay?

"Wait just a moment, I'll write the questions down for you."

CHAPTER 22

16 Bute Street

Within an hour, Mairi was standing outside a row of brown stone cottages built on the edge of a narrow road leading down to Fraser Park. The houses were typical terraced homes, one and a half storeys high with front doors opening onto the pavement. No. 16 was nondescript, with a dark green front door and a pair of stained net curtains fluttering softly through the ground floor window.

She rapped gently on the door, then stood back in anticipation. Soon, the muffled sound of steps approached, and through the frosted glass, she observed a shadowy figure grappling with the lock. Anticipating an elderly resident, she was taken aback when a woman in her early forties, cigarette in hand, peered out from the partially opened door.

"Aye?" she enquired.

Mairi explained that she was looking for someone who might have stayed in the house back in the thirties.

"He wouldn't have stayed long, perhaps a couple of nights but it was possible he had a baby with him."

The woman looked suspiciously at Mairi, wondering why anyone would want to look for someone after so long. Whatever the reason, she was sure it wasn't a happy one.

"That was before my time," she replied with a deep throated cough. "Sorry! Can't help you."

She was about to close the door when Mairi put her foot in the way, imploring her to listen. "Please! I urgently need to trace the young man. You are my only hope."

"You've a bloody nerve," she replied. "Barging into my house demanding information about someone who might have stayed here over twenty years ago. Go away! If you don't leave now, I'll call the police."

"Who is it?" came a gravelly voice from inside.

"A lady looking for someone who might have stayed here twenty years ago. Something to do with a baby."

"There weren't any babies here," the voice inside shouted. "She must have got the wrong number."

"I know but she won't take 'no' for an answer."

Mairi's heart skipped a beat. Keeping her foot jammed in the doorway, she edged further into the hallway. "Are you sure there was no-one staying here with a small baby? A lodger perhaps?"

"Quite sure," came the mystery voice. "And I should know 'cos I've lived here all my life."

By now Mairi was inside the house, squeezed between the indignant woman and the voice of the unknown man.

"Please!" she said. "You are my last hope to find my son.

"He was adopted in November 1933 by the young man I've been talking about and brought to this address. I have no idea how long he stayed here or where he went but your house is the next small clue to a mystery that is tearing me apart."

She lowered her eyes in shame. It was the first time she had spoken about Alexander to a complete stranger. After admitting she was an unmarried mother and a daughter of the Manse, she mentioned that her son, aged three months, had stayed briefly at 16 Bute Street.

"That's all the information I have. After this address the trail goes cold."

"Hang on a mo!" the voice said. "When I was young, we used to take in lodgers and I remember one nice young man who only stayed a few weeks. My parents took quite a shine to him. It was unusual for landlords to have much to do with their tenants but this person was different. He helped around the house and always paid the rent on time. I don't think he ever told us his name."

The woman standing in the hall tried to push Mairi out through the front door. She'd had enough of the stranger asking so many questions.

"Get out of my house!" she hissed. "Can't you see I'm not well."

"Please!" Mairi begged. "It's really important I find this person. A name or an address, anything will do. Please!"

The desperation in her voice softened the lady's initial hostility. Reluctantly she stepped aside to let Mairi pass.

"You'd better talk to my husband," she said, closing the door. "Five minutes, mind you! That's all you're getting."

The simple front room was sparsely furnished with a Bakelite wireless, a two-bar electric heater perched in front of a beige tiled fireplace and a couple of comfy brown armchairs. The lady's knitting lay where she had been sitting. Beside her chair sat an overweight man with a tartan rug covering his knees.

Mairi fixed her eyes on the man who remained seated when she entered the room.

He returned her look.

"Blown off at Dunkirk!" he remarked, pointing to his knees. There was no sign of bitterness in his voice, just weary resignation.

"Bloody awful disaster that was, but at least I made it home which was more than can be said for the other poor buggers!"

The man's wife winced as he swore his way through the account of his rescue at Dunkirk.

Mairi stood and listened, mortified by the way she had been so quick to judge his manners.

"We were left to fend for ourselves on the beach," he said, reliving the events of May 1940. "Not just a few of us but hundreds of thousands of young inexperienced soldiers, desperate to go home and forget they had ever put on a uniform.

"The fortunate secured a place on the rescue boats, the less fortunate faced being obliterated by the Stuka bombers scouring the beaches for anything that moved - tanks, boats, men, or vehicles. I can still hear those bloody Jericho Trumpets screeching across the skies as the planes dropped their bombs.

"God! What a disaster that was! One of those bloody bombs destroyed my legs. It landed close to where I was cowering with my arms wrapped over my head trying to shut out the bloody noise. The explosive ripped the flesh and bones clean off my legs. I felt nothing. Not a thing! I prayed to any God who would listen and asked to live.

"In a remarkable turn of events, despite my lack of faith, an unnamed young officer hoisted me over his shoulder and carried me onto a motor cruiser named 'Westerly'. I don't know if he was a medic but he was my senior in rank and mercifully pumped morphine into my veins, commanding me not to die.

"The captain tried to restart the engines but they had cut out, leaving us bobbing helplessly on the water like a sitting duck. To make matters worse, a fire had broken out in the engine room putting everyone's life in danger. All seemed hopeless until a small motor yacht from Ramsgate, the 'Sundowner', drew alongside our burning vessel and rescued everyone on board, cramming its cabin and decks with exhausted, frightened soldiers. How that little boat made it back to Ramsgate I'll never know but the skipper, who'd been Second Officer on the Titanic, was a genius. He and his son saved our lives."

"Andrew dear," his wife said, interrupting her husband as gently as she could. "The lady hasn't come to hear about Dunkirk. She wants to find someone who lodged here back in 1933."

The animated face that had lit up while reminiscing about the war suddenly looked despondent. His proud upright posture slumped back into the chair.

"Someone who lodged here before the war, you say?"

"Yes dear, someone who might have brought a baby here."

Mairi held her breath.

"The quiet young man I was telling you about, the one my parents liked, caused quite a stir one evening when he brought home a baby. He never said where he found the child or why he was keeping it, only that he needed to spend one night with the child before leaving. My father was furious and threatened to throw him out for breaking house rules but the man pleaded with him and promised to be gone by first light. He was true to his word."

Mairi had already over-stayed her welcome and taken up more than the five minutes she had been promised but she needed one further clue to continue her hunt for Alexander.

"Thank you for your time," she said, heading for the door. "Before I finally leave, can you think of a name or place that would help me in my search?"

"Enough!" the lady said, ushering Mairi into the hallway. "Andrew has told you all he knows. He's not a well man, you know." She stepped forward to open the front door when a voice called out from the living room. "Dora! He said he was taking the baby to Yorkshire to live with Dora."

CHAPTER 23

Mairi's sudden departure left Daisy free to spend her last few days exploring the island. Her senses were heightened by the sound of the sea and birds. She had never felt more alive.

From the moment Mairi left for Inverness, Tavish started pestering his father to take him to school by boat.

"Pleeeease!" he pleaded, jumping up and down with excitement. "Please Daddy, can we take the boat?"

He ran over to Daisy, beaming from ear to ear.

"You'll have to come with us," he laughed. "We can't leave you behind!"

"Hang on a moment," Johnny interrupted, fondly ruffling the child's hair. "First, we need to clear away the breakfast things and do the washing up, then we'll decide how you're getting to school. No promises, mind!"

Tavish's inclusion of Daisy as one of the family was an unscripted act of generosity, typical of his good nature. He liked Daisy and wasn't shy in admitting it. Inch by inch she was being drawn further into the magical world of Kilbackie, an honour that made her blush with private delight. She put her hands up to her hot red cheeks, hoping Johnny wouldn't notice, but he had already left the room.

"Help me, Daisy," Tavish said, racing round the table, grabbing the napkins as he went. His mother would have scolded him for running but he didn't care. She wasn't there to stop him. He could do what he liked.

Daisy stacked the breakfast things onto a tray and carried them into the kitchen where Johnny was filling the sink with hot soapy water.

"Shall I dry?" she said, picking up a tea towel.

"No, it's all right. There isn't much to do. Why don't you go and change into something more comfortable. You'll be cold in that lovely dress."

The compliment lifted Daisy's morale, confirming what she secretly knew – that her presence added vitality and fun to an otherwise drab house.

"You've decided to take the boat then!" she smiled.

"Yes! I don't think Tavish would ever forgive me if I didn't. He can be very persistent, you know."

The idea of joining Johnny and Tavish in a boat thrilled Daisy. What a memory to savour! Travelling to school by boat in the Scottish Highlands. It couldn't get more romantic! She hurried upstairs, determined to repay Johnny's compliment by looking her best. For someone in the middle years of life, she looked incredibly youthful. No wonder Tavish adored her.

She laid a few clothes on the bed trying to put together an outfit suitable for the journey. It wasn't easy. The cotton dress bought specially for Skye now seemed out of place as did her cardigan. They were not warm enough for a boat trip, even if the water was calm. In the end she chose a flattering pair of navy slacks and her favourite cream polo neck jumper, the one that made her skin glow. To complete the look, she accentuated her grey blue eyes with a touch of eyeliner and made a perfect cupid's bow.

She had never felt or looked better.

From the moment she walked into the kitchen she knew she had made an impression. Tavish stared at her with wide open eyes while Johnny, flustered and embarrassed, chose to divert his gaze.

"Daisy! Your eyes look different! They're all sparkly," Tavish said, holding his father's hand.

Johnny was clearly unnerved by the transformation in Daisy's appearance. He stood awkwardly by the sink, unsure what to do or say. In the end he turned his attention to Tavish, whose shirt had come untucked again.

"Get that shirt tucked in," he said. "There's no room on my boat for scruffy crew!"

Tavish grinned, shoving the end of his shirt into his trousers and standing to attention with a salute.

"Yes, Sir!"

"That's better," Johnny said, looking at his smartly dressed son. "You look more presentable."

Tavish wasn't interested in looking presentable. He wanted to show Daisy the boat.

"Can we go now, Daddy?" he asked, tugging at his father's hand.

The small boating party set off at a brisk pace with Tavish running ahead, reaching the moored vessel in double quick time. He put on his life jacket and waited impatiently for his father and Daisy to catch him up.

"You don't mind, do you?" Johnny asked hesitantly, hoping Daisy hadn't felt pressured into accepting Tavish's plan. She shook her head. Her shining eyes told him everything he wanted to hear.

"Are you ready?" he cried, grabbing the mooring rope and hauling the boat beside the slipway. "Let's go!"

Tavish sprung on board as sure-footed as a mountain goat, leaving Daisy cautiously waiting at the water's edge unsure what to do next. She had never been on a boat before. Johnny stretched out his callused hand to steady her as she stepped on board. The softness of her skin bewitched him, the power of her touch overloaded his senses. In an instant, he felt sensually alive. His lips tasted saltier, the air was cleaner, the sky brighter, the wind fresher. The rocking motion of the boat stirred him uncontrollably. Had a six-year-old boy not distracted him, he could so easily have lost all sense of propriety.

"Hurry up Dad! If we don't get a move on, I'll be late for school."

No further words were exchanged during the short crossing. Tavish cosied up to his father, leaving Daisy free to experience, for the first time, the allure of motoring through open waters.

The walk over the moor to school was dominated by Tavish's excited chatter. He trotted beside Daisy like a faithful terrier, teaching her the names of wayside flowers; dog violet, bitter-vetch, speedwell, eyebright and cat's-ear. Occasionally he held her hand for company or pulled her over to examine a small flower partially hidden in a grassy bank.

"What's that one?" he said, pointing to a bluey-mauve lipped flower. Daisy should have remembered but she was distracted by the close proximity of Johnny who had moved within touching distance. Her instinct was to clasp his hand and feel the warmth of his body run through her fingers but she resisted the urge, trying to concentrate on Tavish's guessing game even though she was hopeless at remembering the plant names.

"Come on, Daisy, think! I've already told you once."

"I give up," she admitted but before Tavish could tell her, Johnny cupped his hands and whispered the answer in her ear, lightly caressing her hair with his fingers. She quivered.

"That's cheating, Dad!" Tavish laughed, looking at the coy culprits. "Daisy should have remembered without you telling her."

The boy's enthusiasm for the boat trip captivated Daisy who began to relax for the first time since arriving on Skye. Surrounded by energetic, youthful curiosity, she reflected wistfully on Bill who had once been her rock but was now a disillusioned cynic, too lazy to be curious, too fat to walk. To her shame, she no longer found him attractive. His dull mind and indulged body repulsed her. When they had first met, Bill had been eager to improve his lot by working hard. He never took a day off sick and became a reliable, loyal member of the sales team, someone Mr. Thomas, the Managing Director, could rely on. Promotion seemed inevitable, yet it never happened. All Bill received for his faithful hard work was a curt note, telling him he had been turned down for the position of Head of Sales. No reason was ever given. He tried to explain his disappointment to Daisy who listened sympathetically as he ranted on about the injustice of the decision to appoint Fred Wilson instead of him. Fred Wilson! Someone who had only recently joined the company and was still finding his way. Arrogant and unbearably smug, he had few friends and plenty of enemies. News of Fred's promotion left Bill feeling unappreciated, robbed of a position he felt was rightly his. Eventually he gave up his dreams of a better life and plummeted into a depression that lay beyond the reach of his wife.

"Penny for your thoughts!" Johnny said as Daisy stood wondering if the Highlands could restore Bill back to health.

She doubted it.

"I'm sorry," she replied enigmatically. "I was miles away."

They continued their walk at a slower pace, with Daisy stopping from time to time to compose herself. A great sadness descended over her. The youthful face that moments before had sparkled with mischief had now turned pale. Tavish sensed the sudden change in mood and strode ahead, kicking up clouds of dust as he went.

"Pick up your feet!" Johnny shouted, "You'll ruin your new school shoes."

Things were not going the way Johnny had planned. He had been looking forward to the school run, taking Daisy out in the boat, spending time with her away from Mairi's recent erratic behaviour. The journey had started well with everyone in good spirits but, for some reason, Daisy grew more pensive as the walk progressed.

"I'm not kicking," Tavish shouted back rudely. "I'm shuffling."

"That's enough cheek from you!" Johnny said with sufficient authority to make the child listen. "Now walk properly."

Reluctantly Tavish did as he was told but with little grace.

Had Johnny glanced in Daisy's direction, he would have noticed a wry smile appear on her face as she witnessed Tavish's childish act of rebellion. It pierced her melancholy and lifted her flagging spirits. She called out to Tavish, taking him completely by surprise.

"Come back here! I want to teach you something," she said with an infectious laugh.

"Is it a flower?"

"No, it's a game."

"Then I'm not interested," came the gruff reply.

"All right, have it your own way," she said. "But it's your loss, not mine!"

The frosty silence between them didn't last long. Tavish needed company and he liked playing games, especially with Daisy. She made everything fun.

"What sort of game is it?" he asked with curiosity.

"I'll give you a clue. It's named after me."

Tavish gave her a bemused look and shrugged his shoulders, unable to think of a single game with 'Daisy' in its title apart from Daisy Chains, but that wasn't a game.

"This game is called 'Oopsie Daisy'!" she said, glancing over at Johnny.

"That's a silly name," Tavish giggled.

Johnny watched the two interact and began to relax as things appeared to be getting back to normal.

"Let's see if you like it," she said, holding him under one arm and instructing Johnny to hold him under the other.

The three of them marched up the path shouting, "One, Two, Three," then Daisy and Johnny swung the excited boy high into the air shouting "Oopsie Daisy!" The game was an instant success.

"More! More!" he cried, nestling up to Daisy. She and Johnny patiently swung the child above their shoulders until they came within sight of the school.

"That's all for now," Johnny explained. "It's time to get ready to line up. For goodness' sake, tuck your shirt in!"

A small gaggle of mothers had been watching in astonishment as Johnny and his remarkably elegant companion approached the playground.

"Well, Mr Mitchell, we don't often see you at these gates!" Janet Cameron remarked, giving a knowing wink at the other mothers standing by. "Are you going to introduce us?"

She looked pointedly at Daisy who refused to be intimidated. She had met many Janet Camerons in her time and knew how to look after herself. It was Johnny she wanted to protect. He stood holding Tavish's hand, frozen to the spot unsure how to react.

"Hello!" Daisy said with supreme confidence, holding out a hand for Janet to shake. "I'm Daisy, a friend of

Johnny and Mairi's from way back. I'm sorry, I didn't catch your name."

"That's because I didn't give it," came the surly reply but Daisy's unflappable manner had caught Janet off guard. She paused to work out her next move.

"It's Cameron," a voice called out from the evaporating crowd. "Her name is Janet Cameron."

Johnny turned to see a flushed but defiant Margaret MacLean step forward to apologise for the way he was being treated.

"What's up with Mairi?" Janet asked, determined to have the last word. "She's usually here with Tavish."

There was a short pause before she uttered her damning comment looking directly at Daisy.

"I expect she's left Skye now her replacement has arrived."

Johnny was horrified.

Daisy stood her ground, refusing to reply.

Janet was a known trouble maker but her acerbic comments were usually humorous, hardly ever vindictive. This time, however, she had gone too far. One by one, the mothers who had gathered to witness some sport, dispersed, embarrassed at the way she had insulted a visitor.

"Mairi has a few visits to make on the mainland so she asked me to look after Tavish while she was away."

"That's very convenient," Janet muttered under her breath.

Instead of commenting, Daisy maintained a stony silence, pretending she hadn't heard what Janet had said but Johnny was less confident, less composed. He remained rooted to the spot, decidedly uncomfortable by the way this total stranger had rudely attacked his wife and friend.

Before he could think of anything to say, the school bell rang, ending any further confrontations.

CHAPTER 24

The following day, Mairi returned to Kilbackie House with mixed feelings.

Her search for Alexander had been partially successful. She knew he had been born with Down's Syndrome and been adopted at twelve weeks by someone whose name she didn't know. He had taken Alexander from the orphanage to Bute Street before travelling down to Yorkshire to stay with someone called Dora.

She hung her coat on a peg and called out.

"Hello! I'm back!" Her cheery greeting was met with silence.

No-one was about.

She walked into an immaculately tidy kitchen that smelt of baking. The mood of the house had changed during her short time away. It felt brighter, warmer. Even the vase of daffodils on the well-scrubbed table had been artistically arranged with sprigs of pussy willow. A new drawing by Tavish took pride of place on the dresser. He had coloured in yellow a large sun which shone over two figures swinging a child high in the air. Written in his neat handwriting at the bottom of the page were the words *Oopsie Daisy*.

"Bother Daisy! I was so looking forward to coming home and now she's ruined it all."

Mairi picked up her coat and wandered outside to find Tavish.

The sun had finally broken through the mist that had clung to the hills for over a week. It was good to get outside and breathe in the clean air. She arched her back and loosened her shoulders to allow the peaceful surroundings to relax the buildup of tension.

It was good to be home.

Her thoughts were interrupted by the sound of laughter coming from the beach. It was a spontaneous, merry sound of people enjoying themselves, having fun. Cautiously she climbed a gentle slope to get a better view of the shore. To her horror, she saw Tavish standing on a large rock saluting Johnny and Daisy, who were sitting on a picnic rug, clapping enthusiastically. Mairi wanted to scream at Johnny to get his son down off the rocks, to remind him how dangerous they were but she held her tongue when she saw the delight on Tavish's face.

'I mustn't interfere,' she thought, determined to hold her tongue and supress the panic rising within her. Two days away from Kilbackie had given her time to reflect on why she was constantly over-reacting to normal, everyday events. Her short temper and tendency to judge those around her were changing her into someone she no longer liked.

The high-spirited banter between Tavish, Johnny and Daisy was so joyously infectious, she hadn't the heart to break it up. Even though the sight of Tavish perched high on a rock made her sick with worry, she restrained herself from interfering and walked, as calmly as she knew how, across the beach to greet the picnic party.

"Mummy!" Tavish cried, waving frantically. "Mummy! Look at me!"

Johnny anxiously watched his wife, expecting her to cause a scene but it never came. Instead, she gave him a nervous smile.

"Good to see you back," he said, getting up to kiss her tenderly on the cheek. "I've missed you."

Mairi looked at her husband with new eyes. She saw a good, honest man who had stood by her ever since they arrived on Skye. She affectionately returned the kiss and held his gaze.

"I've missed you too!" she whispered.

The emotional exchange of feelings wasn't lost on Daisy who detected a subtle change in Mairi's behaviour.

Johnny explained that Tavish was playing the part of a General inspecting his troops.

"We are a very small section of his vast army with specific orders to march in close formation. I'm warning you, he's a very fierce General so you had better do as you're told!"

Tavish stood straight-backed on the rock, proudly saluting.

Mairi, Johnny and Daisy saluted back.

"Eyes right!" he snapped. "Forward march!"

The small band of soldiers started marching.

"Mummy, keep in step," Tavish barked. "Left, right, left, right!"

Mairi looked down. The 'General' was correct. She was out of step. Shuffling her feet to match the others, she continued marching, only this time in unison with Johnny and Daisy.

"That's better!" Tavish cried, clearly delighted with the power he held over his parents and Daisy. "Keep going! Left, Right, Left, Right, Halt!"

The trio stopped.

"At ease!" A peaceful calm hung over the bay after the final order had been given. Quietly but still with surprising authority, Tavish informed them that they were all dismissed.

The picnic party returned to the rug, amused at the child's grasp of military language. Within seconds, he had scrambled confidently off the rocks and ran over to his mother.

"You're back!" he said breathlessly, flinging his arms around her. "I've got so much to tell you."

The happy, ruddy-cheeked child sat on the rug next to his parents, telling Mairi all about the boat trip to school, the game Daisy had taught him and how hopeless she was at remembering the names of flowers.

"She kept forgetting," he giggled. "I showed her a Bitter Vetch and she only remembered its name because Daddy cheated and whispered her the answer."

Mairi winced at the thought of Johnny and Daisy walking side by side on the hill track, whispering, being intimate.

To her surprise, she resisted the desire to react critically.

"I'm sure Daisy does her best to remember the names."

Daisy looked bashful and started packing away the picnic things, sensing a shift in the dynamics.

Tavish's ebullient mood was infectious. Mairi had never seen her son so happy, so energetic and relaxed. He was finally beginning to enjoy his life on Skye much to her relief. The slow walk back to the house was accompanied by squeals of delight as he was swung high into the air by his doting parents, leaving Daisy to trail behind with the picnic things.

Johnny had already offered to carry the basket and rug but Daisy had refused his help, sensing the family needed time together. She trudged a little distance behind Johnny who held onto Tavish's hand, gazing lovingly at his wife. It was clear he adored her. The close bond between the three Mitchells reminded Daisy that she was an outsider and had outstayed her welcome. The problem was she had no desire to go home and leave behind the rugged coastline and wild landscape she had grown to love.

The picnic party was halfway across the hall when the shrill sound of the telephone penetrated the silence. Mairi picked up the receiver.

"Rosvaig 914...Yes? … that'll be fine, no problem … thanks for letting us know … Of course! … When shall we expect you?... about ten thirty?... Perfect!"

The caller hung up, leaving Mairi holding the receiver in her cupped hand. She paused a moment to think before replacing it in its cradle.

"Who was it?" Johnny called from the kitchen. "Anyone for me?"

"It was Mr Buchanan. He's in the area and wants to visit the library and chat through a few things."

"Did he give a time?"

Mairi shook her head. "Not exactly. He said he would be over at about ten-thirty tomorrow morning."

The relaxed mood of the beach party didn't last long. Much to Mairi's relief, Daisy made herself scarce and Johnny disappeared into his make-shift office to write a list of questions he wanted to ask Mr Buchanan. Mairi was left alone with Tavish but it soon became clear he didn't want to be with her.

"Where's Daisy?" he asked, aimlessly kicking his chair.

Mairi felt her nerves bristle. "I don't know," she said, praying Tavish wouldn't make a scene.

"Can I go and find her?" he said, still kicking the chair.

"No! Let her have some time to herself. She's spent two days looking after you so I expect she needs a break."

"But Mummy!" he said indignantly. "I like playing with Daisy and I'm sure she likes playing with me. She says I'm a good boy and no trouble."

The kicking continued.

"Stop kicking that chair and sit properly!"

Tavish gave his mother a withering look as she placed a large box on the table. "This looks interesting," she said with faint enthusiasm. "Let's see if we can finish the puzzle before bedtime. I hear you're really good at finding the difficult pieces!"

Not even her cheerful words of praise could draw Tavish out of his bad mood. Mairi tipped all five hundred jigsaw pieces onto the table and started turning them over, suggesting Tavish picked out the ones with the straight edges.

"Let's get the four sides done first."

As the minutes ticked painfully by, it became clear Mairi's heart wasn't in the jigsaw and Tavish was in no mood to help.

He looked at the picture on the lid - a magnificent Monarch stag standing on a rocky crag against a backdrop of Scots pines and flowering heather. He knew exactly how the stag felt standing there on top of the world. He had experienced the same heroic pride when he stood on the rock in front of his father and Daisy.

"Come on, Tavish! Stop dreaming and help me finish this puzzle."

That was it! He had no wish to put together a five-hundred-piece jigsaw without Daisy.

In a gesture of defiance, he swept everything on the floor and left the room, deaf to his mother's cries.

CHAPTER 25

As expected, Mr Buchanan arrived punctually at ten-thirty. He breezed into the hall with an enthusiastic spring in his step.

"It's good to see you, Johnny," he said, shaking him warmly by the hand. "I've just passed Mairi on the causeway. I'm sorry she won't be joining us."

Johnny looked puzzled, unaware Mairi had left.

For a moment Mr Buchanan thought he had said something wrong but Johnny quickly explained that she had gone to visit a cousin near Achnasheen.

"Something to do with an uncle or aunt, I can't remember which," he lied awkwardly.

Mr Buchanan appeared to believe the lie but Mairi's sudden disappearance left a bitter taste in Johnny's mouth. Whatever her reasons for leaving, he vowed he would never cover for her again, especially not with someone as honourable as Mr. Buchanan.

Mairi's abrupt departure had been brought about by the shame of admitting she had been wrong to dismiss Rhona without first discussing the matter with the Trustees. It had all been a terrible mistake, an impetuous miscalculation based on fear but the deed had been done and there was no going back. The last thing she needed was to be told off in front of Johnny or, worse still, Daisy. Like all cowards, she took the easy way out and fled before

Mr Buchanan had a chance to chastise her. Bemused by Mairi's unpredictable behaviour, Johnny stood in front of the house to welcome their visitor alone.

Mairi didn't have an uncle who lived in Achnasheen but she did have a friend who lived in a whitewashed cottage at the end of a short drive near the school on the north side of the mainland. Margaret's front garden, if it could be called a garden, was a barren plot of land that had unsuccessfully been planted up with shrubs and trees. The salty winds had scorched the shrubs, deer had stripped the bark off the fruit trees and slugs had eaten most of the bulbs. Eventually Margaret gave up the idea of a garden, concentrating instead on growing vegetables. The vegetable plot regularly produced a healthy crop of potatoes, carrots, onions and leeks which she made into stews and soups. Despite her success growing vegetables, her true pride and joy was the sturdy washing line that stretched between two hefty poles dug deep into the ground. It was strong enough to carry all her washing despite the punishing winds that blew around the croft.

Mairi attempted to open the door but it was locked. Concerned at being shut out, she called out Margaret's name, hoping for a response.

"Margaret, open up. It's me! I need to speak to you!"

Cautious footsteps approached the door, followed by the sound of a key turning in the lock.

"What are you doing here?" came a voice mixed with annoyance and anger.

"Please, Margaret, let me in. I promise I won't keep you!"

Margaret threw caution to the wind and let her friend in, doubting she would cause much trouble. She was secretly intrigued to know why Mairi had made the effort to show her face.

Mairi appeared highly anxious, her darting eyes were unable to focus, her hands were shaking. She repeatedly thanked Margaret for allowing her to enter her house.

Margaret had never seen her in such a state.

"Stop thanking me. Just say what you have to say and go. I don't have much time to spare."

The two ladies, who had once been so close, sat opposite each other at the kitchen table. Margaret's golden hair was swept back off her round freckled face. Her pronounced cheekbones accentuated the gentleness of her hazel eyes. She had always been the prettier of the two and had aged well, whereas endless stress had turned Mairi's lank hair, grey. Her once fresh flawless face was now lined beyond repair.

"Well?" Margaret asked once they had sat down at the table. "What do you want?"

Mairi nervously picked flecks of wool off her sleeve, unsure where to begin, wishing she had never come. In her confusion she forgot what she wanted to say. Her dry cracked lips tasted faintly of blood.

Margaret waited for her old friend to say something but she remained speechless. The unnatural silence was occasionally interrupted by the muffled sound of footsteps pacing up and down an upstairs bedroom.

'Poor Rhona!' Mairi thought, remembering the seething anger she had felt when her father had unjustly banned her from reading stories. This calculated vengeful act had deprived her of literature and the chance to experience life beyond the confines of the Manse. History was repeating itself but this time she was the oppressor.

"I'm sorry, Margaret. I'm nothing but a nuisance!" she mumbled. "I'll leave you in peace and return another time."

Margaret looked puzzled, then angry.

"Do you mean to say you've come all this way for nothing? The least you can do is stay for a cup of tea and while the kettle's boiling perhaps you'll remember why you came."

Her generous offer was interrupted by the sudden sound of scuffling and yelps.

"Hang on a minute," she said, opening the door to a tsunami of playful puppies who tumbled into the kitchen, causing absolute chaos.

"Are these Bonnie's?!" Mairi exclaimed. "I didn't know she had had a litter. They're gorgeous! How old are they?"

"Seven weeks," Margaret replied, placing a cup of tea next to Mairi. "Do you take sugar? It's been such a long time since you've sat at this table, I've forgotten."

Mairi shook her head.

"May I?" she asked, bending down to pick up the puppy with a white eye patch who had been nibbling her ankles.

"Of course! Go ahead. They're normally kept in the byre with their mother but since Rhona's had so much time on her hands, we've brought them all inside. She adores them and spends hours playing with them."

If there had been a barbed edge to Margaret's comment, Mairi had missed it.

"I'll get straight to the point," she said, stroking the puppy that lay obligingly still in her arms. "Do you know anyone called Dora?"

"Dora? No, I don't think so. Why?"

Mairi couldn't think of a suitable answer and mumbled something about Donny mentioning a distant MacPhee relative called Dora.

"I'm not a fool," Margaret said, "Your brother hates our family. He would never inquire about a random name connected with us. How about telling me what's really going on?"

Mairi suddenly felt trapped. The last thing she wanted was to share her story. It was still too raw. Her visit to Margaret had been a mistake. Reluctantly she put the puppy down on the floor and left the house, leaving her tea untouched.

CHAPTER 26

Johnny announced he would be spending the day in a meeting with Mr Buchanan and wasn't to be disturbed. He looked forward to these meetings because the Trustee had the rare knack of explaining complex issues using a language he understood. At first Johnny was too shy to ask questions or admit he didn't understand some of the things they discussed but gradually he gained confidence and found himself contributing to the meetings, questioning items on the agenda. Always courteous, Mr Buchanan never mocked or belittled him. He treated Johnny as an equal in all matters concerning the Kilbackie Estate.

While Johnny looked forward to spending the day with Mr Buchanan poring over Estate maps and balance sheets, Daisy was left alone with Tavish for the second time that week. He was no trouble. His enquiring mind and even temperament made him good company but she only had a couple of days left before returning home. One of her goals was to explore the largest of the beguiling islands that lay a short distance off the Kilbackie coast.

Mairi could come and go as she pleased. Daisy didn't care but she was not prepared to put her plans on hold to babysit Tavish. If Johnny and Mairi were too busy to look after their son, it was up to them to find someone local to help.

"Come on, Tavish," she said, taking the boy's hand. "Let's see if Daddy is in his office."

She led him down the corridor to the study and knocked twice on the door.

"Come in!" came a distracted voice

Johnny and Mr Buchanan were standing over a large table studying various documents and ledgers. There was paper everywhere.

"Daisy!" he exclaimed, clearly annoyed at being interrupted. "What are you doing here? Is everything all right?"

He looked with concern at his withdrawn son standing in front of him.

"Are you ill?"

The boy shook his head.

"Everything's fine and Tavish is well," Daisy said, giving the child a wink of encouragement.

"So, what's the problem?"

"The problem, sir," she said, using 'sir' for the first time, "is that Tavish has no-one to look after him."

Johnny looked confused. "Why can't he stay with his mother?"

"Because she isn't here. She's disappeared and I have no idea when she will be back."

Then Johnny remembered Mr Buchanan mentioning he had passed Mairi on his way in.

"Could you look after Tavish 'til she returns?" Johnny pleaded.

"No, Sir! I'm sorry, I can't."

Mr Buchanan watched the conversation between Johnny and Daisy with quiet amusement. He had always thought

Mairi's decision to dismiss Rhona had been hot-headed and foolish. Now the chickens were coming home to roost.

"Why not?" Johnny replied, trying to hide his exasperation.

"Because I have already made plans to visit Eilean Torrach today."

"Couldn't you put off the visit 'til tomorrow to help us out?"

"No, sir!" she replied defiantly. "And for the record, ever since I arrived on Kilbackie, I've been expected to look after Tavish, put up with Mairi's moods and oversee the house during her sudden absences. You have been more than generous, allowing me to stay at short notice. Please don't think I take your hospitality for granted, I don't, but I gave up being in service ten years ago and I have no wish to return."

Daisy let go of Tavish's hand and urged him forward. The pitiful look on his face showed a child too young to understand why everyone was cross and too sensitive to ignore the tension.

"Are you sure you wouldn't prefer to be with Daisy?" Johnny asked.

Tavish hung his head dejectedly. He didn't know how to reply.

"I'm afraid you don't have a choice!" Daisy replied firmly. "He is staying with you until Mairi returns."

There was a stunned silence.

"What shall I do with him all day?" Johnny exclaimed,

embarrassed at being shown up once again in front of Mr Buchanan.

"I'm afraid that's your problem, sir. He's your son! Perhaps you could find him something to do while you work in the office and take him with you when you go outside?"

A broad smile spread across Mr Buchanan's disfigured face. Although his mouth and cheeks barely moved, his eyes twinkled with delight as Daisy drove home her point.

She had clearly won the argument. The day was hers.

In order to reach the island, she needed Willie to take her over in *Arctic Tern* but first she had to find him. As predicted, he was in the barn working on the grey Ferguson.

"Good morning, Willie! Are you busy?" she asked, raising her voice to be heard above the running engine.

"May be!" he replied, rummaging in an old tool box for a spanner. "Pass me that bucket. The galvanized one next to the creel over there."

A 'please' would be nice,' Daisy thought but said nothing, seeing she was about to ask a favour.

It was obviously a bad moment.

"Don't come too close!" Willie warned, switching off the engine. "The oil could be hot and I don't want you to get your clothes dirty."

He placed the bucket under the tractor, slipped the spanner round the sump plug and tugged hard. At first it refused to move but gradually the nut loosened enough to be taken off, releasing a torrent of black sticky oil into the bucket.

He patted the bonnet, assuring the tractor that the change of oil would make her run more smoothly.

"Did you want something?" he asked, wiping his hands on an old rag.

Daisy hesitated aware she had chosen a bad time.

"It doesn't matter. I'll come back later when you're not so busy."

"I've got plenty of time," he replied. "I'm just checking the engine oil because the log book says the tractor hasn't been serviced for two years. It's a good thing I checked as the oil and filters were filthy."

The rusty bucket standing under the engine didn't look as if it would be able to hold oil for much longer. It had corroded on all sides.

"What happens to that oil?" she asked, pointing to the bucket.

"Ah! You see that barrel over there. The one full of fence posts. That's where we pour the waste oil."

"Why?" Daisy asked, aware she was asking a lot of questions.

"To extend the life of fencing posts. If the wooden ends that go into the ground are soaked in oil, they take longer to rot."

Daisy enjoyed Willie's company. Although he could be gruff and at times taciturn, he was extremely practical and took pleasure answering questions about cattle, the waters around Kilbackie and the crofting way of life.

"I'm leaving in a couple of days," Daisy explained, "but before I go, I wanted to visit Eilean Torrach. Is there any chance you could take me there this morning? I've already cleared it with Johnny."

Willie nodded emphatically.

"It would be good to get Arctic Tern back in the water."

Eilean Torrach was the largest of the three uninhabited islands lying at the mouth of Loch Rosvaig. No-one had lived there permanently since the kelp boom over a hundred years ago, when seaweed was burned to create alkali which was needed in soap and glass making.

Harvesting kelp had been a family affair with every member fully engaged in the manufacturing process. The men collected the seaweed, the children hauled it onto the rocks to dry, the women managed the fires that burned day and night from June to August. It was back-breaking, demanding work. The thick smoke badly affected their eyes and, in some cases, led to blindness.

The industrial process had involved placing the kelp on a grid over a fire and tirelessly turning it with long iron poles for up to eight hours each day.

Putrid oil would slowly drip through the grid onto the stones below. Eventually the oil hardened into a solid mass called ash which was then broken into lumps and transported south.

During the Napoleonic Wars, an import ban on ash had forced British manufacturers to turn to the West Coast of Scotland for their supply.

Prices rocketed.

At the height of kelp mania, Eilean Torrach had been home to eight families, all working in the kelp industry.

At the end of the Napoleonic War, the government lifted import duties on ash. Prices dropped. The Highland kelp industry collapsed and remote coastal communities like Eilean Torrach became unsustainable.

Its inhabitants left, never to return.

News of John Nicolson's move to the island was received with a mixture of admiration and derision. Those in favour wished him well as he crossed the water to try his hand at subsistence living. Those against, never forgave him for allegedly murdering his brother-in-law, Angus. They believed he got off too lightly when Sir Hugh Hollister secured his release from prison

Arctic Tern rounded the southern tip of the island to the deafening sound of nesting gannets, guillemots and cormorants, all jostling for position on the high narrow ledges. The imposing cliffs gradually sloped down to sea level, forming a natural sandy cove known as Torrach Bay.

John Nicolson sat among tufts of marram grass in the sandy dunes, watching *Arctic Tern* chug into the shallow waters of the bay where she weighed anchor, rocking gently from side to side in the glare of the sun.

Willie switched off the engine, satisfied that the new oil had made the boat move more smoothly through the waves.

"Well," he said with a hint of satisfaction. "Here we are, Torrach Bay."

The glistening sand reminded Daisy of the holiday brochures she enjoyed thumbing through over a cup of coffee.

"It's breathtaking," she said, rolling up her trouser legs to reveal skin as pale as the island's sand. Willie took her hand to help her step over the side of the boat into the clear turquoise waters of the receding tide. It was freezing.

"Five-thirty," he said firmly. "Five-thirty here on the beach and don't be late."

"I'll be here," Daisy said, picking up her shoes and wading onto a beach that stretched as far as the eye could see.

It was paradise.

Under the harsh light of the midday sun, waders scurried gracefully along the shoreline, scanning the shallow waters for molluscs and crustaceans. Step by delicate step, they plunged their slender bills into the wet sand, probing for food, their muted tones blending with the colours of the shoreline. The rhythmic repetition of their feeding mirrored the timeless movement of the waves that eventually erased the tiny footprints left behind in the wet sand.

Daisy ran her hands through the soft warm grains, letting them slip through her fingers.

Her peace was shattered by a sudden unexpected flutter of wings as the waders took off in a single cloud of feathers, flying in close formation over the water's edge, constantly on the lookout for somewhere peaceful to re-settle and continue feeding.

She leapt to her feet and chased the wild birds with her arms outstretched, the way a child might react to pigeons in the park.

Looking up, she saw the silhouette of a tall, lean man with a leisurely gait walking across the sand towards her. It had to be John Nicolson, Katherine's older brother. They shared the same almond-shaped eyes, thick hair and engaging smile. The likeness was incredible. It was as if Katherine had come back into Daisy's life and was walking beside her.

For a brief moment, she wished she had worn her floaty floral dress instead of the dull navy-blue pair of slacks that looked out of place on the sun-baked beach.

CHAPTER 27

"I enjoyed your little performance," John said with a smile.

Daisy hung her face with embarrassment at the thought of someone watching her brief moment of madness.

"You didn't!" she cried in disbelief. "You shouldn't have been watching."

"Why not!" he exclaimed. "You landed on my island without being invited, so it was my duty to keep an eye on you."

He fixed his gaze on Daisy's horrified face.

"Don't worry!" he said, cheerfully. "You passed the test, so welcome to Eilean Torrach."

She looked puzzled.

"What test?"

"The 'you made me smile' test! At first, when you set foot on the island, I thought you were a trick of the light, a mirage on the sand but then I discovered you were a Ceasg."

"A what?" Daisy asked, unsure what he was talking about.

"A Ceasg is one of the wonders of the sea world with the upper body of a beautiful woman and the tail of a salmon. She can change into a human at any time and, if captured, can grant three wishes."

"That's nonsense," Daisy said rather abruptly, wishing John Nicolson would leave her alone. Her stay on Skye was nearly over. Time was precious. Soon, much to her dismay, she would be exchanging these beautiful surroundings for the noise and bustle of urban life.

"I don't believe such a creature exists and even if it does, I'm far too old to be mistaken for one!" she retorted. "Now, if you'll excuse me, I'd like to be left alone to enjoy the peace around me."

John seemed deaf to her request.

"Now I've captured you, you have to grant me three wishes."

Daisy found his manner irritating. The fairy tale about beautiful women with salmon tails granting three wishes was all nonsense.

"I don't know how to say this kindly," she said, "but go away and leave me alone. I've come to this lovely island to enjoy the wildlife not waste my time talking about mythical creatures that don't exist."

"So, you don't want to hear my wishes?" he said with exasperating cheerfulness.

She shook her head and started walking.

John didn't give up. He trotted beside her like a faithful dog, oblivious to her wish to be alone.

"Here they are," he said. "My three wishes.

"First, I wish we could get married here and now. Second, I wish you were kinder to me. Third, I wish you would stay with me forever."

Daisy was speechless.

'The arrogance of the man!' she thought. 'How dare he be so familiar.'

She quickened her step to distance herself from him but he remained cheerfully by her side.

Things were not going to plan.

Every morning, Daisy stood by her bedroom window and gazed wistfully at Eilean Torrach, whose moods were as fickle as the Hebridean weather. The small island would sulk in the mist, dazzle in the midday sun, cower in the pouring rain, groan in the wind and blush at sunset. Daisy felt an affinity with the craggy island whose inhabitants had long since left or died. Ancient lazy beds that once fed the whole community lay forsaken – an abandoned memorial to a past way of life.

"Come and see my home," John said proudly. "Then I promise I'll leave you in peace."

He led her to the cottage he had built by hand with stones salvaged from the homes that lay in ruins after the collapse of the kelp boom. Picking up two rickety chairs, he went outside and placed them against the cottage wall.

"Sit down a moment. I know you want to explore but before you go, tell me why you are really here, apart from wanting to marry me! I presume you haven't come all this way just to wave your hands at waders!"

Daisy tilted her head back to absorb the sun's warm rays. The tension of the past few days began to ease.

"What a place!" she replied drowsily. "It's so calm and quiet."

"You should be here when the wind howls and the rain lashes," John laughed. "You wouldn't call it calm then."

Daisy looked at her watch. It was already midday and

she still hadn't learned anything about Mairi's past or explored the island. She needed to get a move on before it was too late.

"Would you mind if I asked you some questions about Mairi?" she asked, hoping to get the ball rolling. "I know she's your aunt but she's also my dear friend who happens to be in trouble. I'm desperate to find some answers before I leave and you are my last chance."

"I'm not very good at understanding people's emotions," John replied. "But I'll do my best."

"Thank you! You've no idea how helpful that could be. Don't worry! The last thing I want is to cause offence or ask any inappropriate questions. It's just a few enquiries.

"I don't know when you last saw Mairi, but she isn't happy at the moment and I'm trying to find out what's wrong. Can you think of any reason why she might be so miserable?"

John shook his head. He hadn't seen his aunt for years.

"If you can't help, is it worth me talking to her brother, Donny?"

The mention of Donny's name had a profound effect on John who turned deathly white. Not even the warmth of the sun could bring the colour back to his cheeks.

"I'm sorry," Daisy said, aware she might have gone too far. Perhaps she should drop the subject and think of something else to say. Clearly there was little love lost between John and his father.

"I'm fine," John said. "Honestly, I am. It's just that your arrival has come as rather a shock!"

He continued to fidget on his chair staring nervously out to sea. The infectious laughter that had made him so irresistibly attractive and annoying on the beach had disappeared. He now wore the same haunted, tormented look as his sister Katherine when she was struggling to cope. Watching the pain etched on John's face, Daisy wished she had been a better friend to Katherine in the months leading up to Tavish's adoption. The agony she went through would haunt Daisy for ever.

Daisy closed her eyes, aware that John was sitting within touching distance of her. The proximity of his presence released an unexpected surge of pent-up desire. She shivered in the heat of the moment.

John never noticed her flushed cheeks or, thankfully, heard the rapid beating of her heart. He was too wrapped up in his own thoughts.

After a long pause he finally spoke.

"I'd like to talk about Mairi and my father but I don't know where to start."

Daisy patted him lightly on the knee, more as an act of encouragement than affection although the touch and the closeness of his body made her uneasy.

"Why not start at the beginning?"

The pause in their conversation was filled with the soaring notes of a rising skylark singing its cadenza. It wasn't until the bird had fluttered back into the grass that John began to open up.

"My father isn't a very nice person," he whispered, "and yet he is adored by many. I don't know if you've met him but you can't mistake his distinct white hair, artificial leg and a tendency to walk everywhere with a large black bible tucked under his arm. To his credit, he takes the Book very seriously, studying it daily and learning large chunks by heart. He believes it is the inerrant word of God and can never be doubted or questioned. He quotes it to warn unbelievers of hell, to bless the faithful, to frighten doubters and to forgive the penitents. Scripture legitimises all his judgements. It gives him an authority he doesn't deserve. I'm afraid a lot of what he says and does is unworthy of the faith.

"At home he threatened me, Kenny and Katherine with words and looks but he never laid a finger on us, not after an incident that took place when I was three. Apparently, I had insisted on playing in the freshly-dug potato beds with the little spade I had made out of wood. My father didn't want me to get dirty so he ordered me back to the house. I refused to obey him. In his anger he grabbed me by the scruff of the neck, unbuckled his belt and gave me a thrashing. My mother and Angus, who happened to be visiting at the time, thought he had gone too far and killed me. My poor terrified mother gave my father an ultimatum - if ever he touched one of his children again, she would leave him for good, taking us with her. My father reluctantly agreed to her terms but he never forgave Angus for the look of contempt on his face when witnessing the beating.

"Kenny eventually emigrated to Canada and Katherine

accepted Angus' marriage proposal and moved to Shottenden, leaving me to cope alone."

"What was the relationship like between your father and Mairi?" Daisy asked out of curiosity.

"It's difficult to say. I think they were fond of each other as children. My father certainly did his best to protect his sisters, Mairi, Effie and Ishbel. Apart from a tough childhood I can't think of any reason why she should be unhappy. She has everything going for her; a loving husband, a son and a beautiful home."

His voice betrayed the merest hint of resentment as he described Mairi's perfect life.

"Wait a moment!" he said. "There was an occasion, about twenty years ago, when Mairi left Skye for Inverness. I'm not sure why she left but the move didn't work out. After a few months she returned home a much sadder person. No-one discovered what had happened, she never spoke about it but it had obviously been a rough time."

'Inverness', Daisy thought. 'Everything seems to point to Inverness.'

"When did Mairi leave for Inverness?"

"1933."

"One last question," Daisy said but John shook his head.

"No more questions. If Willie is meeting you on the beach at five-thirty we don't have much time and I want to show you my island before you leave. Are you coming?"

He looked down at her bare feet.

"You may need to put your shoes on if we are going to explore."

Daisy still had questions to ask. Time was running out.

She laced up her plimsolls and followed John over the dunes to the sandy beach that stretched the full length of the island.

"I'll leave you here if you want to be alone," he said.

Daisy shook her head, realising how much she enjoyed his company.

At the summit of Cnoc Breac, the island's highest peak, they had a spectacular view of Rosvaig and Kilbackie and further beyond to the Outer Isles. Far below, on the opposite side of the bay, loomed Kilbackie House - the formidable stone fortress symbolising Urquhart power.

"It looks tiny," Daisy exclaimed. "So much power in a building the size of a dot on the landscape." In the short time left, John guided her to one of his favourite places on the island - a magical secluded cove nestling at the base of a craggy cliff.

"Unfortunately, we can only look at it today," he said with regret. "It would take a couple of hours to do it justice as the path down is steep and the return climb is hard work. Definitely a place to visit the next time you are here."

As they continued walking, John surreptitiously took hold of her hand, an act so gentle and natural, it never occurred to her to snatch it back. She found the gesture reassuringly comforting. Strolling hand in hand, he told her about the island's recent history, pointing out a row of ruined cottages that once formed the main street of a thriving community. Not far from the houses, near the shore, stood the abandoned kelp pits, monuments to a bygone age.

John's presence helped Daisy unwind and as she relaxed, he found himself drawn to her fragrant femininity and enquiring mind. She possessed an inexplicable quality that set her apart from any woman he had ever encountered. She seemed to draw conversation out of him, encourage him to open up and reveal his innermost thoughts. He had never met anyone like her.

They sat on top of the dunes holding hands aware of an awakening energy flowing between them. The thought of breaking the spell and parting company was too painful to bear. With the short time left, John shared his plans for Eilean Torrach, the island Sir Hugh had bought for him as compensation for being falsely accused of Angus' death. Under his stewardship, John wanted to reintroduce a herd of cattle, set up a system of crop rotation and experiment with low-intensity grazing, all of which he hoped would enable him to scrape together a meagre living. His vision was to manage the land and live a simple life.

From their viewing point among the Marram grass, they watched *Arctic Tern* chug into view.

"Come on!" he said. "It's time you were going."

Daisy sighed. Her short stay on the island had been an experience she would never forget. The thought of returning to Kilbackie House suddenly filled her with dread. There was bound to be a huge argument between Mairi and Johnny once Mairi returned from wherever she had been. Johnny would accuse her of abandoning Tavish and dismissing Rhona without thinking about their son's welfare. She would retaliate by admitting she had made another wrong decision and wasn't fit to be a mother.

"I'll just check I haven't left anything behind?" Daisy said, climbing over the dune to the cottage. The thought of leaving John, his dreams and the island weighed heavily on her mind.

She deliberately hid her handbag under the table and left.

CHAPTER 28

Mairi drove past clusters of crofts inhabited by families she had known all her life, yet since arriving back on Kilbackie she realised she had never really belonged.

Her life had been shaped by her father's obsession with splitting his parish into two camps – the saved and the unsaved. In his unforgiving world, there was no middle ground. His children were programmed to be suspicious and mistrustful of those in the condemned camp and within this confusing, angry world, 'saved' friends could be reclassified as 'unsaved' on a whim, as was the case with Margaret.

Looking in the mirror, Mairi saw the reflection of her father, the unloving judge who never hesitated to condemn those who challenged his authority. She thought of those she had recently condemned; Johnny, Tavish, Daisy and Rhona and felt deeply ashamed. Her greatest regret was losing Margaret's friendship. The loss marked a turning point in her life. She should never have reacted the way she did to Rhona. It had been a huge mistake. One she bitterly regretted and was determined to put right. All she needed was courage.

She changed down a gear as the car approached the causeway, then accelerated over the uneven track to get home as quickly as possible. Pride and fear had been the driving forces behind her decision to dismiss Rhona. Now she had to find a way to redeem herself.

For the second time in a week, she stepped into an empty kitchen and was faced with a draining board stacked high with dirty crockery and a floor that needed sweeping.

Mairi made herself a hot drink and thought about Dora, the mysterious lady who had played a part in Alexander's adoption. She believed Margaret when she said she didn't know anyone of that name but, without Dora, there was no hope of finding her son. The two were inextricably linked.

Lost in thought, Mairi never heard Johnny return.

"You're back!" he said sarcastically. "Where did you rush off to in such a hurry this morning?"

His question was accusing but Mairi was in no mood for a fight. At first, she ignored him and carried on sipping her tea but then she thought of her father and put down the cup.

"I went to see Margaret to put things right and before you have a go at me, I went because she's my greatest friend and I can't bear the bad feelings between us. If I could turn the clock back, I would never have been so petulant dismissing Rhona the way I did. It was unpardonable."

"Couldn't you have discussed the visit with me before rushing off?"

"No," came the short reply.

"Look, Mairi, I'm trying very hard to be reasonable but when you disappeared this morning, who did you think was going to look after Tavish? You knew Mr Buchanan was coming to see me and Daisy had already made plans to visit Eilean Torrach."

"Daisy never told me she had made plans for today," Mairi said trying to defend her actions.

Johnny tried hard to remain calm but his wife's tetchiness was testing him to the limit.

"Since when has she had to ask your permission to make plans?" he asked exasperatedly. She's a guest. It's your job to run the house and look after Tavish and at the moment, you appear to be failing on both counts."

Mairi stared at her husband in a state of shock. He had never spoken with such brutal honesty before and it hurt.

He was making a deliberate attempt to shame her by eyeing the stack of washing up piled high on the draining board.

"Listen to me! I have no idea what's going on in your mind at the moment but what you seem to forget is Tavish is our son and it's our duty to care for him. You knew I had a meeting planned with Mr Buchanan, you even took the phone message, so why choose this morning to set off without telling anyone?"

If Mairi had decided the time was right to tell Johnny everything, the moment had passed.

Tavish rushed into the kitchen, oblivious to the frosty atmosphere. He sounded excited. "Mummy! I've been on the farm with Daddy and Mr Buchanan. It was the best day ever! Did you know that there is a little blue flower called Selfheal and …?"

"Not now, Tavish," she interrupted. "Tell me all about your day when I'm feeling less tired. All right?"

Hurt by his mother's rejection, the small boy stomped angrily over to Jess who lay curled in front of the range.

He flung his scrawny arms round the collie's neck to draw comfort from her soft coat, oblivious to the earthy smell of fox. His parents soon forgot Tavish was in the room and continued discussing his welfare and the consequences of Rhona's dismissal. Tavish felt uncomfortable hearing his name mentioned over and over again, of being the cause of tension between his warring parents. He tried covering his ears to shut out the words bouncing between his mother and father but it didn't work.

His rescue came when Daisy unexpectedly entered the room, radiating happiness. One look at her glowing face persuaded Mairi and Johnny to draw a line under their differences.

"Daisy!" Tavish cried, running into her outstretched arms. "You've come!"

She lifted him high into the air and hugged him lovingly, ignoring the pungent smell that clung to his clothes.

"I've had the best day ever!" he said, wriggling to get down.

"So have I," she replied with mysterious joy. "Tell me what you've been up to."

He beamed with delight and led her by the hand through the hall to the front steps where they could sit together and watch the light fade on a perfect day.

"Daisy," he said, using a serious voice. "Why is Mummy always cross with me?"

"Oh, Tavish!" she sighed. "I don't know. Sometimes grown-ups get sad and don't like talking about it but you can always talk to me. How about telling me all about your day with Daddy and Mr Buchanan. What did you learn?"

The little face lit up as he told her about the wildflowers he had seen, mentioning in particular, Selfheal with its healing properties on wounds and bruises.

"Isn't that amazing?" he added, his eyes wide open in wonder.

Daisy had to agree.

"What else did Mr Buchanan teach you?"

"There's a tiny bright yellow flower with four petals called Tormentil. It was used to cure tummy upsets and mouth ulcers.

"What are ulcers, Daisy?"

"They are sore white spots that often grow inside your mouth or on your lip."

"Ah!" he replied thoughtfully, pleased that her answer made sense. "Anyway, Tormentil roots can also be used to make Tormentil Red, a dye that stains leather and makes red ink."

Daisy couldn't help laughing. "Oh, Tavish! You really have learned a lot today. Did Mr Buchanan teach you all these things?"

He nodded with a broad smile that lit up his contented face.

"Stay where you are and don't move," he said suddenly. "I'll see if I can find the last flower to show you. Promise you won't move?"

"I promise," she said, amused at his insatiable enthusiasm for wildflowers.

He crossed the drive and searched along a grassy bank for a tiny star-shaped white flower. Eventually he found one and ran back to Daisy who hadn't moved.

"Count the petals," he said breathlessly passing her the flower. She did as she was told.

"One, two, three … eight, nine, ten."

"Ten" she said with premature confidence.

The child's energetic thirst for knowledge was infectious. He clapped his hands with delight.

"Wrong!" he replied. "Count again."

Daisy re-examined the miniature star head and noticed that the petal tips were joined at the base in pairs. She re-counted.

"You little beast!" she laughed, nudging his ribs. "You tricked me! I thought there were ten but there are only five petals!"

Tavish couldn't hide his excitement.

"I know!" he said jumping up and down. "It was a trick question and you fell for it!

"Do you know what the flower is called?"

Daisy shook her head.

"It's called Lesser Stitchwort because when you run very hard and get a sharp pain in your side, it's called a stitch. This little plant is supposed to make the pain go away."

Daisy sat spellbound by Tavish's knowledge of wildflowers. He was like a piece of blotting paper absorbing everything he was told and memorising it. For a six- year- old he was very good company.

"Well, I'm blowed!" she said, putting her arm round his shoulder. "That's the best lesson I've had in a long time. You're a brilliant teacher, Tavish. Thank you."

Instead of being pleased with the compliment, the small child looked worried, his eyes fixed firmly on the causeway leading to the world he had left behind.

"Why do people I love keep leaving me?" he asked, taking Daisy by surprise. The melancholic observation came out of the blue. It was such a sudden change of mood. One minute he was enthusiastic, full of energy, the next, downcast and sad.

"Come here!" she said drawing the boy closer. "Why do you think people you love keep leaving you?"

"I don't know," he said with a forlorn sigh. "I vaguely remember my first Mummy but she left me, Rhona left me, the Mummy I have now keeps leaving me, Daddy is too busy for me and you are soon going to leave me. I'm always on my own. Jess is my only friend."

The poor boy looked totally bewildered, forced to bear the weight of other people's guilt and suffer their pain through no fault of his own. One day he would have to learn the truth about his past but until then Daisy wished Mairi would be kinder and more loving to her son instead of pushing him away.

"Look at me," she said, her eyes filling with tears. "Sometimes grown-ups have a lot to think about. They get worried, even sad. Moving up to Skye has been a big upheaval for everyone. Give your parents time to adjust. They are under huge pressure and haven't always been able to show their love in a way you understand.

"Be patient, Tavish. Everything will work out for the best. Promise."

She pulled Tavish onto his feet and brushed the dust off her clothing.

"No more gloomy thoughts. Let's go and find another Lesser Stitchwort," she said full of optimism. "Who knows, it could heal the stitch in your heart."

CHAPTER 29

Daisy heard the clock strike three, then four and by the time it had struck five she was up and dressed.

Her plan for the day depended on Johnny's goodwill, the weather and Willie.

"Has anyone seen my handbag?" she asked at breakfast.

Johnny shook his head. Mairi looked blank, her mind still distracted by the mixed events of the previous day.

"I'll help you look for it," said Tavish, keen to please. He asked if he could get down.

"Don't forget you've got school in half an hour," Mairi said, "and after I've dropped you off, I'm going to visit Margaret."

"Again?" Johnny queried. "I thought you visited her yesterday."

"I did," she replied, "but we didn't have time to finish our conversation."

She turned to Daisy who was clearing the table. "Will you be all right while I'm away? I should be back by lunchtime."

Daisy nodded, showing little interest in Mairi's need to spend time away from the family.

After a thorough search, Tavish gave up looking for the handbag and set off to school with his mother, leaving Daisy alone to gaze forlornly at the change in the weather. The previous day's sunshine had been replaced by a south westerly gale that lashed the sea, sending the waves into a frenzy. It was wild. Very wild. Too wild to ask Willie to take her across to the island and yet she was driven by an insatiable desire to see John again, to feel his touch and hear his voice.

Memories of her husband's idle evenings listening to the football results, eating pies or fish and chips, unnerved her. It hadn't always been like that. At the beginning of their marriage, Bill was ambitious and successful, working long hours to boost the family income. Having been denied the senior managerial position he coveted, he became disillusioned and saw little reason to go the extra mile for the company that had failed him. He grew depressed and put on weight until he was unable to walk more than a few hundred yards without getting breathless.

Daisy, on the other hand, had reached a senior position within the firm, Warburton, Clark and Paine. She was considered indispensable to Mr Warburton, the senior partner who employed her and paid her handsomely.

The differences in Bill and Daisy's lifestyles placed an enormous strain on their marriage yet, for William's sake, they stayed together.

Meeting John had changed everything.

"What are your plans this morning?" Johnny enquired, aware that their guest had been abandoned by Mairi yet again. Her disregard for Daisy had become an embarrassment.

"I'm not sure," she replied. "I'm worried about my handbag. I can't find it anywhere. It's just possible I might have left it on the island."

"You won't get there in this storm," he replied, "but the wind might die down in an hour or two. The forecast for this afternoon and evening looks promising."

By ten o'clock, the raging seas had calmed down. Jess sensed the shift in the weather and bounded over to Johnny, her ears pricked ready for her morning walk but she would have to wait. Johnny had found an error in the monthly accounts and needed time in the office. The energetic dog tried guilt-tripping him into taking her out but he was too preoccupied to notice. Dejected and dispirited, she sloped back to her basket.

"I'm afraid I'm going to be tied up with accounts all morning," he apologised. "But the worst of the storm seems to be over. Why not find Willie and ask if he has time to take you over to the island to look for your handbag? You might as well make the most of the break in the weather."

Daisy found Willie where she expected him to be - in the barn with the grey Fergie.

"What are you doing out here in such awful weather?" he asked, wiping the grease off his hands.

"What awful weather?" she exclaimed. "You've been shut away in this barn for too long. Take a peek outside and see for yourself. The storm has blown itself out."

"I'll take your word for it!" he said, tidying away his tools.

"I suppose you want me to take you back to the island."

Daisy looked abashed, blushing like a teenager.

"If it's not too much trouble. I think I left my handbag there. Without my purse and train ticket I won't be able to return home at the end of the week."

She tried to sound nonchalant, casual, but the little white lie made her self-conscious. She knew perfectly well her handbag was on the island because she had hidden it there. The search after breakfast had been a farce and the visit to Eilean Torrach staged. All to see John.

Willie poked his head outside to check the waves.

"Mmmm!" he said, stroking his chin. "There's still quite a swell out at sea but I like a challenge and seeing it's you, let's give it a go."

The remnants of the morning storm had stirred the sea into a magnificent show of white horses that jostled and crashed, sending a salty spray into the air.

"Are you sure it's safe to take *Arctic Tern* out?" Daisy asked with concern. "It looks rather rough."

"It's fine," Willie assured her. "The sea won't stay choppy for long now the storm's over. The engine is powerful enough to power the boat through the waves. You'll be perfectly safe."

Daisy heaved a sigh of relief. For a terrible moment she thought Willie was going to attempt to sail to the island. The mention of the engine settled her nerves. It was more reliable than the capricious movement of a taut sailcloth.

She slipped on her life jacket and jumped on board, grasping the side of *Arctic Tern* as it bobbed up and down like a cork in a vast ocean. Willie was in his element. The upward swells gave him a chance to test his nautical skills and feel the power of the propellor driving the boat forward. Through the spray, he guided the small boat to the shallow waters of Torrach Bay where he dropped anchor.

"I'll pick you up from this spot at six thirty this evening. If the weather deteriorates or I'm not here, I'll try and get back at six thirty tomorrow morning. Will you be all right?"

Daisy nodded.

John was already waiting at the water's edge for the boat to arrive.

"Morning, Willie!" he shouted across the crashing surf. "What have you brought me today; another Ceasg?"

"The same," Willie replied with a knowing look.

John waded into the sea and lifted Daisy off the boat, carrying her gently back to the shore. They wandered up to the house where a welcome fire burned in the grate. The sea spray had tangled Daisy's hair and soaked her raincoat. All of a sudden, she looked very pale and vulnerable with blue chattering lips.

"Take these," John said, handing her a large towel and a pile of men's clothing.

"Rub yourself down and change out of your wet clothes. You'll catch your death if you don't dry off quickly."

Daisy looked horrified at the thought of changing in front of John, a man she had only met once before. He seemed to read her mind.

"You're perfectly safe. I'm going to make us both a hot drink."

Daisy was too cold to question his motives. Tired and cold, she peeled off her wet coat and wrapped the towel around her shoulders removing her shirt and trousers. Having changed into one of John's shirts and put on a pair of thick woollen socks, she slipped on the knitted jumper that came down to her knees. Everything felt so reassuringly comfortable, as if John himself were holding her in his arms to keep her warm.

He gazed at her timeless beauty trying to work out why he found her so fascinating. Despite the age-gap, he was drawn to her personality, her honesty and plain speaking. He handed her the mug of hot sweet tea and hung up her wet clothes to dry.

"Well, this is a surprise!" he exclaimed with a hint of mischief. "What brings you back here so soon?"

Daisy cupped her mug in her hands and breathed in the hot soothing steam unsure how honest she should be.

"Could it be this?" he asked, holding a black leather handbag in his outstretched hand. "I found it tucked under the table."

Daisy gave a rather feeble nod and admitted she had deliberately left it behind so she could see him again.

"I know," he said with an unexpected sadness. "What time is Willie picking you up?"

"Six-thirty this evening, if the weather holds."

"That gives us five hours and if the storm returns, longer."

He held out his hand and touched her cheek, kissing her gently on the forehead.

"Finish your tea and then… well, then it's up to you." But Daisy already knew her destiny and put her mug down on the floor to touch the fingers of his outstretched hand. He lifted her off the chair and drew her to himself as if to protect her from harm. His woollen clothes smelt of toil, his awkward embrace was taut but the kisses that wove through her matted hair were light and soft. He waited for her to finish her drink then led her up a narrow wooden staircase to a space under the eaves where a simple rustic bed was strewn with tartan blankets and a thick green eiderdown.

Daisy tucked herself under the eiderdown and shut her eyes as John crawled in beside her. Gently, almost maternally, he removed her heavy clothing, caressing every part of her now exposed body. She had never experienced such tenderness before and as John's kisses reached her lips, she started to cry. She tried to speak but he placed a finger on her mouth, encouraging her to use her body to express her deepest feelings. Timidly, with a great deal of hesitation, she started to explore his body, to feel the leanness of youth, to respond to his desires and allow him to ease her years of neglect. His response stirred within her such an intensity of longing, she ceased to be an individual. The very core of her soul merged with John's.

For the first time in her life, she knew what it was to be loved and feel alive.

"Don't go back to England," he said sleepily. "I need you here."

She lay listening to the rain pattering on the skylight above their bed.

"I wish I could stay here forever," she replied, dreamily.

"But I can't abandon my job, my husband, my son and my unborn grandchild to live with someone I've only just met. Not only someone I've only just met but someone practically half my age."

"Nonsense!" John said, running his fingers over her body. She responded by drawing him to herself, embracing him as softly as she knew how, while he joined her in an intimate movement of oneness. As they rocked in harmony, she felt her whole being disappear into a maelstrom of ecstasy. Their love-making was raw yet so satisfying, she couldn't stop herself letting out a low groan of contentment. As the passion subsided, she whispered, "How old are you?"

"Thirty-six," came an exhausted reply.

"Thirty-six!" she repeated, drowsily. "You're still a child! What am I doing here? I must have lost my mind."

He looked directly into her eyes and kissed her. "I wouldn't call myself a child. Not with all I've experienced so far in my short life."

"Well!" Daisy replied. "I am forty-seven, soon to become a grandmother so I'm definitely not a child!"

John gathered her in his arms, caressing her body with such devotion she was moved to tears. "Age isn't the problem, Daisy. Loneliness is. We've both been leading unfulfilled lives, searching for meaning in a world we barely understand. Together we have created a spark that has re-ignited a passion we didn't know existed. We have added colour to our bland existence and given each other hope. I want you to stay. I need you."

Daisy hadn't the energy to argue about a future that seemed a million miles away from the present. She held his hand, wishing things could stay as they were for ever.

Outside the house a series of short repetitive rasps broke the peaceful silence. The sequence repeated itself over and over again like a rusty hinge on a revolving door.

"What's that?" she asked out of curiosity. He listened. Silence. Then several short rasps.

"There!" she said. "That croaking sound."

John stroked the hair out of her eyes and smiled.

"It's a corncrake," he said. "The first I've heard this year. Have you never heard one before?"

She shook her head.

"I don't even know what a corncrake is."

"It's a strange secretive bird that overwinters in Africa and flies over six thousand miles to nest and lay its eggs in the rough grass around the crofts. The male corncrake makes that distinctive call hoping to attract a female."

He paused, aware of the irony of hearing the first corncrake of the year with Daisy lying beside him.

"Every year it flies from Central Africa to Eilean Torrach hoping to find a mate. It's a perilous journey, full of dangers – deserts, mist nets, shotguns - to name but three."

"What does it look like?" Daisy asked, unsure if John had slipped a hidden message into his answer.

"A bit like me," he replied. "An insignificant loner!"

Daisy smiled, aware of his continuing desire for her. She lay totally still, allowing him to enfold his body around hers in an act of love-making so gentle, she felt spiritually weightless. Her response was woefully clumsy by comparison but the understanding between them spoke the eternal truth of a shared destiny.

Finally, they parted, somewhat subdued by the powerful mystery of love.

Outside, the persistent corncrake carried on calling.

"Were you and your sister close?" she whispered, hoping to change the subject.

"Where did that come from?" he asked, surprised that his sister was being brought into the conversation.

"She was one of my dearest friends," Daisy said, "and I want to know more about her."

"We weren't particularly close as children but looking back, I think Katherine was one of the finest, noblest women I knew but when she needed me most, I let her down. I'll never forgive myself for treating her so badly."

This was not the answer Daisy had expected. From the way he spoke, John was clearly troubled by his past.

"Do you want to talk about it?"

Strangely, he did.

"My behaviour when she and Angus got engaged was unforgivable. At the end of the meal, my father brought out a bottle of whisky for me and Kenny to drink to mark the special occasion. Alcohol was never served in the Manse although my father occasionally had a wee dram in his study, he never drank in public. The whisky had nothing to do with celebration. It was a cynical way of encouraging drunken behaviour. Kenny and I enthusiastically over-indulged until we became boorish, offensive, tearing into Katherine for no reason other than she was there, and accusing her fiancé, Angus, of Devil Worship. We even mocked his virility and her innocence. We were horribly cruel and totally out of control. What we said was unforgivable and our father sat through the whole disgraceful debacle never once defending his only daughter or disciplining his depraved sons.

"Katherine interpreted his silence as a betrayal.

"Later that evening, she confronted our father in his study, demanding an apology or at least an explanation as to why he had served whisky and let such a drunken outburst go unchecked.

"He refused to explain why he had encouraged his sons to consume an entire bottle. As for an apology, none was forthcoming.

"She never set foot in the Manse again.

"The following Sunday, my father stood in his pulpit and publicly disowned his only daughter, wringing his hands of her."

Daisy didn't know what to say. It was obvious that John was still deeply ashamed of the part he had played in her departure.

"What really happened to Angus on the day he died?" she asked, hoping to shed light on the one event that had haunted Katherine's life.

To her astonishment, John held her tight and rested his head on her shoulder, trembling, terrified. He started to cry. She cradled his head and stroked his hair, assuring him that everything was all right but he was inconsolable.

"Whatever's the matter?" she asked. "For goodness' sake, tell me what's up. I can't bear you being so upset."

The rain had stopped and, much as she had feared, the sun came out. Daisy had lost the chance to stay the night. Willie would be over to fetch her in an hour so she had to tread carefully. Instead of making John talk about an event that still troubled him, she decided to tell him everything she knew about Angus' death.

John stopped crying but lay absolutely still in her arms.

"Did you know Sir Hugh wrote to Katherine telling her about his visit to you in prison?"

John cautiously shook his head.

"He agreed to engage the best defence lawyer in the land if you would tell him exactly what had happened. Correct me if I am wrong but according to Sir Hugh, you followed Angus onto Kilbackie Island hoping to 'rough him up a bit' for marrying your sister who was twenty-three years his junior.

"Drunk and in no fit state to fight, you returned to the mainland and settled on a grassy patch near the causeway waiting for Angus to cross.

"What happened then, John?"

The broken man tried to compose himself before talking. "I can't remember. It's all a blank, Daisy. You have to believe me. I was in a terrible state having downed a bottle of whisky earlier in the day. Perhaps I passed out, I don't know but I was in a bad way."

He clung to Daisy like a drowning man.

"Help me!" he cried, sweating profusely.

"Shhhh!" she said, trying to calm him down. "It's all right. I'm here. Take your time and tell me what happened next?"

"All I remember is staggering down to the water's edge where Angus' body was floating in the water. There was nothing I could have done to save him. He was already dead."

He described his panic, Angus' stare and the white skin.

"It was awful. Truly awful."

"Did you see what happened to Angus on the causeway?" Daisy asked, trying to piece together everything that had happened on that fateful day.

"I'm not sure. It's all a blur."

He stared at Daisy with wide hollow eyes, clearly terrified of the images flashing in front of him.

"Are you sure Angus was dead when you left him?"

John took some time to think, then nodded.

"Yes, I'm sure he was dead but I should have gone for help instead of abandoning him."

Here she paused and covered John's wet face with the softest of kisses.

"Is this why you have chosen to live alone on this abandoned island? To punish yourself."

Again, he nodded.

"Don't leave me, Daisy," he cried.

"I've got to go, but I promise I'll be back as soon as I can.

CHAPTER 30

The school playground was full of children letting off steam before the morning bell drew them into an orderly queue. Mairi loved watching Tavish play with his friends in a safe environment. She stood behind a low stone wall opposite the car park, a short distance from Margaret's large group of family and friends. Occasionally, when she felt confident, she would join in their gossip but usually she preferred to stand aloof.

Today, however was different. She hung around the edge of Margaret's group hoping for a word, but Margaret sensed her neediness and withdrew further into the crowd, deliberately excluding her. As soon as the bell rang and the children formed their lines, Margaret's little gaggle began to disperse, giving Mairi the chance she had been waiting for.

"Can I come over to your house? There's something I need to say," she asked, nervously.

"If you have something to say, then say it here," came the terse reply.

"Not here, please, Margaret. Somewhere more private."

"No, Mairi. I'm done! I thought we were friends but now I hardly recognise you. Your move to Kilbackie House has changed you for the worse and your treatment of Rhona was unforgivable. I still can't believe you sacked her on the spot without giving her a chance to explain. If only you could see her now. She's become withdrawn, not wanting to go out, refusing to eat. Her days are spent playing with the puppies or shutting herself in her bedroom thinking she's a horrible person. I can hear her sobbing. It breaks my heart!

"Your family never liked the MacPhees and you are no exception. Poor David! He should never have got involved with Effie. It was bound to end in tears. I often wonder if your family had something to do with his disappearance."

Mairi looked shocked. The idea was absurd yet she had to admit that her family had treated the MacPhees badly in the past and she hadn't behaved any better!

"I know I haven't handled things well, but give me one more chance. Please!"

"Why should I when you refused to give one to Rhona. I'm sorry, Mairi. It's too late! I have nothing more to say to you."

She started walking home leaving Mairi alone, the hardhitting words still ringing in her ears. The true cost of their broken friendship was only just dawning on her. She knew she had treated Rhona badly but until recently she had felt justified in sacking her. If only she had talked things through with Johnny or Mr Buchanan before dismissing the girl, things might have turned out very differently.

The animosity between her and Margaret couldn't continue. It was tearing them apart. She needed to say something before their relationship deteriorated beyond repair.

Summoning up the courage to face her friend again,

Mairi left her car in the layby and walked up the winding road to Margaret's croft, fearful of what she was going to say but determined to put an end to the pointless feud.

The house was a typical white building, one and a half storeys high with small windows either side of the front door. It had a large fenced-off garden with a rickety old gate which was closed to keep out the sheep. Mairi tried lifting the rusty latch but her hands were trembling so much she couldn't grip the bar. Things weren't going well. The knot in her stomach grew tighter. She felt sick. After several attempts, she managed to push open the gate and walk up the path.

"Go away!" Margaret shouted. "I don't want to talk to you."

"I won't leave until I've said what I've come to say," Mairi replied, keeping her distance.

Margaret stood next to the washing line clutching a large washing basket in her arms. She looked crest-fallen and sad, her hollow eyes were swollen and red. Both women felt the unbearable tension festering between them and could do nothing about it.

Help came from an unexpected source. A sudden gust of wind blew a pair of unpegged knickers off the line. They tumbled across the grass towards Mairi who ran to catch them.

Waving them triumphantly in the air, she cried, "Got them!

"Pass me some pegs, Margaret, and I'll help you finish the job, then I promise I'll leave."

There was little Margaret could say. She gave Mairi a handful of pegs and the two women worked side by side as if the rift had never existed.

"I don't know where to begin," she said humbly, pegging half a dozen socks onto the line as a way of distraction. "Promise you won't interrupt me until I've finished what I have to say."

Margaret nodded, welcoming the more contrite tone in Mairi's voice.

"Do you remember the St Andrew's Night Dance in 1932? The one Effie had to miss because she was ill in bed. You decided to stay the night with your friend Seonaid, leaving me to walk home alone with David."

She spoke in hushed whispers afraid the wind would spread her shame across the hills.

Margaret nodded but said nothing.

"David and I set off at a good pace but it was bitterly cold and my flimsy party frock was totally unsuitable for a November night. If I hadn't tried to look sophisticated, I would have worn warmer clothes but I had set my heart on one particular cotton dress.

David realised right from the start that I was going to struggle in the cold. He did his best to keep me warm by wrapping his coat around my shoulders but I was getting sleepier, swaying from side to side. Whether he knew it or not, I was drunk. It was the first and last time I had ever had so much to drink and I felt awful. All through the dance, I sat in the shadows, worried someone would see me and tell my father. I was a twenty-three-year-old adult yet I was still afraid of his judgement. Although he had banned me from attending dances, I think I would have got away with just a reprimand had I not been with a MacPhee.

"Am I boring you?"

Margaret shook her head. She had stopped hanging clothes on the line, preferring to give Mairi her full attention.

"Several people took pity on me and bought me a drink. I have no idea how much I drank but alcohol became my companion for the evening and by the time I was ready to leave, I could hardly walk.

"I'll never forget how cold and sick I felt!

"By now David knew I wouldn't make it home. His only option was to take me to the shieling on Gillen Moor where we could find shelter until the morning. Inside was bleak but the stout walls protected us from the bitterly cold wind."

"Oh, God!" Margaret whispered, turning the colour of the sheets on the line. "You didn't, did you?"

"You promised to let me finish my story. If you interrupt me once more, I'll leave."

Margaret held her tongue.

"For years I had lived dutifully at home, caring for my ageing parents without receiving a word of thanks. I was preached at, mocked and belittled on a daily basis, while Effie was free to do whatever she liked. My fate as the youngest daughter was to stay at home, deprived of love and affection. It was no life for a young woman.

"I had loved David for as long as I could remember and envied Effie's close relationship with him. Envy and jealousy are ugly words but they raged within me, destroying what little peace I had at the time. I tried to get him out of my mind - to forget him but he haunted my waking hours and disturbed my sleep. I lived in daily dread that he would marry Effie but he never did. He and I were both free so, to answer your question, yes, I did."

A strong gust of wind came from nowhere and lifted the laundry high into the air giving the sheets a good thwack. Margaret stood frozen to the spot, speechless.

Mairi explained that she and David left the shieling at dawn, having promised each other never to speak about what had happened.

It was their secret.

"Shall I continue?" she said, watching Margaret struggle with what she had heard so far.

"No!" Margaret said, burying her face in her hands. "I've heard as much as I can take."

She and Mairi had been friends since primary school, long enough to share confidences yet what she had just heard shocked her to the core.

"I can't believe it! After all these years! I never thought for one second that you and David had had an affair." She paused and asked the one question Mairi dreaded.

"Does Effie know?"

Mairi's shame was now complete.

"No," she whispered, "and before you go mad, it wasn't an affair! It was one night of confusion, loneliness and cold. All right, if you want to add lust to the list then I'll admit I longed to experience love. I'm not proud of what happened and have spent the past twenty-two years regretting it but I can't turn the clock back."

"Of course you could have helped it!" Margaret said, showing little sympathy. "You were old enough to know the difference between right and wrong, old enough to know what you were doing. You were the Minister's daughter, for goodness' sake. A role model, someone I looked up to. Effie's sister!"

"I was never a role model. I was an unhappy, lonely young woman, deprived of love and affection."

"I don't believe you! You were highly respected, a good woman who cared for others. I envied your life and now look at you!"

Mairi was determined to hold herself together graciously.

"I thought your hurting my daughter was bad enough," Margaret continued, "but now it turns out you and my brother deceived everyone you loved." Her voice rose with anger. "You've gone too far, Mairi. I'll never forgive you for this."

"I understand," Mairi replied, her eyes welling up with tears. "It's a lot to take in and I don't come out of it well."

She handed back the spare clothes pegs, relieved that her secret was finally out. There was no way of telling what Margaret would do with the truth but Mairi, having braced herself for the worst, felt strangely at peace.

CHAPTER 31

"Where are you going?" Margaret called out as Mairi reached the rickety gate. "Come back!"

Mairi turned round with her head hung low.

"You could do with a cup of very, very sweet tea!" Margaret said with unexpected generosity. "What you have just told me must have taken courage. You are braver than I could ever be. Come inside and finish your story."

Mairi's throat and eyes prickled. She lifted her jumper up to her face and let the tears flow.

Once inside, Margaret put on the kettle.

"I'm glad you told me," she said. "Friends should be able to share their secrets. You've been incredibly brave sharing yours with me. It can't have been easy. I've missed you so much, Mairi. All those wonderful times of laughter. Where did they go?"

Whilst waiting for her cup of tea, Mairi worked her way through a box of tissues.

"Do you really want to be friends with me after all the terrible things I've done?"

Margaret managed a weak smile.

It was a start.

"Yes," she whispered, stretching out a hand to hold Mairi's. "Of course I want to remain friends with you. Our disagreements have torn us apart and made us miserable. If you are able to continue, I'd love to hear the rest of your story."

Mairi shuffled on her chair to get comfortable. She took a sip of tea and drew in a deep breath.

"I hardly saw David in the weeks following the dance. I wanted to talk to him, to find out if he had any feelings for me but he shut himself away on his croft, refusing to see me. Whether he was feeling guilty for what had happened I'll never know but he made no effort to contact me.

"I carried on being the model Manse daughter, smiling at parishioners, helping in the Sunday school, visiting the elderly. Yet deep down I knew my body was changing. I was so frightened, I stopped eating. Perhaps I was trying to starve myself to death, who knows? I lost so much weight, my mother insisted I visited the doctor."

Mairi paused to compose herself. The strain of talking was beginning to tell.

"You don't have to continue if you don't want to," Margaret said with surprising sympathy.

"It's all right. I need to talk. I've kept things to myself for far too long.

"I made an appointment to see Dr MacNeil who took less than a minute to diagnose my problem."

Margaret held her tongue, horrified that Mairi could be talking about a nephew or niece she didn't know existed.

"His diagnosis was what I expected. I begged him not to tell my parents. The shame would have killed me. The dear man was true to his word and said nothing. My pregnancy remained a secret."

Margaret sat spellbound.

"Why didn't you tell me!" she said so softly that Mairi barely heard her.

"Because I was too ashamed of what I had done and David was your brother.

"My parents noticed a change in my behaviour. I had become lethargic, tired and nervous.

I needed to get away. They agreed to let me go to Inverness if I found the money for the journey, but working unpaid for the church, I never had any money of my own so travelling to Inverness was out of the question. In the end I managed to see David and told him everything. He was surprisingly supportive and agreed to pay for me to go to Inverness as long as I promised never to have an abortion. The very idea of a termination horrified him but he never advised me how to find work or what I was meant to do with the baby once it had been born.

"I travelled to Inverness, bought a curtain ring from Woolworths which I wore on my wedding finger and called myself Mrs Una Fraser - the first two names that came into my head. David had given me two months' rent before I left Skye but he was hopelessly out of touch with the cost of renting a room in Inverness. The money barely covered the rent for the tiny damp attic space I found near the town centre. The elderly landlady was delighted with the advanced payment. After making me sign a list of rules and regulations, she handed me my key. I immediately started looking for a job and eventually found work as a waitress at the Station Hotel, a short distance from my digs. My plan was to scrape together enough money to see me through to the end of the pregnancy.

"All went according to plan until the hotel owner, a horrid fastidious little man with a thin moustache, noticed my increasing bump and sacked me on the spot. He felt my 'condition' would spoil the genteel atmosphere of his renowned establishment!

"Back on the street, I visited tea rooms, hotels and shops looking for work but my growing waistline gave the game away and no-one was prepared to employ me. It was getting dark. My final call was Maggie's, a popular tearoom on Academy Street which served tea, hot chocolate, scones and cake. The proprietor, Maggie Ferguson, listened to my story and took pity on me. I'll never understand why she was so generous but she took me on and paid me well, giving me a daily hot midday meal and allowing me to take home a few leftovers - sponge, teacakes and scones. She never asked me about my private life nor the pregnancy which, by then, was clearly visible.

"Those four months were the loneliest, most frightening time of my life but I had promised David I would go to full term and I was determined to keep my promise.

"Alexander was born in a bleak attic room at 9.00 a.m. on 1st August 1933 with Maggie in attendance. She stayed with me throughout the labour and helped with the delivery although later, she admitted she didn't know what she was doing! Without her care, I don't think I would have made it. Two days later, we wrapped Alexander in the blanket David had given me as a present and walked to St Joseph's House, the orphanage where I had already planned to leave him. Maggie waited outside while I went in. Matron asked me some questions and made notes. I signed a couple of forms without knowing what I was signing, then handed over the sleeping baby to a complete stranger in a bleak institution devoid of maternal love. That was the last time I saw my son. I returned to my digs a few hours later and spent the next two weeks being cared for by Maggie, who heroically nurtured me through the trauma of losing my newborn child. It was Maggie who fed me, clothed me and bathed me. Her love kept me alive in body, mind and spirit until I was strong enough to return home.

As far as my parents were concerned, my trial period of independence hadn't worked out. They were delighted to have their unpaid helper back again and before long it was as if I had never been away."

Mairi looked at Margaret for some kind of reaction but was met by a blank stare.

"I know what you want to ask me, Margaret, and the truthful answer is I don't know. The last time I saw David was April 1933, a month before he went missing. I haven't seen or heard from him since."

Mairi suddenly felt drained and cold, knowing that her words could never be taken back and Alexander's existence was no longer a secret.

"Come here!" Margaret said warmly, beckoning Mairi to her. She wrapped her friend in a loving embrace. "I've missed you, Mairi. I really have. To think we were once so close and yet you've had to go through all this pain without telling me."

"I've said enough for now but at least you know the

truth," Mairi replied. "I have led a vain and foolish life, treated Effie and Rhona unfairly and been a rotten friend. I don't deserve any favours from you but I would appreciate it if you didn't tell anyone until I've told Johnny and Effie."

Margaret nodded, assuring her friend that she would keep her secret.

"Who is Dora?" Margaret asked out of curiosity.

"Another time," Mairi replied, getting ready to leave.

She had just walked past the rusty barbed wire fence when she shouted back.

"Tell Rhona there's a job waiting for her if she would like to return to Kilbackie House. I'd be delighted to see her on Monday morning."

CHAPTER 32

Arctic Tern motored round the headland into the glaring sun. The deep waters off Torrach Point were alive with seabirds squabbling over a shoal of fish. A frenzy of beaks and feathers plunged into the churning waters, creating a breathtaking scene of organized chaos. Willie brought the boat into the shallows where Daisy and John were waiting. Daisy looked strained. Gone was the irrepressible joy that had captivated Willie the first time he took her to the island.

"Did you find your bag?" he asked, taking her hand to help her on board.

"Yes, thank you. I would have been lost without it."

She wrapped her coat tightly round her waist and moved to the stern of the boat, clutching her bag as if it were a comforting hot water bottle. Her eyes never lost sight of John who stood forlornly at the water's edge, hands in his pockets, waiting for Willie to pull the starter cord.

"When do you return home?" Willie asked, watching her stare longingly at John's fading silhouette.

"On Tuesday."

"We'll miss you," he said generously. "You add a touch of gaiety to our dour lives."

Daisy was touched by the crofter's kindness but kind words alone weren't enough to lift her spirits. She closed her eyes, hoping to keep the intense intimacy of the past six hours alive but every second took her further from John, and nearer to No. 36 Windsor Avenue, the house she shared with Bill.

Back on dry land, Daisy took Willie's weather-beaten hands in hers and thanked him for being so understanding.

"John's a good man," he said. "He's got great plans for that island of his. I hope you'll come back one day soon."

Daisy had gained an ally.

Unnoticed, she tiptoed back into Kilbackie House and headed upstairs to spend some time reflecting privately on her momentous day. The loving attention she had received from John was unlike anything she had ever experienced before. It had drawn her into a relationship she knew she could never end. From her bedside, she gazed wistfully at the jagged outline of Eilean Torrach surrounded by the reddish hues of the setting sun.

The evening meal was a sombre affair. Everyone seemed preoccupied. Tavish refused to eat, complaining he wasn't hungry, Daisy wanted to be back with John and Mairi was worried she still had to tell Johnny about Alexander.

She waited until they were in bed before deciding whether or not to disclose the secret, she had kept from him for so many lonely years.

"Have you a moment?" she asked, turning towards her husband who had already switched off his light and was ready for sleep.

"Not now, Mairi, I'm too tired. Can it wait till tomorrow?"

"No, it can't," she said firmly, sliding between the fresh sheets. "What I have to say needs to be said now."

Johnny lay awkwardly by her side waiting for her to disclose whatever it was that was troubling her.

"That plasterwork still looks dangerous," he said. "If we don't get it seen to, the whole ceiling could fall down."

Mairi had noticed a few new cracks above her head. Johnny was right, the ceiling had started to bow badly. She shifted nervously towards the middle of the bed where her husband lay half asleep.

"Forget the ceiling. It's the least of my problems."

"Not if it falls on you it isn't," he joked.

If it falls, it falls," she replied pessimistically. "There's absolutely nothing we can do about it this evening.

"Are you awake?"

"No!" came the drowsy reply.

"I'm being serious, Johnny. Are you awake?"

There was a low groan, followed by a grunt.

"I am now!"

Mairi shifted further under the blankets, dreading the thought of telling Johnny about Alexander.

"Johnny!" she said nervously.

"Go to sleep," he whispered. "And don't worry about what you were about to tell me. I've known about your secret for the past four years. It's fine by me. I love you, Mairi. Everything's going to be all right so don't worry. Go to sleep!"

"What do you mean you know?" she replied, shocked by the casual way he spoke about the most traumatic event in her life.

"Exactly what I say. I know you gave up a child for adoption twenty-two years ago."

Mairi sat up with a jolt, unable to believe what she was hearing.

"But how can you possibly know when I've never told a soul?"

"Sir Hugh told me." He said, patting the pillow to persuade her to lie back down beside him.

'Sir Hugh?' she exclaimed in disbelief. 'How on earth did he know about Alexander?"

She racked her brain to think who else could possibly have known. No-one.

The orphanage knew of his existence but they were sworn to secrecy by a confidentiality clause in the contract she had signed. Maggie Ferguson knew about his birth but then she didn't know Mairi's true identity.

The bedroom's damp chill made her shiver. She stretched her feet to the bottom of the bed to find the hot water bottle and slid back under the bed clothes to keep warm.

"Can I carry on?" Johnny asked drowsily, shifting next to his wife so that she lay nestled in his arms. "Lie still and promise you won't interrupt.

"The night before we got married, Sir Hugh came over to see me at the cottage. He seemed genuinely worried, weighed down by a secret he had carried for many years. He knew he was dying. I could see the anguish in his eyes as he struggled to do the honourable thing. After much soul searching, he decided the only way forward for all concerned was to break a promise and tell me the secret.

"He made me promise never to tell a soul. It was to be our secret but I told him I never made promises. If he really wanted to tell me something confidential, he would have to trust my discretion.

"This was not the answer he was expecting. He paced up and down the room with his hands clasped behind his back, battling with his conscience.

"In the end, he had no choice but to trust me.

"He told me that Angus had visited the Estate office with a problem he couldn't resolve. He had a friend from Skye who had fallen in love with his fiancée's sister, a predicament fraught with complications right from the start. The friend had known the girl all his life but had been too shy to declare his love and too frightened to break off the engagement to her sister. After one unplanned encounter, the girl became pregnant and left Skye for Inverness, leaving the friend distraught.

"Without the girl he had no future. Without her love he had no present.

"He was in a fix. The only way out, as far as he could see, was to fake his own death and start a new life far away from Skye and the woman he loved."

Mairi buried her face in her hands, hearing her husband talk about David's love for her in the intimacy of their marital bed. It all seemed deeply inappropriate, yet knowing that Alexander, despite the clumsy, naïve circumstance surrounding his conception, had been born out of a genuine love, brought her a profound sense of peace.

"At first the young man didn't go far. He made his way to Inverness, where he hoped to start a new life but he couldn't get the girl out of his mind. Against his better judgement he set out to discover where she worked so he could catch a glimpse of her from time to time. After a while he discovered she had found a job at Maggie's Tea Room. Every day after his shift at the fish factory, he stood on the pavement opposite the tea room and watched her serve customers with efficient grace. She seemed happy in her work, unaware that he was nearby.

"After a while, things began to change. She seemed to lose confidence, her face became pasty, she took more breaks and required comforting. Maggie Ferguson, the proprietor, kept a close eye on her, put an arm around her and consoled her. It was clear that her advanced pregnancy was making life difficult.

"Then one day she didn't turn up for work. For the next three days, the young man stood on the pavement as usual, hoping to catch a glimpse of the woman he loved but she never showed up.

"Unknown to him, his regular appearances on the pavement opposite the tea room had been noticed by Maggie who, one wet afternoon, walked across the road to invite him in for a cup of tea and a scone. He willingly accepted. Angus didn't know what was discussed but for the next two weeks, the girl received a full wage even though she no longer turned up for work."

Mairi took her hands away from her face and stared at her husband in total disbelief. She could not believe that David had moved to Inverness after faking his own death and had sent money to support her in the two weeks after Alexander's birth. It was unbelievable!

"Shall I continue?" Johnny asked gently, caressing her hand.

She nodded, unsure how much more she could take without bursting into tears and making a fool of herself.

"The young man knew he was the child's father. Apparently, the girl had told him before she left for Inverness. Eager to remove his new-born son from the orphanage, he wrote to Angus asking if he was aware of anyone who would be willing to adopt his child. He knew it was a long shot but if Angus was unable to help, perhaps he could ask around. Angus showed the letter to Sir Hugh who used his formidable contacts to find a devout, childless couple wishing to adopt a baby. Within weeks of writing to Angus, the young man took twelve-week-old Alexander down to Yorkshire to meet his new adoptive parents. They welcomed the baby with open arms. After kissing his son good-bye, the young man disappeared and Angus never heard from him again."

Mairi wriggled closer to Johnny and held onto his hand.

"Did Sir Hugh ever tell you the name of Alexander's adoptive parents?"

"No!"

"When did you know I was Alexander's mother?"

Johnny folded Mairi in his arms and whispered, "The night Sir Hugh told me about the baby. The evening before our wedding."

"Why didn't you tell me?"

"It wasn't my story to tell but I knew you would let me know when the time was right."

CHAPTER 33

Effie gazed at her three dogs lying fast asleep on the sitting room floor. There was no doubt where her heart lay.

Dogs were less complicated than people.

She caught sight of the photo on the mantlepiece. The one with her and David MacPhee sitting on a rug enjoying a picnic. With hindsight, she hadn't handled her engagement particularly well. Although they had been best friends for as long as she could remember, her betrothal had been more an act of rebellion than a declaration of love. Ever since her father, Rev Tommy Nicolson had put the MacPhee family firmly in the 'non-saved' camp, Effie sought a way to restore the strong bond that had previously existed between the two families. She exacted her revenge by pledging herself to the one man her father had forbidden her from seeing.

David had also handled the engagement badly. He should have had the courtesy to ask the minister for his daughter's hand but knowing the likely response, he lost his nerve. The engagement went ahead as planned amidst a great furore from the Manse. Effie suspected the engagement would never lead to marriage, because she wasn't in love with David.

Over the months and years, she grew to enjoy the comfortable familiarity of his company. His listening ear, wise choice of words and sound advice. Perhaps the two of them had been destined never to marry but they spent so much time together, friends assumed it was a forgone conclusion.

When David disappeared, the whole community mourned his loss, offering Effie their condolences and support. Without a body, there was no closure or burial. Gradually those who had shown an incredible amount of sympathy, slowly distanced themselves from Effie, finding it hard to know what to say.

Effie bore her unusual situation with dignity and grace. Although at times she had felt lonely and sad, she could never have described herself as grief stricken. This was mostly due to the close bond she had with her dogs and her love of crofting.

Bess became restless. She arched her back, curled into a ball, the white-tips of her ears twitching in time to the gentle snores of an exhausted sleep. Effie had spent the whole day gathering sheep on the hill behind the croft. The main flock, although scattered, had been easy to gather but Effie kept a sharp eye on the stragglers who had strayed onto the furthest hill where a patch of lush grass grew beyond the scree. This area was too dangerous to cross on foot, so Effie had to rely on Bess. With a wave of her stick, she watched her favourite collie tear into the outrun along familiar contours, powered by instinct and adrenalin. Bess raced over the springy heather towards the grazing ewes but in her haste to reach them, she failed to notice a small herd of roe deer nibbling the green shoots of low growing plants. These nervous black-eyed creatures with white rumps lived in a permanent state of fear, always on the lookout for danger although their natural predators - wolves and lynx - no longer roamed the Highlands.

Acutely alert by nature, they pricked their ears in alarm as Bess crept closer. All of a sudden, they sprang into the air and scattered in different directions, unsettling the sheep.

Effie shouted at Bess to 'lie down' then 'walk up', encouraging her to get above the sheep without causing them to panic. One false move could spook the dumb creatures and scatter them over a wide area. The sheep looked edgy and confused, unsure what to do. It was up to Bess to creep forward paw by paw until she had them under her control. With effortless ease, she steered the ewes over the stony escarpment and across the gully towards Effie who was watching their progress from her vantage point on the other side of the scree. The last leg of the journey, leading the sheep off the hill, went smoothly. The entire flock followed Bess and Effie down the well-worn track to the fank where they were securely penned until the shearers arrived the following day.

Effie loved the crofting way of life, especially the long summer days out on the hill among the wildflowers that bloomed reliably year after year. Sulphur-yellow Bog Asphodel, white Bogbean, red Marsh Lousewort, yellow Globeflowers and silky wisps of white Cotton-grass - blooms that created a floral map of an unchanging landscape.

During the winter months, prolonged periods of rain soaked through the sheep's fleeces, stripping their skin of its protective layer of wax, causing dermatitis, an intensely itchy infection which no amount of scratching or biting could alleviate. It wasn't surprising that the infected skin eventually tore, producing a discharge that attracted pregnant blowflies to bury themselves deep inside the fleece and lay their eggs. The hatched eggs produced maggots that fed voraciously on the sheep's protein-rich flesh, secreting ammonia into the blood supply. Quite literally, the maggots ate the sheep alive. It was a pitiful, painful death.

Shearing the heavy woollen coats was an effective way of preventing the blowfly larvae from taking hold. Shorter fleeces enabled infected areas of skin to dry quickly.

Mairi walked up the path to pay her sister a visit but her timing couldn't have been worse. Effie had hurried home to collect the clootie dumpling she had boiled for the morning break. The last person she wanted to see was her sister. Now was not the time.

"I can't talk," she said, grabbing the clootie. "The shearers will be taking their break in twenty minutes so I must get back."

"Not to worry!" Mairi replied, trying not to show her disappointment. "I'd forgotten you were shearing today. Perhaps another time."

Effie's bronzed and weather-beaten face bore witness to an outdoor life well-lived, a contented life that embraced simplicity. Unlike Mairi, she had never wished to leave the close-knit Gaelic community surrounding her croft. Here, amidst the mist-covered hills, the crofting traditions of a bygone age still held sway. In a world of rapid change, Effie stood for a past way of life, displaying the resilience of tradition.

She knew every mound, path, bog and crevice on the hill above her croft and could read the weather in the clouds. She and Kilbackie fitted like a hand and glove. To Effie, life was a gift to be lived to the full. At night, her sleep was deep, free of guilt and regrets.

"Why don't you come with me?" she exclaimed enthusiastically. "We can chat while I open and close the race gate. Please come, for old time's sake."

Considering their recent exchange of words, Effie's generosity touched Mairi and she agreed to walk with her sister to the stone fank crammed with bleating sheep waiting to be shorn. The whole hillside rang to the deafening sound of agitated ewes who, given half a chance, would have jumped the stone walls in a bid for freedom. Fortunately, they were packed so tightly together, escape was impossible.

The community had gathered around the fank for one of the highlights of the crofting year - shearing. It was a day of feverish activity but despite the apparent chaos, everything seemed to go smoothly. The sheep were released down the race towards the shearers, who clamped the panic-stricken animals deftly between their knees and started clipping the long straggly wool. It all looked so easy but shearing was not for the faint-hearted.

It required strength and stamina especially if the heavy winter fleeces were damp. As the hours passed, an elderly crofter who had proudly shorn sheep for over forty years, began to slow down, showing signs of fatigue and pain.

"All right, Uncle Donald?" his nephew enquired, seeing the older man pause to catch his breath, "I'll take over from here." He took the shears, saying, "You've earned a break. Iona has just made a fresh brew. Go and rest your back."

Donald didn't protest. The crippling pain in his back made him wince every time he breathed. His ruddy cheeks turned an unhealthy grey. He knew his days of physical hard work were numbered and accepted the inevitable with grace. He believed the Scriptures when they said that there is nothing better for people than to be happy and to do good while they live, that each of them may eat and drink and find satisfaction in all their toil.

Donald had always found satisfaction in his work even though it hadn't always been easy. The ancient rhythms of the Gaelic way of life defined his identity so completely that he couldn't understand why the young chose to leave Kilbackie for jobs in the English-speaking south. It was heart-breaking to see so many fine young men pack their bags, hoping to find a better standard of living in far off towns and cities. Soon there would be no-one left to cut the peat, thatch the roofs, shear the sheep or plant the potatoes.

Effie and Mairi rounded the corner to see plumes of smoke rising from the burning fires. It was a marvellous sight. White wisps floating like dandelion seeds in the wind. The place was teeming with people busily getting ready for the shearers' break. Effie slipped her clootie in amongst the cakes and shortbread displayed on a trestle table and offered to help Janet MacAskill, who was organising the refreshments. The men helped themselves to hearty slices of cake, preferring to eat together away from the women and children. Mairi recognised them all - Donny MacAskill, Hamish Gordon, Alec MacKay, Findlay Murchison, Ruairidh Campbell and Ally MacSwan. Men she had known since childhood. Men who kept alive the oral tradition of story-telling by recounting tales passed down through the generations. The names and tales were well-known but the manner in which they were told varied, keeping audiences entertained for hours. The rich expressive Gaelic language drew its listeners into a close-knit, humorous world of misdemeanours, eccentric characters and drunken escapades, a far cry from the stilted anglicised life Mairi was living in Kilbackie House.

It was here, among the shearers, over thirty years ago that she had first fallen in love with David. At the time he had been a relaxed, easy-going sixteen-year-old, stripped to the waist with a pair of braces covering his torso. The sight of a half-naked man rolling up fleeces aroused, in the young Mairi, feelings of delight tinged with horror. It was as if her eyes had been opened to the power of physical attraction. David had been a MacPhee. He and his family had been placed in the 'non-saved' camp by Mairi's father and he was, by definition, an untouchable.

Looking back, Mairi now realised with a surge of emotion just how much of a role fear had played in her failed life.

"Is now a good time for you to say what you came to say?" Effie asked, ready to release a sheep through the gate and send it down the race to the waiting shearer.

"I don't know where to start," Mairi said, raising her voice to be heard above the din.

"Why don't I tell you what I know and you can fill me in on all the things I leave out?"

Mairi nodded in agreement. She disliked talking about David and Alexander. Their stories made her appear immoral and uncaring.

"It would be good to listen for a change," she replied, relieved she didn't have to explain herself any more.

Effie's understanding of Mairi's story was pretty accurate. She instinctively knew that her sister had gone to Inverness to have David's baby and was generous enough to admit that she had never loved David the way Mairi had.

"As it turned out," she confessed, "his refusal to commit was a blessing. I was never cut out for marriage. I would have been miserable. I'm much happier on my own with Bess, Peg and Nell. A husband would only have complicated things and restricted my freedom."

Mairi filled her in on the missing facts and finally asked if she knew anyone called Dora.

Effie shook her head.

CHAPTER 34

The morning of Daisy's departure started badly. Mairi spent a restless night battling her conscience, regretting the way she had left Daisy to babysit while she tried to make amends for her past mistakes. Looking back, she realised how often she had taken Daisy for granted, treating her like a member of staff rather than a good friend. She had behaved shamefully.

Daisy too, had slept badly. She had lain awake most of the night remembering the passionate way John had overwhelmed her with a love she had never experienced before. He had become her instant soul mate someone she could totally trust. With him by her side, she had felt invincible but now she was leaving Kilbackie to face an uncertain future with a charmless husband whose sedentary life repulsed her.

One by one she folded her expensive clothing in tissue paper and packed them in her suitcase. She loved quality and was fortunate that Warburton, Clark and Paine paid her well. Her generous weekly cheque was enough to cover the household bills and indulge in a few fashionable extras. In a moment of madness, she bought a very expensive pure silk nightie hoping its opulent softness would compensate her for having to share a loveless bed with Bill

Her fears for the future were interrupted by Tavish calling up the stairs.

"Get a move on, Daisy! If you don't come down soon, you'll miss me. It's nearly time for school."

She could hear Mairi telling Tavish off for being cheeky then asking him if he had cleaned his teeth and washed behind his ears?"

Tavish assured her he had.

Daisy checked her watch. Time was passing too quickly. It was already 8.15 am.

"I'll be down in a minute," she replied catching a glimpse of herself in the dressing table mirror before closing the suitcase. The face staring back at her no longer reflected the fashionable pallor of Elizabeth Taylor or Grace Kelly. It had become browner and healthier, displaying the characteristics of someone who enjoyed the great outdoors.

She liked what she saw.

Daisy took one last look through the window at the distinct outline of John's isolated island. She would miss lying in bed listening to the howling gales pounding the window panes, rattling their rotten frames. Instead of hearing the evocative sound of curlews or the eerie mewing of buzzards soaring high above the trees, she would wake up to the honking of car horns and a world addicted to noise and speed

Deep in thought, she closed the bedroom door for the very last time and made her way downstairs.

"You've come, at last!" Tavish said flinging his arms round her waist. "I've got to go to school now. Will you still be here when I come home?"

Daisy explained that she had a train to catch and would probably be in Inverness by the time he finished school.

Mairi held Tavish's hand and walked to the car.

"Ready?" she said, switching on the engine.

"Ready," he replied.

Daisy sat with Johnny on the front step, watching the car disappear into a plume of smoke. In a nearby field the repetitive rasps of a hidden corncrake floated over the grass, reminding her of John's challenge to return.

"We'll miss you," Johnny said with feeling. "We really will! You've added colour and fun to our rather dreary way of life. I hope you won't judge us too harshly and that we haven't spoiled your holiday. Please come back and visit us soon. Hopefully, by then, we will be over the worst of the teething troubles."

Daisy was touched by his contrition but not surprised. Johnny was the linchpin of the family, thoughtful, courteous, long suffering - qualities she hoped Mairi would learn to appreciate more.

Mairi's return signalled the dying moments of Daisy's stay at Kilbackie House. Johnny put the luggage in the boot of the car and checked the oil and tyre pressures.

"Have we time for a cup of tea before you go?" Mairi asked, hoping for a chat before Daisy finally left for the ferry.

"Heavens, yes! We don't have to leave till ten. The ferry departs at two."

Mairi sat with Daisy in the kitchen, nursing her tea. She had lost count of the number of cups she had drunk over the past few days. They had become synonymous with confession and regret.

"I hope you have an easy journey home."

"Thank you! I'm sure everything will be fine," Daisy replied. "Once I'm on the train it's plain sailing, if you know what I mean?!"

She forced a smile but the pun was lost on Mairi.

The two friends sat in silence, wondering what they had left to talk about.

"Have you finished?" Daisy asked pointing to the tea cup. Mairi nodded.

"Pass me your cup and saucer. The least I can do is wash up before I leave."

Her small act of kindness was interrupted by a high-pitched yapping sound.

"What on earth!" Daisy exclaimed as a small puppy appeared out of nowhere. It tore round the room, followed by a very flustered Rhona crying "Come here!" but the tiny bundle had no intention of obeying its mistress. It scurried around the room sniffing the chair legs and cupboards, then promptly squatted on the stone floor and puddled.

"Oh my God!" Rhona cried, rushing to the sink to fetch a floor cloth, "I'm so sorry, Mrs Mitchell. I promise I'll clean it up."

She got down on all fours to wipe the floor but the tiny dog sank its razor-sharp teeth into the corner of the cloth and started tugging.

"Go away!" Rhona cried, trying to hold the puppy

by the scruff of its neck and clean at the same time. It was hopeless. The puppy wriggled free, yapping with excitement as Rhona blushed with embarrassment.

In the midst of all the chaos Mairi started to laugh. Not just a chuckle but a real fit of the giggles, with tears streaming down her face. All the while Rhona was dancing on the floor trying to stop the puppy from biting her, Mairi kept laughing.

The young girl finally disentangled herself and stood up, patting down her dress and rearranging the loose strands of hair that had fallen out of her ponytail.

She gave a little curtsy.

"I'm so sorry about the mess, Mrs Mitchell. The puppy was meant to be a surprise for Tavish but everything seems to have gone wrong. Shall I take her home with me?"

"Absolutely not!" Mairi said, wiping the tears of laughter from her eyes. "Give her to me."

She stroked the wriggling bundle until it had calmed down.

"Oh, my goodness!" she said, talking to the puppy, "you've done me so much good. I don't think I've laughed so much since I was a child playing with Margaret. We used to laugh until our sides ached and our tummies hurt."

She looked up at Rhona who was standing aghast at Mairi's unexpected reaction.

"This little puppy," Mairi chortled, burying her face in its soft fur "has brought laughter back into the house. And about time too! I never thought such a transformation would happen in my lifetime.

"Of course she can stay! Does she have a name?"

Rhona shook her head.

Mairi asked Daisy if she would pick a name for the puppy before she left. She wiped her hands and sat down at the table to think. It didn't take her long to come up with a suggestion.

"What about Dora?"

Mairi turned a ghostly white. Her mood changed from laughter to fear, a terrible fear that dulled her eyes, making her fitful and nervous. Daisy wondered what she had said to make Mairi act so strangely.

"Not Dora! Anything but Dora!" Mairi said with an urgency Daisy didn't understand.

"All right," she conceded. "Not Dora. How about Bella? That's a good name."

She tried calling the puppy. "Bella! Come here, Bella," but the dog was far too busy playing to respond. It continued racing round the room, sniffing the furniture and tugging at Rhona's jumper.

"Stop it, Bella!" Rhona cried. "You'll tear the wool and unravel the stitching."

Mairi watched the commotion pensively, as if weighing up what to say next. Her strong dislike of the name 'Dora' had ended her irrepressible fit of the giggles.

The more she heard the puppy being called Bella, the more she preferred the name Dora.

"Bella's a good choice," she said, "but can I change my mind please and go with the name Dora. It suits her better."

After more chaos and cuddles, Mairi asked Daisy why she had picked the name Dora.

"Easy!" Daisy replied, relieved the name no longer caused such a negative reaction. "Do you remember Gladys's sister Agnes who ran the post office in Shottenden?"

Mairi wasn't sure she did.

"Well, everyone called her 'Dora.'"

"Why 'Dora?'" Rhona asked out of curiosity.

"It was quite sweet really. She used the abbreviation 'dora' to describe anything she thought was adorable. Children, cats and dogs were all 'dora'! She used to say, 'You are so dora and What a dora child!'

"You must remember her, Mairi. She used to cycle round the village delivering cakes, eggs, flowers and honey to anyone in need. She also did the most amazing flower arrangements in St Thomas' church. I believe her husband Derek was one of the churchwardens but I can't remember. Anyway, they never had children but I believe they adopted a baby but I don't know what happened to him."

Mairi gave a short gasp. The coincidence was too great to ignore. She rushed out of the room to find Johnny, leaving Daisy and Rhona utterly bemused.

"I've got to catch the ferry with Daisy and travel south," she told him, her words tumbling out incoherently. "Daisy believes she knows who Dora is. She lives in Shottenden of all places! I've got to meet her. Can you look after things until I get back?"

CHAPTER 35

Mairi's decision to leave Kilbackie and head south with Daisy had been so sudden, she hadn't had time to make arrangements for Tavish, who had become an obstacle in her quest to find Alexander. She pleaded with Johnny to back her, begging him to take charge of Tavish until she got back.

Alexander had become her sole focus, her priority. She would never find peace until she discovered what had happened to him.

Johnny finally lost his temper.

"We chose to be Tavish's parents. No-one forced us – we chose him because we loved him right from the start. The poor boy has been through a lot recently, as a result of the adoption, the move to Skye, your mood swings, losing Rhona and starting a new school. Can't you see he needs consistency, routine and lots of love, particularly maternal love? How can you be so heartless, standing there and telling me that the son you gave up for adoption over twenty years ago has more claims on you than our own son?

"Shame on you!"

Mairi didn't know what to say. Alexander had completely taken her over, leaving her powerless to resist.

If it hadn't been for the arrival of Rhona and the puppy, Johnny would have refused to let his wife go south, insisting she stayed behind to care for Tavish.

Her strange, irrational behaviour and obsession with Alexander, convinced him that Tavish would be happier alone with Rhona and the puppy.

Plockton! Plockton! Next stop Plockton. The train slowed down, its brakes screeched to the sound of hissing and gasping as huge clouds of steam billowed into the sky. A row of heads leant out of the carriage windows, waiting for the train to stop before turning the brass handles that opened the doors onto the bustling platform.

The announcement was repeated. *Plockton! Plockton! This is Plockton! All alight here for Plockton.*

Much to Daisy's relief, the few passengers who boarded the train found seats elsewhere, leaving her and Mairi alone to reflect on their lives. Mairi's decision to travel south with Daisy only added to her dread of returning home.

As the train gathered steam, it passed a row of neat cottages nestling in a secluded bay. Daisy rested her head against the window, staring at the tall palm trees that gave the village its exotic Mediterranean flavour. In the distance loomed the towering mountains of Wester Ross and the Applecross peninsula.

The guard reminded passengers that the train would be calling at Duncraig, Stromeferry, Attadale, Achnashellach, Achnasheen, Achanalt, Lochluichart, Dingwall and finally Inverness, where it would terminate. The soft pronunciation of the stations, mingled with the clacketing wheels, made Daisy sleepy but she had no wish to close her eyes and lose sight of the world that linked her to

John. Plockton's breath-taking beauty increased her sense of loss. Her mood worsened as the engine pulled the coaches over the desolate moorland between Achnasheen and Achanalt. She loosened the top button of her blouse to help her breathe more easily but it made no difference. The pain of leaving Skye was affecting her more than she thought it would. As the train passed Muir of Ord and the banks of the Beauly Firth towards its final stop, she prepared herself for the next leg of the journey. They had plenty of time to catch the train to Edinburgh and then on to York where Bill had promised to pick them up. He would be waiting in the station car park to avoid being seen in public. Ever since he had put on so much weight, he had steered clear of public spaces. It would never occur to him to make an exception, for his wife's sake, and meet her on the platform. There would be no kiss or words of affection telling her how much he had missed her. The most Daisy could hope for was a grunt, followed by news of the latest darts match at the club.

The more she thought about Bill, the more she yearned for John.

CHAPTER 36

Agnes Thwaites lived at No. 1 Church Street. It was an attractive old sandstone cottage with mullioned windows and an unpruned rose climbing chaotically over the red front door. It had been built in a peaceful setting, overlooking the flood plains of the river Fisk where cattle grazed rich meadows and vast flocks of geese and wigeon swirled across the wide-open sky before settling on the waterlogged grass. When the ground started to dry out, lapwing, curlew and snipe would arrive to probe the soft mud for food.

The view was such a contrast to Kilbackie!

Mairi took her time before knocking on the door. It was opened by a handsome woman of medium height with short wavy hair pinned off her broad face by two kirby grips. Her slate grey eyes were tinged with blue and although the passing years had dried her skin, her soft wrinkles gave her a homely look.

"Can I help you?"

"I hope so," Mairi replied. "Are you Gladys' sister, Agnes?"

"Yes," she replied, "but everyone calls me Dora. I don't think I've been called Agnes for over thirty years."

"Would it be possible to come indoors and talk? There's something I need to ask you."

Dora ushered Mairi into the sitting room where she offered her a cup of tea.

"That's very kind, but I've just had one with your sister who said you might be able to help me."

Once again, Mairi told her story and waited for Dora to respond.

Her response was totally unexpected.

"Oh! My word! You have no idea how long I've wanted to meet Alexander's birth mother!" she exclaimed, her warm eyes sparkling with delight. "Thank you so much for bringing our son into this world."

Her choice of words sounded strange to Mairi who had never considered Alexander's birth to be such a gift.

"Come and sit down. Are you sure I can't offer you a drink; tea, coffee or hot water?"

"Can I change my mind?" Mairi replied, feeling slightly more relaxed. "A cup of hot water would be lovely."

Dora disappeared to put the kettle on, leaving Mairi alone to examine the photos of Alexander displayed on the mantelpiece. He was instantly recognisable, having David's thick hair and smile. She picked up a particularly lovely photo of him standing on a platform next to a steam engine."

"Ah!" Dora said, carrying in a tray of drinks and homemade biscuits. "I see you've found the photos of Alex, not that you could miss them! I don't think there's a photo in the house that doesn't include him.

"That one," she said, pointing to the photo Mairi was looking at, "was taken next to the 'Flying Dutchman' when it stopped at York. Alex must have been about eleven."

She handed Mairi the cup of water and sat down.

"I expect Gladys told you that Derek and I couldn't have children so Alex's arrival was an unexpected blessing. We don't know what we would do without him."

"Where is he?" Mairi asked, betraying a sense of urgency. "I need to see he's all right before I return home."

"Of course you can see him but he's not here," Dora replied.

Mairi's heart sank. In her dreams she had imagined the reunion with Alexander to be a joyous occasion of instant recognition, empathy and joy. He would fling his arms around her, tell her he loved her and forgive her. She imagined such a love would free her of guilt and restore the maternal love that had dried up since his adoption.

"What do you mean 'not here'?"

The thought of her son being institutionalised with no-one to love him terrified her. Beads of cold sweat formed on her brow. She took another sip of water.

"Please put my mind at ease and tell me where he is?"

"Be patient!" Dora said calmly. "Let me tell you my story in my own words and when I have finished, I'll answer all your questions. But before I start, you need to know that Alexander is safe and well."

Mairi looked visibly relieved.

"In early autumn 1933, Derek and I received an unexpected visitor. Sir Hugh Hollister knocked on our front door and asked if he could come in. I was all of a flutter, never having had such an important visitor before. I managed to work myself into such a state that I left him standing on the doorstep in the rain! Thank goodness

Derek was around to take charge. He immediately welcomed Sir Hugh into our home and led him to the exact chair you are sitting in now. His manners were beautiful and he had such a lovely turn of phrase. He got straight to the point and told us about a newborn baby who desperately needed a home. The boy had been born in Inverness to a young Scottish mother whose situation prevented her from keeping her son. The child's parents came from the same village as Sir Hugh's manager, Angus MacLeod.

Sir Hugh was a man of few words but he was highly respected in the area so when he asked us straight if we would consider adopting the boy, we didn't hesitate. We had been waiting a long time to adopt a baby and the fact that Alexander had Down's Syndrome made him even more special. It made no difference to us.

"You see, Mrs... Oh dear, I don't even know your name."

"It's Mairi, Mairi Mitchell."

"You see, Mrs Mitchell," Dora continued, "God has given Derek and me so much love, we needed to share it with a special child, like Alexander. He joined us on 6th November 1933 and it was literally love at first sight. We adored him. He was the sweetest, calmest baby imaginable and has grown into a kind, affectionate young man with a passion for gardening, something neither of us know much about.

"Six years ago, when he was fifteen, I happened to mention his love of gardening to my cousin, Sheila, who is the Abbess of Malvingborough Abbey. She suggested a trial period working in the Abbey gardens to see if he really had a flare for horticulture. He took to it like a duck to water and has been there ever since. Derek takes him every Monday morning at nine and I pick him up on Thursdays at three. He has a small bedsit in one of the outbuildings which he loves. It's his safe place, a place where he can live independently from us. When I say independently, I mean he wakes and sleeps there but eats all his meals in the abbey.

"It's Thursday today. Would you like to come with me to pick him up and have tea with us afterwards? He's usually famished after a day's work in the garden."

CHAPTER 37

"Welcome to Malvingborough Abbey," the Abbess said as they entered a spacious hall. The word 'Abbey' was misleading. Mairi had imagined an imposing church as cold and oppressive as Kilbackie, so she was pleasantly surprised to see, at the end of a tree-lined drive, a sprawling honey-coloured house built of the same stone as Dora's cottage. Its welcoming facade reassured Mairi and gave her hope. Cherry, apple and plum blossoms, daffodils, tulips and bluebells filled the fields and orchards with colour, releasing a heady blend of floral sweetness and the earthy scent of new growth.

She had forgotten how beautiful England was in late spring.

The Abbey's interior was airy. Mairi followed the Abbess down a bright corridor into a small cosy room filled with comfortable chairs, a well-stocked bookcase and vases of flowers freshly picked from the garden. A vast window dominated one wall, presenting a panoramic view of the enclosed garden where nuns and residents, referred to as 'guests', worked together on a variety of tasks.

The walled garden was central to the Abbey's healing philosophy of fresh air, manual labour, a balanced diet, order and companionship. Most of the thirty-five 'guests' were ex-soldiers who had been referred to the Abbey by psychiatric specialists interested in rehabilitation. All were casualties of war, suffering from trauma and injury.

"I thought you would enjoy watching Alex work in the walled garden before he clocks off for the day," the Abbess said, beckoning Mairi to the large window where she could look out over a patchwork of vegetables, fruit and flowers.

The Abbess explained that the centre of the garden was divided into four rotational plots. Each plot was planted with different vegetables; root, legumes, brassicas and potatoes. Rotation helped reduce a build-up of crop-specific pests and diseases and conserved nutrients in the soil.

Mairi wasn't interested in vegetables. Her only interest was Alexander; he was all that mattered. As the Abbess continued her lecture on horticulture, Mairi scanned the men working along the rows of produce to see if she could spot anyone bearing a likeness to the boy in the photo on Dora's mantlepiece. She looked everywhere in the hope of seeing someone who would make her heart miss a beat. Then she saw him! A small, stocky lad loading boxes onto a wheelbarrow. Mairi stared and stared. He was definitely her son, totally absorbed in what he was doing, serious but with a look of contentment.

The Abbess stopped talking about horticulture after it became clear Mairi was no longer listening.

"I see you've found him!" she said, focusing on the young man with the wheelbarrow. "He'll join us as soon as he's finished for the day. Say in about twenty minutes."

Mairi watched Alexander's every move, his facial expressions and body language. She was determined to condense twenty-two years into a few precious moments. Dora had been right when she said how much he loved gardening. Pleasure was written all over his face. While he packed up for the day and changed out of his work clothes, the Abbess arranged for Mairi to meet his new mentor, the lady who would act as his guardian during his time at Malvingborough.

"She has only just joined the Abbey but the two of them have already established a strong bond of trust. I hope, when you meet her, you will be reassured that Alexander is well cared for and a much-loved member of our community."

She looked at her watch. It was a quarter past three.

"She'll be here any minute."

Mairi stood with her back to the door when Alexander's mentor walked in.

"I hope I'm not too early," said a voice she instantly recognised.

"Katherine?" she cried, instinctively reverting to Gaelic, "It can't be! I knew you had joined the Abbey but had no idea you were mentoring guests!"

The two women looked at each other in disbelief, unsure how to react. It was Katherine who made the first move, giving her aunt a warm hug of acceptance. Mairi responded by holding Katherine's lovely face in her hands and kissing her forehead. She was still painfully thin, worn down by the mental trauma of her unhappy stay in the Summerdale Mental Hospital. The result of her breakdown after the deaths of Angus and Hugh had been catastrophic. The doctors in the asylum had put pressure on her to give Tavish up for adoption, pointing out that she would never cope alone and was unworthy to be a mother. It was in the Summerdale Hospital that she had finally signed Tavish's adoption papers and handed him over to Mairi and Johnny. Without their love, he would have disappeared into a bureaucratic labyrinth. An untraceable statistic cut off from his family roots and rich cultural heritage.

"What are you doing here?" Katherine asked, shrinking back in fear thinking something terrible had happened to her son. "Is Tavish all right? He's meant to be safely living on Kilbackie with you and Johnny."

The panic in her voice was raw.

"Tell me, Mairi!" she pleaded. "Is he all right? I don't think I could cope if anything happened to him."

Mairi assured her that Tavish was well and safe.

The Abbess looked on in amazement.

"Do you two already know each other?"

"It's a long story," Katherine said, quietly. "But Mairi is my aunt and I have no idea what she's doing here! Is there a chance we could have a few moments alone together in private?"

Dora and the Abbess discreetly exited the room leaving the two ladies to piece together the broken parts of their extraordinary lives.

There was nothing Mairi could do other than tell her niece the truth about the St Andrew's Night dance and Alexander's birth.

Katherine listened attentively without interrupting as her aunt struggled to find the words to explain her shame. It was clear from the start that she found it hard to share her past with her niece but she needn't have worried, Katherine's serene acceptance made the ordeal more bearable. When she had finally finished telling her story, Katherine walked over to her aunt and embraced her warmly, sending a wave of indescribable peace through her tense body.

"So, Alexander is my cousin," she said, her eyes dancing with joy.

"Yes! He's the son I share with David MacPhee."

"Ah!" Katherine replied, sympathetically. "A MacPhee! You don't need to tell me how complicated that relationship must have been with my father. Does he know about Alexander?"

"No, and he never will, not if I have my way. He has already said some very hurtful things probing into Tavish's past, trying to find out if he is his grandson. So far, he doesn't have any proof and I pray it will stay that way."

Holding Mairi's hands, Katherine said, "Keep Tavish safe for me. I want him to live his life free from the catastrophic effects of judgement. Too many lives have been scarred by ignorance and prejudice."

Mairi felt a pang of guilt, wondering what kind of mother she had become.

"You may find this difficult to believe," Katherine continued, "but your sweet, kind Alexander has transformed my life. Really, he has! Over the past few weeks, he has eased me, inch by inch, out of the dark abyss I fell into after losing Angus, Tavish and Sir Hugh. It's still early days but the memories of Summerdale Mental Hospital are gradually fading, although the experience has given me a greater empathy for those struggling to cope with physical and mental scars.

Although, technically, I am Alexander's mentor, there are times when he mentors me. Through his non-judgemental support, I am beginning to eat and sleep more. I have been told, although I can't see it, that I have put on a bit of weight. I love Alexander dearly and now I know he is my cousin, the bond will grow even stronger."

The irony wasn't lost on Mairi.

Her abandoned son had found his way to Malvingborough Abbey where he was being cared for by her niece, the one person who meant the world to her. He couldn't be with anyone more special.

The sound of footsteps resonated down the corridor.

Their time together was coming to an end.

"We have both made mistakes," Katherine said, speaking a little faster, "and we will have to live with the consequence of our actions, as will the two boys we brought into this world. Neither of them lives with his birth mother but somehow things have turned out better than we could ever have believed possible. I thank Sir Hugh for that."

The conversation was cut short by a knock on the door and in walked Dora and the Abbess with Alexander who stared shyly at Mairi.

The Abbess formally introduced his mother as Mrs Mitchell. The confident smiling young man she had seen loading a wheelbarrow in the walled garden had become an awkward, child-like man with nervous, shifting eyes.

He stared briefly in Mairi's direction before going over to Dora and hugging her.

"Remember what I told you about meeting someone for the first time."

He looked bemused.

"You shake their hand," she whispered encouragingly.

Mairi felt the formal touch of his white clammy hand and winced. Instead of a loving embrace, she was faced with a weak, floppy handshake that lacked the intimacy she had yearned for. Deep down she felt a strange aversion to the unusual young man standing in front of her. Although he was her own flesh and blood, the cold distance between them was something she hadn't expected after so many years' dreaming of a loving relationship. They were complete strangers. Mairi was forced to accept that she had lost her son the moment she had handed him over to St Joseph's House all that time ago.

"I'll leave you to get on with your visit," Katherine whispered, moving away from the group but before she had time to reach the door, Alexander ran over to her and flung his arms round her.

"I love you, Katherine," he said spontaneously.

CHAPTER 38

Mairi left the Abbey knowing she would never be fully reconciled with her son. The best she could hope for was a few hours of his company in the relaxed setting of Dora's cottage. Dora couldn't have been more friendly. She welcomed Mairi into her home with unexpected kindness and sat her down at a table laden with more food than was necessary.

"Derek will be here soon," she said, "and I did ask Katherine to join us but she was on duty and sent her apologies. How strange that the two of you already know each other but then I suppose it isn't surprising, seeing you're both from Scotland."

Dora's conclusion that Scotland was no bigger than a small village amused Mairi but she let the comment pass, preferring to focus on Alexander.

"Come and sit down next to Mrs Mitchell," Dora said, pulling out a chair for her son to sit on. "Perhaps you could tell her what you've been up to today. Did you help Dave in the walled garden?"

"Dave Simpson is the head gardener," she whispered to Mairi. "Such a nice man. As patient as a saint!"

Alexander appeared not to be listening. His eyes were fixed on a plate of egg, mayonnaise and cress sandwiches, cut into neat soldiers with their crusts trimmed. He wasn't happy.

"Don't like sandwiches!" he exclaimed, picking one up, sniffing it, then throwing it back onto the plate, wiping his eggy fingers on the tablecloth. "Yuk!"

"Nonsense, Alex! You've always liked sandwiches. You eat them for tea every time you come home."

It soon became clear that Alexander was in no mood to enjoy the food that had been so lovingly prepared. The problem wasn't the tea, he liked sandwiches and cake. It was more that he had been looking forward to scrambled egg on toast and nothing else would do. He stomped around the room shouting, "Don't like sandwiches. Don't like cake!"

Dora tried to appease him by explaining that the special tea was for a special visitor but he was having none of it.

"Don't like sandwiches. Don't like cake!" he repeated over and over again before adding, "I want scrambled egg!"

"You'll get nothing if you continue this nonsense," Dora said firmly. "Now sit down quietly and enjoy your tea."

Alex's high-pitched scream pierced the air like a little owl in the stillness of the night.

Mairi was horrified.

She had witnessed Tavish having a full-blown meltdown but never a grown man. To her horror, he threw himself on the floor, thrashing about like a drowning man, out of control. One of his legs caught Mairi's shin. She wanted to cry out in pain but for Dora's sake she bit her lip and said nothing.

Dora made no apology for Alexander's behaviour nor, seeing Mairi wince and rub her shin, did she enquire if she was hurt. Instead, she knelt beside her son's contorted body, massaging his back, shoulders and neck whilst reassuring him with soothing words. Mairi watched, in admiration, at the sympathetic way Dora dealt with her son.

"Would you like me to make scrambled egg on toast?" she asked, helping him back onto his feet.

He nodded with his head hung low.

"What are the magic words?"

"Yes, please," he said meekly.

"Wait here with Mrs Mitchell while I get your tea," she said, hoping a few minutes alone with Alexander would compensate for the disastrous start to the afternoon.

Mairi didn't know where to begin. She tried engaging with her son but he was in no mood to talk. Eventually she gave up and waited for Dora to return with his tea.

"How have you two got on?" she asked cheerfully but one look at Mairi told her things had not gone well.

Alexander took his food and started walking to the other end of the room.

"Stop where you are!" Dora said firmly. "Do I get a 'thank you' for cooking you a separate tea?"

Alexander blushed a deep shade of red.

"Thank you!" he said sheepishly.

"I should think so," Dora replied.

He walked over to the corner of the room and sat down facing the wall.

"Best let him cool off," she said to Mairi who was clearly annoyed with Alexander for ruining their reunion. She rubbed the spot on her shin where his flailing leg had kicked her.

"I'm so sorry about the outburst!" Dora said, embarrassed by the turn of events. "He isn't usually like this. Ask anyone who knows him."

Mairi had no intention of asking anyone. She had had enough. The long search to find Alexander hadn't turned out the way she had hoped, in fact the whole trip had been a disaster. The only highlight was seeing Katherine again.

"Sit down and have a drink. You look totally exhausted," Dora said, handing Mairi one of her special teacups, part of a set she had been given as a wedding present. Shafts of afternoon light illuminated the delicate flowers painted on the wafer-thin porcelain, a feature that usually produced a comment from guests but not from Mairi whose thoughts were elsewhere. Dora had known enough heartache in her life to recognise the pain on Mairi's face as she glowered at Alexander who was still sitting cross-legged in the corner of the room. Such rejection would be hard to bear for most people. It was particularly hard for Mairi who had waited so long and travelled so far to see her son.

"The man who brought Alexander down from Scotland," she asked, "are you still in touch with him? His name was David."

Dora looked blank. She didn't know anyone called David.

Mairi visibly crumpled - Dora was her last hope. She had no-one else to ask.

"We only ever dealt with Sir Hugh," she said with a hint of pride. "Did I ever tell you how he brought Alexander to us?"

Mairi shook her head.

"It was late one freezing November evening. Derek and I were reading by the fire when there was a knock at the door. Derek went to see who was there and, much to his surprise, he discovered Sir Hugh standing in the porch with a small bundle in one arm and a bouquet of flowers in the other.

"I've bought these for Dora," he said proudly, waving the bouquet in the air and folding back the corner of a blanket to reveal an adorable little boy.

"Flowers and a son!"

"I'll never forget the look of pride on his face when he handed Alexander over to me. He was clearly smitten with our little boy and true to his word, even though he is no longer with us, God Bless his soul, he has provided for him ever since."

Mairi was unsure what was meant by *'provided for him ever since'*.

Dora continued. Talking about Alexander was something she clearly enjoyed.

"After Sir Hugh died, we were contacted by Fergus Buchanan, a Trustee of something called the Applecross Trust that Sir Hugh had set up to look after Alexander and Tavish. I don't know what a trust does but I know the Applecross Trust supports Alexander by paying for things that might improve his quality of life, including his four days' working at Malvingborough Abbey. I've only met Mr Buchanan once but Derek speaks highly of him. He sends the Trust regular updates on Alex's progress which Mr Buchanan writes down in a book. I expect there is a similar book for Tavish."

Mairi had no idea. She left all Trust matters to Johnny but listening to Dora, she wished she had paid more attention to the meetings between Mr Buchanan and Johnny.

"The biggest bonus of the Trust, according to Mr Buchanan," Dora said, wishing to push home her point, "is that it will continue to support Alex even after we have died. The relief, knowing he will receive care for the rest of his life, is enormous."

Mairi had a fit of pique on hearing that Alexander and Tavish were beneficiaries of the same Trust. It didn't seem fair that the grown man who had flung himself on the floor because he wanted scrambled eggs for tea, was receiving the same support as Tavish who had only just started school.

"You don't seem very pleased," Dora said, surprised at Mairi's furrowed brow. "I thought you'd be relieved to know that Alexander will be well cared for even after we've gone."

"I am pleased," she replied wearily, "but it's been a long day and, to be honest, I'm slightly overwhelmed by everything I've seen and learned."

Alexander remained on the floor and Mairi had to accept that she would never enjoy a close bond with her son.

She had given up her right to be his mother twenty-two years ago. It was only by an extraordinary twist of fate that he had arrived back in Shottenden to be brought up by Dora and Katherine, two exceptional women whose selfless love had given him a quality of life she could never have managed.

Watching Alex with his back turned against her, Mairi wondered if she had ever been maternal or had just liked the idea of having a child. Her night with David in the shieling had been doomed from the start. Perhaps Downs Syndrome had been God's way of showing his disapproval. She hoped not.

"What are you thinking about?" Dora asked, with an understanding smile that radiated serenity.

"Nothing in particular. I was just watching the calm way you dealt with Alexander's tantrum and thinking I could never have loved him as much as you do. There's no doubt in my mind that he's where he belongs, with the parents he deserves. He's a very lucky young man."

A sudden wave of nausea overcame Mairi. The journey south, the unfamiliar food, the anxiety and tension, had finally caught up with her.

"I think I'm going to be sick!" she spluttered getting up from the table and heading to the sink. Quick as lightning, Dora was by her side, supporting her as she threw up all over the dirty dishes. Alex remained where he was, absorbed in his own little world, unaware of anything happening around him.

"Oh God! I'm so sorry. I should never have come. It's all been a huge mistake."

"Nonsense!" Dora said, massaging her back. "You've been through a lot today. It can't have been easy finally meeting Alex only to discover him behaving like a spoiled brat. You're probably secretly glad you gave him up for adoption! I wouldn't blame you thinking that way. If I'd been in your shoes, I might have felt the same."

Mairi stuck her head under the tap to wash the bile out of her mouth.

"I'm so tired," she said. "For twenty-two years, I've carried the shame of Alexander's birth, wondering what had happened to him. My obsession with finding him has alienated me from my husband and my son. They don't understand how debilitating guilt is. Who can blame them? I've become impossible to live with.

"Do you know what really saddens me?"

Dora shook her head.

"After all the pain of searching, I find that Alexander neither loves nor needs me."

Dora took Mairi by the arm and gently guided her back to the table.

"What you need is a good night's sleep. Things always seem different after a rest. When you return home, concentrate on your family and leave Alexander where he belongs - with me and Derek.

The celebratory tea had not turned out the way Dora had planned. The food lay untouched on the table, Alexander refused to join in, Mairi had completely lost her appetite and Dora wished she had listened to her husband who told her to keep things simple.

"Have a sandwich to line your stomach," she said. "Then try and persuade Alex to join us for a game of Ludo. It's one of his favourites."

Mairi struggled to swallow the thinly cut ham sandwich Dora had placed on her plate. The bread turned pasty in her mouth. It stuck to her tongue and was difficult to swallow. Eventually, after many sips of tea, she finally managed to wash it down and rid herself of the taste of bile. She had no appetite for any more food. The sight of such a huge spread made her queasy.

Alone in the corner of the room, Alex cut a lonely figure. Mairi tried talking to him, suggesting he joined her and Dora for a game of Ludo but he made no effort to respond.

She racked her brains trying to remember how Rhona dealt with Tavish when he was in a bad mood. As far as she could remember, she lowered herself down to his level in an attempt to calm his tantrums and avoid unnecessary conflict. It usually worked so there was no reason why it shouldn't work with her other son. Mairi picked up the Ludo board and settled down on the floor next to Alexander.

"What colour do you want to be?"

"Blue!" came the instant reply.

From that moment, Alex became a totally different person - animated and charming. Very slowly during the game he drew closer to Mairi and nestled his head affectionately against her cardigan. It was the sign of acceptance she had hoped for.

"Would you like to play another game on the table where it's more comfortable?" she asked, hoping his good humour would last. He looked into his birth mother's eyes and smiled. It was the same smile she had seen in David all those years ago. For the briefest of moments, with David present in Alex's beaming face, she experienced the love of a family unit that could never be.

"Yes please," he said, giving her his hand. This time his grip was firm, his hand warm. She pulled him up off the ground and they walked hand in hand to join Dora.

CHAPTER 39

"How did you get on?" Daisy asked, folding a slice of white bread and butter in half and washing down each mouthful with a slurp of hot sweet tea. Mairi looked at the chipped crockery and wondered how long the rancid yellow butter had been left out of the fridge.

"Tea, coffee and sugar are all there," Daisy said, pointing to three enamel tins half-hidden among the clutter on the shelf. The kitchen was chaotic. Stacks of newspaper tied up with string stood on the lino floor next to the cat bowl. Odd pieces of crockery, mixing bowls, packets and dishes perched precariously on the narrow shelf that ran the full length of the kitchen wall. The stained sink was full of dirty plates and mugs. No-one had bothered to wash up for a very long time. To make matters worse, there was a lingering smell of Tom cat rising from an overused litter tray by the door.

"Help yourself to a drink," Daisy shouted from halfway up the stairs. "There're a few things to eat in the larder - eggs, vegetables, bread, cheese. Nothing special but enough to keep you going this evening."

Mairi wasn't hungry. She still felt queasy after throwing up at Dora's.

The smell of urine and cat faeces made her nauseous. It was difficult to believe that the elegant woman who had stepped effortlessly into Kilbackie House ten days ago could live in such a mess. It didn't make sense. The kitchen windows were so dirty Mairi could barely see the overgrown back garden, if it could be called a garden. Half-hidden among the weeds lay an abandoned bicycle, an old ironing board and the wheels of a broken pushchair. It was a depressing sight. The only colour among the weeds and rust was a vivid blue flowering Ceanothus.

Mairi turned towards the approaching footsteps to see Daisy standing in the doorway, looking much younger than forty-seven. Slim-legged and slim-waisted she wore an elegant blue cocktail dress matched with an exquisite sapphire necklace that lay just above her cleavage. She shone like a diamond but her eyes were cold.

"I'm off," she said with little grace. "See you when I get back. Don't wait up. I'll probably be late."

There was no apology for abandoning her friend on the first evening of her visit. No indication of where she was going. With a flirtatious flick of hair, she flounced out of the house, leaving behind a waft of her familiar scent.

Mairi looked at her watch. Seven thirty. It was too late to change her ticket and catch the later train to Edinburgh. Whether she liked it or not, she was staying the night in Daisy's lonely house with only the lingering smell of cat for company. The sterile, sparsely-furnished lounge was as unappealing as the rest of the house. Its Highland colour scheme of greens and browns were painfully unappealing. Mairi failed to understand how someone as immaculately dressed as Daisy could live in such a drab and soulless environment.

The jangling sound of a key turning in the lock made her jump. Much to her surprise the front door was opened by an exhausted Bill who hobbled down the corridor towards the kitchen. Mairi had totally forgotten Daisy's husband. She rarely spoke about him and when she did, it was never flattering.

He was of medium height, about fifty, grossly overweight with closely cropped hair and a puffy face. He reeked of tobacco, stale beer and sweat.

"I suppose she's out again," he muttered, lighting the gas ring. Mairi poked her head round the doorway and watched him pace impatiently up and down while he waited for the kettle to boil. He must have known she was in the house because he kept talking.

"I bet that bloody woman didn't tell you where she was going! She's always out, never here. Seems to forget she has a husband who has needs of his own."

He fumbled for a mug, shoved a tea bag inside and filled it with boiling water, adding three heaped teaspoons of sugar. Mairi noticed his hand was trembling as he carried the hot tea towards the lounge. She backed away from the door as the great hulk of a man slumped on the sofa, wheezing from the effort of walking a few yards.

He was in a bad way.

"I've no idea where she goes half the time. She didn't tell you, did she?"

Mairi shook her head.

He carried on the conversation without acknowledging Mairi's presence.

"She seems to be treating you as badly as she treats me. Don't be fooled by her smart clothes and confident looks. Underneath all that makeup and expensive clothing lies a scheming bitch."

He was in no mood to tone down his language.

"She makes me so bloody angry! You must have noticed the terrible state of the house and garden when you first walked in. We used to have a lovely home with good friends who occasionally came round for supper but all that ended when Daisy lost interest in housework, saying she was too busy. Bull!! She finds plenty of time to get dolled up, apply makeup and buy expensive perfume but she won't lift a finger to clean."

He took a sip of tea.

"All those hours I slogged to pay off the mortgage. And for what?" he continued, thumbing through a copy of the Radio Times to see what was on.

"God knows where she spends her evenings. I tried following her once but she must have spotted me because I ended up on a wild goose chase, running up and down side streets and alleys I never knew existed. In the end I ran out of breath and lost her. I'm still none the wiser."

He switched on the Home Service and settled down to a documentary on the fight against polio.

"I had a work mate once who caught polio," he explained. "He had a terrible time - six weeks in total isolation, unable to move, followed by a further year in hospital. Throughout the whole ordeal he only saw his wife twice. When, finally, he returned home, he had to wear callipers on his legs and a brace on his back. What kind of a life is that? Poor bastard!"

Mairi remained cowered in the doorway, determined not to engage with the loathsome man, unless really necessary.

"Bloody selfish woman!" he continued, lighting a cigarette and filling the room with smoke. Mairi wasn't sure if he was referring to her or Daisy but it made no difference. From the way he spoke, it was clear he had little regard for women.

The nicotine haze made her cough. If she hadn't had such a difficult day, she might have asked him not to smoke but she let the matter go. At least it masked the obnoxious smell of cats.

Bill was dug in for the evening and wasn't going anywhere.

"God, polio is depressing!" he said, shuffling to get comfortable. Several buttons on his shirt popped open, revealing a large roll of stomach fat that spilled onto his lap. It was not a pretty sight. Once the programme was over, he asked Mairi to turn the volume down so they could talk. Hesitantly, she did as she was told, fearing what he might say if she refused.

"Tell me what you get up to in Scotland." he sniggered, "Nothing naughty, I hope."

Mairi chose to sit as far away from Bill as was physically possible. She pressed her legs tightly together, wary of the way he was ogling her.

"Daisy said you live on a farm. Is that true?"

"Yes!" she replied, keeping her voice low to avoid attracting more unnecessary attention.

"You'll have to speak up. I can't hear you!"

She raised her voice a fraction and described their remote way of life and Johnny's work on the farm. When she had finished, Bill gave her his full attention. He seemed genuinely interested in the work Johnny was doing on Kilbackie. Perhaps she had judged him too harshly. She had no idea if his inappropriate humour was malicious or harmless banter.

"God your accent's sexy!" he exclaimed, taking her completely by surprise. "Come and sit next to old Bill and tell him things you wouldn't want Daisy to hear. Keep talking 'cos your accent really turns me on. I've waited a long time to feel this way!

"Let's indulge in a bit of hanky-panky and see how things develop from there."

"How dare you!" Mairi exclaimed. "You disgust me! One more comment like that and I'll leave! Do you hear?"

He nodded, pretending to be contrite.

"Your place in Scotland sounds just Daisy's cup of tea. No wonder she came back looking so damn well. All that exercise and fresh air. Doubtless she managed to find someone to flirt with. I hope you locked your husband away and hid the key!"

"I meant what I said," Mairi warned.

Bill laughed.

"If you could see your face! Don't worry, Daisy never leaves me for long. Once the novelty of the chase wears off, she always comes back to her Bill. Her problem is she gets bored and I'm in no state to offer her the excitement she craves.

LUCY MONTGOMERY

"I've tried often enough, if you know what I mean," he winked. "But she always refuses me.

"You wouldn't mind giving an old man a bit of pleasure, would you?" he said with a glint in his piggy eyes.

Horrified and slightly afraid, Mairi glanced down at her watch. Seven forty-five.

As long as Daisy's husband stayed seated, Mairi was prepared to sit out the next three hours listening to the wireless and flicking through Daisy's magazines.

"Would you like something to eat?" she asked, conscious that preparing supper would kill time and keep her occupied.

"Are you going down the chippy?"

"No!" Mairi replied. "There are eggs and vegetables in the larder. I could rustle up an omelette."

Bill loathed eggs. The thought of a stranger making him an omelette with a few leftover vegetables turned his stomach. He was looking forward to a healthy portion of cod and chips from 'Jimmy's Fries'.

"You can eat what you like," he said, sounding feeble. "But I want a healthy portion of fish and chips. Be a dear and get me some. I'm knackered."

The word 'dear' raised Mairi's hackles.

She wasn't his 'dear' nor would she ever be but for the sake of peace, she decided to get the fish and chips he craved, although they were the last thing his bloated body needed.

She had half a mind to refuse to go until he had cleaned out the cat litter or done something useful around the house but it wasn't her role to criticise her host.

"Don't forget the salt and vinegar!" he cried as she was halfway down the hallway.

Out on the tree-lined street, Mairi took in long deep breaths to calm her nerves. She had never come across anyone as repugnant as Bill before. His smutty jokes and leering looks had repulsed her. She was used to her brother's bullying but this was something on a different level and it scared her. If only Daisy hadn't left her alone with him.

Her fear turned to fury.

Daisy knew exactly what Bill was like. She had spoken often enough of his revolting habits and lazy ways, so why did she choose to go out on the one evening Mairi was staying as her guest?

As she walked down the road, thinking about Daisy, she passed three giggling girls skipping over a long piece of rope, their cotton dresses floating up and down like floral parachutes. A few older boys had gathered in the middle of the road to play football, using their jumpers as goal posts.

Children's voices echoed across the street, their infectious laughter mingling with the pink blossom of the flowering cherries. Kilbackie House never echoed to the sound of children's laughter. It had become too serious, too quiet, devoid of humour, a mirror image of her childhood in the Manse.

Mairi felt sorry for Tavish who had had very little to laugh about in his short life.

She promised she would become more relaxed, more focussed on her son, more light-hearted. All was possible now she knew Alexander was safe.

By the time she reached 'Jimmy's', the line had stretched half way down the street. Right at the end of the queue stood an elderly man holding onto a child no older than five. Mairi took her place behind them.

"You all right, Colin?" he asked, drawing the lad closer to him. The child nodded.

"Nana won't be pleased if I keep you up too late. I promised her we'd be home before your bedtime. You know how worried she gets when you're out of her sight."

He checked his watch.

"We've still got time," he whispered, ruffling the boy's hair.

The child gazed up at his grandfather, nestling his head against the old man's waist. There was an intimacy between the two that touched Mairi.

'Jimmy's Fries' was located in Trinity Street, a typical row of Victorian two-up two-downs, all packed tightly together. The functional, industrial housing scheme made Mairi long for Kilbackie's wide-open space, its hills and islands.

As the queue grew shorter, the air turned greasier. Colin's grandfather shuffled forward, struggling to breathe through his diseased lungs. After several attempts, he managed to cough up a mass of green mucus and spit it out into the gutter.

He glanced down at his grandson.

"Sorry about that, Colin. My lungs aren't what they used to be. The doctor says it's the mines but nothing he says can help me now."

The child rewarded the apology with a tender reassuring smile.

The old man rolled a cigarette to calm his nerves.

"Blow rings!" Colin pleaded, tugging at his grandfather's arm. "Please, Pops! Blow lots of rings."

Much to his amusement, the elderly miner obliged by taking in a large amount of smoke then releasing it in short bursts, producing perfect rings that floated away into the evening sky.

Inside 'Jimmy's', two red-cheeked women with greasy hair were lowering battered fish and chips into large vats of boiling fat. Each generous portion was wrapped in newspaper. Onion rings, mushy peas and pickled onions were extras. Salt, pepper, vinegar and ketchup were available on the Formica counter.

Mairi picked up her two bundles and retraced her footsteps, hoping to prolong the journey as long as possible yet deep down, she knew Bill would not take kindly to cold cod and chips.

Inside the hall, the unbearable smell of Tom cat combined with fish, fat and vinegar made her gag. Bill was sitting on the sofa exactly where she had left him, holding a beer in his podgy hand, his eyes fixed on the door.

The wireless had been turned up to a level that made conversation impossible. The volume hurt her ears but she didn't dare turn it down.

"You took your time," he shouted, ungratefully, not bothering to make eye contact. "I hope the chips aren't cold. Can't stand cold chips."

Grease started to seep through the newspaper, drawing Mairi's attention to an article about a young mother who had been hospitalised with a broken jaw and eye socket after years of domestic abuse. It seemed unfair that the woman's trauma was being used to attract readers. No-one really cared. Her agony would soon be forgotten. One battered woman today, another tomorrow. She wondered what her news headline would be: "Callous mother abandons tragic son."

The thought horrified her.

"I'll fetch a plate," she said nervously but Bill had no time for refinement. He was hungry.

"Don't bother with all that fancy stuff. Newspaper will do."

Before handing over the fish and chips, Mairi asked Bill to settle up.

"Two shillings," she announced with an authority that surprised her.

"Don't be so bloody petty! Give me my fish and chips and be quiet!"

Mairi stood her ground.

"Two shillings!" she mouthed.

The standoff lasted a few minutes before Bill reluctantly produced a shilling, sixpence, a thruppenny bit and three pennies from a handful of loose change.

"Take your money, you grasping cow!" he snarled, thrusting the coins in her hand. "You'll pay for this. I'll make sure of it."

Mairi failed to pick up the warning signs.

Everything happened so quickly.

A sudden urge of unexpected excitement took control of Bill. After years of rejection and ridicule, he finally felt aroused and decided to act. It was a case of now or never. He grabbed Mairi by the wrist and hauled her onto the sofa beside him. She lashed out in protest but lost her balance and fell across Bill's lap, knocking his fish and chips onto the floor.

"Now look what you've done!" he screamed. "You've ruined my supper!"

He pinned her down with his fat arms leaving her legs kicking aimlessly in the air. Despite his soft flabby stomach, Bill was remarkably strong, making it impossible for Mairi to escape. She shouted at him to let her go but he was enjoying himself too much. Very slowly he lowered his face and brushed his lips against her mouth, rubbing his nose gently against hers as a teaser. He was in no hurry. He shuffled on the sofa to get more comfortable, all the while keeping Mairi pinned down. Very slowly he undid the pearl buttons on her blouse and caressed her warm breasts, letting out a low ecstatic moan of unbridled pleasure. Mairi froze.

Emboldened by her fear, Bill rubbed his face against her cheeks, her lips, her hair. He reeked of tobacco and a poor diet, an odour she would never forget. It invaded her nose, infecting her like a virus. When she tried to scream, Bill clamped his free hand over her mouth. His blubbery bulk trapped her against the back of the sofa. Aroused by a feeling of predatory power, he slipped a hand beneath the waistband of her skirt and quivered.

Every cell in Mairi's body fought against the intrusion.

In the corner of the room, the radio continued to play music so loudly, she knew her cries would never be heard. Even if someone did come to her rescue, she would rather die than have a stranger witness the assault.

Bill pushed Mairi further against the back cushions to stop himself falling onto the floor. Once he had secured himself on the narrow cushions, he started to remove Mairi's shirt.

"For God's sake, keep still," he cursed with frustration.

"You won't get away with this," she hissed with cold accusing eyes. "Let me go!"

But Bill had no intention of releasing his victim. He had become addicted to the warmth of her body and like all addicts, he was driven mad with the desire to satisfy his need. He wanted Mairi more than anything else in the world.

"Let me go!" she screamed, struggling to sit up. "Wait till I tell Daisy. You won't get away with this!"

For a moment, Bill hesitated. The thought of Daisy's reaction unnerved him but it was too late, he had already reached the point of no return. Mairi's fear and the feel of her naked flesh against his chest quite literally took his breath away.

His heart rate increased rapidly. He started to pant. Then quite suddenly he felt a sharp pain squeeze his chest so hard, he could hardly breathe.

"Oh God!" he thought. "Please, dear God! Not a heart attack now I'm so close." Beads of perspiration gathered on his forehead before trickling down his face, over his eyes and into his mouth. He ran his tongue over his lips to catch each salty droplet while his chest continued to pound like a bass drum. Powerful beats. Boom! Boom! Boom!

Within an instant, Bill's all-absorbing quest for pleasure turned to terror. He dropped his guard briefly to concentrate on his health. In that moment of hesitation, Mairi managed to wiggle an arm free and fling it amorously round his neck, drawing his face towards her.

"Kiss me," she panted with an urgency that distracted the preposterous man from worrying about his heart. He basked in the glory of being desired, of feeling alive, purposeful, in command. It all felt so good. So very good!

Mairi knew she was playing a dangerous game, but it was vital to make him believe she craved him so she could draw him into her trap. Much as she hoped and dreaded, Bill responded to her advances with renewed vigour, exploring her mouth with his tongue, spreading salt and vinegar onto her saliva, making her retch. Extraordinary survival instincts kicked in as she shut her eyes, held her breath and bit hard into his lower lip.

She never heard the horrific scream that tore through the small terraced house as Bill put his hands up to his torn lip. Her sensory functions had shut down during the assault. Now all she could think of was going home to the peace and safety of Kilbackie. She eased herself free, buttoned up her shirt, straightened her clothing and walked into the kitchen where she grabbed a knife and returned to her abuser, lying slumped on the couch, clutching his mouth. Blood poured onto a cushion from the gash in his lip.

"Bitch!" he spluttered, spitting blood. "You bloody bitch! Wait 'til I get my hands on you!"

But Mairi was beyond caring. She had no wish to spend another second in the company of the man who had just assaulted her.

For ten long minutes, he had played out his warped fantasy with supreme confidence. Now he lay crumpled on the sofa, a snivelling wretch, crying out in pain.

"I'm going upstairs!" she said, waving the knife in the air. "If you dare lay a finger on me again, I'll cut your tongue out. Do you hear?"

Mairi's unexpected fightback had deflated his ego, left him deeply ashamed and utterly humiliated. Struggling to fight back the tears of self-pity, he gave a weak nod.

CHAPTER 40

"Did you sleep well?" Daisy asked with no sense of irony. Mairi nodded, too tired for the truth.

"What can I get you? Eggs, bacon, cereal, toast? There's a pot of tea already on the table."

Mairi asked for a couple of slices of toast and sat down at the small kitchen table to nurse her cup of tea, relieved that the cat litter had finally been taken outside, although the feline smell still lingered. She was beyond talking and Daisy looked drawn and troubled.

"What happened last night?" she asked with surprising concern.

"What do you mean, 'what happened?'" Mairi replied, abruptly. "Nothing!"

"So how come there's blood on the sofa, a sheet of newspaper full of fish and chips on the floor and a man with a bleeding lip out cold in the sitting room!"

Mairi kept her head bowed and took another sip of tea.

Daisy gently shook her arm.

"Tell me what happened?"

"Why?" Mairi replied, trying to keep herself together. "To make you feel better? Last night you abandoned me, knowing full well what sort of man Bill was. How could you? I might have been a rotten hostess when you stayed with us on Kilbackie but I never put you in danger. Was last night your way of paying me back? If so, I paid a heavy price!"

A few tears slipped down her cheeks but she refused to cry.

"What did he do?" Daisy asked, trying to keep her voice calm. "Did he take advantage of you, the bastard? Wait 'til I get my hands on him. He'll wish he'd never been born."

Mairi put her hands to her ears, not wanting to get drawn into a domestic dispute.

"Please, Daisy, leave it. What's done is done! All I want to do now is go home to Johnny and Tavish."

But Daisy hadn't finished. She needed to know the truth behind the harrowing pain in Mairi's eyes, no matter how uncomfortable that truth might be. Leaving Mairi alone with Bill had been a deliberate, cruel and vindictive act of vengeance for the way Mairi had treated her on Skye. She wanted Mairi to realise how lucky she was living with Johnny in such a beautiful house and glorious surroundings. She hadn't thought for a moment it would turn out the way it had.

"Tell me the truth, Mairi," she said with genuine contrition. "Did Bill hurt you? I mean really hurt you." The question had been haunting her ever since she saw the chaos in the sitting room. "I need to know. I promise I will stay calm and not go ballistic."

Mairi looked at her friend and shook her head.

"No," she said so quietly Daisy had to concentrate hard to hear what she was saying. "He didn't hurt me but he took advantage of me. If I hadn't bitten him, he would have gone the whole way."

Daisy shook her head in utter disbelief.

"I'm so sorry. I should never have left you alone last night!"

"No, you shouldn't," Mairi whispered, too tired to raise her voice.

"I suppose Bill told you a lot of nonsense about me being too grand to clean the house, that we used to have friends until I lost interest in seeing them. He probably delighted in telling you that I work as an escort and disappear at night all dolled up without saying where I am going. That I neglect him etcetera etcetera."

Mairi nodded.

Daisy took her hands in hers.

"I thought so. Some of it's true, Mairi, but most of it isn't. I'll explain everything later but first I need to look after you.

"Can you trust me?" she asked, keeping hold of her hands.

The softness of Daisy's voice, combined with a genuine concern for Mairi's welfare, ended Mairi's silence.

She finally allowed herself to let go, unleashing an unstoppable deluge of tears.

"Finish your toast," Daisy said, passing her a hanky, "then let's get out of this awful house."

The two ladies walked past *Jimmy's Fries'*, took a left turn which led to the huge entrance gates of Fitzroy Park.

"I thought you could do with some fresh air and green space after spending so much time cooped up in my smoky house," Daisy said.

"And just in case you are wondering why our kitchen

smells of cat, I can explain. Bill loves cats, or at least he loves the idea of owning a cat. I can't stand them. After a lot of arguments, I finally agreed he could have a cat as long as he fed it and regularly emptied the litter tray. That was my first mistake. From the moment the cat entered our house, Bill has refused to feed it or clean up after it. I don't think he ever really wanted a cat. It was all a power game to get back at me for leaving him in the evenings but I couldn't let the poor creature starve. I feed him but I refuse to empty the cat litter which has now become a stinking pile of 'you know what!'

"What do you think I should do?"

Mairi couldn't help. Her thoughts were focussed on breathing in the restorative air that blew through the majestic ash, elm and beech trees whose green shoots had already started to unfurl into fresh leaves. Hardy plants were slowly emerging through the well mulched soil of the herbaceous borders, thousands of blooming daffodils and tulips added much needed colour to the uncut grass.

"Do you mind if I sit beside you?" Daisy asked, aware that Mairi might prefer to be alone. Mairi patted the space next to her, her mind lost in the song of a chaffinch perched high in the branches above. It reminded her of Kilbackie where the same infectious melody marked the end of the long Hebridean winter.

"Remember what I said, I'm on your side. Trust me!"

They left the park and proceeded to Trinity Close, stopping outside No. 57, a modest, well cared for terraced house.

"This is where William and Dorothy live."

She knocked on the door. It was opened by a pretty woman with thick dark shoulder-length hair, pale skin and mischievous brown eyes.

"Daisy!" she cried with obvious delight, flinging her arms around her mother-in-law. "What brings you here at this time? Come on in. William is out at the moment but I'm expecting him back soon. Gosh! It's lovely to see you."

"Dorothy, this is my friend Mairi, you know, the one I've been staying with on Skye."

Dorothy took Mairi's hand in hers and gave her a warm embrace.

"Any friend of Daisy's is welcome here! Let me take your coats."

"And this," Daisy added, patting Dorothy's neat bump, "is my soon-to-be grandchild."

The affectionate bond between the two ladies took Mairi by surprise. She had never met anyone as fun as Dorothy before. Her dress sense and home reflected her out-going personality. Everything about her was modern and bright, a total contrast to the solemn, dull tones of Kilbackie.

"You'll stay for a cuppa, won't you? I don't know what it is about being pregnant but I'm always thirsty!

"Why don't you two go into the garden while I get things ready!"

"Can I do anything to help?" Daisy asked.

"No, I'm fine. Honestly, I am."

Daisy led Mairi onto the lawn and drew up a couple of folding chairs.

"I don't know where to start," she said. "It's all so complicated but what isn't these days?"

"I suppose I should start with William's return from Burma. Bill struggled to accept that the fit, healthy young man he waved off to war in 1941 had returned, four years later, a nervous, haunted skeleton. He couldn't accept that his child was mentally ill and needed specialist psychiatric help. It took immense courage to admit that his beloved William had volunteered to be a patient at Malvingborough Abbey.

"Bill's hope for the future ended the day William left for Malvingborough."

"Tea's ready!" Dorothy cried from the French windows.

"Can we take it out here?" Daisy said. "I'm filling Mairi in on my life history!"

"No problem! Stay there and I'll bring it out."

"Dorothy's the best thing that's happened to me." Daisy said with pride. "I could never have coped without her support. She knows everything."

"Where was I? Malvingborough...ah yes, Malvingborough Abbey.

"The Abbey staff saved William's life. They understood his demons, encouraged him to talk about his war experience and put him on a programme of healthy eating and physical hard work. At first, I thought the whole thing was a waste of time but little by little he began to get better.

"During William's time at the Abbey the nuns never lost faith in his rehabilitation. I'm sure there were times when they wanted to give up on him but they persevered, patiently encouraging him to take the first steps towards a full recovery.

"Their serenity was humbling. The spiritual peace of the Abbey made me realise that my life was a mess. Bill was still blaming me and everyone else for his son's condition. Nothing was right, nothing was fair, nothing was his fault. He turned bitter, drinking and eating for comfort. I know I should have tried to help him more but my focus was on William who was making progress. Hope is easier to support than despair.

"Once William was home, I contacted the Abbess to see if I could volunteer at the Abbey. She wrote back saying nothing came to mind but she would let me know if anything turned up.

"A year ago, she wrote to say that the Abbey had formed a charity to help unmarried mothers. Would I be interested in becoming a Trustee? Naturally I leapt at the chance to do something positive with my life.

"Philomena's, the home for unmarried mothers, isn't very far from here. Most of the babies are given up for adoption but a few remain with their mothers. I volunteer three evenings a week to do the books, which I love. It isn't all work. I find time to get to know the mothers, listen to their stories and answer their many questions.

"Bill knows nothing about Philomena's and for a good reason. He vehemently disapproves of unmarried mothers. I'm afraid, if he knew there was a place nearby where they were housed, he could do something really stupid especially if he knew I worked there."

Daisy poured out the tea and offered Mairi a chocolate biscuit.

"Why, if you are volunteering at Philomena's, do you dress to kill and wear makeup?" Mairi asked, engrossed by Daisy's story.

"It's difficult for you to understand, living in a beautiful house with daily help, a husband who adores you and a healthy son. I have none of these."

She corrected herself.

"Or at least I didn't, but thanks to Dorothy and the Abbey, I now have a healthy son.

"The atmosphere at home is awful. Bill and I don't talk. No-one visits us anymore, the house reeks of stale beer and tobacco, not to mention the cat! It's a tip! I know I should clean and freshen the place up but what for? The few friends we have still wouldn't visit, Bill would still spend his evenings over-indulging and we still wouldn't have anything to talk about.

"There has to be more to life than sitting on a sofa inhaling smoke in silence! When I look at Katherine, I see a beautiful woman inside and out and I want to be like her. You're probably thinking I have a long way to go and you'd be right but helping at Philomena's is a start and I love it."

Mairi sat mesmerised. She had no idea Daisy and Katherine were in touch and didn't know what to make of Daisy's desire to change.

"I can see from your look that you don't believe me," Daisy said. "You asked me why I dress up to visit the home. I didn't give you the real reason because it sounds rather pathetic, even sad. I dress up to feel good about myself. Living with Bill saps my confidence. He draws me into his shabby world of lazy despair, depriving me of hope and purpose. When I wear flattering, fashionable clothes, I am transformed into an achiever, a woman of substance, someone who can change the world and attract attention. I'm know it's all an act, but who cares, as long as it works.

"On my way to Philomena's, I drop in to see William and Dorothy who are, bless them, a breath of fresh air. They let me use their spare room to change into casual clothes and remove all traces of makeup!

"I love the feel, cut and style of expensive clothing. It's worth paying the extra to feel emboldened and I'm lucky enough to earn a good salary but the time will come when I'll have the confidence to dress down and reduce the amount of make-up I wear but I'm not there yet!

"Do you think me very shallow?"

CHAPTER 41

The phone rang.

"Rosvaig 914."

"Good morning!" came a familiar clear voice on the other end. "I'm sorry to ring so early but I wanted to know how the cattle are settling down. Any problems with the bull?"

"No! Everything is fine," Johnny replied.

The two-year-old bull had arrived from Dingwall the previous morning. He was a massive beast with heavy shoulders, strong legs and a straight back. Willie checked him over thoroughly. As far as he could tell, Dynamite was healthy and should have no problem siring sturdy calves.

"That's good," he repeated. "Don't forget, if you have any problems, I'm here to help."

It was on the tip of Johnny's tongue to ask about David MacPhee but he held back, unwilling to talk about Mairi's private life behind her back. He respected her too much for that.

Mr Buchanan sensed the hesitation and delayed putting the phone down until he was sure Johnny had nothing else to say.

The long awkward pause that followed played on Johnny's mind. He had nothing to do with David MacPhee, yet he continued to haunt Mairi. The least he could do was find out what happened to him and pass the information on to his wife. At least she would then have closure.

"There is something you could do for me." Johnny said. "It's a rather random question but important to Mairi although I'd prefer it if she didn't know I was making enquiries. Could you find out if David Angus MacPhee, born 16th May 1906 is still alive and if not, when he died? Any information will do - change of name, war record, marriage certificate, contacts with the Merchant Navy. Anything. David disappeared while fishing off the Kilbackie coast in 1933. Some people believe he faked his own disappearance because his body was never found. Others believe he drowned and was washed out to sea. I still haven't made up my mind what to believe. The search party found his boat, the 'Effie Joan' drifting in the Minch two days after his disappearance but David was nowhere to be seen. He had simply vanished into thin air."

Mr Buchanan listened with interest.

"You probably know that David was or is Margaret's brother. I want to help her find out what happened to him. It's the least I can do for the family after everything Mairi and I have put them through."

"Leave it with me," Mr Buchanan said. "I'll make a few discreet enquiries and get back to you as soon as I have some news."

Johnny put down the receiver, relieved that he had summoned up the courage to mention David's name. Any snippet of information could only be positive. He returned to the dining room where Tavish was drawing circles in the porridge with his spoon, looking thoroughly wretched.

"Hurry up and finish your breakfast. It's time for school," he said, goading him into action.

"Who's David?" Tavish asked with the curiosity of an inquisitive six-year-old.

"Eat your porridge and don't ask questions," Johnny said, surprised that his conversation with Mr Buchanan had been overheard.

"I'm not hungry," Tavish replied, pushing away his bowl.

"I don't have time for silly games," Johnny said firmly. "You have a choice, so listen carefully. Either you finish your warm porridge now or have it cold for supper. It's up to you."

Tavish knew he would never win against his father. His mother was a pushover but not his father. Reluctantly he finished the unappetising porridge and waited to get down from the table.

"Daddy," he said, fiddling with the cuffs of his jumper. "Is David my real father? Is that why you want to find him?"

Johnny looked aghast! This was not what he was expecting.

"Of course he isn't! What put that idea into your head? David used to fish the waters around Kilbackie a long time ago, long before you were born. One sunny morning he went out in his boat and disappeared. No-one has seen him since."

Tavish thought hard before saying: "You'll never leave me, will you, Daddy?"

"Of course I won't! You're my son."

He was about to engulf the earnest little boy in a reassuring bear-hug when the puppy, bound into the room, yapping with excitement. The moment was lost. David was instantly forgotten in favour of Dora and Johnny was left wondering why his son wanted to know who his real father was. Perhaps he was reading too much into the six-year-old's question but in future he would have to choose his words with care.

At the end of the following day, Johnny was reading a magazine in his favourite chair. Tavish had finally fallen asleep, the puppy was quiet, the cows were content, their stomachs full of fresh spring grass and the bull was docile.

The silence was interrupted by the phone.

"Rosvaig 914."

"Good evening!" Mr Buchanan said with a hint of excitement. "I think I have found the information you wanted on David MacPhee. Do you have a pen handy? You may wish to write a few things down."

Johnny sat up straight in his chair and grabbed a pen and a piece of paper. He hadn't expected such a quick response.

"I'm ready! Go on!"

"David joined the steamship SS Hartlebury as a merchant seaman soon after its launch in January 1934. During the first two years of the war, the Hartlebury transported grain and steel from the United States to Britain. These long transatlantic voyages were extremely dangerous and vulnerable to U boat attacks. For extra security, merchant ships joined together to form convoys which were protected by British and Canadian Navies and Air Forces. In 1941 Hartlebury was transferred to the Arctic convoys. Do you know anything about them?"

"No," Johnny replied, truthfully. "Obviously I've heard about the appalling subzero conditions and unimaginable hardship endured by everyone on board but that's about all."

"The sailors aboard the Arctic convoy ships were some of the most courageous and resilient men of the war. They endured freezing temperatures, ice storms, cramped living conditions and constant attacks from German U boats, ships and aircraft.

"More than a hundred vessels and three thousand British seamen perished in their heroic attempt to deliver supplies to the Soviet Union via the Russian ports of Murmansk and Archangel.

"Nine percent of all the seamen who took part in this supply chain lost their lives, including, I'm sorry to say, David MacPhee. It was the highest casualty rate of any maritime campaign in the war.

"There is no record he ever married but a letter of condolence was sent to his next of kin living at the time on Kilbackie, Isle of Skye. It seems, from what Mairi has said, that his family never received it.

"I'm sorry to bring you bad news."

It took Johnny a few moments to take it all in.

David was dead.

CHAPTER 42

"Would you like to come to Philomena's with me this evening?" Daisy asked, not sure it was a good idea but Mairi could always say 'no'. Eye contact was still awkward between them but at least they were on speaking terms again.

"I've arranged for you to stay here with William and Dorothy as I promised you would never have to set foot in my house again. I could pick you up when I call round to change."

The relief on Mairi's face was instant.

"Can I decide at the last minute?"

"Of course you can," Daisy replied, hoping a positive experience might draw them closer together.

"I'd really like to come but a home for unmarried mothers brings back memories I'd rather forget - long corridors, disinfectant, cabbage, cries of abandoned children. No thanks. I think I'd rather stay here with Dorothy."

"I understand but if you decide to come, I don't think you will regret it."

In the end it was Dorothy who persuaded Mairi to give the visit a try. Daisy never discovered what was said but by the time she called round to change into casual clothes, Mairi was ready and waiting.

Philomena's Home for Young Unmarried Mothers was an ordinary brick townhouse. Nothing special to look at. No different from any other house on the road. It didn't stand out as institutional nor did it pretend to be anything other than a home.

Daisy pressed the buzzer and announced her arrival. The door was opened by a plain dishevelled young woman carrying a fractious baby in her arms.

"Hi, Daisy," she said with genuine pleasure. "Go on through. I'm trying to get this little bugger to sleep but he won't have any of it. I'm at my wit's end. If I don't get some sleep soon, I swear I'll go mad."

Mairi raised an eyebrow but followed Daisy into a communal sitting room where young mothers sat nursing mugs of hot tea or cradling their newborns.

"Come and meet Peggy," Daisy said. "She's good value. I'm sure you will have lots to talk about."

She introduced Peggy to Mairi, then disappeared into the back office to check the orders for the following week. Daisy visited Philomena's three times a week to check the accounts and order anything needed to run the charity as smoothly as possible.

Its income came from well-wishers and generous benefactors who felt the women needed unconditional, 'no questions asked' support. Their faith in the home inspired Daisy to keep a close eye on every penny so nothing was wasted. Her accounting skills and fastidious eye for detail soon made her irreplaceable.

Mairi, meanwhile, did her best to relax in the unfamiliar surroundings of the cosy, brightly decorated home where residents could sit and chat. Memories of St Joseph's long cold corridors, the sound of children sobbing in an atmosphere of fear, still haunted her. Gingerly, she pulled up a chair next to Peggy whose long red hair tumbled over her shoulders highlighting her rosy cheeks and cheerful smile. The two started talking. Awkwardly at first but it didn't take them long to discover their stories were identical! Lonely childhoods, autocratic fathers, distant mothers, ignorance, pregnancies, births, rejection.

"How old?" she asked gazing at the baby's perfect face.

"Eight weeks."

"Boy or girl?"

"A little girl called Rebecca."

"That's a lovely name. Can I hold her?"

Peggy placed the swaddled child in Mairi's arms and watched the maternal instincts kick into action. Within seconds Mairi had reverted to Gaelic, singing the same haunting lullaby she had sung to Alexander moments before she handed him over to the matron of St Joseph's House.

A sudden peel of laughter broke the tender moment.

"She didn't!?" a woman shrieked in disbelief. "That's awful. I never thought she had it in her!" The comment was followed by more howls of raucous laughter.

Mairi instinctively gathered the sleeping baby closer, shielding her from harm.

"Shhhh! No-one will harm you," she cooed in Gaelic. "Carry on sleeping!"

Aware that Peggy was looking at her, she added, this time in English, "You have such a beautiful baby."

The thought of this precious girl being wrenched from her mother and given to another family filled Mairi with rage. It shouldn't be allowed to happen. Not to Peggy and Rebecca. Her mind flashed back to Tavish and Alexander. Two boys given up for adoption by two loving mothers. Why?

The thought had preyed on her mind for over twenty years. Perhaps if Philomena's had been around during her time of need, things might have ended differently.

She handed Rebecca back to her mother.

"Isn't she gorgeous?" Peggy said with pride. "Rebecca is the greatest gift God could have given me. I'm so lucky."

Mairi couldn't help but feel a pang of jealousy as she watched the intense love between Peggy and her perfect little daughter. If only Alexander had been as perfect!

"What will you do when you leave here?"

"I don't know," came the honest reply. "Philomena's have advised me to have Rebecca adopted but so far, I've refused to give my consent. I want to bring her up myself but I have no money, no job and nowhere to live."

She looked down at the baby nestling in her arms.

"We'll find a way, won't we, darling?"

As they were talking, a visitor slipped quietly into the room.

"Mairi?" she said in total surprise, automatically reverting to Gaelic. "What are you doing here?"

"I came with Daisy. She wanted me to see where she worked. More to the point, what are you doing here?"

Katherine threw her arms around her aunt with unexpected joy.

"I'm a trustee of St Philomena's and visit the home as often as I can. This evening is one of those occasions."

"Excuse me!" Peggy interrupted with a few fake coughs. "I have no idea what language you're speaking or what you are saying but I presume you know each other."

"I'm sorry," Mairi said with breathless excitement. "I didn't mean to leave you out. We're speaking Gaelic and Katherine is my niece."

"Oh wow!" Peggy said. "What a coincidence! I could tell from your accent that you weren't English. Where do you come from?"

"The Isle of Skye," Mairi and Katherine replied in unison.

"Never heard of it. Where is it?"

"It's a small island off the West coast of Scotland," Katherine said with unexpected pride.

"Never been there," Peggy said, implying it was a place she had no intention of visiting. "I hear it rains a lot."

After nodding in agreement, Katherine asked Peggy if she could borrow Mairi for a few minutes.

"Of course!" Peggy replied, lowering her face to sniff her sleeping daughter. "Actually, you couldn't have timed it better. I think young Rebecca needs a nappy change."

Katherine took Peggy's chair and sat down.

"We don't have much time, but before you leave, I want to reassure you that Alexander is deeply loved. He's financially secure, thanks to Sir Hugh, and happy in his work. Dora and Derek are wonderful parents, showering him with love and devoting their lives to his welfare. He's a lucky young man, as is Tavish. With you and Johnny as his parents, I know he is loved and will have the best possible life back on Kilbackie where he belongs. You will never know how much that means to me.

"If these babies," she said looking round the room, "are half as lucky as Alexander and Tavish, then my life will have been worth the struggle."

Mairi was gripped by a pang of guilt.

She thought of Tavish, isolated in a rambling house, having to cope with a dissatisfied, unhappy mother who seemed to alienate everyone she loved.

Things would have to change.

Katherine delved into her pocket and brought out a well-worn envelope addressed to Mrs Katherine MacLeod.

"I want you to have this," she said passing the letter to Mairi. "It's from Sir Hugh. He wrote it soon after Angus' death. In parts it's personal but it contains information that might interest you. Keep it. I don't want it back."

Mairi took the letter and slipped it into her handbag unsure what to say in return. The past couple of days had left her too exhausted to dwell any more on the past.

"Tell me about Rebecca," she said. "Peggy's so lucky to have such a beautiful baby. I hope she never has to give her up."

"Ah! the bonnie Rebecca!" Katherine replied. "You're right, she is a very pretty baby. Did Peggy tell you about her condition?"

"No! She said nothing about a condition."

"Rebecca was born with Spina Bifida. I'm not breaking any confidences by telling you this. Peggy is quite open about it."

Mairi looked horrified.

"That perfect baby can't have Spina Bifida. It's not fair."

"It's hard, I know," Katherine replied. "Rebecca's prospects aren't good. It's unlikely she'll ever be able to walk unaided and her chances of reaching adulthood are slim, yet Peggy loves that child with all her heart and is determined to bring her up single-handed. But she needs to be realistic. Her father has refused to acknowledge his grand-daughter, mostly because she was born out of wedlock. The fact she isn't normal has driven him over the edge. He is furious and bitter, wallowing in resentment and blaming his daughter for bringing shame on the family. He hasn't shown an ounce of compassion towards Peggy and has even forbidden his wife from visiting their grand-daughter. Without her mother's help, Peggy will find it almost impossible to keep Rebecca."

Katherine's demeanour remained calm. There was little she could do for Peggy other than encourage her to make the right decision.

Peggy returned with a contented Rebecca.

"Am I interrupting?"

"No, of course not! Come and join us.

Peggy went to look for another chair.

"Take this one," Katherine said, standing up. "Mairi and I have finished talking."

The nappy change had lifted Rebecca out of her deep sleep and brought her back into the real world. Her large bright eyes darted from side to side before focussing on her mother's devoted face.

"If you'll excuse me," Katherine said. "I have a few jobs to do."

CHAPTER 43

The long journey back to Skye gave Mairi time to reflect on her brief stay with Daisy - a time of extreme terror, immense joy, debilitating sickness and tender love. Sitting in the railway carriage, she toyed with the idea of opening Sir Hugh's letter to Katherine. At first, it seemed wrong prying into her personal correspondence but if she hadn't thought it important, she would never have handed it over. She obviously trusted that Mairi would make good use of the information.

She slipped the single piece of paper out of its envelope and read.

My dear Katherine.

Forgive the thoughtless way I handled this evening. The dinner invitation was meant to give us an opportunity to discuss your future but I never made this clear, leaving you feeling threatened and afraid, for which I am truly sorry.

Can we be friends again?

Mairi wasn't sure she could go on reading something so personal. The next few lines were concerned with Sir Hugh's mother's future. Then he mentioned Kilbackie.

I have led an exceptionally privileged life and when the Kilbackie Estate came on the market, I bought it with my own private funds and sent Angus to look over the estate to see if it were somewhere you might wish to call home.

His death destroyed this plan and I will never recover from the shock of losing the finest man I have ever had the privilege of meeting. I am tormented, knowing I unwittingly sent him to his death. There are many times I find the guilt too heavy to bear. Death, when it comes, and I hope it comes soon, will be a relief.

I have no fear of dying and believe all will be understood and forgiven in the after-life.

I have placed Kilbackie House, its buildings and land in trust for Tavish until he reaches the age of twenty-five. The Trust will be managed by three Trustees: my cousin, the Reverend Hubert Hilton, the Reverend Alasdair Mackie from Gairloch; and my solicitor, Mr Simon Knowles of Knowles, Barton and Waghorn in Richmond. After my death, I want you to contact Hubert Hilton who will offer you wise advice.

I have also set up an annuity for you, giving you financial security for the rest of your life.

After Angus' funeral, do you remember I went to Inverness to interview your brother, who had been arrested for Angus' murder? He told me he was innocent but refused to say what he had seen on that fateful day, apparently fearing the truth more than the hangman's noose.

I made a pact with him, promising to engage the best defence lawyer in the land if he told me exactly what had happened.

John said very little at first but eventually he broke down and told me everything and, however hard you find the truth, I feel you should finally know what happened to your husband.

Your brother followed Angus onto the island hoping to give him a 'good hiding' for humiliating the family but after downing a bottle of whisky, he wasn't in a fit state to start a fight and decided to return to the mainland to sober up. He found a sheltered grassy patch overlooking the causeway and settled down to wait for Angus' return.

He didn't have to wait long before he saw Angus strolling back along the causeway, followed by an agitated man, shouting and waving his arms wildly in the air.

Angus continued walking, showing no sign of fear and never once quickening his step.

His pursuer's pronounced limp made it difficult for him to keep up. Determined not to let Angus get away, he picked up a stone and threw it with all his might. It struck the back of Angus' head and he slumped to the ground where he remained motionless. We shall never know if the culprit intended to harm Angus or just frighten him but the impact of the blow was catastrophic.

The man looked round to see if he had been spotted and then dragged the body down to the lower slopes of the causeway, leaving it to the mercy of the incoming tide.

It was a brutal act of cowardice, witnessed by your brother who remained hidden in the grass until all was clear.

By the time John made his way down to the water's edge, the rising tide was lapping over Angus' body. As he was lying face-down, John rolled him over. He thought he heard a moaning sound and was going to take his brother-in-law's pulse for signs of life but the sight of the deathly white face staring back at him terrified him so much, he fled the scene without checking.

I leave you to come to your own conclusion as to the identity of the murderer. As yet he has evaded justice. Perhaps this is for the best. I don't know. All I can say is that a great wrong was done that day.

CHAPTER 44

Mairi entered the kitchen to the sound of barking and laughter.

"You're back!" Tavish shrieked, running into his mother's arms and hugging her as if he would never let her go.

"I am," she laughed, unable to hide her delight at being back with her family.

"Welcome home, Madam," Rhona said in her calm, controlled way.

"It's good to have you home, darling," Johnny said, pecking her lightly on the cheek. "You're looking well."

Mairi beamed back at her family with a confidence that made her eyes sparkle. All the things she feared most about returning home hadn't happened. Tavish was thrilled to see her, Rhona hadn't left and Johnny appeared uncharacteristically affectionate. He had called her 'darling', something he hadn't done for a long time.

"Thank you for looking after Tavish," she said to Rhona. "Why don't you clock off early and have the rest of the day free. You deserve it. We'll see you tomorrow."

The young girl gave a half curtsy which made Mairi smile.

"Go on! Off with you! Go home and enjoy some time with your family."

Rhona took off her pinny, hugged the dog and headed home.

"Anyone ready for a walk?" Mairi said with an enthusiasm that took Johnny by surprise. Dora barked at the word 'walk' and hurtled towards the front door.

"You've got one volunteer," he grinned. "How about you, Tavish? Are you coming with us?"

"Of course I am!"

They walked beside the burn, then over the stile to the beach. It was a mild drizzly evening. The wind was light. The air was clear. Mairi held Johnny's hand and gave it a knowing squeeze as if to remind him how happy she was, finally to be home.

"It's so good to be back. I missed you."

He kissed the top of her head.

"I missed you too."

That evening, Tavish was too excited to go to bed. He did everything possible to delay the inevitable. First, he was thirsty, then he demanded a story, finally he said his tummy hurt.

Johnny was having none of it.

"Enough!" he said firmly. "It's bedtime. Run upstairs and brush your teeth and we'll come and kiss you good night in a few minutes."

Reluctantly the boy did as he was told, protesting all the way that he wasn't tired although the dark circles around his sleepy eyes told a different story.

Within minutes of his head touching the pillow, he was fast asleep.

"At last!" Mairi sighed as she joined her husband in the kitchen.

"Let's open a celebratory bottle of wine," Johnny said, raising a glass in the air.

"To my beautiful wife!" he toasted.

"Your good health Johnny," Mairi replied, taking a welcome sip.

They sat close together by the range, enjoying a new kind of intimacy. Johnny wanted to hear all about her journey south - Daisy's life in England, her home and husband Bill. Although he had many questions, he promised not to interrupt.

Mairi told him about her visit to Malvingborough Abbey and Philomena's, of seeing Alexander, Katherine and Agnes. She left nothing out, not even her terrifying ordeal with Bill. Johnny was true to his word. He refrained from interrupting her long ramble even though, at times, he had to bite his tongue.

"If ever I come across that conniving bastard," he said when she had finished, "I swear I'll knock him out!"

"Well, let's hope you never do. Two wrongs don't make a right, not even when it comes to Bill. Forget him! He's not worth it. It's over, finished! I've got the rest of my life to look forward to."

Johnny was unconvinced but reluctantly accepted Mairi's wishes. She had returned home a different woman - more self-assured, positive, even happy. He wondered how long it would last before she slipped back into a dark place.

"Katherine has left me with a problem," she said, handing the envelope over to Johnny. "It's rather personal in parts but she was very keen that I read it and acted upon the information."

She watched Johnny's knitted brow grow more tense as he read through the letter. By the end he was fuming.

"Damn that man!" he cried. "He has caused so much misery yet still struts around Kilbackie pretending to be a beacon of virtue."

Mairi nodded in agreement.

"I shudder to think of the number of people he has condemned to hell for falling short of his ideals or holding a different point of view! I can't believe my brother has acted the saint all this time while secretly hiding the fact that he's a murderer! I can't believe it. My own brother!"

"What are you going to do with the knowledge?" Johnny asked. "Katherine has lumbered you with a huge burden."

"I ought to forgive him," Mairi exclaimed. "But then I think of the way he treated Tavish when we first arrived. Do you remember?"

"I'm hardly likely to forget," Johnny said, slipping the letter back into its envelope.

"My brother was cruel and heartless. Who in his right mind would try and trick a six-year-old into revealing his birth mother's name? And if that wasn't bad enough, he threatened to cut out Tavish's tongue if he told a lie. The poor boy was terrified. Goodness knows what would have happened if you hadn't walked into the kitchen and found him quivering behind the door!"

"He's a dangerous, troubled man," Johnny said. "Will you confront him or leave things as they are?"

"In time, with your help, I hope I'll be able to forgive him but right now, Donny needs to own up to murdering Angus and being the cause of unimaginable grief to

Katherine, Tavish and Ailsa. He also needs to apologise to John for letting him take the blame when he knew all along, he was innocent. Without Sir Hugh's intervention, John would still be in prison.

"Let me sleep on it tonight. Hopefully tomorrow I'll have a clear head and make the right decision."

She got up to leave when Johnny asked her to remain seated.

"I won't keep you long," he said "but I too have some news although it isn't pleasant!"

"Oh goodness!" Mairi panicked. "Not more bad news!"

"I don't know if I did the right thing but I asked Mr Buchanan to look into David's disappearance."

"You did what?"

"I asked Mr Buchanan to look into David's disappearance."

"But why? Why would you want to do that?"

"For two reasons," Johnny explained. "His disappearance is the missing piece in Alexander's story and I felt we owed it to Margaret to find out what happened to her brother."

Mairi wasn't sure she could cope with more revelations. Her visit south had been successful but emotionally draining. All she wanted to do was lie down and go to sleep.

"I know you are tired," Johnny sympathised. "And this isn't probably the right time to talk about David but I'll be brief.

"Mr Buchanan phoned me yesterday to say that David joined the Merchant Navy in 1934 and was killed in action aboard SS Hartlebury in 1942. I wrote down a few details but they can wait until tomorrow. I'm so sorry to be the bearer of bad news, Mairi."

CHAPTER 45

The rising sun had turned the morning sky crimson, with streaks of orange, yellow and mauve. It was a promising start to the new day but as the saying goes, 'red sky in the morning, shepherd's warning.' It didn't take long for dark clouds to gather over the hill and spread across the warm sky, smothering its glow.

Mairi had promised Johnny there would be no more secrets. All future decisions would be taken together and any differences of opinion would be discussed.

After dropping Tavish off at school, Johnny tried to persuade Mairi to visit John on Eilean Torrach.

"You need to talk to him about Donny. I know you hate everything to do with boats and the sea but I promise I'll take great care of you. The crossing won't take more than half an hour!"

The dark waters looked unforgiving, even menacing in the morning light. Mairi couldn't help thinking about David drowning in the icy waters of the Barents Sea.

Since confirming his death, Mr Buchanan had made discreet enquiries into the sinking of SS Hartlebury.

"I thought you would like to know what happened to David's ship," he said to Mairi during a phone call.

"Forgive me if I ramble on a bit. I don't wish to prolong your grief but the more you know, the easier it will be to understand what David went through and why. Promise you will tell me if I talk too much.

"The Hartlebury was part of Arctic convoy PQ 17 that left Iceland in June 1942. It was huge, consisting of 35 ships loaded with 297 aircraft, 594 tanks and 4246 lorries and gun carriers.

The heavily escorted convoy had passed Bear Island on its way to Archangel when it was ordered to scatter. The Hartlebury broke away and headed towards Novaya Zemlya where on 7th July it was hit by two torpedoes fired in quick succession from a German U Boat.

"Are you still following me?" he asked, aware he was going into more detail than necessary. "I can stop right now if you wish."

"No, it's all right," came the faint reply. "Carry on."

"The initial damage to David's ship was enormous. However, shortly after the first onslaught, another torpedo ripped through the ship's bow, sending her to the bottom of the Barents Sea, a marginal sea of the Arctic Ocean.

A few survivors managed to clamber aboard the only available lifeboat but during a moment of panic, the boat flipped over throwing its occupants into freezing water. Those who had jumped ship before she sank, managed to swim ashore but the loss of life was heartbreaking. Of the forty-two souls on board at the start of the journey, only thirteen survived the sinking. Unfortunately, David was one of the unlucky ones.

"There's lots more I could say," Mr Buchanan said, "but I suspect you have heard as much as you need to hear.

"Let's call it a day!"

He put down the receiver, leaving Mairi to muse on all she had heard.

"Poor David!" she thought. "He had faked his own death in the calm waters of Kilbackie only to die in a battle zone thousands of miles from home. What a waste of life!"

Johnny was true to his word.

He steered Arctic Tern effortlessly through the calm, water, weighing anchor in Torrach Bay where John was waiting to greet them.

"What are you doing here?" he said helping Mairi step ashore. "You're the last person I was expecting."

"Sorry to turn up out of the blue but I need to talk to you," she said, hoping her sudden appearance didn't alarm him. "You're impossible to get hold of by telephone or by post so Johnny brought me over in the boat."

"I saw you enter the bay," he said warily, wondering why his aunt had decided to visit him. "First Daisy and now you. I am popular!"

He looked quizzically at Johnny then at his aunt, waiting for an introduction.

"Have you two never met?" she asked, horrified. "John, this is my husband, Johnny. Johnny, this is my nephew, John."

The two men eyed each other positively.

"It's good to meet you at last," John said, shaking him firmly by the hand. "I've heard so much about you. All positive I might add, except for your accent and not having the Gaelic."

"Ah!" Johnny replied with a smile. "My accent's as Yorkshire as Wensleydale cheese but you're right, I can't speak a word of Gaelic!"

The two men exchanged pleasantries before the heavens opened and they were forced to find shelter in John's house.

"Come in," he said, opening the door. "It may look rough and ready but it's dry and comfortable. Pull up a chair by the fire and get warm."

Mairi and Johnny did as John suggested.

"Now," he said, looking at his aunt. "What's so urgent you've taken all this trouble to visit me?"

"It's difficult to know where to start," Mairi said. "Perhaps it's easiest if Sir Hugh speaks for himself."

"Sir Hugh?" he asked, looking confused. "What's he got to do with your visit? I thought he was dead!"

Mairi handed the envelope over to John.

"Have a look inside. This is the letter he wrote to Katherine not long after Angus died. She gave it to me a couple of days ago and I don't know what to do with the information. Read it for yourself and tell me what you think."

Seated in his chair by the fire, John absorbed the contents of the letter in silence - a furrowed brow being his only sign of emotion. When he had finished, he put his head in his hands and let out a long, drawn-out moan.

"Oh, my God! It's all coming back."

He closed his eyes and took in a few deep breaths before continuing.

"I've always struggled to remember what happened after I drank the bottle of whisky. I seem to have blanked everything out. Perhaps it was better that way. Who knows?"

He looked down at the two sheets of neat handwriting.

"Where did you say you got this letter?"

"From Katherine."

"Dear, kind Katherine. She never did anyone any harm," he said with a hint of remorse. "Yet we treated her appallingly. Her only fault was to fall in love with my father's best friend and arch enemy. What a tragedy! Reading Sir Hugh's letter has brought it all back. I saw everything. He was there on the causeway with Angus."

"Who was?" Mairi asked, trying to get as much information as she could out of her nephew.

"My father!

"He followed Angus over the causeway, waving his cane in the air, shouting. I couldn't hear what he was saying because I was too far away but he appeared to be very angry, acting like a madman."

"What happened next? Think, John, it's very important."

"My father frantically tried to catch Angus' attention but he never looked back. It's difficult to say if he knew he was being followed or heard the shouting. He just kept walking at his usual brisk pace, while my father gradually lost ground, unable to keep up. His artificial leg was uncomfortable at the best of times but crossing the rough surface of the causeway must have been agony. As he fell behind, he suddenly stopped, picked up a stone and threw it with all his might, hitting Angus on the back of the head."

"Are you quite sure it was your father who threw the stone?" Mairi enquired.

"Quite sure!" John replied sweating with the stress of recalling events that took place six years ago. "Poor Angus didn't deserve to die."

"What did your father do after the stone hit Angus?" Mairi asked, trying to keep John focussed.

"I can't remember," he said, placing his hands over his ears to shut out Mairi's questions and all the painful memories he wished to forget. "Can we talk about something else? I honestly can't remember what happened after Angus stumbled and fell. You're asking me to talk about an event that would make my father a murderer. I can't do it! It's too awful!"

"John, this is important. Listen to me. Did your father walk away from Angus, once he had fallen or, did he stop to see if he was hurt?"

Again, there was a long pause.

Johnny gave Mairi a gentle nudge as if to say 'enough is enough, be kind,' but she wanted answers.

"Did he stop to help? I know I'm asking a lot of uncomfortable questions, but I have my reasons. There is just a chance we can get Donny to face up to his crime and admit he committed a terrible sin."

For the first time since Mairi entered the small house, John began to relax. It was as if the twin burdens of guilt and fear had been lifted off his shoulders. Slowly he began to trust his aunt and share with her his recollections.

"My father panicked when he saw Angus crumple to the ground. I believe he only meant to scare him but he disliked his son-in-law so much, he let his renowned temper get the better of him. He raced over to the body lying motionless on the stony ground and shook it hard, trying to get it to move but it was all hopeless. In the end, he picked up the offending rock and threw it into the sea but I can't remember what happened next."

John's facial expression betrayed his agonising struggle to recall the past. All the while, Johnny patiently listened, observing the interplay between aunt and nephew. He was wise enough not to interfere but sensitive enough to encourage Mairi to back off so John could steady his nerves.

For a few minutes, nobody talked. The insufferable tension was only broken when John blurted out: "He grasped Angus' wrists. That's it! I remember now. He grasped Angus' wrists and dragged him off the causeway."

"Who grasped Angus' wrists?" Mairie asked.

"My father."

John let out a long sigh and closed his eyes.

"He dragged Angus to the edge of the causeway and left him there. I remember thinking that Angus would get wet if I didn't scramble down to help him."

Mairi held her nephew's hand and said very gently, "Was Angus alive when you saw him last?"

"I don't know. I was drunk, frightened and angry. The look on his pale face was so awful I ran. That's what's haunted me all these years. I don't know if he was alive when I left him."

"The reason I'm asking all these questions," Mairi said cautiously, "is that I want Donny to admit to murdering

Angus and face justice. Will you come and confront him with me?"

John looked aghast at the thought of visiting his father.

"I'm sorry, Aunt Mairi, but I can't! It's not that I don't want to. Nothing would give me more pleasure than seeing that bastard locked up but I'm scared stiff of him. I can't be in the same room as him without feeling sick. He terrifies me."

Mairi didn't push the point. She remained by the fire, giving her suggestion time to sink in.

"Donny has been living a lie for too long. It's time we made him face the truth. He's not above the law you know.

"For Katherine and Angus' sake, please come with me.

"Johnny says he'll give us moral support but he won't take part in the meeting. That will be between you, me and Donny."

John turned the letter over and over in his trembling hands.

"Did you know I haven't touched a drop of alcohol since the day Angus died," he said nonchalantly. "I often wonder what would have happened if I'd been sober that day. Could I have saved him? Probably not but the question still haunts me."

"Think of the lives Donny has ruined," Mairi pleaded.

"He murdered Angus, deprived Katherine of a husband, Ailsa of a son, Tavish of a father. Not only that, he publicly humiliated the MacPhee family, tormented Tavish, bullied me and tried to frame you.

"Please come with me."

While John mulled over his options, Johnny quietly stood up and went into the kitchen.

Before long the kettle was singing and three mugs of steaming hot tea were brought in on a tray and placed in front of the fire.

Outside, it continued to rain.

John cupped his mug in both hands, his mind spinning with indecision. After a long pause he finally agreed to go with Mairi.

"I know it's none of my business," she asked, "but what made you change your mind?"

He considered the question before answering.

"My father has bullied me all my life. Nothing I've done was ever good enough for him. I am, what is called, a disappointment, a failure. He thrashed me within inches of my life as a two-year-old, criticised me all through childhood, disowned my sister, and murdered my brother-in-law. What a role model!

"Since Angus' death, my life has spiralled out of control. I've found it hard to hold down a job, trust people, form lasting relationships and free myself from a perpetual feeling of hopelessness and guilt.

"Through the dark moments two people have given me hope. Sir Hugh Hollister, who never stopped believing in my innocence and went the extra mile to win my release from prison. He was what I call a true Christian gentleman.

"Secondly and more surprisingly, Daisy. I've only met her twice but, on both occasions, she has encouraged me to pursue my dreams."

CHAPTER 46

Rev Donny Nicolson laid a clean sheet of paper on his desk, picked up his pen and wrote the opening sentence of his sermon. It was the highlight of his week. Meticulous research enabled him to expand that first sentence into forty minutes of instruction and warning. The feeling of elation never left him. It was an honour to serve God and direct his flock in the ways of truth.

When Donny first took over from his father, he developed a stutter which got steadily worse as he struggled to find his voice in the pulpit. The speech impediment affected the potency of his message. It diminished his authority and failed to drive home the points he wanted to make. Over time, he honed his writing skills, polished his delivery and worked on his stutter until his sermons became masterful speeches on salvation. No-one could accuse him of being a lightweight preacher.

As he grew older, his sombre study became a sanctuary of tranquillity, far removed from the rigorous demands of daily life. His long-suffering wife, Edith, ran the household, taught in the Sunday School and visited the poor and sick, leaving him free to prepare his sermons.

He looked around the room with satisfaction. Books were everywhere. They lay on every available surface, filled the bookcases and lined the shelves. Scores of them.

Biblical commentaries, biographies and concordances which Donny had inherited from his father as well as more modern editions bought over the past twenty-five years.

Every book had its own reference index card which was carefully filed away in a box.

The library was his pride and joy.

His thoughts were interrupted by the unexpected intrusion of Mairi, John and Johnny. Their unannounced presence in his Holy of Holies made him apoplectic with rage.

"How dare you barge in without knocking," he snarled. "Get out!"

"No, Donny, we're not leaving until you've heard what we have to say."

The minister's worn face grew crimson. He thumped his desk and glared at his sister.

"What's all this nonsense about? Get out, all of you! Do you hear? Get out!"

Mairi sat down opposite her brother while Johnny closed the study door.

"Listen carefully," she explained slowly and deliberately. "In my handbag I have a letter from Sir Hugh Hollister telling Katherine that you were responsible for Angus' death!

"Is this true?"

Donny looked totally shocked. He stared through his sister at the inspirational books that only a few minutes earlier had given him so much pleasure but had now lost their appeal.

"How dare you storm into my study accusing me of untruths! Leave, at once - all three of you. I have nothing to be ashamed of for it is said: *Blessed are ye, when men shall revile you, and persecute you, and shall say all manner of evil against you falsely, for my sake. Rejoice, and be exceeding glad: for great is your reward in heaven.*

"Stop quoting and listen to what John and I have to say." Mairi said with an authority that surprised everyone. "We won't be long.

"According to Sir Hugh, you hit Angus on the back of the head with a rock. The blow either killed him or knocked him out, he didn't know which but either way, you dragged Angus to the edge of the causeway and left him there. His body was later found floating on the incoming tide."

"It's not true!" the Minister protested. "Angus was my son-in-law, I loved him. Why would I want to hurt him?"

"Because you were jealous of him and resented his marriage to Katherine," Mairi said calmly.

Johnny watched in amazement as his wife took control of the situation. Ever since her visit south, she had become a happier, more confident person. He couldn't have been prouder.

"Angus returned from the war without a scratch on his body." Mairi continued. "He had charisma, a well-respected job and all the status that went with it. To add insult to injury, he married your only daughter who was twenty years his junior.

"You didn't love Angus, you loathed him and his success!"

Donny was speechless. For a while he didn't know what to say.

"Get out! Your letter is meaningless. It is circumstantial evidence. You have no proof."

This time it was John who spoke.

"You're wrong, Father. I witnessed everything. You tried to catch up with Angus as he was leaving the island but your leg slowed you down. You called out to him. You waved your stick at him but he ignored you and kept walking. How you must have hated him for not showing you the respect you craved. I have no idea what went through your warped mind but you deliberately picked up a rock and hurled it at him, hitting him on the back of the head. He stumbled and fell. You dragged his body to the edge of the causeway and left him there."

For a brief moment a glint returned to Donny's tired eyes.

"Did you bother to check Angus was all right?"

"Of course I did," John replied. "After you had left the island, I went to see if he needed help."

"Was he alive when you saw him?"

"No! He wasn't breathing and his body was unnaturally white and lifeless. I ran to find Willie and together we dragged Angus out of the water but he was already dead."

Mairi took over from John.

"Listen, Donny. All John and I want is the truth. To hear you confess to killing Angus. We have written evidence and John's witness statement to say that it was you who threw the fatal rock, so there's no point denying it."

"I have no intention of admitting to something I never did," Donny replied. "Do what you want with your so-called evidence. Who will believe you? John went to prison for allegedly killing Angus! It wouldn't take much to convince the good people of Kilbackie that his testimony is worthless. John's word against mine? I don't think it would carry much weight. As for Sir Hugh, his letter is hearsay. He was tucked away on his estate in England at the time of Angus' death so, again, I don't think the good people of Kilbackie will take much notice of what is written in his letter to Katherine.

"And don't forget the scandal he caused when he turned up at Angus' funeral in a chauffeur-driven Rolls Royce with Angus' pregnant widow by his side. Tongues were wagging then as to the paternity of the unborn child. I expect they could wag again!"

"How dare you speak of your grandson like that!" Mairi cried.

"Well, well, your little outburst has confirmed, what I've always suspected, that Tavish is Katherine's son and my grandson. How the tables have turned! Now you've confirmed I'm the boy's grandfather, I think it is only right and fair that I see him more often.

"Go home, all of you and leave me to get on with my sermon."

Mairi could hardly contain her fury. She had been convinced her brother would cave in and confess to killing Angus rather than face the community. He was right. Sir Hugh's letter and John's testimony carried little weight. It was unlikely that Kilbackie would side with John against their Minister.

The impasse was broken by a familiar voice.

"The good people of Kilbackie might believe you are innocent, Donny, but Almighty God and your wife don't believe for one minute that you are speaking the truth." Edith said.

This time, Donny looked terror-struck.

"Edith!" he said in a strangled high-pitched voice. "What are you doing here?"

"I heard the commotion in your usually quiet study and decided to see what was going on and I'm pleased I did. You may be able to fool your sister and your son but you can't fool your wife!"

Mairi and John looked at her in amazement. Gentle, hardworking, downtrodden Edith had finally found her voice.

"Lying lips are an abomination to the Lord," she said. "I should know. You have told me often enough. So, Donny, before Almighty God, who is the judge of all men, will you answer this one simple question?

"Did you kill Angus?"

The monotonous ticking of the grandfather clock signalled the passing of time. Each tick brought Donny nearer his Maker. Nearer judgement. He began to sweat, felt the tightening of his dog collar as his heart beat faster. He wanted to cry out for forgiveness but pride held him back. He grew hotter, his fingers started to swell, his hands grew clammy, his mouth dried up, his tongue burned. The clock continued ticking.

Time was passing.

In his distress he thought of the passage from Proverbs: *'The LORD detests lying lips, but he delights in people who are trustworthy.*

Donny looked at his wife, who had faithfully stood by him all these years.

And still the clock ticked.

Donny was burning in torment.

"Well?" Edith said. "Are you going to speak the truth?"

Donny bowed his head and nodded.

"Yes!" he whispered. "God forgive me!"

After confessing, Donny broke down. His life's work had shattered into a thousand pieces. He had been humiliated by his wife and exposed as a liar and a murderer.

Mairi, John and Edith felt no pleasure in seeing a grown man crumple under the weight of guilt but they got the justice they were looking for.

Edith had reminded her husband of the promise she had made back in 1919 when he thrashed two-year-old John with his leather belt. She warned him then, that if he ever laid his hand on one of their children, she would leave him.

"Angus was my son-in-law and I loved him," she said, "not that you ever bothered to find out what I thought. Your temper, mixed with jealousy and resentment, got the better of you and you killed him!"

Donny pleaded with his wife to stand by him.

"I meant what I said, Donny, after you beat John. I am leaving you."

Donny was past words. The agony in his soul was so all-consuming, he feared it would kill him. While he waited for death, he clung to the hope that his confession was enough to save him.

"My sister, Shirley, has invited me to live with her," Edith said. "She has a large empty house just outside Bedford with plenty of spare rooms. Her grown-up children have left home and since her husband's death she has been lonely. I have no idea how things will turn out but I'm going to start a new life back where I belong, in Bedfordshire with my family."

CHAPTER 47

The unexpected departure of Rev Donny Nicolson was announced in church, much to the surprise of the congregation.

No reason was given.

He just left.

Mairi helped her sister-in-law clear out the Manse after Donny had accepted a call to become the minister of a small church near Golspie. He left with honour as Mairi, John and Edith were true to their word, agreeing to keep his confession a secret.

"Let's burn all the paperwork," Edith said, sifting through piles of notes and correspondence. "As for the books, they can stay in the study for the next incumbent. I'm sure he will find some of them useful."

Mairi rummaged through Donny's desk, removing old bills, memos and jottings. Edith made it quite clear that everything had to go. Right at the back of Donny's desk, in a small drawer half hidden behind a hole puncher, Mairi found an opened envelope addressed to Mr and Mrs MacPhee. She pulled out the letter dated 20th July 1942.

Dear Madam,

It is with the deepest regret that I have learned that your son, Mr David Angus MacPhee, who was serving in the Merchant Navy, has been recorded as supposed drowned whilst on service with his ship.

By command of His Majesty the King, the names of those members of the Merchant Navy who have given their lives in the service of their country are recorded in the Merchant Navy Roll of Honour. I am now adding Mr MacPhee's name to the Roll of Honour, and, as I do so, I wish to express my admiration for the services he rendered and to convey to you and your family my profound sympathy in your sad bereavement.

Your son worthily upheld the noble traditions of the Merchant Navy and I hope perhaps that this fact may help to soften the heavy blow which has befallen you.

Believe me,

Yours sincerely,

'Leathers'

Minister of War Transport

Mairi thought of all the pain she, Effie and Margaret had endured not knowing what had happened to David. Here was the proof they needed. Mr Buchanan had been right. David went down with his ship off the coast of Novaya Zemlya in the Arctic Circle. She prayed he hadn't suffered but feared he might have burned to death in the explosion or frozen to death in a sub-zero sea. In either case, he would have experienced a deep fear of the unknown.

"Have a look at this," Mairi said, showing Edith the letter. "Donny must have intercepted it on purpose to spite the MacPhee family. Was there no end to his cruelty?"

Edith read through the letter and sadly shook her head.

"I thought Donny was being compassionate when he asked the postman to give him all the condolence letters. He gave the impression he would deliver them in person and offer the bereaved families comfort and prayers. I had no idea he never delivered this one."

The clearance continued. Drawers and shelves were hastily stripped of their contents. More bills, receipts, letters, cheques and sermons were hurriedly taken outside and thrown on the pyre. It was a cathartic moment watching the smoke rise above Kilbackie and disappear into thin air.

"Do you want to take this?" Edith asked, pointing to the large Nicolson Family Bible standing on the top shelf of the bookcase. "One day, when he's older, Tavish may like to look at the names inside. They will tell him all about his Skye roots. What do you think?"

Mairi thought hard before answering.

"Let's take it," she said suddenly. "I promised Johnny there would be no more secrets between us. I want Tavish to be brought up knowing the truth."

As Edith pulled the book off the shelf, five bundles of unopened envelopes fell onto the floor. "What on earth are these?" she asked, picking them up.

Mairi came over to have a look. There must have been at least a hundred letters, all neatly tied up with string and addressed, in the same handwriting, to Rev Donny Nicolson.

"Shall I open one?" Mairi asked, taking out an envelope. Edith nodded.

The letter, written in Gaelic, was from Angus. In it, he asked Donny for news of his parents, the community and the church. He said nothing about his life at Shottenden but mentioned significant moments of change in the natural world - the first 'candles' flowering on the horse chestnut trees, cow parsley growing in the lanes, speckled eggs lying in neat tidy nests. At the end of the letter, he prayed that one day, the wound that had placed a barrier between them would be healed.

The room went deathly quiet as Mairi translated the letter to Edith.

"What shall we do with them?" she asked.

"I honestly don't know," Mairi replied. "I knew Donny was lying when he told me that Angus had cut all ties with him and here's the proof." She flicked through the envelopes looking at the postmarks. The earliest was dated May 1920, the last, March 1948, just before his death.

"Dear Angus!" Mairi said. "He loyally wrote to his friend and kept in touch for nearly twenty-eight years and never, as far as we know, received a single reply. It's so sad."

The two ladies stared at the letters in disbelief, unable to comprehend Donny's mind.

"Burn them!" Mairi cried, taking Edith by surprise. "Burn the lot of them. They belong to the broken past that struggled to make sense of the Great War. We both have a chance to put those times behind us and move forward, so now is the time to cauterize the wound once and for all."

Mairi and Edith took the letters outside and placed them gently on the fire, watching the paper brown and curl before bursting into flames.

CHAPTER 48

The long light summer months were calm, the air filled with a heady mix of bird song and drowsy bees collecting pollen from the wildflowers that carpeted the grassland. Clovers, vetches and orchids grew in abundance among meadow fescue, rye grass and crested dog's tail. Hidden deep within the tall quivering grass, secretive male corncrakes continued to lift their heads and repeat their irritating song. The strange rattling sound cut through the stillness of the day.

The Storr Lochs Hydro Scheme on Skye had opened in 1952, using water from Lochs Leathan and Fada to provide the first general supply of electricity to the island. Before long, poles and wires criss-crossed the townships, hills and glens until eventually it arrived on Kilbackie, just in time for the delivery of the twin tub, fridge and Hoover. Once the light bulbs, wires and sockets were in place, the kitchen became the beacon of modernity Sir Hugh had planned.

The labour-saving devices weren't the only changes. Alasdair MacPherson and his son, James, arrived to create a new bathroom and link the pipework to the hot water tank in the attic. Throughout the upheaval, Rhona volunteered to run the Hoover over the upstairs carpets after the builders had gone. She loved the sound of dust being sucked into the bag, a novelty that still hadn't worn off.

"Can I have a word?" Mr MacPherson said in Gaelic. "I don't want to be a nuisance but we need to lay some pipes in an attic room that's full of furniture. If you have a spare moment, could you help us sort through what's to keep and what's to throw away.

There's no hurry but obviously we need to get a move on."

Mairi checked the time.

It was 10.00 am

"There's no moment like the present," she said, keen for the building project to end. "I've been meaning to sort out that attic room but keep putting it off. Now is as good a time as any."

She followed Mr MacPherson into a room stacked high with furniture, books, curtains and pictures. He was right. It was a shambles.

"I don't think anyone's been up here since the Great War." Mairi said. "Where shall we start?"

"Why not divide everything into two groups?" Mr MacPherson suggested helpfully. "'To burn' and 'to keep'. James and I will help if you want an extra pair of hands."

Sorting through the room took all morning but by lunchtime two distinct piles had emerged out of the chaos. The largest pile by far was the one destined for the bonfire. It included moth-eaten evening dresses and curtains, broken furniture and mouldy books. The items were placed in a heap near the stone byre ready to burn. Mairi hesitated about adding the Scottish landscape paintings, fearing they could be worth something.

"Let's leave these until I've had a word with Mr Buchanan," she said. "I'd hate to burn an Urquhart heirloom, although looking at the broken frames and torn canvasses, they don't look very valuable."

Stacked at the back of all the clutter, stood a large full-length portrait of a young man dressed in formal Highland attire. There was no mistaking the sitter, Douglas Urquhart. Mairi pulled the picture clear and leant it against the wall for a better look. It was an exquisite painting of a handsome young man in full Urquhart Highland dress. Central to the image was the highly polished silver Urquhart buckle depicting a lady, from the waist up, emerging out of a coronet. In her right hand she brandished a sword, in her left, a palm sapling.

Mairi gazed in awe at the extraordinary work of art that had cleverly captured the sensitive, proud young sitter. Despite its artistic beauty, something was not right. She took a second look at the painting, focussing on the hand that rested on the wide leather belt.

"It can't be!" she exclaimed in a state of shock. "Oh my word! It is!"

Mr MacPherson was too busy, sorting through the attic to hear Mairi's comment. He picked up a pair of Alexander Peter chairs and examined the woodwork.

"I'm afraid these will have to go," he sighed. "They are so riddled with woodworm I doubt they would support anyone sitting down."

He looked at Mairi for permission to put them on the 'to burn' pile but she was too distracted by the portrait.

"Is everything all right?" he asked. "You look as if you've seen a ghost. You're as white as a sheet."

"I'm fine," Mairi assured him. "But if you can spare me a while, I need to speak to Mr Mitchell. Something's turned up which could be important."

She raced down two flights of stairs and ran straight into Johnny's study without knocking.

"Have you a moment?" she exclaimed, pausing to catch her breath. "I've been clearing out the attic with Mr MacPherson and there's something I need to show you."

"Can't it wait? I've a lot on my plate today."

"No, it can't!"

Reluctantly, Johnny stood up and followed her to the attic room where Mr MacPherson and James had collected another armful of mouldy books.

"This had better be good," Johnny whispered. "You know I don't like being disturbed."

"Believe me, it is," Mairi replied.

They squeezed past Mr MacPherson and James who were struggling to hold onto the books they were holding.

"Good morning, sir," Mr MacPherson said. "Not much left to do once we've moved this lot and connected the pipes to the new hot water tank. I expect you'll be glad to see the back of us after all the disruption."

"Thank you, Alasdair," Mairi said in Gaelic, as the plumber and his son went downstairs leaving Johnny and Mairi alone in the attic.

"Well?" said Johnny.

"There!" Mairi said pointing to the oil painting.

"What am I supposed to be looking at?"

"The painting."

Johnny was in no mood for games. He was clearly annoyed at having his morning disturbed just to look at another tartan portrait.

"It looks the same as all the others in the house," he said.

"I know," Mairi replied, "but look carefully. Look!"

"I am looking," Johnny replied in exasperation, "What am I supposed to be looking at?"

"The hands!"

Johnny took a close look at the hands but couldn't see anything odd about them.

"So?" he said. "They each have the correct number of fingers and thumbs and seem to be attached to the arms. Look, Mairi, I was in the middle of working out the winter-feeding programme. Please tell me the hands are worth the interruption."

"I've seen those hands before," she said, unable to contain her excitement.

"Now you've totally confused me. Hands don't move without a body so where have you seen them before?"

"You remember when Tavish cut his knee?"

"How could I forget. It was probably the worst day of my life!"

"I agree. The day is best forgotten but do you remember how Mr Buchanan took control of the situation and stitched up Tavish's wound. I watched every tiny movement of his hands as he cleaned the wound and made the sutures.

"These," she said pointing to the picture, "are the same hands.

"Mr Buchanan is Douglas Urquhart!"

"He can't be!" Johnny said. "Douglas died in 1915."

"I'm telling you. They are the same hands and if you don't believe me, look at the signet ring on Douglas Urquhart's little finger."

She pointed to the gold ring in the painting.

"Mr Buchanan wears that exact ring on his little finger. Why would he wear an Urquhart ring if he wasn't an Urquhart. Now do you believe me! Mr Buchanan and Douglas Urquhart are the same person."

"I don't know," Johnny said doubtfully. "It all seems rather far-fetched. How did Douglas Urquhart come back to life with a different name?"

"I have no idea but it's him, I know it is! What shall we do?"

"Nothing!" Johnny said. "Without proof we can't do anything, so leave it alone and whatever happens, don't interfere."

Mairi knew Johnny was right but she didn't like thinking of Mr Buchanan living in fear of being found out. She wanted to help.

"Perhaps I could talk to him," she said hesitantly.

"Absolutely not!" Johnny replied. "Don't even think about it! You'll only make matters worse. Do you hear me, Mairi. Say nothing."

CHAPTER 49

A week later, during one of Mr Buchanan's visits, Johnny discovered the farm had run out of cattle feed. It was an oversight that should never have happened. He blamed himself and took full responsibility for the failure but deep down he felt some of the blame lay with Mairi, whose frequent absences, poor decision-making and overall dissatisfaction with life had distracted him. Without her support he had struggled to juggle meetings, child minding and farming.

"I can't apologise enough," he said, full of contrition. "It won't happen again."

Mr Buchanan gave an enigmatic look, as if to say, 'It had better not.'

It was then Johnny noticed the signet ring.

Mairi was right.

It was identical to the one worn by Douglas Urquhart in the portrait - the half-naked lady rising out of a coronet, holding a sword and a palm sapling.

He couldn't think how the two men were connected. For the first time since arriving on Skye, he questioned whether he could ever belong to the clan way of life, a culture that had existed for centuries through blood-ties and marriage. The Urquhart, MacLeod, Nicolson, MacDonald and MacKinnon families had all been shaped by the crofting way of life. He was an outsider making careless mistakes under the watchful eye of the man he thought he knew and understood. It was a wakeup call. If he wanted to continue farming on Skye, he had to be more focussed on the job, more professional. Mairi would have to make her own arrangements to look after Tavish.

He looked at his watch.

3.30 p.m.

"Please stay for tea," he said knowing how much Mairi and Tavish would enjoy the company.

"I need to drive over to MacAllister's to collect the feed before they shut. Hopefully, if the mist doesn't get any worse, I'll be back before you leave. Once again, I am truly sorry for the error."

A heavy cloud had descended over Kilbackie reducing visibility to a few yards. Mr Buchanan took one look outside and decided to take up Johnny's offer to stay for tea, a domestic ritual he thoroughly enjoyed. He relished the opportunity to spend time with Tavish, answering his many and varied questions. He had never met a child like him. Not only did Tavish retain a huge amount of information, he enjoyed exploring a wide range of subjects, the latest being the history of Kilbackie House.

Mairi made a pot of fresh tea whilst Tavish went to the larder to fetch the cake tin, giving his mother a pleading look.

"All right," she conceded. "But only because we have company. Do you want help cutting the cake?"

Tavish shook his head, determined to show how grown up he was.

He handed Mr Buchanan a slice of Rhona's chocolate cake, then cut two more slices - one for himself and the other for his mother.

The three of them sat at the kitchen table taking their time to taste the sweet mixture of fondant icing and sponge, an experience they and the nation had been denied during the long years of austerity and rationing.

Mairi told Mr Buchanan about the latest building work in the attic, describing the room Mr MacPherson had just cleared to link the bathroom pipes to the hot water tank.

"You've never seen so much clutter!" she said. "Most of it was only fit for the bonfire - mouldy soft furnishings, broken furniture, books and clothes that had been attacked by mice and moths. It was disgusting! We've burnt the whole lot of them. As soon as the bathroom is installed, Rhona and I will give the attic a thorough spring clean.

"She will be so happy to use the Hoover! The girl is obsessed with it. If she had her way, she would spend all day, running up and down carpets, listening to the dust being sucked into the bag. I don't blame her. Everything feels so much fresher after the house has been vacuumed.

"If you have a spare moment after tea, could you help me with the paintings? I think one or two of them may be valuable but, to be honest, I haven't a clue! I've been meaning to ask Johnny but you know what he's like - either too tired or too busy."

After answering Tavish's questions on when the house had been built, why the Urquhart family lived there, who had built the causeway and where did all the stones come from, Mr Buchanan paused to enjoy his tea.

"No more questions," he said with the hint of a smile. "I need a break."

Tavish reluctantly accepted the decision although his head was still full of questions. They would all need answering eventually but he was happy to wait for now.

Once tea was over, Mr Buchanan followed Mairi up to the attic to look at the paintings. Much to her relief he agreed they were pastiches of little value, but suggested she stored them away in case at some time in the future they became fashionable.

"I doubt they will ever see the light of day but it seems a pity to burn them."

He stopped in his tracks when he saw the portrait of the man in full Highland dress.

"Where did you find this?" he asked.

"Behind those landscape pictures," Mairi said, pointing to the paintings they had been looking at. "I nearly added it to the pile destined for the bonfire but it looked too valuable to burn."

The room fell silent as Mairi's revelation hung in the air.

Mr Buchanan continued to gaze at the portrait, obviously moved by its discovery. The weight of his secret grew heavier, surrounded by memories of his past life. He glanced at Mairi whose understanding look conveyed a sense of empathy and trust.

"Do you know who he is?" she asked, trying to sound casual.

"I'm not sure but it could be Douglas Urquhart, although I've never seen this portrait before."

Mairi took a moment to consider her next move. Here was her chance to probe into a possible link between the two men. She could hear Johnny warning her to leave things alone, not to interfere but the urge to solve the mystery was too great.

It was now or never.

"Are you related to the Urquharts?" she asked, aware she was straying into dangerous waters.

Mr Buchanan didn't give an immediate answer but the way he stared at the portrait convinced Mairi she had touched a nerve.

"Why do you ask?" he enquired, unable to keep his eyes away from the picture.

"Your ring."

There was no turning back. She had disobeyed Johnny and trusted her instincts.

"I noticed the Urquhart signet ring in the portrait was the same as the one you're wearing. It can't be a coincidence."

Mr Buchanan said nothing.

In that brief moment, buried memories involving Kilbackie, Festubert, a hospital, a friend and a split-second decision began to surface. He had nowhere to hide now the truth was out.

The relief was enormous.

"You are Douglas, aren't you?" Mairi said. "Tell me what happened but only if you want to."

Mr Buchanan studied the woman standing in front of him. Her direct question had come out of the blue. He hadn't been prepared to face his past in such a simple way.

It all came down to the portrait. The one his mother had commissioned from her cousin, Cowan Dobson, a few weeks before Douglas was due to leave for France. Cowan Dobson arrived on Kilbackie and immediately set to work making sketches. He was a popular artist and much in demand. The trip over to Skye had been an inconvenience, but he was fond of Douglas' mother and wished to please her. He had intended to stay no more than a week but after three days, Douglas had unexpectedly been ordered to join his regiment in Inverness. His early departure forced Cowan Dobson to rely on the hastily drawn sketches he had made. The result wasn't only a masterpiece, it also bore a remarkable likeness to Douglas.

Now, forty-one years later, he was back at the beginning, in the attic of his childhood home, facing himself in the portrait he had never seen before.

He started to speak.

"My parents' love for me was obsessive. They kept me a virtual prisoner here on the island, always fearing I would come to harm without their protection. My decision to break free and join the army quite literally changed my life. During my time away, I met so many characters - most of them first-class men - but Fergus Buchanan stood head and shoulders above them all. He was such an extraordinarily compassionate man, full of wisdom and dreams. We were opposites in every way but became the best of friends, sharing the highs and lows of trench warfare right up to the end.

"Am I boring you?" he asked, aware he was talking too much.

Mairi shook her head.

"Fergus was killed instantly when a shell exploded as we ran across No Man's Land towards an enemy trench. He took the brunt of the blast which shredded him into tiny pieces. I fared better, suffering extensive wounds and burns to my face.

"As I crawled on all fours among the bone fragments, tissue and flesh that had once been my friend, I cried for help across a desolate landscape occupied by the maimed and dying. No-one came to my aid. Those still breathing had been abandoned to their fate, discarded, no longer fit for service. In the brief time left to them, they prepared for the Great Unknown with dignity, holding on to happy memories, maternal love and faith in God.

Amidst the carnage, I came across Fergus' dog-tag and made a decision that would change my life. The wrong man had been killed that day. Fergus, the great humanitarian, had so much to live for. He wanted to heal the broken world that has sent so many young men to their deaths. His worthy vision, along with the energy to make it happen lay shattered in tiny pieces.

"I, on the other hand, had very little to offer. I was devoid of dreams. I had no plans, no focus, no ambition.

"To a needy world, I was dispensable.

"In a moment of madness, I swapped dog tags, believing I could honour his short life by taking on his mission. We were both only children. He had been born in Glasgow to an alcoholic mother and an unknown father. It had become clear early on in his life that his mother was unfit to care for her only child. Against her wishes, Fergus had been forcibly sent to a children's home where he spent ten years, unloved and unnoticed. As soon as he was old enough to get a job, he left the home and started out on his own. The war couldn't have come at a more convenient time. Like me, he joined up to escape. He died unloved by his fractured family. I was his only mourner."

Here, Mr Buchanan paused to compose himself.

"How did you become a Trustee?" Mairi asked.

"Sir Hugh Hollister was my Commanding Officer in the war, so after the explosion when my name was added to the list of dead, he dutifully wrote to my parents telling them I had been killed in action. In the meantime, I, now known as Mr Buchanan, was lifted off the battlefield and sent to a field hospital in Rouen where I received treatment for my injuries before being sent to The Queen's Hospital in Sidcup where I stayed for two years. In the early days, I hovered between life and death, slipping in and out of consciousness but the nurses never gave up. They worked tirelessly to keep my wounds clean and prevent infection."

Again, he paused to compose himself. "Are you sure I'm not boring you?"

"Quite sure!" Mairi exclaimed.

"After my discharge from hospital, I trained to become a chartered surveyor and found work near Carlisle. Looking back, I wish I had been kinder to my parents whose only fault was to love me too much. They weren't bad people and they didn't deserve to be deceived the way they were but had I returned home, injured and scarred, they would have imprisoned me to protect me. I couldn't have coped.

"It was through work that I read about the sale of the Kilbackie Estate, so you can imagine my surprise when Sir Hugh Hollister, my old Commanding Officer, bought my family home and sent Angus, whom I had known all my life, to survey the land. I had no idea what was going on but was intrigued enough to write to Sir Hugh and offer my services as a surveyor should he ever want help managing the estate. He wrote such a charming letter back, thanking me for my interest in Kilbackie, promising to be in touch should he need my help. Not long after receiving his reply, Angus died. His death drew a line under our correspondence and I heard nothing from Sir Hugh for months.

"Little escaped the attention of that wily gentleman. Although I never told him and he never asked, he instinctively seemed to know my true identity. After the death of Rev Hubert Hilton, he offered me a seat on the board overseeing the running of the Kilbackie Estate which I willingly accepted.

CHAPTER 50

The warm sun hadn't yet set on the lengthening day, the night was as bright as the morning.

"It's too light to sleep," Mairi said, encouraging Johnny to sit beside her. A bird was singing its melodious song outside their bedroom window, unaware of the lateness of the hour. "Is that a blackbird or a song thrush?" he asked out of curiosity. "I still can't tell the difference. They both sound the same to me."

Mairi didn't know. She only recognised with certainty, the cuckoo, the corncrake and the chaffinch.

"I'm afraid I ignored your warnings and went with my instinct," she said out of the blue. "He told me everything. I got the feeling he was relieved to share the truth with someone at last."

"Who are you talking about?" Johnny replied, sounding confused.

"Mr Buchanan, of course! While you were collecting the cattle feed, I showed him the portrait in the attic and asked about the signet ring. He confessed everything."

Mairi told Johnny about the exploding shell, Fergus Buchanan's death and Douglas Urquhart's decision to swap dog tags.

"Come here!" Johnny said, embracing her with a passion that had lain dormant for so long. Mairi quivered as he traced his fingers gently over the contours of her breasts.

Her intimate response to his touch made him gasp with pleasure. For the first time since arriving on Skye they were driven mad by a desperate longing to satisfy each other's deepest needs. Their love-making was frenzied - an explosion of suppressed lust that took them both by surprise. When calm was finally restored, they lay exhausted but totally fulfilled in each other's arms.

The tautness of Johnny's muscles slowly relaxed as Mairi continued her intimate exploration of his body.

"Johnny," she whispered. "What are we going to do about Mr Buchanan?"

"At the moment – nothing," he replied, kissing her tenderly on the lips to stop her talking. Mairi looked at her husband with new eyes and saw a man whose love for her had never wavered. Loyal, kind and long suffering, he had stood by her through thick and thin and borne the brunt of her chaotic emotions.

'If only I had been kinder,' she thought. 'Less selfish. Dear Johnny, he deserved far more than I could ever give him.'

"I'm sorry I've been such an awful wife," she said, their bodies still entwined. "Will you forgive me?"

Johnny was unable to reply. For months he had wanted to express his love for Mairi but she had been too preoccupied with her own troubles to hear his voice. Now he had a chance to show her what words could never say. With every nerve and sinew tensed, he poured his love into his wife, completely overwhelming her with sensations that made her cry out with ecstatic pleasure. She had never felt so complete, so accepted. Johnny's love-making quite literally took her breath away.

Within minutes he was asleep, leaving her to think about Mr Buchanan's unique association with the future of Kilbackie. The next morning started early with the bright rays of dawn shining through their bedroom window. It didn't take long for Mairi to bring up the subject that had dominated her waking hours.

Mr Buchanan.

"What do you suggest we do?" Johnny asked, diplomatically, having learned over the years that when Mairi asked for his opinion, she usually expected him to agree with her.

"I think we should invite him to live with us," she said, having given the matter much thought. "After all, Kilbackie is his home, it's where he grew up and I suppose, it's where he still belongs. It can't be easy living so far away on his own. I'm sure if you asked him, he'd love to be part of a family and get more involved in managing the Estate. He has made it clear that he's keen to pass everything on to Tavish as a profitable concern."

"Let's discuss it today and see how we feel tomorrow," Johnny replied. "It's a huge decision that will affect us all so it's important we get it right."

In the end, after going over the pros and cons of Mr Buchanan living with them, Johnny agreed to bring up the subject of a possible move back to Kilbackie at the next Trustees' meeting. For Mairi, the wait was impossibly long and tense. She didn't want to raise her hopes too high but the thought of a new member joining her family was exciting.

A few weeks later, the two men met. Johnny asked Mr Buchanan if he would consider making Kilbackie his permanent home, living with him, Mairi and Tavish.

"It was Mairi's suggestion," he said enthusiastically. "But all three of us would love it if you would consider moving back."

There was a moment's silence as Mr Buchanan grasped the enormity of the invitation. He was genuinely moved by the generous offer, saying he would give it some thought and let them know by the end of the week.

"What did he say?" Mairi asked eagerly after Mr Buchanan had left. "Did he agree to come?"

"Not exactly, but he seemed pleased to be asked and said he would let us know soon."

A few days later a car made its way cautiously across the causeway.

"It's Mr Buchanan!" Tavish cried, running outside to greet him. Mairi could feel the knot in her stomach tighten. She had set her heart on the wise trustee living with them but as the days had passed without any news, she began to lose heart.

Tavish ran up to the unexpected visitor who enthusiastically lifted him high in the air before embracing him warmly. They chatted effortlessly as they walked towards the front door where Mairi was waiting.

"Were we expecting you?" she asked, looking confused.

"No," he replied, "but I wanted to sit down with you and Johnny and explain the decision I've come to following your very kind offer."

Mairi tried to hold herself together, nervously shaking, desperate not to be disappointed by his answer.

"You'd better come in," she said apprehensively. "Tavish, could you go and find your father and tell him Mr Buchanan is here?"

They all gathered round the kitchen table, including Tavish at Mr Buchanan's insistence. Mairi put the kettle on. Whilst she was making tea, they talked aimlessly about the weather, Tavish's school, Hoovers, washing machines and the new bathroom.

"Time and time again I have considered your extraordinarily thoughtful invitation to move back to my childhood home. I can't tell you how touched I am at the suggestion but, before I tell you what I've decided, I need to explain a few things."

For forty years, I have based my character and life on Fergus Buchanan, a remarkable man who sadly never lived to see his dreams fulfilled. Since taking on his name I have tried, with limited success, to make a difference in my only area of expertise - Estate Management. If Fergus had lived, I'm sure he would have created a storm in whatever career he chose. If he were in my shoes, he would have pioneered changes to Kilbackie, focussing on cattle breeding, grassland management, use of outbuildings, tree planting and wetland drainage. Not a day goes by when I wish he had lived. If I continue to be known as Fergus Buchanan, I will do my best to make Kilbackie fit for the present and well-prepared for the future."

He paused to take a sip of tea.

"I apologise for deceiving you. My whole adult life has been a lie, but living as Fergus has freed me from all the restraints and expectations my family once piled upon me. My parents, with all their faults, loved me but their love was misguided. They kept me a virtual prisoner on this island, believing I couldn't live without their protection. In fact, the opposite was true, I couldn't live *with* their protection.

"Returning to Kilbackie after forty years, I have become aware of the importance of my heritage. I'm an Urquhart by birth and my family have run this estate for the past three hundred years. I know the names of every crofter, their familial links, loyalties and ties. There isn't a knoll, boulder, burn or bog on Kilbackie that I haven't explored. The Gaelic language defines me. When I speak it, I am aware of an unbroken thread linking me to my ancestors. Like so many Kilbackie residents, I am created out of its timeless mist.

The Urquharts were traditional Highland lairds who enjoyed a privileged way of life. Before the First World War, they embraced all the trappings of wealth with house parties, duck shoots, otter hunts and balls. They even moored a yacht in the bay.

If I revert back to being Douglas Urquhart, I will no longer be living a lie. My vision for the Estate would be in keeping with the past. All I ask is the approval of ancestors who look down at me from the dining room walls. Life would be lived at a slower, more Highland pace. It would be as it has always been, less pioneering yet more sustainable. I have no idea which way farming is going. Using time-honoured methods might work, although something tells me it will not build up enough capital to equip the Estate for the next generation.

"I have to decide who I want to be. Whether I want to retain my family's traditional identity or be free to be progressive."

"Have you decided yet?" Johnny asked, desperate to know which way Mr Buchanan was leaning.

"Yes, I've finally decided who I am."

Johnny, Mairi and Tavish sat in total silence, their eyes fixed on Mr Buchanan.

"And?" Mairi blurted, hardly able to contain her curiosity.

"I am Fergus Buchanan."

CHAPTER 51

You could have heard a pin drop while Mr Buchanan was talking. Mairi hung on his every word. One moment elated, believing he had decided to live with them, the next downcast, convinced he had decided to stay where he was. The suspense was killing her.

"I'm glad you're not changing your name," Johnny said. "Fergus Buchanan is someone we have grown to admire and trust. I can work with Mr Buchanan but I'm not sure I could have worked as easily with Mr Urquhart. He sounds rather intimidating."

Mr Buchanan smiled, thinking of the portraits of his austere ancestors scattered around the house. They all shared the same haughty look and accusing eyes. He could understand why Johnny might be intimidated by them.

Tavish had sat spell-bound throughout Mr Buchanan's explanation of his true identity. He liked a good story and this was a really good one. Although most of what was said went over his head, he had clearly understood why Douglas Urquhart had swapped dog tags with Mr Buchanan. He would have done the same.

"If you are really Douglas Urquhart, does that mean you lived in this house when you were my age?" he asked.

"Yes," came the reply. "When I was your age, I used to sleep in your bedroom and like you, I'd spend hours outside exploring the island.

"Your parents give you more freedom than mine ever did," he said, smiling at Mairi. "But we used to have a stockman called Iain MacKinnon who was illiterate, but he knew the names of all the wildflowers on Kilbackie, where to find birds' nests, what wild plants and mushrooms were edible, how to snare and skin a rabbit, which plants to use on a sick cow. He could predict the weather, name the constellations, interpret the clouds, make honey and build haystacks. As an only child, Iain was my constant companion."

They finished tea in silence, not daring to bring up the one subject uppermost in all their minds. Tavish took the dirty crockery to the sink where Mairi had started washing up.

He was the first to speak.

"Are you coming to live with us?" he asked with forthright honesty.

There was an audible intake of breath from Mairi as she awaited the reply.

"Ah!" Mr Buchanan said. "I don't want to sound obtuse but the answer is yes, and no."

Three pairs of eyes looked at him, eagerly wishing he would hurry up and put them out of their misery. They wanted to know whether he was joining their family.

"What do you mean 'yes' and 'no'?" Tavish asked. "You can't be in two places at the same time." Mairi could have kissed her son for saying what she didn't have the courage to ask.

Fergus tried to find the words to explain his plan.

"I love Kilbackie. It was where I was brought up. It's where I belong and, yes, I would like to take up your offer and move back." He paused to allow the full effect of his words to sink in. Mairi couldn't believe her ears. He was coming home. She was ecstatic!

"But," he continued with caution. "I'll only stay until I've made the necessary arrangements to move out."

Mairi's heart sank. She had no idea what he was trying to say. It all sounded so cryptic.

Once again Tavish spoke on behalf of everyone.

"I don't understand. Are you planning to live with us or move away?"

"I've decided to renovate the old steadings so I can live on the estate and remain close to you all. Until my house is sold and the restoration completed, I'd like to take up your offer and live with you here in Kilbackie House," he said enthusiastically. "The steadings will give me the best of both worlds. I will be back where I belong, on Kilbackie but will keep my independence and hopefully won't be a nuisance by getting in your way."

Tavish ran over to the man sitting awkwardly at the table and flung his arms round his neck.

"I knew it!" he cried. "I knew you would move back and become a part of our family. Can I visit you when your new home is ready?"

"Of course you can! That's the whole point of the move. My home will be an extension of your home. We can see each other as often as we like. From now on," he added, "I would like you to call me Fergus. After all, it is my name."

Once Tavish was tucked up in bed, the three adults discussed how they should deal with Douglas Urquhart whose name was recorded on a list of soldiers 'Missing in Action'.

"I feel there should be some memorial to the fact he existed," Fergus said. "A statue seems a bit over the top but a plaque doesn't give him the credit he deserves. Any other ideas?"

They went round and round in circles discussing benches, urns, herbaceous borders and trees. Nothing appealed. Finally, Mairi suggested a sundial, an idea that caught their imagination. Fergus said he would design it and ask John MacDiarmid, the stonemason, to make it as a lasting memorial to Douglas James MacLeod Urquhart of Kilbackie House, lost at the Battle of Festubert 1915 aged 18 years.

In the woods surrounding the house they decided to plant eighteen horse chestnuts, one for each year of Douglas' short life. The trees would mark the end of the Urquharts' tenure of Kilbackie. Fergus remarked rather poetically that the trees' late summer candles would light the way for a future generation.

From the moment Fergus decided to live, albeit temporarily, with the Mitchells, the veil of grief that had stifled the house for so long finally lifted. Years of broken dreams and loss were replaced by humour and fun. The sound of laughter swept through the corridors like a torrent of irrepressible joy.

Mairi thrived on the extra company but more importantly, she saw a change in Tavish, whose confused, unsettled life was finally responding to a stable routine. Day by day he grew in confidence, trusting that his parents, Fergus, Rhona and Willie were permanent fixtures in his life and would never let him down.

Not long after Fergus arrived, Mairi received news of Susan Louise Smith's birth on 31st August 1955, weighing a healthy 8lb 14oz. Mother and daughter were doing well. Daisy described in detail the new addition to the Smith family, her placid temperament and Dorothy's natural maternal instincts. The arrival of a granddaughter finally gave Bill a reason to live. Before her birth he had been told he would never make old bones, a fact he had accepted as inevitable. Death had never worried him. That was, until Susan's arrival which changed everything. She reinvigorated him, made him desperate to live long enough to see her grow up and get married.

"I'm staying with Bill for the sake of my family," Daisy wrote. "He has made a huge effort to lose weight and get on better with William and Dorothy. He still has a long way to go but there are glimmers of hope which, I believe, are worth preserving. Things between us are far from perfect but they have definitely improved since you last stayed with us. Poor you! What a terrible time that was! I'm afraid you saw us at our lowest. I still dress up before leaving for Philomena's but I no longer need the clothing to feel special. Perhaps Susan's arrival will give me the contentment I've craved all these years. Who knows?

"I still dream of returning to Kilbackie with my family but Bill will never move, so for the moment I am staying put."

Mairi tucked the letter behind a jug on the dresser. It looked as if she and Daisy were both changing for the better. She returned to prepare the evening meal.

"Hurry up Mr Buchanan!" the young excited voice called out from the hall. "You promised you'd teach me how to skin a rabbit. I want to learn everything Iain MacKinnon taught you when you were my age."

ASK NOT HOW